BAD HOMBRES

A SLASH AND PECOS WESTERN

**LOOK FOR THESE EXCITING WESTERN SERIES
FROM BESTSELLING AUTHORS
WILLIAM W. JOHNSTONE AND J.A. JOHNSTONE**

The Mountain Man

Luke Jensen: Bounty Hunter

Brannigan's Land

The Jensen Brand

Smoke Jensen: The Beginning

Preacher and MacCallister

Fort Misery

The Fighting O'Neils

Perley Gates

MacCoole and Boone

Guns of the Vigilantes

Shotgun Johnny

The Chuckwagon Trail

The Jackals

The Slash and Pecos Westerns

The Texas Moonshiners

Stoneface Finnegan Westerns

Ben Savage: Saloon Ranger

The Buck Trammel Westerns

The Death and Texas Westerns

The Hunter Buchanon Westerns

Will Tanner, Deputy U.S. Marshal

Old Cowboys Never Die

Go West, Young Man

WILLIAM W. JOHNSTONE

AND J.A. JOHNSTONE

BAD HOMBRES

A SLASH AND PECOS WESTERN

PINNACLE BOOKS
Kensington Publishing Corp.
www.kensingtonbooks.com

PINNACLE BOOKS are published by

Kensington Publishing Corp.
119 West 40th Street
New York, NY 10018

PUBLISHER'S NOTE: Following the death of William W. Johnstone, the Johnstone family is working with a carefully selected writer to organize and complete Mr. Johnstone's outlines and many unfinished manuscripts to create additional novels in all of his series like The Last Gunfighter, Mountain Man, and Eagles, among others. This novel was inspired by Mr. Johnstone's superb storytelling.

Kensington hardcover printing: August 2023
First Zebra mass market paperback printing: October 2023
ISBN-13: 978-0-7860-4955-4
ISBN-13: 978-0-7860-4956-1 (eBook)

10 9 8 7 6 5 4 3 2 1

Printed in the United States of America

Chapter 1

Harlan Benson sat astride his horse in the middle of the road, reached into his coat pocket, and pulled out a fancy notebook bound in soft lamb's skin. From another pocket he took a short pencil, hardly more than a stub, pursed his lips and touched the tip to his tongue. Properly lubricated, the pencil slid smoothly across the first blank page in the notebook recording his initial impression.

He liked what he saw.

Twice he glanced up at the neatly lettered sign by the roadside proclaiming this to be PARADISE. He wanted to be certain he copied the name properly. After he entered the name in a precise, small script at the top of the otherwise blank page, he carefully wrote "532" centered beneath it. The declared population of Paradise was 532. A few more observations about the condition of the road, and the likelihood of this being a prosperous town because of the well-maintained sign, were added.

He took out a pocket watch and noted the time it had taken him to ride here from the crossroads. All the data were entered in exactly the proper form. Nothing less than such precision would do. The Colonel expected it, and Benson demanded it of himself.

Harl Benson tucked the notebook back into the inside pocket of his finely tailored, expensive cream-colored coat, with beige grosgrain lapels and four colorful campaign ribbons affixed on his left breast. The pencil followed the notebook into the pocket.

"Giddy up," he called to his magnificent coal-black stallion. The horse balked. It knew what lay ahead. He booted it into a canter. He was anxious to see what Paradise had to offer, even if his stallion was not.

After climbing a short incline in the road, he halted at the top of the rise. Paradise awaited him. The town lay in a shallow bowl. A river defined the northern boundary and provided water for the citizens. Straight ahead to the east lay open prairie. The next town over was far beyond the horizon. To the south stretched fields brimming with alfalfa and other grain to feed livestock. That told him more about the commerce in this peaceful Colorado settlement. It was prosperous and enjoyed a good standard of living in spite of the railroad bypassing it and running fifteen miles to the north.

Giving his horse its head, they eased down the far side of the incline into town. Into Paradise.

His sharp steel-gray eyes caught movement along the main street. He never missed a detail, especially the pretty young woman who stepped out of the grain store to give him the eye. He touched the brim of his tall-center Stetson, appreciating the attention she bestowed on him.

Benson was a handsome man and knew it. Handsome, that is, except for the pink knife scar that started in the middle of his forehead and ran down across his eye to his left cheek. He had survived a nasty knife fight, enduring only that single wound. His opponent hadn't survived at all.

Most women thought that thin pink scar gave him a dangerous look. If they only knew.

He was a real Beau Brummel in his dress. The cream coat

decorated with the mysteriously colored ribbons caught their eye, but he wore trousers of the purest black with a formal silk ribbon down the outsides. His boots were polished to a mirror finish, the leather a perfect match to his ornate gun belt. The six-shooters holstered there hardly looked to be the precision instruments of death that they were. Silver filigree adorned the sides of both Colt .44s. He wore them low on his snake hips, the butts forward on both sides.

Most of all, he was proudest of the intricate gold watch hidden away in a vest pocket lined in clinging velvet to prevent it from accidentally slipping out. A ponderous gold chain swung in an arc across his well-muscled belly. A diamond, the size of his little fingernail, which was attached to the chain, swung to and fro, catching every ray of light daring to come close.

He was quite the dandy and was proud of the look. It was only natural that all the ladies wanted to be seen with him—wanted to be with him.

Benson slowed and then came to a halt. He turned his stallion toward the young lady openly admiring him.

"Good afternoon, ma'am," he said. "Do you work at the grain store?"

"If you need to purchase some seed, I'll fetch my pa. He owns the store."

"No, dear lady, that's not true." He enjoyed the startled expression.

"Whatever do you mean? Of course he does. He's Neil Paulson, and nobody else in these parts runs a store half as fine."

"You misunderstand me, miss. I meant that *you* own everything within your sight. How can such beauty not dominate everyone who chances to cast his gaze on your female loveliness?"

She blinked and pushed back a strand of mousy brown hair. The surprise turned into a broad smile—a smile that promised Benson anything he wanted. Then she looked dis-

comfited. Quick movements brushed dust off her plain brown
gingham dress. Her clothing was no match for his finery,
and here he had ridden into town off a long, hot, dusty summer road.

"Do I take it you are *Miss* Paulson?"

The wicked smile returned and she nodded slowly. She
carefully licked her ruby lips and tried to look coy. Eyes bat-
ting, she gave him a look designed to melt the steeliest heart.

"Clara," she said. "Clara Paulson."

Harl Benson took his notebook from his coat pocket and
made a quick notation in it. He looked up from her to the
store and made quick estimates of the store's size and its inventory. As enticing as it would be to have the girl give him
a tour of the store and detail its contents, in private, of
course, he had so much work to do and time pressed in on
him.

"You want to check the grain bins out back?" She sounded
just a tad frantic. A quick look over her shoulder explained it
all. A man so large his shoulders brushed the sides of the
open door glared at Benson.

"That is a mighty neighborly invite for a stranger," he
said.

Another quick entry into his notebook completed all the
details he needed about Paulson's Grain and Feed Store, and
its burly owner. Benson caught sight of the shotgun resting
against the wall just inside the door. The feed store owner
had the look of a man able to tear apart anyone he disliked
with his bare hands, but that shotgun? It showed intent.

"I must go, but one parting question, my dear."

"Yes?" Clara Paulson stepped a little closer, leaning on
the broom. She looked expectant that he would offer to take
her away from this small town and show her a city where all
the best people dressed like Benson—and she could show
off a fancy ball gown and flashy diamond and gold jewelry
like European royalty. "What is it?"

"Do you have any brothers?"

"What? No, there's only Grant and Franklin working here, but they're cousins. I had a brother, but he died when he was only six. He fell into a well. It was two days before Pa found him."

"Good day," Benson said, again pinching the brim of his hat. He glanced in her father's direction and evaluated the man's barrel chest and bulging arms. In a fight he would be a formidable opponent. But did he have a box of shells nearby to feed the shotgun after the first two barrels were discharged? Benson doubted it.

Benson had faced off with men like Neil Paulson before, men who toiled moving heavy sacks of grain or bales of hay. Their vitality often required more than a single bullet to stop them, even if the first shot was accurately directed to head or heart.

As he made his way down the middle of Paradise's main street, he took note of the buildings and their sizes. How far apart they stood, the construction and position. Quick estimates of the employees in the businesses were probably within one or two of actual employment. He was expert at such evaluations, having done it so many times before with great success. Not a single man walking the street or working in the businesses along the main street slung iron at his side. Perhaps this town really was Paradise and men didn't have to strut about carrying iron.

Harl Benson made more notes in his precise script.

The horses tethered outside the stores generally had a rifle thrust into a saddle scabbard. Travelers into town needed such firepower out on the plains and especially when they worked their way into the tall Front Range Mountains to the west. Dangerous creatures, both four- and two-legged, prowled those lonely stretches.

He dismounted, checked the horses' brands to find out where the riders had come from, and entered a new notation. All these horses belonged to punchers from a single ranch. Where the Double Circle ran its stock, he didn't know, and it hardly mattered. The hands probably carried sidearms in addition to their rifles and had come to town to hoot and holler. They'd be gone by Monday morning.

Benson entered the saloon. The Fatted Calf Saloon and Drinking Emporium looked exactly like any other to him. Eight cowboys bellied up to the bar, swapping lies and nursing warm beer. That meant they hadn't been paid yet for their month of backbreaking labor. Walking slowly, he counted his paces to determine the size of the saloon.

It stretched more than forty feet deep, but was narrow, hardly more than fifteen feet. He settled into a chair with his back to a wall where he had a good view of the traffic outside along the main street.

"Well, mister, you have the look of someone who's been on the trail long enough to build up a real thirst." A hand rested on his shoulder.

Benson turned slightly to dislodge the woman's hand and looked up at one of the pretty waiter girls. She wore a bright red silk dress with a deep scoop neckline. White lace had been sewn along the cleavage, since the dress was so old it was coming apart at the seams. If she had let the seams pop just a little more, she would have shown her customers for free what she undoubtedly charged for in private. Benson quickly evaluated everything about her. Her worth matched the cheapness of her dress.

"Rye whiskey," he said. "Don't give me the cheap stuff." He dropped a twenty-dollar gold piece onto the table. The tiny coin spun on its rim and then settled down with a golden ring that brought him unwanted attention from the cowpunchers at the bar.

That gave him a new tidbit to enter into his notebook. Twenty dollars was unusual in Paradise.

"For that, dearie, you can have anything you want," the doxie said. She ran her tongue around her rouged lips in what she thought was a suggestive, lewd manner to inflame his desires. It did the reverse.

"The shot of rye. Then we'll see about something . . . else."

She hurried over to whisper with the bartender. The short, mustached man behind the bar looked more prosperous than the usual barkeep. Benson guessed he owned the Fatted Calf.

He sighed when two of the cowboys sauntered over, thumbs thrust into their gun belts. They stopped a few feet away from him.

"We don't see many strangers in town," the taller of the pair said. The shorter one said something Benson didn't catch. This egged on his taller partner. "You got more of them twenty-dollar pieces?"

"Are you desperate road agents thinking to rob me?" Benson moved a little to flash the twin six-shooters. The dim light caught the silver filigree and made the smoke wagons look even larger than they were.

"Those don't look like they get much use," piped up the short one. "You one of them fellas what brags about how many men you've cut down?"

"I don't brag about it," Benson said. He took the bottle of rye from the floozie and popped the cork with his thumb. He ignored the dirt on the rim of the shot glass she brought with it and drank straight from the bottle. He licked his lips. "That's surprisingly good. Thanks." He pushed the tiny gold coin across the table in the woman's direction. "Why don't you set up a round for everyone at the bar? And keep the rest for yourself."

"Yes, *sir*. And if there's anything more you want, my name's Hannah."

He tipped his head in the direction of the bar in obvious dismissal. Benson looked up at the two cowboys and said, "The drinks are on the bar, not here." He took another pull from the bottle and then placed it carefully on the table with a move so precise there wasn't even a tiny click of glass touching wood.

"You ever killed anybody with them fancy-ass six-guns?" The short one stepped closer. "Or are they just for show?"

Benson didn't answer.

"How many? How many you claim to have gunned down?" The man shoved out his chin belligerently. At the same time he moved his right hand to his holster, as if prepared to throw down.

"How many men have I killed? How many men and boys? Well, now, I can't give a good answer about that."

"Why the hell not?" Both men tensed now. Benson had seen his share of gunmen. These two might be good at rounding up cattle, or even rustling them, but they weren't gunslicks. They'd had a beer too many and thought to liven up their visit to town by pestering a tinhorn dude.

"I stopped counting at a hundred."

"A hunnerd? You sayin' you've killed a hunnerd men?"

"Only with these guns. The total's considerably greater, if you want a count on the total number I've killed." Benson laughed at their stunned expression.

"Hell and damnation, Petey, he's pullin' our leg." The tall one punched his partner in the arm.

Petey's expression was unreadable. The flash of panic mixed with disbelief. A sick grin finally twisted his lips, just a little.

"We got drinks waitin' fer us back at the bar," Petey said.

"Yeah, right, thanks, mister. You're a real friend. You got a good sense of humor, too." The tall one punched Petey in the arm again and herded him away. They got to the bar and the free setup erased any intention of upbraiding the stranger. In a few seconds they joked and cussed with their partners from the ranch.

Harl Benson added a new notation in his notebook about the quality of the whiskey at the Fatted Calf. He knocked back another shot of the fine rye and started out the swinging doors. A thin, bony hand grabbed his arm. Again he shifted slightly and pulled away.

"You ready for more fun, mister?" Hannah looked and sounded desperate. "I got a room down the street. It's a real fine place."

"A sporting house?"

"What? Oh, yeah. That's a mighty fancy term. Nobody in these parts calls Madame Jane's that."

He looked over his shoulder toward the rear of the saloon.

"What's in the back room?"

"You wanna do it there? If you cut Jackson in for a dime or even two bits, well, maybe we kin do it there." Hannah looked hesitantly at the bartender. "Better if we go to my place."

"Madame Jane's?"

Hannah bobbed her head.

"Ain't much in the back room 'cept all the whiskey and other stuff. It's crowded right now. Jackson just got in a new shipment."

"Of the rye? How many cases?"

"Hustle the customers on your own time. Get back to work, you scrawny—" the barkeep bellowed. He fell silent when Benson held up his hand.

"'Nuff for a few months. Ten cases, maybe more?" Hannah looked back at her boss. "Listen, I'll be outta here in another hour. You wait fer me at Madame Jane's. There's a real fine parlor and she bought a case of that liquor you've taken such a shine to. Fer the payin' customers. Like you."

Benson stepped out onto the boardwalk. A new description in the notebook and he was ready to check on the whorehouse. But first he had one final stop to make.

With Hannah calling after him to enjoy himself until she got to the brothel's parlor, the finest in this part of Colorado, she claimed, he walked directly to the bank down the street. Benson counted the paces and made measurements of the street's width and the location of other stores. When he stepped into the bank, his work was almost completed.

Bustling over when he saw his new customer's fancy clothing, the bank officer beamed from ear to ear. A quick twirl of his long mustaches put the greased tips into points equal to a prickly pear spine.

"Welcome, sir. We haven't seen you before in these here parts. What can we do for you?" The plump bank officer pumped Benson's hand like he could draw deep well water. He released the hand when Benson squeezed down. Hard.

"I'd like to make a deposit."

"A new account. Wonderful, wonderful. How much, sir? Ten? Twenty?"

Benson heard the pride in the man's voice. Those were the big depositors in the Bank of Paradise.

"I was thinking more like five."

The banker's face fell, but he hid the disappointment.

"This way, sir. Our head teller will handle your deposit. Excuse me, but I have other business to—"

"Thousand," Benson said.

This brought the banker up short.

"You want to deposit five *thousand*? That's almost as much as Mr. Rawls out on the Double Circle has in our safe."

"You have other deposits of equal size, I take it? I certainly do not want my money placed in a bank without . . . ample assets."

"Five other ranchers, all quite prosperous. Yes, very prosperous. Come this way, sir, let me handle your account personally." The banker snapped his fingers. The man wearing the green eyeshades and sleeve protectors came from the middle cage.

"You," Benson said sharply. "I want you to show me the safe where you'll keep my money. I don't like to deal with underlings."

"I . . . uh . . . underlings? Oh, no, not that. This way." The bank officer ushered Benson to the side of the lobby and through a swinging door set in a low wood railing. "This is our safe. You can see how sturdy it is." The banker slipped his thumbs into the armholes of his vest and reared back, beaming.

"A Mosler with a time lock," Benson said, nodding slowly. His quick eyes took in the details, the model of the safe and how it had been modified. The safe itself wasn't as heavily constructed as many back East, probably due to the cost of freighting such a heavy load into the foothills of the Front Range.

"You know the product, sir?" The banker's eyes widened in surprise. "Then you recognize how sturdy it is and how, excuse the expression, *safe* your deposit will be. Five thousand, you said?"

"That's correct." Benson walked from one side of the safe to the other. It wasn't any different from a half-dozen others of its ilk he had seen.

"Let's get the paperwork started," the banker said, rubbing his hands together. He circled a large cherrywood desk and began dipping his pen in the inkwell and filling out forms.

Benson seated himself in the leather chair opposite and made his own notations in the lambskin notebook. He glanced up occasionally as he sketched the safe. While not an artist of great skill, he captured the details quickly and well from long practice.

"Now, sir, your deposit?" The banker looked expectantly at him. A touch of anticipation was dampened by fear that Benson wasn't going to hand over the princely sum. The banker positively beamed as Benson reached into his inner coat pocket and drew out his soft leather wallet. Making a big show of it for both the banker and his head teller, he counted out a stack of greenbacks onto the desk until he reached the agreed-upon sum.

Benson almost laughed when the banker visually tallied up how much money remained in that wallet. Only through great exercise of willpower did he restrain himself from asking Benson to deposit even more.

"Affix your signature to the bottom of the page. Here's a receipt for the full amount. And a bankbook. See? The full five thousand dollars is indicated right here with the date and my initials to certify it. Should you wish to withdraw any amount at any time, show the passbook. Or," the banker said, winking slyly, "if you want to add to your savings at any time. That will be entered and officially noted, too."

Benson tucked the deposit book and receipt into the same pocket with his wallet. He stood and held out his hand to shake.

"I look forward to doing more business with your bank soon," he said.

The banker hesitantly shook, remembering the bone-crushing grip. This time Benson made no effort to cripple the man. Sealing the deal with the handshake, Benson turned his back on the man, who babbled about what a fine place Paradise was and how Benson would prosper here, as long as the bank was part of his financial plans.

Walking slowly, Benson took in every detail of the buildings and how they were constructed. A few more notations graced his notebook by the time he reached a three-story building that might have been a hotel. He saw immediately this wasn't the case. On the second-story balcony, several partially clad women lounged about, idly talking until one spotted him down in the street.

"Hey there, handsome, why don't you come on in? I'll show you a real good time." She leaned far over the railing and shimmied about to show what she offered. "I'll show you a good time if you're man enough to handle a real woman like me, that is!"

The other Cyprians laughed.

Benson started to make a few more notes, but an elegantly dressed blonde stepped into the doorway. She had a come-hither smile that captivated him. Benson had seen his share of beautiful women, but this one ranked easily in the top five. She wore a shiny-green metallic flake dress that caught the sunlight and made it look as if she stood in a desert mirage. The shimmering only accentuated her narrow waist and womanly hips. For a woman in a brothel, she sported an almost-sedate décolletage. Only the barest hint of snowy-white breasts poked out.

He couldn't help comparing her with the blatant exhibitionism of the whores on the balcony.

She tossed her head back, sending ripples through the mane of golden hair. Eyes as blue as sapphire judged him as much as his steel-gray ones took her measure. He liked what he saw. A lot. From the tiny upward curl of her lush, full lips, she shared that opinion.

"You're Jane?"

"I hadn't realized my reputation was that big. A complete stranger to town knows me? I'm flattered." She batted her eyes. Long, dark lashes invited him closer.

"It's my job to know things," Benson said, slowly mounting the steps to the front porch. He stopped a pace away. A tiny puff of breeze carried her perfume to him. His nostrils flared and he sucked in the gentle fragrance. His heart raced.

"It's French perfume," Jane said. "I buy it from an importer in Boston."

"And I thought it was your natural alluring scent that is so captivating. I am crushed. How could I have been so wrong?" He turned to leave, as if in abject defeat.

"Don't go," Jane said. "Come in. Have a drink and let's talk. You might even persuade me to forgive you your . . . mistake."

"I've already sampled the rye whiskey. There's more that I want to sample, and my time is running out."

"You don't look like the sort of man who . . . hurries."

"Not in all things," Benson said. He stepped up and circled her trim waist with his arm. She leaned slightly into him. Their bodies fit together perfectly.

"I'm not cheap," Jane said.

"'Inexpensive,'" he corrected. "And I never doubted it. I'm willing to pay for the best."

"I can tell that you're a gentleman."

Pressed together, they went through the parlor into an expensively decorated bedroom.

"My boudoir," Jane said.

"A fitting place for one so lovely," Benson said.

They worked to undress each other and sank to a feather mattress, locked in each other's embrace. Afterward, Benson sat up in bed.

"I wasn't wrong about you, Harl," she said. Jane made no effort at coyness by pulling up the sheet to hide her voluptuous breasts. "You're a real gentleman, and about the best I've ever found."

"This town is well named," Benson said, climbing into his clothes. "It might not be Paradise in all respects, but it certainly is when it comes to . . . you." He turned and put his forefinger under her chin. She tilted her head back for him to lightly kiss her on the lips. "You are both lovely and skilled."

"You come on back anytime you want. I don't say that to just everyone." Jane's bright blue eyes watched as he completed dressing.

"Thank you for the fine afternoon. I enjoyed your company so much, I am going to give you something special."

"More than my usual?" Jane glanced at the stack of ten-dollar gold pieces on the table beside her four-poster bed.

"More than I usually give, because you deserve it," Benson said.

He drew his six-gun and shot her between those bright blue eyes.

Harl Benson settled his clothes, smoothed a few wrinkles, retrieved the fee from the bedside table, and tucked it away in a vest pocket, then walked quickly from the brothel. His work in Paradise had just begun, and he wanted to complete it soon.

Chapter 2

"Let me drive," James "Slash" Braddock said peev-ishly. "I swear, you're hitting every last hole in the road. And them holes got even deeper holes at their bottoms. They might just reach all the way to the center of the earth, they're so deep."

Melvin "Pecos River Kid" Baker looked out the corner of his eye, then hawked a gob with admirable accuracy so that it missed—barely—his partner's boot braced against the bottom of the driver's box of their Pittsburgh freight wagon.

"If I let you drive, them mules would balk. And rightly so. They don't much like you 'cuz you don't have a lick of sense when it comes to treatin' the lot of them with dignity."

"Dignity!" Slash roared. "They're *mules*. Mules don't have 'dignity.' They're as dumb as . . . as you."

"I wouldn't have to drive so fast if you kept a better look-out." Pecos reared back and sent his long whip snaking out over the heads of his team. The cracker popped as loud as a gunshot. The mules tucked back their long ears, put their heads down, and pulled a little harder.

"What are you goin' on about?" Slash gripped the side of

the box and hung on as the wheel nearest him hit a deep rut. If he hadn't braced when he did, he would have been thrown out of the wagon.

Still minding the team, Pecos swept graying blond hair out of his bright blue eyes and then half turned on the hard wood seat toward his partner. This freed up the Russian .44 settled down in its brown hand-tooled leather holster. He reached down. His fingers drummed angrily against the ornate shell belt. Arguing with Slash passed the time on a long, dusty trip, but calling his ability into question inched toward fisticuffs. Or worse.

After all, there were limits.

"For two cents I'd whup your scrawny ass," Pecos said.

"You don't have that much, not after you lost everything but your underwear to that cardsharp last night at the Thousand Delights."

"He cheated. Anybody could see that. Jay should never have let him set down at a table, not the way he dealt seconds."

"If you knew he was cheatin', why in the blue blazes did you stay in the game? Ain't you ever heard the gamblin' advice, 'Look around the table. If you don't see the sucker, you're it.' And you leave my missus out of this argument." Slash glared at Pecos.

"I think she let him play just to humiliate you. Did you and her have a tiff? That'd explain why you're bein' so disagreeable." Pecos thrust out his chin, as if inviting his partner to take a swing.

"Me and Jay are on the best of terms. Every night's like our honeymoon. And don't you go makin' crude comments 'bout that." Slash felt like posing to show off how much younger than Pecos he looked. His thick, dark brown hair poked out around his hat. Streaks of gray shot through it, but nothing like what Pecos sported. His temples and sideburns showed the most. To make his point, he crossed his arms across a broad chest and glared back at his partner.

His brown eyes never wavered under Pecos's equally flinty look.

"That's why you've been daydreamin' and not payin' a whit of attention to anything around you. You're rememberin' what it's like to have a woman as fine as Jay snuggled up alongside you in bed." Pecos swerved and hit another deep hole. Both men popped up into the air, putting space between their rear ends and the seat for a long second.

"What's stuck in your craw? You're always a mite cantankerous, but this is goin' way too far, even for you."

"You're not payin' attention, that's what," Pecos said. He drew his lips back in a feral snarl. "We got company and you never mentioned it, not once in the last three miles when they started trailin' us."

Slash swung around and leaned out past the flapping canvas covering over the wagon bed. A few seconds passed as he studied the matter, and then he returned to his seat beside his partner.

"Your eyes might be gettin' old, but they're still sharp." Slash touched the stag-horn grips of the twin Colt .44s he carried, butt forward on either hip, then fumbled around behind him in the wagon bed and brought out his Winchester Yellowboy. He drew back the rifle's hammer and took a deep breath to settle his nerves.

"There's three of them. Which one do you want me to take out first?" Slash cracked his knuckles to prepare for the sharpshooting.

"You got an itchy trigger finger all of a sudden? What if they're peaceable travelers and just happen to be headin' in the same direction as we are?"

"You're the one what called my attention to them and bawled me out for inattentiveness." Slash leaned out again to get a better idea of what they faced. Still, only three riders.

Or was that three road agents? In this part of Colorado, that was as likely as not.

"It don't change a thing if they're on the road to Potero the same as us, their business bein' in the town and not bein' road agents."

"You have a time decidin' your mind, don't you?" Slash asked. He gripped the rifle and studied the terrain ahead. "Let me drop off at the bend in the road."

"Those rocks make good cover," Pecos said, seeing his partner's plan. "You can knock two out of the saddle before the third twigs to what's what."

"If they're just pilgrims like us, I can save my bullets."

"If they're like us, they're cutthroats."

"That's *former* cutthroats," Pecos corrected. "We've given up ridin' the long coulee."

"I gotta wonder why we gave up such an excitin' life," Slash said, jolted so hard his teeth clacked together when the wagon rumbled over a deep pothole. "Haulin' freight shouldn't be this exasperatin'."

He came to his feet, then launched himself when the freight wagon rounded a sharp bend in the road. Slash hit the ground and rolled. He came to a sitting position, moaning from the impact. Such schemes were better for youngsters full of vim and vigor, not old knees and an aching back like his.

He struggled to his feet and close to fell behind a waist-high boulder alongside the road. It was closer than he liked for an ambush, but he didn't have time to hunt through the rocks for a better vantage point.

Slash knelt, rested his Yellowboy on top of the rock, and took a couple slow breaths to calm himself. Before he sucked in air for a third time, the riders rounded the bend.

He hadn't decided what to say to them, but it didn't matter. They were more observant than he had been. All three spotted him right away. The leader held up his hand, made a fist, and brought his two companions to a halt.

"You have reason to point that rifle at us, mister?"

"I ain't fixin' on robbin' you," Slash said, though the thought fluttered through his mind. He and Pecos had given up the owlhoot life and gone straight, as much through threat as desire. They had run afoul of an ornery U.S. federal chief marshal by the name of Luther T. Bledsoe, who had promised to stretch their necks unless they did "chores" for him, all of which were outside the law. Chief Marshal Luther "Bleed-'Em-So" Bledsoe used them to go after road agents and rustlers and other miscreants in ways that he could deny, should any other lawman protest the methods.

In return, Bleed-'Em-So paid them a decent wage for carrying out his secret orders and let them run a legitimate freight company the rest of the time. And he bragged he wouldn't see them doing the midair two-step with nooses around their necks.

But Slash still felt the pangs of giving up the excitement of robbing a bank or sticking up a train or stagecoach. There had always been more than stealing the money. Nothing matched the anticipation after pulling his bandanna up over his nose, drawing his gun, and going after someone else's money. The uncertainty, the promise of danger, even the sheer thrill when they stashed the loot in their saddlebags and raced off seconds ahead of a determined posse, made it unlike anything else he'd ever done.

It was always his wits against the world. And he waltzed away with enough gold and scrip to keep him going for months until the next robbery. That had been quite the life.

"I'm married now," he said under his breath. That should have given him all the more reason to close the chapter of his sordid past and move on.

"What's that? You're married?" The lead rider looked at his partners. They shrugged.

"Don't pay that no nevermind," Slash said. "Tell me why you're trailin' us. Are you fixin' to hold us up?"

He expected a denial. The leader surprised him.

"That depends on what you're carrying. Gold? Something worth stealing?" The man laughed as if he'd made a joke.

"Truth is, we don't rightly know what's in the crates we're haulin'. They're too light to be loaded with gold and too heavy if they're stuffed with greenbacks."

Slash watched the three cluster together and whisper among themselves. He got a better look at them. If they were road agents, they were prosperous ones. More prosperous than he and Pecos had been, except in the best of times. The riders wore beige linen dusters. The leader had his pulled back to show a coat and vest that cost a young fortune. At his hip rode a smoke wagon big enough to bring down a buck. And, curiously, on his left coat lapel he wore two colorful ribbons.

A quick look showed the other two also had similar ribbons, though the rider to the left had only one and the third horseman two of different patterns.

"You boys Masons or do you belong to one of them secret societies?" Slash tried to hold down his curiosity about their decorations and failed. He'd never seen anything like them except on army officers' full dress uniforms. Never had those officers worn their medals or ribbons on civilian clothing.

The question caused the leader to whirl around. His hand went toward his holstered iron, then he caught himself. The Yellowboy aimed at his heart kept things from getting too hot, too fast.

"He's asking about our campaign ribbons, Hutchins," the rider with only one decoration said. His tone put Slash on edge. Mentioning those ribbons was worse than accusing them of being thieves.

"What we wear doesn't concern you," the leader—Hutchins—said sharply. His hand moved closer to his six-shooter.

"We got other things on our mind than your fancy duds,"

came Pecos's drawl from the far side of the road. He had parked the freight wagon and come back to catch the trio in a cross fire.

Hutchins looked from Slash and half turned in the saddle to find where Pecos had taken cover. The huge man saw the rider's move toward his piece and swung around the sawed-off shotgun he slung across his shoulder and neck from a leather strap. The double barrels carried enough firepower to shred the three men and parts of the horses they rode.

"Whoa, hold on now," Hutchins said. "We're peaceable travelers on our way to Potero. If you happen to be going there, too, that's purely coincidence."

"Why don't you gents just ride on into town," Slash suggested. "We'd feel easier if you stayed in front of us."

"Damned back shooters, that's what they are," grumbled the rider with the single ribbon.

"We don't have time to discuss the matter," Hutchins said. "The Colonel's waiting for us."

"Trot on along," Slash ordered. He motioned with his rifle. "Sorry to have misconvenienced you," he added insincerely.

Hutchins raised his arm as if he were a cavalry officer at the head of a column. He lowered his arm smartly, pointing ahead. The two with him obediently followed.

Before leaving their cover, Slash and Pecos watched them vanish down the road.

"Now, don't that beat all?" Slash said. "You'd think them boys was U.S. Army, only they weren't wearin' blue wool coats and brass buttons."

"You're right about that," Pecos said. He lowered the rabbit-ear hammers on his shotgun and tugged it around so it dangled down his back in its usual position. "No officer I ever saw dressed in such finery out of uniform. And none of them wear their combat ribbons. Now, I ain't an expert in such things, but I didn't recognize a single one of them ribbons."

Slash nodded.

"Let's deliver our freight and collect our due. I just hope you don't get any ideas about spendin' the money to buy fancy togs like that just to impress your new wife."

"I'll let Jay get all gussied up," Slash said.

"She'd appreciate you takin' a bath more 'n wearin' a frock coat," Pecos said.

Again Slash agreed, then added, "Even one with fancy, colorful ribbons." As he hiked all the way back to their freight wagon, Slash pondered why the three riders wore those decorations. He came up empty about a reason.

Chapter 3

"We shoulda cut them down," Pecos grumbled. He snapped the team's reins and kept the mules pulling slowly up the steep hill. "They're gonna ambush us. Wait and see."

"We've turned over a new leaf," Slash said. "Taking care of them was the old us. The new us, the law-abiding us, did the right thing." He heaved a deep sigh. "More 'n that, I'm a married man."

"So because you got yourself a lovely bride waitin' for you back in Camp Collins, you won't defend yourself? They wanted to steal our cargo. You could see it in their eyes. But we had the drop on them, so they brushed us off like we was a pair of greenhorns." Pecos glanced over his shoulder into the wagon bed at the rows of crates.

"If we don't know what's in them boxes, why would some footloose bunch of cutthroats?" Slash considered their cargo for a moment. "We might open one crate to see what's in it. Just to make sure nuthin's got all banged up from the way you're runnin' into every last pothole on the road."

"For once, you have a good idea," Pecos said. "There's only one problem I see."

"What's that?"

"That's the sign tellin' us we just entered the Potero town limits. We're not more 'n a couple minutes from deliverin' the load. It'd cause some gossip if we was seen openin' the boxes within sight of the rightful owner." Pecos pointed to a large building at the edge of town.

Slash's lips moved as he read the sign painted in bold red letters on the side of the barnlike structure.

"That's the place we're deliverin' to, all right. McCall's."

"And there's the owner. You can spot them a mile away." Pecos sniffed the air like a hound dog. "Yup. He's doused all properlike in sweet stinkum to impress the ladies."

"I'm glad I don't have to do that no more," Slash said. "I always got a rash when the barber splashed that on after I got a haircut and shave."

"It's a good thing you hardly ever got a haircut, then," Pecos said. He stood, shoved his foot down hard against the front of the driver's box, and tugged hard enough on the reins to convince the mule team to stop. They rolled to a halt a few feet from the fancy-dressed business owner.

"It's about time you lazy oafs got here. Pull around to the side and unload." McCall jerked his thumb over his shoulder to let them know where he meant.

"You got anyone inside who kin help out?" Slash hopped down.

McCall glared at him, spat a gob of chawin' terbacky, and shook his head before stalking off.

"A real friendly cuss," Slash opined. He went to the lead mule and gripped the bridle. A few gentle tugs got the team moving around to the far side of the warehouse.

"Too bad," Pecos said. "There's already a door, and it's open. I'd've enjoyed knockin' a piece of the wall out." He held out his huge hands and slowly clenched them. Men had died when he hit them with those muskmelon-sized fists. If

Pecos got a good swing, he could batter down the rickety boards.

Slash lowered the tailgate and climbed into the wagon. They had lashed down the crates. It took a few minutes to untie the ropes. Cutting them with the bowie knife he carried in a sheath at the middle of his back was quicker, but rope cost money. He bent low, put his full weight into the effort, and scooted the crates to the rear, where Pecos waited impatiently.

"He's got a whole damned warehouse full already. Findin' a place to put these will take some effort."

"Let's jump to it, then. It'll be worth it to be done with Mr. McCall and his attitude," Slash said.

"His smelly attitude," Pecos corrected. "Do you think the sweet smellum draws women?"

"More likely, it draws flies," Slash said. They wrestled the crate from the wagon and together carried it inside. "Do you think Miss Abigail would tolerate you if you drenched yourself in it?"

"She likes me the way I am," Pecos said defensively.

Before Slash could reply, he stopped dead in his tracks and stared across the yard toward McCall's business office.

"You slackin' off already? I ain't doin' all the work myself. Hold up your side, will you?"

"Lookee yonder, Pecos."

Twisting around, Pecos watched three men dismount and go to the door. McCall waited there, hand outstretched. He shook with each, in turn, before ushering the trio into his office.

"Hutchins and his gold dust twins," Pecos said. "We mighta knowed they were friendly with McCall."

"All the more reason to unload quick as a rabbit and get on home." Slash grunted when the taller Pecos lifted his side of the heavy crate a tad and put more of the weight on him.

They wrestled the crate inside and looked around the large room. Coming to a silent agreement, they lugged the box to a space at the rear of the warehouse. Almost a half hour later, backs aching and fingers cramped, they finished.

Slash sank down on top of one low box and wiped sweat from his forehead.

"It's not like we're gettin' old," he said, "but doin' a day's work keeps gettin' harder. That must mean the day's are gettin' longer."

"We're gettin' old," Pecos argued. He held out his hands and flexed them to get some feeling back. He stood six-six, a goodly four inches taller than Slash's six-two, and outweighed him by sixty pounds, and even he felt the strain of grappling with the cargo.

"Rocks," Slash said suddenly. "That's what's in them boxes."

"There's no reason to bring rocks to Potero. The whole damned town's set in a canyon with the whole Front Range circling it. Or do you mean there's gold nuggets in the boxes?"

"Maybe McCall deals in cast-iron pots. Those'd weigh a ton, and I swear we hauled a ton of crates in here."

"Two. It's got to be two tons," Pecos declared.

"I might have known you two would be slacking off." McCall stomped into the warehouse and looked around. "Where'd you put the boxes?"

"In the back," Slash said, speaking up before Pecos got riled. "We're done. Pay us and we'll be on our way."

McCall harrumphed, pushed past them, and began counting the boxes they'd stacked along the back wall. After a second count, and examining the crates to be sure they hadn't been opened, he spun around and returned to where the tired freighters waited.

"The crates are all banged up. I'm not paying."

Slash and Pecos exchanged a quick glance.

"Let's open them boxes and see what condition the contents are in," Slash said. He shrugged his shoulders and moved his coattails away from the twin Colts slung low at

his hips. Beside him Pecos rested his hand on his Russian
.44. His fingers drummed nervously, making a hollow sound.

"You calling me a liar when I say the crates are damaged?"

"We treated them like they was newborn babes," Pecos
said. "They're in the same condition now as when we picked
them up. Now pay us so we can leave."

"You're not getting a penny!" McCall bellowed.

"Kindly rethink that," Slash said. He put his hands on
both his six-guns. He was getting toward middle age, and
not as fast as he once was when he and Pecos rode with the
Snake River Marauders, but his reflexes were still good and
he never missed. With a six-shooter in either hand, he was a
crack shot.

"Don't you dare throw down on me. You'd be dead before you cleared leather," McCall said.

"So you ain't gonna pay us our due? We signed a contract
with your agent back in Denver. We delivered your cargo.
You owe us. That's simple enough, even for you to understand." Slash started to pull his smoke wagons. He stopped
when he caught movement out of the corner of his eye.

Pecos was slowly raising his hands high over his head.

Slash craned his head around and saw the reason. Hutchins and his two partners had them covered. From the arrogant expression on Hutchins's face, he wanted nothing
more than to kill the two freighters who had backed him down out
on the road.

"Get in your wagon and get those moth-eaten, lop-eared
mules pulling you out of town. I won't tell you twice."
McCall pointed to their rig.

Slash considered what to do. He hadn't lived this long by
taking foolish chances. Back when he and Pecos held up
trains and robbed stagecoaches, he had been the one to consider the risks and plan for the inevitable surprises.

Slash had a chance of dodging and getting his six-guns
into action, but with three pistols pointed at his partner, he

knew Pecos was a surefire goner if he tried. Pecos wouldn't have a chance to even whip that gut-shredder of a shotgun around and get it into action before a curtain of bullets took him down.

"Come on," Pecos said. "Let's go."

"He owes us." Slash held his anger in check. Barely.

"Slash, we have to go. Now."

Snarling, Slash turned his back on the cheating business-man and glared at Hutchins. The gunman showed a hint of disappointment that McCall had driven them off so easily. Like a hungry wolf on a chain, he scented blood and was furious at being denied the chance to spill it.

The two former cutthroats climbed into their freight wagon and swung it around. Pecos hesitated when they reached the main street running through the middle of Potero.

"What do we do? We're not gonna let no-accounts like them cheat us."

"It's bad for business," Slash agreed.

"We can take 'em. All of 'em."

"We showed that out on the road, Pecos. But we're sup-posed to keep our noses clean. Bleed-'Em-So would hang us in a flash if we took 'em down." Slash rubbed his neck where the chief marshal had come within seconds of actu-ally stringing them up. Hanging them for real was part of the hold he used to force them to do his bidding.

"I don't want my neck stretched because of a whim," Pecos said. "What do we do?"

"There's a marshal in town. There must be."

They looked at each other and shook their heads.

"What's the world comin' to, sorry old desperadoes like us beggin' a lawman to collect money owed us?" Pecos grumbled a bit more under his breath, then started the team pulling down the street. There had to be a marshal's office somewhere nearby.

They found it sandwiched between two saloons.

"That makes the lawdog's life easier. He don't have to

walk more 'n a few feet to collar rambunctious drunks to throw into the calaboose."

"There he is, Slash," Pecos said. "You do the talkin'."

"I always do because I'm what they call 'glib.'"

"If that means you don't stutter much, you're almost right for a change." Pecos fastened the reins around the brake and joined his partner in front of the jailhouse.

"We got a contract, Marshal," Slash said. He held up the paper they'd signed to haul the crates. "See? It says McCall's supposed to pay us a hundred dollars upon delivery. We delivered—"

"And he won't," Pecos cut in. He looked a bit sheepish when Slash glared at him. "Well, he refused to give us our due."

"We stacked close to a ton of freight in that warehouse of his. We went to get our money and his henchmen threw down on us. We're lucky they didn't shoot us in the back when we protested."

The marshal held up the contract, squinting as he read it. He balled it up and tossed it into the street. A sudden gust of wind caught it and caused it to tumble along in a tiny dust cloud.

"You can't do that! You just destroyed a legal document!" Slash was outraged. Without realizing it, he reached down to the pistols snugged away in his holsters.

"Think twice before you draw them hoglegs," the marshal said coldly. He glanced into the jail. A deputy stood just inside the door with a leveled Greener goose gun. At this range the twelve-gauge double barrel would leave him a bloody mess in the street before Slash had a chance to draw.

"We told you. McCall is cheatin' us out of our due. You and that shotgun-totin' deputy of yours need to march right on down there and tell him to fork over our money."

"Mr. McCall's a fine, upstanding citizen in this here town. We all think highly of him and how he conducts his business. What none of us, and that means me, don't think highly of is a pair of shabby strangers bad-mouthing him. I can't order you two to drive on out of Potero this very minute, but I can't guarantee what'll happen if you decide to stay.

"And I sure as sin and death can't guarantee you'd live to see the dawn if word gets out that you're calling our finest citizen a cheat."

"He owes us," Pecos said doggedly.

Pecos's cold stare caused the marshal to take a step back. The lawman looked around like a trapped skunk, then motioned to his deputy. The deputy stepped from the jailhouse, clutching his shotgun so tightly his hands shook. With a finger on the trigger, such shaking threatened to discharge the shotgun.

Pecos wasn't sure that if the deputy did fire, it would be accidental. The wild look on his ugly face signaled that he'd enjoy cutting down anyone the marshal asked him to.

"That's what you say. If you want to collect this fee that you claim he owes you, sue him."

"What?" Both Slash and Pecos spoke at the same instant.

"Get yourself a lawyer and take Mr. McCall to court. If you're interested, there's only one in town, and he's Mr. McCall's half brother. Don't let that deter you. Benjamin's an honest lawyer."

"One lawyer in town?" Pecos said skeptically. "Is there any chance he's bein' paid by McCall?"

"Especially since he's a relative," Slash added.

The old marshal grinned, showing two busted front teeth and a blackened canine.

Slash pulled Pecos away. They got their wagon rolling out of town. Uncharacteristically, neither of them had a word to say as they both stewed in their personal anger.

Chapter 4

"Are you gonna tell her?" Slash asked, nursing his beer. A quick move dipped his finger into the foam. He ran it around the glass rim until he produced a squealing sound that irritated Pecos, which was his intention.

He and his partner sat at the back of Jaycee Breckenridge's establishment, the Palace of a Thousand Delights Saloon, Brothel & Gambling Parlor. Anyone unable to remember the entire name was declared too drunk to be served any more of the potent liquor, but turning away customers right now wasn't a problem. The early morning kept much of a crowd from populating the saloon.

Pecos and Slash had driven all night from Potero and had returned to Camp Collins just as the sun peeked up over the horizon, giving the promise of a bright new day. Neither of the former bank robbers felt one whit of that promise. They had hardly spoken all the way back after being cheated by McCall.

"Me? Why should I tell her anything?" demanded Pecos. "You're the one who's married to her. Most times I envy you. You might even say I'm green with jealousy, but not now."

"If Myra had been at the yard, we coulda had her tell Jay. Myra has a way about her that calms folks right down. Even Jay."

Myra Thompson was their business manager, and as cute as a button. They had "acquired" her when she was a few years younger and had gotten tangled up with a gang not known for their mercy when it came to unarmed men or defenseless women. Hiring her as their business manager was an unplanned boon. Myra had proven to have the wit needed to prevent them from going bankrupt with their freight business, and she kept the books, negotiated contracts, and generally did everything the two older men weren't comfortable handling.

"She's been slackin' off, Myra has," Pecos complained.

"You don't begrudge her and young Del their fling, do you? It surprised me when I heard they was sparkin'."

"She's smart and pretty and he's got buckteeth and a goofy look." Pecos drained his schooner and held it up. The barkeep nodded and drew another for the boss's husband's partner.

"He's also the town's deputy marshal. Once upon a time, not so long ago, that would have made him suspect in our minds."

"Del Thayer's a decent fellow. They look mismatched at first glance, but they fit together real well, Myra fillin' in all the places Del's lackin'." Slash leaned back and ran his finger around the wet stain on the table in front of him, lost in their problem.

"Just like you and Jay," Pecos said.

"You refuse to tell her?"

"Tell me what?" Jaycee Breckenridge—Mrs. James "Slash" Braddock—bent over and gave her hubby a kiss on the lips. She grabbed the front of his coat and pulled him upright. "That's no way to return your ladylove's affection." She kissed him again.

Jay released him after an indecent amount of time and stepped away. She looked hard at both men, her jade-green eyes flashing. The early-morning sun caught her russet hair and turned it into a firestorm matching her expression.

"What aren't you telling me? What trouble have you two upped and gotten yourselves into now?"

"It's like this, Miss Jay," Pecos began. "Slash there's got something real important to tell you, while I get my beer." He shot out of his chair as if launched from a mountain howitzer and almost ran to retrieve the beer waiting for him at the bar.

Slash started to curse Pecos for leaving him like this, but his wife occupied his full attention when she sat on his lap. Her arms circled his neck. When they began tightening, he wasn't even able to look away. The lovely woman was a vision to behold. Even with her hair in a bit of disarray, showing she had just gotten out of bed—a bed without him beside her—she was about the prettiest he had ever seen.

No, he corrected himself, she was *the* prettiest. That made it all the harder to lie to her.

"Don't you dare tell me a fib, Slash darling. I'll know. What's wrong?" She tightened her grip. If he had wanted to get away, there wasn't any chance in hell now without her breaking his neck.

Bit by bit, he worked through the story. Most of it he even got out in the proper order.

"So the three gunmen were the ones who tried to hold you up on the road? But they actually worked for this skunk, McCall?"

"That's the way I see it. We was wrong about them fixin' to rob us. Why'd they steal what we had in the wagon when they were beholden to McCall?"

"They *weren't* going to rob you," Jay said with emphasis. "I've got a question, dear."

Slash grinned weakly. He knew he wasn't likely to appreciate whatever she asked.

"Why'd you sign the contract instead of letting Myra handle it?"

"Well, she and Del, and there wasn't time, except . . . we had the chance to pick up the crates right away. Botherin' her in the middle of the night didn't seem right."

"You signed a contract to deliver the crates from a man who showed up at midnight?"

"Yeah, that's about right," Slash said. He peered past Jay. His partner pretended to be lost in a deep conversation with the bartender, but the way Pecos kept sneaking a look over his shoulder showed he waited to see what Jay would do before he came back.

"I wondered where you'd gotten off to. Your side of the bed was cold."

"It wasn't supposed to be like this, honey. We reckoned we'd earn a quick hunnerd dollars, and I could buy you that dress from Boston you've been ogling."

"You mean the one you've been ogling, imagining me—almost—wearing it." She shook her head, then continued. "I hope you got a clause in the contract giving you a bonus for such quick delivery."

"That might have gotten mentioned. Or maybe he just promised he'd see we got a few bucks extra, and never put it in black and white. A man's word's got to be his bond—only, McCall's word wasn't worth the paper it was written on."

"So, what are you going to do about it?"

Jay pushed back when she saw his expression harden.

"You're not going to do any such thing, James Braddock!"

"The marshal wouldn't collect our debt. He said to sue, and the solitary lawyer in Potero's a relative."

"*Potero?* That's where this McCall fellow hangs his hat? It's worse than that, having the only lawyer be his kin," Jay said.

Pecos stopped a few feet away. He started to return to the bar, but Jay said sternly, "Sit yourself down, Pecos. You're as much to blame for this as Slash." She swung around and settled into a third chair. Her grip on Slash's arm kept him from slinking away like he wanted.

"What can be worse? McCall owes us. We intend to pay him a visit and take our due out of his cash box."

"I'll tell you what's worse. The marshal's an old geezer, short and stocky? Not much in the way of hair on top of his head, but with bushy gray sideburns?"

"That's a fair description. Do you know him?" Slash asked his wife.

"He's McCall's uncle Jerome Welles. I think he married into the family, but the McCall family's tight, real tight. Welles fits right in with that den of thieves. You mess with McCall and you're taking on the law in Potero."

"We've tangled with more dangerous lawmen," Pecos said.

"Look at the mess you made dealing with Chief Marshal Bledsoe. He's got you by the short and curlies," she pointed out. "Steal the money from McCall and he'll have a posse on your trail before you reach the town limits."

"She has a point, Pecos," Slash said. "With everyone in that danged town related to everyone else, we'd be prime suspects."

"And if the marshal wired Bleed-'Em-So, every federal lawman in Colorado would be on our necks." He ran his fingers around inside his collar, remembering the feel of hemp tightening as he stood on a gallows trapdoor. Avoiding that demise was high on Pecos's list of things he wanted to make sure he achieved.

"I'm not lettin' that thief keep our money," Slash declared.

"We can't ride in and stick 'em up, not the way we used to," Pecos said. "We're honest businessmen now."

"But McCall stole from us! We're not letting him get away with that. If it gets out how he hoodwinked us, we'll be laughingstocks from Denver to Laramie. Worse, anybody thinkin' on usin' our services would take advantage of us."

"This is a dilemma," Pecos said. "What are we gonna do?"

Jay cleared her throat. A sly smile crept onto her ruby lips. She began outlining her scheme how they could get their revenge on McCall—and recover their money.

Both men's frowns slowly turned into broad grins. They slapped each other on the back and Slash kissed his wife good and proper as a reward for such fine skullduggery.

Chapter 5

Harl Benson checked his compass, then cut due north off the road. Within a few minutes he saw evidence of men high in the rocks watching him. He continued riding on the narrow trail, then turned to go higher into the mountains. The sentries here made no pretense of hiding. They stood boldly, rifles in hand, watching his advance.

He ignored them. There was no reason to give passwords or otherwise identify himself. They knew him. He knew most of them, even the new recruits not wearing campaign ribbons showing their history with the Colonel. It was his job to recruit and keep the men, both veterans and newcomers, in their place.

The path widened into a meadow surrounded by trees. This close to the tree line, the forest was sparse. Scattered among the lodgepole pines camped a dozen men. More. And a huge tent, its canvas sides flapping in the breeze gusting down from higher elevations, dominated the grassy terrain.

Benson rode directly to the tent and jumped to the ground. He held out the reins to his magnificent black stallion. A silent man took them. Benson knew the horse would receive the best of care, grain, currying, a farrier checking the shoes before . . .

Before the attack.

He stopped before pushing through the tent flap. A quick touch to his coat pocket assured him he had his notebook. Only then did he enter. The sunlight filtering through the canvas turned everything inside a dull brown. Four men huddled around a table with a map spread on it. Three looked up as he entered; then they stepped back to give him room for his report.

The solitary man still poring over the map wore a butternut coat that might have graced the shoulders of a rebel soldier during the War of Northern Aggression. A broad leather belt supported a holster on his right hip. The butt of the Smith & Wesson thrust into the holster faced forward in the style of a cavalry officer. A quick draw wasn't needed. Easier access while mounted mattered more.

The man looked up when Benson halted across the table with its topographic map. His dark eyes burned with determination. The broad face and flat cheekbones gave him a slight Oriental look, but Colonel Belvedere Raymond was Kentucky born and bred. His face was weathered from long hours in the elements, and every move he made showed military precision, no wasted effort, nothing but arrow-straight aim for his goal.

"You made good time, Harl. Does that mean your reconnaissance went well?"

"Yes, sir." Benson looked down at the map showing the region surrounding Paradise. At the corner of the map, a small red-green-gold rectangle designated the campaign. Every campaign carried its own colors. Automatically, he reached up and touched the ribbons on his left breast. Soon enough he'd add the one for Paradise. The Colonel had a good sense of color.

Red, green, gold.

Benson approved.

"Is this an accurate layout for the town?" Raymond's finger stabbed down onto the center of the map. Benson came around and gave it a once-over.

"It is, sir. If we enter the town from the east, first there'll be a grain store." He began making notations on the map, adding, in a precise hand, his appraisal of the opposition they'd encounter when the wagons began loading the grain to feed their horses.

"A family?" Raymond scratched his chin. A stubble of brown bristles grew. He hadn't shaved in a few days. Benson took this to mean his leader had worked straight through. This added emphasis to how important it was for them to take Paradise.

He felt a glow of pride. His work would make the assault the easiest they had carried out since arriving in Colorado six weeks earlier.

"Three men, shotguns and rifles. A woman. A girl," Benson corrected.

"Is she likely to put up any resistance?"

"If she's not stopped, she'll sound an alarm." Benson checked his notes to verify that was his belief about how Clara Paulson would respond.

Raymond bent over and made a new note on the map in red ink, this one above Benson's.

"The saloon is stocked with excellent whiskey, about the finest I've found in these parts. No opposition expected, if we strike quickly enough."

Harl Benson continued with his report, often checking his meticulous notes from the lambskin book. He marked the location of the telegraph office, where the jail and its lawmen were situated, everything.

"How wide are the streets?"

Benson checked again, then said, "More than wide enough for our wagons. Even if they rolled side by side, the streets are big and accommodating. Whoever repairs the roads in and approaching Paradise earns his pay." He transferred measurements to the map so Raymond could verify widths. Every detail had to be guaranteed.

"Excellent work, Harl," Raymond said. "As usual, very good work. What are your estimates for our takings?"

"Every man will see at least two thousand dollars."

"After our take is levied, of course."

"Of course," Harl Benson said. He grinned wolfishly.

Colonel Raymond took a final look at the map, rolled it up, and tucked it under his arm.

"Let's roll the war wagons."

"Sunrise in twenty minutes, Colonel," came the report.

Raymond raised his rifle and discharged it into the air. The report rolled across the stillness and echoed off boulders standing sentinel along the road ahead. Three ponderous armored wagons began rolling. Inside the armored behemoths men began loading Gatling guns and preparing explosives. Behind the wagons rolled a caisson, preceding a howitzer capable of firing a three-pound shell. In response to the rifle report came the whinnies of more than two dozen men festooned with pistols.

Raymond had read how Quantrill's Raiders each carried a dozen pistols during an assault. That made every rider equivalent to a squad of men. Seventy or more rounds fired from each attacker before they had to reload. He had modified the attack so only half his force swept through to reach the far side of town. There they reloaded, while the other half of his men attacked.

Two passes were usually enough. With the added firepower from the Gatlings, not much ever remained standing—or alive.

"Ready to begin, Harl?"

Harl Benson nodded. He pulled on a heavy canvas duster to protect his fine clothing. This wasn't his first rodeo. He knew what lay ahead. The attack would be over soon enough, but until that hour or two passed, things got very messy.

"Lead the way, sir!" Colonel Raymond fired twice more into the air.

Benson booted his horse to a gallop. Four handpicked, and dependable, gunmen flanked him as they rode. He rushed past the lead war wagon and took the last curve into town at a dead gallop.

"There. Grain store. Out back."

"Got it, Mr. Benson. The Colonel showed us your notes." Three raiders circled behind Paulson's store and went to secure the supplies in the rear.

Benson and the remaining man hit the ground running. He went to the door and kicked it in so hard, it partially came off its hinges. Benson plowed in and looked around.

"What the hell's goin' on?" The owner blundered from a back room, sleepily clutching his shotgun.

Benson shot him. When the first round failed to knock down the burly Neil Paulson, Benson emptied his six-gun into his chest. With a well-practiced move, he holstered the empty gun and drew the one holstered just above it. By knowing which guns were empty and which were loaded, he ran little risk of making a mistake that'd prove deadly for him.

He spun when a door along a long hallway opened. Clara Paulson stepped out, eyes wide.

"What's going on? You! You came back for me!" She rushed forward and threw her arms around his neck. "I thought you'd left me. Take me away. I can't stand being here one more second."

"Your pa abused you?" he asked.

She pulled away slightly and stared up at him with an expression of utter devotion.

"You're my savior!"

He caught her around the waist, lifted, and spun. He

threw her over her pa's dead body. She stumbled and fell to her knees.

"Take her, if you want," he told his partner. "She's as good as any of the whores."

Benson shut out the woman's screams as he searched the rest of the building. He found a strongbox in a back room, shot the lock off and stuffed several hundred dollars into his pockets. When he left the way he came, there were two bodies stretched on the floor.

He ignored his partner working to button his jeans. This was part of the attack, and he had owed it to the man.

They mounted and followed the last war wagon as it rumbled past. Gun ports on either armored side had dropped open. The chatter of the Gatling guns was enough to wake the dead—only the dead left in Paradise would never know what happened to them. The heavy bullets blasted down walls and reduced entire buildings to rubble.

Benson saw a freight wagon pulled up to the saloon. A steady stream of men worked like ants as they loaded cases of whiskey. When they emptied the gin mill of anything drinkable, as well as the tasty rye whiskey, they'd move on to the general store. By then, axles creaking under the heavy load, they'd head back the way they'd come. With luck they'd form a wagon train with several more wains from the feed and grain store.

Looting Paradise would give them all the supplies they needed for another month of scouting new towns . . . and looting them.

"The bank's over there," Benson called to his companion.

"The cannon's already set up." The words were hardly out of the man's mouth when a thunderous roar rolled back, along with a cloud of dust and gunsmoke.

Benson rode to the bank, made sure the howitzer crew wasn't preparing another round, then went through the blasted-open front doors. The shell had torn through, not only the heavy oak doors but the tellers' cages, and knocked down a large section of the rear wall.

He vaulted over the low wood railing and went to the safe. He whistled. Two men rushed in with just enough dynamite to blow open the steel-doored safe. They were hand-picked experts in blasting open this model of safe.

"The gunner wants to load another round," his partner for this raid called from the sundered oak lobby doors.

"There's nothing more in town that needs so much firepower. Save the shell and powder for another day. Order them to retreat. Their job here's done."

Benson approved placement of the dynamite, flicked his thumb across a match head, lit the fuse, and walked quickly from the bank. Again his measurements proved exact. He exited the instant the dynamite ripped open the top of the safe. His two blasters and his partner all rushed back in. By the time Benson got to the safe, they had emptied the contents.

His partner looked up, grinning ear to ear. "There must be thirty grand in here, Mr. Benson."

"Give me five thousand," Benson ordered. "That was my seed money. And the rest? Pack it up. You two, retreat."

"Aw, Benson, do we have to go right now? You reported there's a big whorehouse with some mighty fine-looking doxies looking for men to pleasure them. We've earned 'em."

He drew a second gun. With legs spread wide and a six-shooter in each hand, he said, "Get the money out of here. Straightaway."

The men grumbled, but did as they were told. Benson glanced at his partner, who was smirking.

"You can go with them or join the wrecking crew."

"At the brothel?" The man hitched up his drawers, then rubbed himself. "It can take a goodly while, making sure there's nothing left behind."

"Go," Benson said. He owed the man these extras. His partner was either very lucky at cards that night or had cheated. Either way he had earned his reward. Benson vowed to play more conservatively. He knew better than to draw to an inside straight, but he had been sure he'd fill that diamond flush. He hadn't.

After they finished with the town, there wouldn't be any witnesses to anything done.

As he stepped outside into the new dawn, he saw a portly man rushing up.

"You! It's Benson, isn't it? What happened, Mr. Benson? Did my bank blow up?"

"I came to make an early withdrawal," Benson said.

"I . . . I don't understand. You aren't making a deposit?"

"Yeah, you might say that I am," Benson said. He shot the banker in the head. Benson made a face. The blood spattered his duster. He was glad he had the foresight to wear it over his expensive clothing. Getting a bloodstain off a cream-colored coat was impossible. With a quick hop he vaulted onto his stallion's back and trotted off.

Half of Paradise was aflame now. The buildings that survived so far were riddled with bullet holes. Bodies lay everywhere. As Benson rode by the looted general mercantile, he saw a man, likely the owner, though Benson couldn't tell because of the soot smeared on his face, fumbling with a six-shooter. The man cried incoherently and tried to lift the weapon. A single bullet ended that vain attempt to defend his business.

"Lucas, Lucas!" A woman with a shawl pulled around her quaking shoulders, but still wearing her nightgown, dropped beside the man.

"Was he your husband, ma'am?" Benson called.

"Yes, yes, get the marshal. Get him!"

Benson shot her twice, just to be sure. It was the most merciful thing he could do for her, just as it had been merciful when, during his scouting of the town earlier, he'd shot the whore and saved her the horror of seeing her girls raped and her business burned to the ground.

He continued through town, being sure nothing was over-looked. The men ahead of him, led by Colonel Raymond, were thorough. If so much as a dime remained unclaimed in Paradise, it would be a miracle. Similarly, not a building escaped destruction or a life remained untaken.

Benson saw the ramrod-straight rider through the dust and choking smoke and made for him. He drew rein along-side Raymond.

"You've ordered the war wagons to withdraw, sir?" Benson asked the question needlessly. Of course his leader had. Belvedere Raymond was a brilliant tactician, and his battle plans were things of utter beauty. In, out, complete looting. Every detail of the plan ran like a fine Swiss watch.

"I have. It's now time for us to leave." Raymond checked his pocket watch. "From entry to exit, ninety-four minutes. Excellent scouting, Harl. Excellent work, as usual."

"Thank you, sir." He started to follow the last of the heavy-laden wagons leaving with loot from town. Raymond reached out and stopped him.

"Excellent work," Raymond repeated. He held out his hand. Resting in his palm was a red-green-and-gold campaign ribbon. "For Paradise."

Harl Benson took the colorful decoration with some pride. It'd look good pinned on his chest with the other four ribbons.

Chapter 6

"The whole danged town's on fire." Chief Marshal Luther T. Bledsoe lowered the spyglass and shook his head. The white cotton-wool thatch atop his otherwise bald pate moved about as if a summer breeze rustled the hair. He clenched his teeth and almost shook from the frustration burning inside him. "It's like I was told. It's got to be them."

He held out the spyglass in his skeletal, pale-skinned hand. It trembled just a little. He turned his cobalt-blue eyes up to his lovely assistant. She looked out of place standing on the dusty Colorado road, clad in a forest-green cloak over her impeccably tailored rust-colored jacket. A bleached white blouse beneath billowed forth, a fine lace cascaded down the front, accentuating her bosoms. The matching split riding skirt swirled about her flaring hips as she moved with glacial precision. Nothing rushed her, nothing upset her. She was a gorgeous force of nature.

"Here, take it. Tell me what you see." Bledsoe thrust it out insistently. "My old peepers are a bit misty today."

Abigail Langdon moved from behind the chief marshal's

rolling chair and reached for the telescope. She had to tug just a little to pry it loose from the old man's hand. Arthritis froze his joints enough to be obvious. He grumbled at his weakness and shifted around in the chair, staring off in the direction of the column of rising black smoke. He pointed, his bony finger stabbing out as if he pressed someone against a wall.

"There. Tell me what you see there."

The tall Nordic beauty lifted the 'scope to her right eye and peered through it. In spite of the horrific scene revealed, she showed little emotion. It was as if she had been chiseled out of pure white ice, befitting her heritage. She slowly panned around to take in the entire scene of carnage, then lowered the spyglass.

"They are still in the town. They haven't completed their pillage." Her words were soft and tinged with a disdain that would have cowed anyone other than the chief marshal.

"What? Gimme that!" Bledsoe yanked the spyglass from her long-fingered hands. "Where're they? Tell me where!"

Miss Langdon stepped behind the chair and shifted it so Bledsoe stared straight at what she had seen.

"By all that's holy, you're right. That's gotta be a wagon train loaded with everything they stole from the town."

"Their loot," she said softly. "Those wagons trail the military force. One wagon farther ahead shines like a silver dollar."

"Armor. Them varmints have an armed wagon. It won't do them a lick of good against the right attack." He held out the spyglass, no longer interested in watching the raiders retreat with their plunder. She took the telescope and slid it into a wooden tube used as a carrying case, slung over the back of the rolling chair. "Hansen! Hansen, git your lazy butt over here."

A tall, lanky deputy rushed over. He pushed his tall-crowned Stetson back up onto his forehead to get a better look at his boss.

"You called back all your scouts?" Bledsoe pointed at the criminal caravan rolling away with the wealth of an entire town.

"All of 'em," Hansen said. "Fifteen deputies in the posse, sir."

"Mount 'em up, git 'em to that town. I want every last mother's son of them raiders brought down. There's no tellin' how many are still pillaging. It don't matter to me. Take prisoners if you have to, but don't go out of your way. They're downright vicious killers."

Hansen nodded and whirled away, running to mount. He yelled out orders to the entire posse. They lit a hurry and were gone in a dust cloud within a minute.

"Don't just stand there, woman," Bledsoe snapped at his secretary. "Get me into the wagon. I've got to see what them cutthroats have done." He cleared his throat and said in a lower voice, "I gotta see with my own eyes to appreciate how ruthless I gotta be to bring the lot of them to justice."

Abigail Langdon coughed genteelly and waited behind the rolling chair. Bledsoe craned his scrawny neck to look back up at her.

"Well, what are you waitin' for? Push me. I can't do it myself."

She coughed once more and looked off into the distance at Paradise—or what remained of the once-prosperous town.

"Please. Is that good enough? *Please?*" Bledsoe let out a yelp of surprise at how fast his secretary pushed him along to the rear of his fancy-outfitted wagon. His driver waited uneasily, looking toward Paradise.

"Get me into the wagon, consarn it. Has everyone gone deaf?" Bledsoe grumbled as the driver and Abigail positioned him on a wooden platform and secured the wheels of his chair. Once Bledsoe was settled in place, the driver began yanking on the pulley to get the chief marshal level with the bed. By the time he finished hoisting the chief marshal, Abigail had circled around, climbed up to the driver's box, and worked her way through the interior. She snared the rope and swung the cranky old lawman in.

Bledsoe rolled forward and secured himself at the front of the wagon, where he could look out. The luxurious furnishings were ignored. Decorative lamps swung from the supports for the canvas canopy. A table with carved-out holders for a half-dozen whiskey bottles began to shake as the driver got the team pulling. Miss Langdon sank onto a red-velvet-covered settee and stared at the back of her boss's almost-bald head.

"Go on, say it," Bledsoe snapped, without turning. "Tell me what a mean old rattlesnake I am."

"You don't rattle," she said softly, her voice almost drowned out by the clatter of the iron-rimmed wheels against the rocks in the road. "Unless you mean your lungs when you breathe. You're more like a sidewinder and attack without warning."

"That's more like it," the chief marshal said, hunched forward to look past the driver. The column of black smoke thickened. "I can't stand havin' everyone bootlicking all the time."

"Just most of the time," she corrected. "You demand complete loyalty."

"*Loyalty?* What's that? I keep everyone in line by convincing them their lives'd be worse if they don't. If that takes a little blackmail now and again, so be it."

Miss Langdon said nothing. He had a hold over her, and they both knew it. As long as she did his bidding—within limits—her secrets would never be revealed. She clung to the back of the padded settee as the wagon took a sharp turn. The road straightened and she tried to lean back.

"I don't believe it," Bledsoe said in a choked voice. "I seen what them jackals have done before, but it's never been this bad."

Miss Langdon made her way forward, her shoes making

soft sliding sounds as she walked across the thick Persian rug spread on the wagon bed. She gripped the handle on Bledsoe's rolling chair for support.

"Makes the nose wrinkle up and wiggle, don't it?" He craned his wattled neck to see past the driver.

"It turns my stomach," she said. "The stench of burned flesh is terrible."

"The stench of burned *human* flesh," Bledsoe corrected.

In the distance rapid gunfire drowned out the crackle and pop of fires already beginning to die down. The town of Paradise had burned itself out, with few buildings remaining unscathed.

"Do you want to see the . . . carnage?" Miss Langdon swallowed hard as she stared out at the devastation.

"Drive on through town," Bledsoe ordered. "I can see plenty from here. There ain't nothin' more I can do for any of these blighted souls." His hands gripped the arms of his rolling chair until his bony knuckles turned pasty white. His breathing became ragged as they drove past a saloon. Its sign once said THE FATTED CALF SALOON AND DRINKING EMPORIUM. So many bullets had ripped through the wood sign that it dangled by a few splinters.

"The 'something Calf Saloon something something' has seen better days," Miss Langdon said. "From the huge number of bullet holes in that sign, they used a Gatling gun indiscriminately."

"More 'n one rapid-firin' gun caused that kind of damage," Bledsoe said. "They blew the sign to holy hell, but left the main room intact. Why'd they spare it?"

"They wanted something. Liquor?" Miss Langdon leaned out and looked at the structures on either side of the saloon. They had been reduced to kindling. More than one arm or leg or other body part poked out from under the destruction.

"They'll whoop it up on what they stole then," Bledsoe said. "I hope Hansen catches at least one of them alive. I want to know everything about the mangy cayuse that'd leave behind so many bodies." He spat. "And they did all that killin' just for booze? They murdered every last man and woman in town to steal liquor?"

"Children too," Miss Langdon said. "And dogs. There's one body I think used to be a dog," she said in a tiny voice. "It might have been a small child. I can't tell."

"Marshal," the driver said, leaning back. "Deputy Hansen's comin' back like his tail's on fire."

"Good. I want to hear a complete report on how he sent the lot of them into Satan's burnin' clutches. All of them."

"Marshal! Marshal Bledsoe," cried the deputy. He rode close enough to the driver's box to look inside. His face was pasty under the layer of soot and gunpowder residue.

"Dammit, man, where's your prisoners? How many of those snakes did you kill?"

"They . . . they . . . all . . ." Hansen wobbled in the saddle. The driver reached out to steady the deputy to prevent him from taking a tumble to the street.

"Good riddance," Bledsoe said. He looked back at Miss Langdon when she gasped. He seldom heard her react with such emotion. "What is it, woman?"

"The deputy means the posse's all gone." Abigail Langdon spoke in a low, choked voice.

"Not possible. That's not possible. There were fifteen ornery deputy U.S. marshals. They weren't greenhorns. Every last one of 'em has seen gunplay before."

"She's right," Hansen choked out. "We caught up with the trailing wagon. We stopped it and were fixin' to take prisoners, but they brought up one of them armored wagons. Slits dropped open on the sides." He closed his eyes, then forced them open. Hansen had seen hell on earth. "They cut through us like a scythe through winter wheat. They chopped us all down with just two passes. All of us."

Bledsoe sat still, stunned at the report. He had lost men

before, but never an entire posse. Never so many deputies, all armed and raring to get into a fight. They had been slaughtered as surely as every last, lost soul in Paradise.

"Driver, get me outta here. Right now. As fast as you can drive. Kill the horses. I don't care." He slumped into a bony pile and shook his head.

Then anger burned away his shock.

"They're gonna pay for this. I'll swear that on a stack of Bibles. They're gonna pay for slaughterin' my posse and burnin' down Paradise and the other towns."

"How, Marshal? What are you gonna do?" Deputy Hansen got out in a strained voice.

"I got a secret weapon I'm gonna unleash on them." He sat a little straighter. "I got *two* secret weapons named Braddock and Baker."

Chapter 7

"It's too dangerous. Let's turn back 'fore we get ourselves in a world of trouble," Slash said.

Pecos looked at him as if he had been out in the sun too long without his Stetson.

"Am I hearin' you all right? This from the fearless cutthroat who held up trains and robbed banks?"

"You know what I mean. It's too dangerous for Jay to get herself tangled up in our problems."

"Her and you are hitched. Your problems are hers now, aren't they? Ain't that the way marriage works? You share everything?"

"Not this. We was the ones that got skunked outta our due. McCall owes us and we ought to collect from him without her gettin' shot at." Slash ground his teeth together and rested his hands on the butts of his twin Colts.

"I wanted to mosey on in and stick a gun under his nose, but who was it what disputed that as a decent plan? Was that you? I'm gettin' old, so maybe my think box is leakin' memories." Pecos snapped the reins and pulled the mule team off the road leading into Potero.

"You know it wasn't me."

"Who was it, then? Did some little birdie fly down and chirp a new plan in your ear? Maybe all the hair growin' there made you hard of hearin'."

"You know good and well that it was Jay. She was the one what concocted this scheme."

"If it wasn't for her warnin' us off, Slash, we'd've ended up in a stew pot cookin' our corns off. She knew that the marshal was McCall's uncle. That whole town's related to one another. Any big church social must come real close to bein' a family reunion for the McCalls."

"Even the preacher's family. She said he was the marshal's half brother."

"I rest my case. You didn't know that. I sure as death and taxes didn't. Jay not only knew all the gossip about Potero, she came up with the plan for us to get back our property. She's got the facts we lack."

"Ain't our property. We just hauled it for McCall. I'd rather be paid," Slash said. "Ain't no tellin' what junk he had stashed in those crates."

"Accordin' to the law, it *is* our property, since we didn't get paid for our haulage services. We load it all back and drive off with it."

"Whatever *it* is. Those wood boxes creaked, they was so stuffed."

"That, Slash, is the beauty of it. Anything that weighs that much has to be valuable. We haul it back to Camp Collins and sell it to the army sutler. Or take it to Denver. There's always somebody there that'll buy durned near anything."

"Easterners floodin' into town have money burnin' a hole in their pockets," Slash said, nodding thoughtfully. "We find what's in those crates and sell it to 'em as gen-you-wine Indian artifacts. Maybe dab some paint on it and call it war paint."

"They'll believe anything, if you're sincere enough."

Pecos laughed. "See, you're comin' around to our way of thinkin' on this matter."

"*Our?* If it works, it's my blushin' bride's idea."

"And if it doesn't," Pecos said, "it's got to be yours!" He laughed even harder, then settled down and squinted into the setting sun.

Neither said a word. They had to arrive at McCall's warehouse after it got dark. Jay had gone into town ahead of them to look out for Hutchins and McCall and Marshal Welles. If any of them showed his ugly face before Jay had set up things for them, there'd be such an uproar, only gunplay would settle it. But she was lovely and had a friendly way about her that soothed ruffled feathers. Nobody'd think twice about two old freight drivers sneaking around when there was such a beguiling woman in their midst.

"Let's go," Pecos said. "I'm gettin' all nervy settin' and doin' nothin'."

Slash only nodded. He snapped the reins and got the mules pulling. Every creak of leather and snort from a mule made them jump just a little.

"We're a fine pair," Slash said. "We weren't ever this nervous when we stuck up a train or robbed a bank."

"It's tryin' to make a legitimate livin' that's stealin' away our nerve," Pecos said. "Courage is like a muscle. Use it enough and it gets stronger. But with us haulin' freight all day long, we forget how to face up to trouble."

"Slash, old pard, we keep our hand in performin' chores for Bleed-'Em-So Bledsoe. This ain't any more dangerous than what he makes us do."

"Whoa, pull up!" Slash grabbed Pecos by the arm and pointed to the problem.

"That's Jay! What's she up to?"

"Looks the world like she's bein' escorted by McCall!"

"And these old eyes ain't lyin' when I say that's Hutchins trailin' them to the saloon." Pecos had to restrain Slash to keep him from leaping from the wagon. "She's decoyin' them snakes away for us. We got to make the most of her sacrifice."

"Sacrifice?" Slash snarled. "If they touch one curly red hair on her head, I'll show 'em sacrifice!"

Slash settled down and gripped the reins, then steered the wagon toward McCall's storage building. He drove around back to the double doors where they had unloaded the freight earlier.

"There'd better be a barrow or some way to move them crates easy. I don't want to strain my old, creaky back again." Pecos jumped down and tried the doors. They were barred on the inside. He glanced back, then motioned.

Slash joined him, his thick-bladed knife flashing in the dim light. Thrusting the blade between the door, he lifted until he met resistance. Grunting, he increased pressure until the locking bar popped out of place. The doors swung wide.

"I swear, there's even more in here than when we left the cargo for McCall." Slash swiveled around, taking in the merchandise stacked from floor to ceiling. There were so many rows of crates, it took a bit of wiggling to squeeze past and move deeper into the warehouse.

"He must be cheatin' more 'n us," Slash said. "Those four stacks of boxes weren't here before." He leaned against one pile, then dug in his heels and pushed harder. "What's he up to? Don't he ship anything but anvils?"

"The crates we unloaded were heavy enough, but these are like mountains. And lookee there. Do you think your little bride'd like some new furniture for your livin' quarters?"

"He's got davenports and sofas, and I don't know what all, that's for certain-sure," Slash said. He turned glum. Pecos realized why his partner's mood changed so fast. At the best of times, Slash wasn't a cheery sort. Accidentally reminding him where his wife had gone made him down-right sour.

"Jay won't stay with them sidewinders much longer,"

Pecos said quickly to ease some of the hurt he'd caused. "We'd better get to movin' some freight. Here're the boxes we delivered."

Slash found a barrow. Wrestling the crates into the wheelbarrow let them move the freight to their wagon. Lifting it into the back caused them both to moan and groan from the effort.

Pecos stepped away and rubbed his back.

"I swear, I'm gonna need more liniment than's in the entire town of Camp Collins. My muscles got muscles achin'."

"You have to rub it in, all by your lonesome. Me, I got Jay to do it for me." Slash gloated over that.

"Talk about rubbin' something in," Pecos said. He stood on tiptoe and measured the space left in the wagon. "We got plenty of room for some of that fancy furniture."

"And a few extra crates. It's only fair," Slash said.

"It ain't stealin'," Pecos agreed. "It's more like collectin' interest on our unpaid bill."

"A penalty for not payin' up quick and proper," Slash rationalized.

They returned to the warehouse and moved the furniture. After having tackled the heavy crates, the furniture only proved awkward, not difficult to carry. Then they retrieved a couple other boxes near the warehouse doors.

"Think we oughta see what it is we're stealin', Pecos?"

"Ain't stealin', I tell you. We're not stickin' a gun in anybody's face, or boldly stridin', with masks on, into a bank. This is like what the sheriff does when he goes out to serve process. Repossessing things that don't belong to the one with them."

"It might not be thievery, but it's sure not you doin' your part. Put your back into heavin' this into the wagon." The two bent and slid their hands under the crate. Together they got it to the edge of the wagon bed. It teetered there and threatened to come tumbling back onto them.

"What's going on? Why're you loading up that wagon?"

Slash gave Pecos a quick glance and called out, "Don't just stand there, pard. Give us a hand. You don't want to make Mr. McCall mad because we're takin' too long, do you?"

"He never said there'd be a new delivery tonight. The last one was supposed to be this afternoon."

"We're pickin' up early, that's all. Put your shoulder into it. You ain't any help at all, standin' around and just watchin'. McCall can't abide by a slacker."

Both Slash and Pecos stepped back so the guard fought the entire weight of the crate. He grunted, turned red in the face from exertion, and heaved, sliding it into the wagon on his own.

"The Colonel won't need any of the supplies for a week," the guard said.

"We do what we're told," Slash said.

"Plans change," Pecos added.

The guard stepped back and brushed off his hands. For the first time he got a good look at them. He grabbed for his smoke wagon.

Pecos wrapped a brawny arm around the man's neck and squeezed hard. Slash plucked the man's six-gun from his numbed fingers. In seconds the once-helpful guard sagged to the ground.

"He recognized us," Pecos said. "At least he recognized your ugly face."

"It's hard to forget such a manly aspect," Slash said. He tossed his head and ran his fingers through his hair, posing for his partner's admiring gaze. "What are we gonna do with him?"

"We could cut his throat."

"We could do that, pard, we could, but that seems too criminal. We're legitimate businessmen now."

"It *is* something we'd have done when we rode with the Snake River Marauders," Pecos agreed. He stared down at the unconscious man. He came to a decision. "Help me load him into the wagon. We'll dump him outside town. By the time he walks back, we'll be long gone."

"You reckon he'll admit to knowin' what happened?"

"Maybe, Slash, old buddy, but he sure as the sun rises every morning won't fess up to helpin' us load the wagon. One confession gets him a beatin'. The other, well, if McCall don't do it, Hutchins would." He drew his forefinger across his neck and stuck out his tongue to enact the man's fate.

Getting the wagon moving took considerable coaxing. The mules strained and almost found the load too heavy. Then with a snort and a snap, they pressed forward and the freighter began rolling. Slash and Pecos sat all stiff and tense, sure that they'd be spotted. When they reached the outskirts of Potero, they slowed.

"Should we wait for Jay?" Slash was anxious about his wife.

"We keep rollin'. She's ridin' Dorothy. That horse can gallop the whole way back to Camp Collins and never tire. You wait and see, Slash."

They rattled along for fifteen minutes before Pecos leaned far out and peered at their road from Potero.

"A rider's after us."

"Can you see who it is?" Slash reached for a holstered six-gun.

"No need," Pecos said. "Ain't two women that good-lookin'. That's got to be your lovely wife."

Jaycee Breckenridge galloped up and then slowed to pace the wagon. She leaned over and gave Slash a quick peck on the cheek and then sank back into the saddle.

"You've been drinkin'," Slash accused.

"I have. With a gentleman willing to buy a po' li'l outlaw lady like me a sip of whiskey." She grinned like a wolf. "Or two. It could have been three drinks. I lost count."

"You don't have to pretend to have liked it," Slash said, grumpy.

"Did you get the cargo back?" Jaycee tried to peer around the two men in the driver's box. The wagon's interior was too dark for her to see anything.

"We did," Pecos said. "And your lovin' hubby even got you something special."

"Just for me? A present? What is it?"

"Pecos, don't—"

"Stop the wagon. I'll fetch it for her."

"You stay here." Slash hopped down and walked to the rear of the wagon.

"You didn't have to get me anything special, darling. I—" Jay caught her breath when Slash lowered the tailgate. He grabbed a handful of the guard's coat and pulled him straight out, to land heavily in the middle of the road.

"That's for me?"

"Throw him back. He's too small to keep," Pecos called from up front.

"It was real thoughty of you to bring him, but Pecos is right. I have all the man I need." Jay bent low and pulled Slash over. Kissing from horseback didn't satisfy either of them, but she whispered in his ear details of his reward when they got home.

Slash climbed back into the wagon and, in spite of the overloaded axles, made good time all the way back to Camp Collins.

Chapter 8

"Are you sure you don't want to say where all this came from?" Myra Thompson balled her hands on flaring hips. She looked up at Slash disapprovingly. "I get the feeling I need to talk to Del about this. What's he going to say, do you think?"

Slash caught his breath and looked at Pecos. They came to a decision who was to tell their general manager about the stack of crates piled at the rear of their storage shed. When they had "gone straight," they started a freight company and quickly found they were good at moving and hauling and, even getting on in years as they were, able to tote heavy boxes.

When it came to running a business, they were babes in the woods.

They had rescued Myra from a vicious gang when she was only a teenager and had given her a safe place to stay until she found her way. The temporary quarters became permanent as she took over more of their business, keeping ledgers and arranging contracts for the company they'd bought from Emil Becker with the first bounty money earned from Bleed-'Em-So Bledsoe. Because of her background and the illegal things Myra had been forced to do, she was willing to look the other way—most of the time.

But ever since Deputy Sheriff Delbert Thayer had started sparking her, they'd walked on eggshells. The young lawdog had eyes only for the petite and perky girl, and she spent more of her free time with him than in the freight yard, but stealing so much cargo that it overloaded a Pittsburgh wagon until the axles creaked crossed the line.

"It's for Jaycee," Slash blurted.

Pecos closed his eyes and tried not to groan. They should have practiced their lies. Slash wasn't good at lying. For all that, neither was the Pecos River Kid, but he knew he'd do better. Slash looked like a little boy caught stealing a pie cooling on a windowsill.

"Jay Breckenridge? Your wife? Is that who you mean? Jay?" Myra gave them "the look" that she knew they were lying to her.

"That's right. She's my wife," Slash said lamely.

Pecos horned into the disastrous excuse making.

"It's a surprise for her. We got all this from . . . an estate sale."

"An *estate sale*? I haven't heard a peep about anyone dying around here. And nobody's died in the last few months that didn't have a family to pass on everything they owned." Myra stood on tiptoe and looked around Slash and into the shed. "That's mighty fine furniture."

"All for the Thousand Delights," Pecos said. "Where else would we take it? Who else'd have it?"

"How much did you pay for the load? There must be a half ton stored in there. I need to issue a credit voucher and be sure the bank account's in balance." She fixed Slash with her steely stare. He looked even more like the guilty little boy.

"We got it for nothin'. They wanted to pay us to haul it off, but we done it for free." Slash looked at Pecos, who only shrugged.

"I need to see what all's in them other crates. If we're selling it all, I have to put a price on it."

"All the furniture's a gift. For Jay," Slash said hastily.

"It'll look good upstairs in the sitting room," Myra said. "That padded chair she has there is getting a little worn—"

"Like Slash," Pecos cut in.

"How do you know what she's got up in the brothel? You ain't been there to . . . ?" Slash sounded outraged.

"More 'n *that* goes on upstairs. You ought to know. You live there." Myra was frustrated with both of them. She pushed past and picked up a pry bar.

"You got no call pokin' 'round in them crates," Pecos said. "We'll handle it all."

Myra ignored them and applied the iron lever to the nearest crate. Nails ripped free of the wood with a loud screech. She pushed the lid off and poked around inside.

"If this isn't Jay's, I can get top price for it. This is mighty fine silverware." Myra pulled out a gleaming spoon. More fishing around produced a handful of forks and butter knives. "That's a fine-looking gravy boat, too." She heaved a deep sigh. "Me and Del aren't talking about getting hitched. Nothing like that, not yet. When we do, I'd love to have this for Sunday meals and holidays." She smiled and got a dreamy look. "And it would be perfect for big family dinners. I want a big family."

"Rich folks use spoons like that," Pecos said, frowning. He pulled Slash away, while Myra continued inventorying the crate's contents.

"What do you suppose McCall was doin' with all that?" Slash sounded perplexed.

"Considerin' how easy he found it to cheat us, I got ideas how he came about it."

"But, Pecos, this is silver. I got a nose for it."

"You got a big nose, I'll grant you that," Pecos said. "Sets of china, I can understand. Every ship from Shanghai uses plates and cups and saucers as ballast. I've been told there're mountains of it at the Embarcadero in San Francisco."

"It's the first thing to be dumped from settlers' wagons when they get into trouble, too," Slash said thoughtfully. "That's china. This ain't the kind of thing any woman parts with. Look at the way Myra's moonin' over it, imaginin' family reunions and Sunday socials."

"She'd dump it just 'fore she left her bratty son behind," Pecos agreed. "Though if that kid was you, your ma'd likely keep the silver and let you set out in the middle of a desert."

"I can get top dollar for this!" Myra called. She'd opened two more crates. "That was an incredible estate. Where was it?"

"We got to haul the furniture over for Jay," Pecos said, trying to distract Myra from her questions. He elbowed Slash, who grunted.

"Yeah, right. We promised her."

"You said it was a surprise gift," Myra said. "I don't know where all this came from, but get your stories straight, will you?" She stepped away and pointed at another crate. "That one's got my mark on it. This is the shipment you took to Potero. Why's it still in the shed?"

"We'll get around to it," Slash said. "After we get the furniture over to the Thousand Delights."

"You two aren't telling me anything like the truth," Myra said.

"We're not lyin' to you, I promise you that, little darlin'," Slash said.

"You're *trying* not to lie. Not telling the truth is the same as lying. That's what Del says, and he ought to know."

"He listens too much to what Marshal Decker tells him. Decker's a bad influence, even if he is Del's boss."

"Jimmy Braddock, you don't know what you're saying. You tell Jay to put you straight."

"Oh, she'll do that for him, mark my words," Pecos said, chuckling. Both Myra and Slash glared at him. He pointed to the davenport and chairs. He made a silent motion to get to work moving them.

Slash joined him lugging the furniture to the back of the wagon to escape Myra's sharp questions and her outright doubt about how they had come by everything in the shed. As long as they struggled to load the furniture, they were safe from her keen observations.

"That little girl sure can be a thorn in your paw," Slash said. "All the time askin' questions 'nd thinkin' about the answers. It's enough to give a fellow the collywobbles."

"It's good havin' her do that. I can't do all the thinkin' by myself," Pecos said.

They heaved the davenport into the wagon and followed it with several chairs, a fancy cherrywood table, and a desk.

"I can see Jay settin' behind this desk, like one of them regal European queens, runnin' every little thing in the Thousand Delights," Slash said. "She deserves the finest."

"And here she ended up with you," Pecos shot back.

"She gets my finest. I don't deserve a fine woman like her, but unlike Pistol Pete Johnson, I know it. All he ever did was mistreat her. She should never have stayed with him so long, not him and not his gang of cutthroats. She's better off that he came to the end of the trail and didn't take her with him."

"She truly loved him, though. He came to a sorry fate, that's for sure," Pecos said. "It was well deserved, even if it did pain her something fierce at the time." He settled in the driver's box and took up the reins. A quick glance into the shed made him sigh. Myra continued to rummage around in the boxes they'd taken from that double-dealer McCall's warehouse.

"Jay's got me now," Slash said. He sounded glum.

"She's movin' up in the world," Pecos said. "What woman wouldn't want you?"

"You're the one what always has a woman hangin' on his

arm. That's changed since you started sparkin' Miss Abigail."

"She might be more than I can handle, and I don't fess up to that easily." Pecos heaved a sigh thinking about the Nordic queen and her regal ways. It was safer handling old dynamite sticks dripping nitroglycerin, but that was part of his attraction to her. Sneaking around behind Bleed-'Em-So's back added to the thrill, not that Abigail wasn't a handful all by her lonesome.

He took the team down an alley beside the Thousand Delights and stopped at the rear of the saloon and pleasure house.

"We wouldn't have so much work to do unloadin' in front," Slash said. "This is like we're sneakin' about, thieves in the night."

"Your memory's leakin' out, old pard. We did steal all this, and it was in the middle of the night."

"But we didn't steal it here. Nobody who matters here in Camp Collins knows. Jay helped us, so she's not gonna tell the marshal. It's not his jurisdiction anyway—all the way out there in Potero."

"Quit flappin' your gums and give me some help." Pecos slid the first of the furniture to the edge of the wagon bed. The two wrestled the heavy desk down and into the Thousand Delights' back room.

As they were stacking the last of the furniture, Jay rushed in, out of breath and looking flustered.

"We brung along the best of the furniture. It'll look real fine up—"

Jay cut off Slash by hugging him close.

"They're here," she said. "Out in the main room."

"Who might that be?" Pecos asked, but he had a good idea. He reached around and pulled the sawed-off shotgun slung by a lanyard around his neck and over his left shoulder, where he could use it.

"The gunmen I had a drink with back in Potero," she said. "They didn't spot me, but they were asking too many questions."

"With the crowd you get in the saloon, every last customer'd fall all over themselves gossipin' 'bout us," Slash said. "All it'd take would be the offer of a free drink and those owlhoots would get quite an earful."

"How'd they ever trail us here?" Pecos wondered. "Once we got out on the road, there were a dozen places we might have driven."

"They're on the way to the shipping yard," Jay said. "Is Myra there?"

Both Slash and Pecos left without another word. They took one look at the mule team and lit a shuck on foot. Running got them back to their business headquarters faster than letting the balky mules pull the empty wagon.

"I recognize that horse," Pecos said. "What was his name? McCall's henchman?"

"Hutchins. He had the look of a fork-tailed son of Satan."

A pistol report sent them running even faster. Out of breath they got to the shed. The door swung in the afternoon breeze. Quite a commotion came from inside.

As they raced forward, both of them cried, "Myra!"

Another shot filled the small shed with white gunsmoke. Almost immediately came a yelp of pain and a string of sulfurous profanity that turned the air blue. They slammed into the wall and peered inside.

"Myra, you all right?"

"I'm all right, but one of your friends got a busted wrist. Trying to grab me wasn't too smart."

"That's something only Delbert's allowed to do," Slash said. He drew his six-shooters and slipped around the door and went left. Pecos hefted his gut-shredder and ducked right, taking cover behind a crate Myra had already opened.

"We got her. Throw down your guns and lift those hands high," came the shouted order from the back of the shed.

"That's a lie! They don't have me." A loud crash was followed by another yelp of pain. "I just smashed another one in the head."

"Next time hit him where it'll do some damage," Pecos called. He moved along the wall and finally caught sight of an owlhoot rubbing his gun hand. Myra had whacked him good with the pry bar.

Something warned the man of danger from somewhere other than the fierce young girl with the crowbar. He turned. Moving awkwardly, he drew his pistol with his left hand. That was as far as Pecos allowed. Both tubes of his shotgun discharged and left a very dead body plastered against a crate.

"Got one. How many are there, Myra?" he called.

"I only saw two."

"Outside!" Slash yelled. "Hutchins done kicked the wall down like a mule and is gettin' away."

Pecos let the shotgun dangle from the lanyard and drew his Russian .44. Rather than retrace his path to the door, he did as Hutchins had done. He kicked out a couple planks in the flimsy wall and tumbled into the dirt beside the shed.

He propped himself up on his left elbow and raised the .44 to take aim at Hutchins. Pecos got fleeting images. The man pointing his six-shooter. A couple pretty ribbons pinned on his chest. The lips pulled back in a snarl. And the eyes. The cold, flat, snake killer eyes.

They both fired at the same instant.

Then came reports like a string of Fourth of·July firecrackers going off. Hutchins stood stock-still for a moment. Pecos saw the light go out of the gunman's eyes. He crumpled bonelessly to the ground without so much as a dying twitch.

"You're slowin' down, old man," Slash said, coming around the shed. Both of his Colts smoked from being fired repeatedly. He blew the smoke away from the muzzles and tucked the irons away on either hip.

Pecos got to his feet and brushed himself off. "All I needed was one shot. Got him right through the ticker. He was deader 'n a doornail by the time you showed up."

Both of them turned. Myra stood at the shed door, pry bar in her hand. Her eyes were wide. She stared at them and asked in a soft voice, "What the hell have you two old reprobates gotten yourselves into?"

They didn't have a good answer. Not a quick and easy one, at any rate, since they had no idea.

Chapter 9

"It surely does look like you told me," Deputy Marshal Delbert Thayer said, staring at the two bodies. "That one got blowed all apart." He looked up at Pecos. The tall man tried to look innocent and failed. "Yup, that scattergun of yours did him."

Pecos instinctively reached around and rested his hand on the sawed-off dangling around his neck.

"I killed the other one, too," Pecos said.

"I had a part. What are these?" Slash held up both his Colt .44s and waved them around. "Don't let him take all the glory, Del."

"You two, hush up," Del said. His buckteeth about clacked as he spoke. "I'm working on how to put all this to the marshal so he won't clap the pair of you into jail. Right now, I don't know what to say. The one with the bullet holes in him had his six-shooter out, but the one cut smack-dab in two?" He shook his head. "Ain't no way I can see that this was in self-defense." The deputy snorted. "You should leave more evidence behind when you turn a fellow into a chopped steak, Pecos."

"Del, honey, it's like they said. Those two tried to kidnap me. Slash and Pecos stopped them." Myra Thompson rubbed up against the lawman's flank. She was at the point of purring like a contented kitten, but stopped before she reached that point. "The one Pecos shotgunned? I whacked him when he grabbed me. I wasn't able to fight them both off. Pecos and Slash saved me, Del. They saved me!"

"I believe you, Myra. I got to believe all of you, but this is pretty extreme." He kept staring at the gunman Pecos's double-ought buckshot had almost cut in half.

"It was done in our storage shed. Unless we herded them inside to kill them, they was trespassin'," said Slash.

"If you ask me, they wanted to do more 'n kidnap Myra. They wanted to steal our freight," added Pecos.

"I'm sure they wanted to do more with Miss Myra," Slash said. "If you know what I mean." He blushed, just a little.

"No need to spell it out for me," Del said. His arm circled Myra's waist and drew her close. "I don't know why that one's got military ribbons on his coat." The deputy pointed to Hutchins's decorations.

"Might be he was in the U.S. Army back in the day, but he wasn't now. He's not in uniform," Slash said.

"Everything tells me this was self-defense. You two fellows killed them cutthroats not only to keep yourselves from gettin' plugged, but to save Myra. I can see why they'd want to kidnap her and have their way with her."

"You're right, Del. You're right as rain," Slash said.

"I'll see to disposin' of them bodies," Del said. "I don't want my sweetie havin' to see them one minute longer 'n necessary. Truth is, it kinda sickens me lookin' at their corpses."

"You're a good man, Del," Slash said. The deputy and Myra stepped away and conversed privately. Slash pointed out into the street. "We got more trouble comin' at us, pard."

Pecos slumped and shook his head. "The old sayin' 'It never rains, but it pours' is—"

"'Right as rain,'" Slash finished for him.

They left the deputy and Myra and walked to meet the small posse out in the street. The five men wore badges that showed they were deputy federal marshals, but Slash and Pecos recognized them as being part of Bleed-'Em-So Bledsoe's personal army. They had tried to count the number of deputies Bleed-'Em-So put into the field and had stopped when they got to thirty. The Denver District's chief federal marshal had both money and manpower to spare.

And they were all tangled up in his sticky spider's web.

"I don't have to ask what brings you this way, Donahue," Slash said.

"Mount up. Marshal Bledsoe wants a word with you out in Saguache." The flinty-eyed deputy made no effort to turn his horse's face and leave town. He had been sent to do more than pass along the summons. The rawboned giant of a man, almost as tall and bulky as Pecos, provided an escort. He and the other four wouldn't let their wards stray even an inch until they faced Bledsoe and found out what the chief marshal wanted of them this time.

"It goes without sayin'," Slash said. "He wants to see us this very minute."

"Sooner," Donahue said. His weathered face might have been chiseled from stone. Not a hint of emotion flickered across his lips or forehead. His eyes tried to bore holes in the unfortunate pair he'd been ordered to fetch.

Both Slash and Pecos refused to be cowed by the intense looks, but they began to wilt a little after ten solid seconds of that glare.

"Get Buck and my Appy," Slash said. "We've got a ride ahead of us."

Donahue motioned. Two of the badge-toting hard cases with him trailed Pecos on his way to the stables, where the horses and mule teams were housed.

"Where are you goin', Pecos? I got more questions to ask." Del Thayer stepped out and put his hand on his holstered six-gun.

Seeing the men with Pecos, Myra gripped Del's wrist and tugged enough to get his attention. He looked at her, then back at the small posse. He swallowed hard when he got a better look at the men with Pecos. His Adam's apple bobbed up and down. He tried to say something more, but words jumbled up. Myra moved closer and whispered in his ear. He moved his hand from his iron, but the concerned girl refused to let loose of his wrist.

Pecos nodded curtly, letting them know everything was all right. He saddled his horse and then Slash's mount he refused to name. "Horse" reluctantly allowed someone other than his owner to prepare him. Pecos made sure the cinch was tight around the Appaloosa's middle, since they'd be riding fast, if not too far.

"Hurry up," one of Bledsoe's deputies barked. "You don't want to keep the boss waiting."

Pecos took the man's measure. Like Donahue, he looked as if he worked as a blacksmith before having the deputy's badge pinned on his chest. His hand was steady and his gaze unwavering. Pecos nodded curtly. If it came to a showdown, he believed he could take the man, either with a pistol or bare knuckles. It was like that with all of Bledsoe's small army. Together they were formidable. Taken individually, they weren't a match for Pecos. Or for Slash.

That was why the federal marshal had recruited them to do dirty work that an ordinary deputy wasn't able to do.

Pecos forked his saddle and led the Appy back to where Slash was staring down Donahue. His partner had barely mounted when the deputies all whirled about as if controlled by a single thought and galloped out of town.

"Tell Jay!" Slash called to Myra.

"Where're you going?" The young woman took a half

step forward, as if she had the power to stop them from leaving.

"She'll know," Pecos said. He put his head down and set his buckskin to full gallop.

They approached the ghost town. It wasn't a surprise that the town of Saguache wasn't entirely deserted. An old geezer ran the saloon. How he made enough to stay alive wasn't a matter of much concern to either the Pecos River Kid or Slash. Catering to Federal Chief Marshal Luther Bledsoe might be the sole source of income.

Bleed-'Em-So Bledsoe's fancy wagon was parked outside the saloon. Inside hung a lantern so he could read as the ponderous wagon made its way from his headquarters in Denver. Carpeting on the wagon bed soaked up some of the bumps and rolls as the wagon crossed uneven terrain. A special table with holes drilled in the top let Bledsoe set glasses down so they wouldn't slide around.

Slash and Pecos exchanged a knowing glance. Both laughed at the same instant.

"What's funny?" Donahue hadn't uttered a word during the three-hour ride from Camp Collins.

"If he sets a glass down in one of them holes, it don't budge," Slash said.

"But he's gonna spill the whiskey in the glass," Pecos finished. He mimicked a man licking his hand. It was childish, and he enjoyed seeing how it irritated Donahue.

"Inside. Now." Donahue dismounted and hitched up his gun belt.

His two unwilling riding companions pushed open the swinging doors and went directly to the rear. They'd had more than one meeting with Bledsoe in this deserted town, away from prying eyes and journalists thinking on spying for their newspapers.

Luther Bledsoe sat in a push chair, his spindly legs twisted in front of him. He had tried to stop a bank robbery and had thrown a few rounds in the direction of the perpetrators, one of whom happened to be none other than Mr. James "Slash" Braddock. During the exchange of lead, a bullet had ricocheted off a wall and struck Bledsoe in the middle of the back. The stray bullet had left him paralyzed and bitter.

Bleed-'Em-So Bledsoe's cottony white hair fluttered as wind gusted through the cracks in the saloon's back wall. His keen eyes fixed on the pair.

"I was beginnin' to think you were reneging on our deal. I was all ready to burn this." He pressed his bony hand down on a sheet of paper—the presidential pardon exonerating Slash and Pecos for all their crimes. It was his hold over them. They had been rescued from swinging from a gallows crossbeam at the last instant by a gang of Pinkerton agents. Bledsoe had hired the Pinks to save Pecos and Slash so he could threaten them to work for him in ways that were seldom legal.

If they ever refused, the pardon vanished, and they'd be dancing at the end of a rope.

Bleed-'Em-So took his hand off the page and stared hard at his two slaves, for that's what they were as long as the threat of canceling their pardon remained.

"A cigarillo, Miss Langdon." Bledsoe held out his skeletal hand, thumb and forefinger spread apart just a tiny bit.

For the first time Pecos and Slash saw the lovely blonde. Abigail Langdon had remained in deep shadow at the rear of the saloon, a cape of purest sable over her shoulders. A hood pulled up over her abundant blond hair had further hidden her. The hood fell away to her shoulders as she stepped forward. Her long, lustrous locks shimmered as if made from the purest spun gold.

Pecos gasped. Her sudden appearance took him by surprise. He and Miss Abigail had been sparking every time he went to Denver. Neither had seen fit to tell her employer. Pecos had no idea what Bledsoe's reaction would be if he found out of their indiscretions. Amusement was a possibility. Fury was more likely. The chief marshal staked out his territory, marked it like a hound dog lifting its back leg, and defended it jealously. The statuesque blonde was certainly part and parcel of what he considered his possessions.

She reached into a fold of the cape and drew out a thin cigarillo. She let it dangle from the corner of her mouth. Her red lips barely held it as she struck a lucifer and puffed the smoke to a fiery coal. Somehow she made it seem sensuous as she took the cigarillo from her mouth and placed it carefully in Bledsoe's grip.

"Thank you, Miss Langdon. As always, you are indispensable."

Slash elbowed his partner in the ribs and stepped between him and the scrawny old man trapped in the push chair. Nobody wanted Bledsoe to get even an inkling of his beautiful assistant's indiscretions with Melvin Baker. The way they looked at each other raised the temperature in the room to that rivaling desert heat in the middle of summer.

"You didn't ask us here so we could watch you smoke," Slash said.

"Mr. Braddock, I didn't *ask* you here. I *ordered* you here." Bledsoe took a puff. A smoke ring rapidly expanded and disappeared in the air currents inhabiting the old saloon.

Slash held his tongue. He stepped to the side to block Pecos's view of Abigail. Betraying the attraction between the two was a sure way for Bleed-'Em-So to consider other orders . . . orders that'd get them outfitted with hemp neckties.

"Have you heard anything about Paradise?" Bleed-'Em-So puffed a couple more times, then knocked the ash onto the floor. As he smoked, he watched them with an eagle eye.

"Can't say that we have. It's up in the Front Range. Out of the way for a pair of honest freight haulers like us," Slash said.

"It is gone."

"What do you mean 'it's gone'? An avalanche wiped it out? A flood? There hasn't been that kind of storm in a month of Sundays."

"No, Mr. Braddock, none of those things. I was too late to save it. My men, close to twenty strong, got there after a plague of locusts stripped it bare."

"Bugs?" Slash and Pecos looked at each other.

"Carrion bugs," Bledsoe said. "No, not that. Carrion bugs dine on dead flesh."

"They missed a meal with him," Pecos said under his breath.

Slash tensed. Miss Abigail smiled at the remark from her lover. A quick look relieved Slash when he saw Bledsoe hadn't heard. Whether the years took away the old reprobate's hearing, or he was too caught up in his tale, hardly mattered. He waved his cigarillo around, stabbing with it like it was a knife.

"They were just leaving."

"Who?" asked Pecos.

"Town killers. They swept in and murdered every man, woman, and child that got in their way. They used Gatlings to reduce the buildings to rubble. They looted all the stores and houses, robbed the bank, knew where to find every penny in cash anywhere in Paradise. Oh, yes, they were locusts. They dined well on the carcass of the town."

"You said you and your deputies got there as they were leavin'?" Slash tried to piece together the story and wasn't having much luck. "You stopped them dead in their tracks, didn't you?"

He let out a soft "Oh" when he realized what had happened.

"They killed most all of my men. They have war wagons plated in steel armor, firepower any cavalry unit would be proud to field, and they had howitzers. It was an invading army."

"A destroying army," Abigail said.

"I can't match them. They've got too many guns and men. It's like a military unit."

"Get the army to track 'em down," said Pecos. "You don't need us."

The fury grew until the marshal's face turned fiery red. His hand shook and his eyes bugged out. For a second Slash thought the man's anger would give his legs strength enough to stand. Bledsoe rose halfway out of his push chair before falling back.

"They made me look weak. I want you to stop them. You two cutthroats are perfect to weasel your way into their ranks, then rip their guts out. I want them all dead. Dead, I tell you!" Spittle formed at the corner of his mouth. His forehead turned into a plowed field of furrows with his fierce scowl.

"I've heard tell of other towns bein' wiped out like that. Over in Kansas. Most folks disregarded such tales and figured a tornado did the damage," said Slash.

"You reckon they're movin' into Colorado from Kansas?" asked Pecos.

"And Nebraska," Bledsoe said, his anger muted now. "Nobody's got any idea who's responsible. Anyone tryin' to desert gets cut down and their carcass left for the coyotes. About all I know is what one of them not-quite-deads said to a deputy what found him alongside a road. 'High Mountain.' He squeezed out those words and then keeled over."

"Never heard of any High Mountain," Pecos said.

"Colorado's filled with 'em," Slash countered. "That doesn't mean a danged thing."

"Worm your way into their confidence, then kill 'em. Kill every last man. A thousand dollars each, as usual, when you finish your assignment." Bledsoe leaned back in his push chair. "Do it quick. Paradise was too easy for them. If you don't stop 'em real quick as a bunny, the thought will fester that another Colorado town's easy pickin's. There won't be no stoppin' them if they get a taste for Colorado towns."

"There ain't no way two of us can stop a goldanged army," protested Slash. "If you lost twenty deputies, we don't stand a snowball's chance in hell."

"You're refusin' me? Is that what you're tellin' me, Mr. Braddock? Mr. Baker?" Bledsoe leaned back in his chair and held the burning cigarillo over the pardon laid out flat on the table.

He slowly lowered the flaming tip until it touched the edge of the pardon. The dried paper flared and began turning to powdery ash.

Pecos had never moved faster in his life. He slammed his hand down over the burning document. He drew back to see if he'd extinguished the fire. Bleed-'Em-So Bledsoe lowered the cigarillo again. Pecos slid his hand under the coal. Tiny curls of smoke from his burning flesh rose. He never flinched. That would give Bledsoe too much satisfaction.

"So? You're takin' the job? I knew you would. Miss Langdon, give them each one thousand dollars."

Her polar-blue eyes welled with tears, but her every move was precise. From somewhere inside her sable cape, she pulled out an envelope and handed it to Pecos. As his hand left the pardon, she slid the paper off the table and tucked it into her cape.

Pecos wondered how much lead would fly if he grabbed the woman and claimed the pardon.

"No" was all Slash said. He read his partner's intentions all too well.

Pecos tore his eyes off the beautiful Nordic woman and saw a half dozen of Bledsoe's deputies all with pistols drawn arrayed along the far saloon wall.

"Miss Langdon, it's time to return to Denver so these two can get on with their jobs." Bledsoe's thin lips drew back and showed yellowed teeth in a feral smile. "Get it done quick. I won't tolerate any more towns bein' razed."

Abigail gripped the handles on the push chair and shoved Bleed-'Em-So Bledsoe to the door.

Slash plucked the envelope with their pay from his partner's hands.

"I'll hang on to it for safekeepin'."

"What makes it safe in your hands?" Pecos asked.

"I'm lettin' Jay hang on to it for us."

"That's safe, bein' with your missus," Pecos agreed. "I hope we live long enough to spend it."

Chapter 10

"I've asked everyone around town," Myra Thompson said, shaking her head. "Nobody's heard of a place called High Mountain. Are you sure you heard right?"

Pecos nodded glumly. His mood only darkened after getting back to Camp Collins. Bleed-'Em-So Bledsoe had ordered them about and tormented them with putting a burning coal to their pardon. He held up his hand. A scorched spot on his palm showed how he had smothered the first fire to save their pardon from going up in smoke. A fiery circular red burn mark on the back of his hand reminded him vividly of what an utter low-life, no-account, sleazy snake in the grass Bleed-'Em-So was. And worst of all, he hadn't had a chance to say a single word to Miss Abigail.

"Even Miss Jay's not heard of it," Slash said. "Last night, when things quieted down, we had a long talk."

"Is that what you call it?" Pecos said.

"Don't sound so grumpy," Slash said. "We was takin' it easy and reminiscin' 'bout what all's happened. That's all I meant." Slash grinned broadly. "Then we got down to scarin' the cat most of the night."

"Are you sure it's a town?" Myra chewed at her lower lip in thought. "Maybe it's something else. I don't know all the names of the tall mountains around here. It doesn't sound like Pikes Peak or anything like that, but if it's translated from one of the Injun tongues, you might find it straightaway."

"I know four or five different lingoes," Pecos said. "That doesn't tell me anything in a single one." He began using sign language. His fingers flowed until he gave up when his joints began hurting him some.

"That's what High Mountain looks like in sign language?" Myra asked.

He nodded. "We got other business to tend to. I didn't want nothin' to do with Bleed-'Em-So's latest way of puttin' us in early graves, if two cranky old-timers like us can ever be considered fit and proper for an early grave."

"What are you going to do?" Myra looked toward the shed where they had yet to repair the broken walls. "The company can use some cash flowing in."

"*Flowing in?* You make it sound like we've dammed up a river," Slash said.

"What she's sayin', pard, is that we need to be busy as beavers and get to work haulin' freight. You have any contracts for us, little darlin'?"

Myra admitted that business was sparse right now.

"We've got the money Bleed-'Em-So handed us," Slash reminded them.

"That should be put in the bank until you earn it," Myra said. "If we use it to keep the business going, without you delivering what he asked for, the marshal might take offense."

"That scrawny old buzzard'll take offense even if we do catch those town killers."

"They sound like a scary bunch," Myra said. "I can't imagine what it'd be like standing around in a town minding your own business and having them swoop down like a hawk. You said they killed everybody? Even women and children?"

"Then they burned the town to the ground after looting it." Slash rested his hands on the butts of his six-shooters. "Desperadoes like that don't stay in one place long. If we ignore 'em, they'll go away."

"Because they've run out of places to destroy?" Myra's voice carried an edge. "You owe it to Marshal Bledsoe . . . and the folks around here . . . to find them."

"How are we gonna stop an army? There's only two of us and a couple dozen of them. Hell, they ripped up Bledsoe's posse." Pecos's funk deepened. Not only were they signing their own death warrants by tangling with a gang like that, he hadn't so much as given Miss Abigail a peck on the cheek.

If he and Slash ever found the killers with their Gatling guns, and a desire to leave behind only dead bodies after burning down a town, he wasn't likely to ever feel her cool, smooth fingers caressing his brow again.

"Pecos. Pecos! If your mood gets any darker, lightning clouds will start to thunder overhead," Slash said.

"If we can't touch the two thousand that Bledsoe gave us as an advance, I know a way to make some money," Pecos said. "And if Bleed-'Em-So has spies trackin' us, it'll look like we're scoutin' around." He pointed to the shed. "We delivered furniture to Miss Jay. Let's figger out what else we can sell."

"It is ours," Slash said. "We came by it all honestly. By that, I mean we took it all as payment McCall cheated us out of. But we've been forgettin' one teeny little thing."

"The gunslicks," Myra said. "McCall sent a couple stone-cold killers after you. How long's it gonna be until he wonders what happened to them and sends more?"

"Hutchins was the ramrod of that outfit," Slash said. "Anybody could see that by the way he strutted around and pretended to be so ornery."

"He was ornery, Slash," said Pecos. "Myra's right about them bein' killers. We'd never have crossed them, given the chance."

"But they weren't any match for two old cutthroats like us," Slash said.

"Ain't many over the years that were our match." Pecos chuckled. "Reckon we showed 'em who was top dog, since they're in the ground and we ain't."

They looked at each other and spoke at the same instant.

"Where'd McCall get all that furniture?"

"And everything else," Myra said. "I surely do appreciate fine silverware. That's about the best I've ever seen." She heaved a deep sigh. "When Del and me get hitched, it'd be a fine wedding present."

"We had something even better in mind," Pecos said.

"We did?" Slash looked puzzled. "What was that? I don't seem to recollect."

"Why, yes, you do, pard. We agreed. If Myra enters into wedded bliss with the deputy, we was gonna give her two whole days off."

"Naw," Slash said, catching his partner's drift, "that'd be way too generous. One day, and not a second more. We don't want to spoil her."

"You two are joshing me," Myra said. "Besides, Del hasn't sprung the question yet. Not exactly."

"What was in the crates we took back from McCall?" Slash asked, going into the shed and kicking at a box here and there.

"Them other crates was household fixin's," Pecos said. "There must be more in what we carted up to Potero for that thievin' skunk. Maybe we have things we can sell around town and not have to haul off to Denver."

"Why are you lookin' for excuses to avoid a trip to Denver?" Slash asked. "Miss Abigail's tender attentions got you spooked? Afraid if you mentioned you had a shed full of china and silverware and furniture, she'd entertain ideas about gettin' hitched? That she might take the bit in her teeth and ask you to marry her?"

"Like Miss Jay did you? If she'd waited for you to find your tongue, she'd be waitin'—"

"Slash," called Myra. Her voice was small and choked. "Pecos. Come take a gander at this. Now. You're not going to believe your eyes."

Myra stood on tiptoe and peered into another crate they'd retrieved from McCall. She had a stricken look on her face.

They sauntered over, thinking she had discovered more household goods.

Both of the old bank robbers looked into the open box. That single glance caused them to react just as their business manager had. No words came out from either of them.

Stunned at the discovery, Pecos reached in and jerked out a long metal device from the shredded paper cradling it against being jostled around. It came out oily from preservative.

"Is that what I think it is?" Myra asked. She stepped back another pace, as if it might bite her, and stared, wide-eyed.

"It's a hopper all loaded with .30-caliber rounds," Pecos said.

They stared at each other, then at the metal column.

"We got ourselves a crate bustin' at the sides with fifty magazines all primed and ready for a Gatling gun," Slash said softly.

Chapter 11

Colonel Raymond leaned forward, fists on the edge of the table. The map of Colorado stretched out in front of him, held down with rocks at each corner. The map was distressingly void of marks showing movement of troops, approaches, or even a decent target. He straightened, pulled an ornate watch from his vest pocket, and snapped open the engraved lid.

A woman's face stared at him from inside the lid. He smiled a little. *Mara.* Poor, doomed Mara lost in the chaos of Reconstruction. Raymond ran his finger over the photograph, then held up the watch to see the time. With an impatient snap he closed the lid and returned the watch to its pocket.

"Matthias!" He bellowed for his aide a second time before the smallish man entered the tent.

As always, Matthias looked as if he, and he alone, knew the joke. A tiny smile curled the corners of his lips under the thin mustache. His chin bobbed up and down like a cow chewing its cud, making the dyed-dark Vandyke beard wiggle obscenely. A thin face added to the look of constant mischief, but his brown eyes danced. His eyes were always darting about, taking in every detail. He moved like a snake, lacking bones and slithering about. Raymond tried not to shiver just looking at him.

If he hadn't needed the man's expertise in moving equipment and supplying troops, Raymond would have shot him down. If any of his staff ever betrayed him, Raymond knew it would be Dane Matthias.

"Yes, sir? What is it?"

"Hutchins. Has he returned? I need his scouting report for the next town. Without a list of potential towns, how can I send out Benson to do the final pre-assault reconnoiter?"

"Nobody's heard from him since Paradise," Matthias said. "That's not unusual. He's always very thorough when he finds a new target. I appreciate his detailed reports. It gives me a chance to anticipate supply problems before they happen."

Nothing in what Matthias said was true, other than Hutchins not reporting back after the Paradise campaign. Hutchins only located possible targets and made cursory examinations to determine the potential for a worthwhile raid. Then he galloped on to find another and another. His sketchy reports were what Raymond used to home in on an actual location. For some reason Matthias thought heaping praise on every one of Raymond's subordinates somehow elevated him in the Colonel's estimation. He was wrong.

"You're a fine quartermaster, Matthias," Raymond said. That much was true. He was undeniably slimy, but Matthias knew his job and did it well. "But we must keep moving. The federal deputies we tangled with at Paradise won't take their defeat easily. If they get angry enough, they can call out every cavalry trooper in the territory to track us down."

"Our men are trained well enough and outfitted to defeat any such attack. Give me the route and I'll see that supplies are placed for a hasty retreat. Wyoming? Or do you prefer to head farther west and venture into Utah?"

The Colonel shook his head. He saw no reason to undertake a campaign in New Mexico Territory. The low-hanging fruit in Colorado still beckoned. And once he finished here? He needed Hutchins to locate the next town. Only after consultation with Benson would he tell Matthias where they relocated next.

"Do you want to send out a courier to find Hutchins?"

"There's no need. He might have gone to Potero. Yes, he must have."

"I asked for an inventory of our supplies there," Matthias said. "Did you order him to check for me?"

"No, he's out ranging on his own. But Potero. Yes, he might have gone there."

"Sir, it's not good dealing with family like that. Wasn't Hutchins related to the marshal?"

"Everyone there's related. Hutchins is the marshal's half brother." Raymond sucked at his teeth. "I didn't like dealing with relatives in this fashion, but they were Hutchins's clan, after all. He's a good man and vouched for his uncle and the others in Potero."

"Hutchins," Matthias said so low that Raymond almost didn't hear. Louder, "I need to know what's stored there. I have a buyer for much of the Paradise loot, too, but I need an inventory."

"We'll go there," the Colonel said.

"*We*, sir?"

"Muster a squad. We leave in fifteen minutes." Raymond turned from his quartermaster and studied the map again. So many possibilities, but he needed scouting reports. "Where are you, Hutchins? It's not like you to be out of touch for so long."

Colonel Raymond flipped the rocks at the map's corners off the table and rolled up his battle plans. Or what would be his battle plans.

Damn, Hutchins!

* * *

"Spread out, circle the warehouse. Stay at a distance," Raymond ordered his troops. It pleased him to see every last one of them sported at least two campaign ribbons. These were tried-and-true soldiers in his sweep across the West. They knew their jobs and what he expected of them.

"Orders, sir?" asked a hulking brute of a man. It took him a second to remember his name.

"No one in or out while Matthias and I are conferring with the warehouse owner. Any other questions, Bunton?"

"Does that include the law? That can get dicey."

"Everyone," the Colonel said, steel in his voice. Bunton wore three ribbons, but he had not distinguished himself enough to question orders the way he now did.

Bunton nodded curtly, then rode away to position the sentries. Raymond held up his hand to shield his eyes from the setting sun. This was the perfect time for his inspection. The town shuttered stores for the day and everyone sought an evening meal. That reduced the chance of being disturbed as he spoke with Earl McCall.

The Colonel sat his horse ramrod straight, looking directly ahead and paying no attention to minor details on his way to McCall's business. The large warehouse cast a long shadow. By the time he dismounted, the Colonel was cloaked in twilight. In a few minutes, the stars would provide the only illumination for a moonless night.

He marched to the office building and came to a halt a few feet from the steps leading up.

"Mr. McCall, I'd like a word with you." He sucked in his breath when the man burst out, waving around a rifle. Raymond showed no hint of emotion at being threatened.

"What is it?"

"I need an inventory. A dozen wagons are on the road to remove our most recent plunder."

"That you, Colonel?" McCall peered nearsightedly. "Step around to where I can see you in the light."

A pale yellow glow from a kerosene lamp inside the building spilled out onto the steps. Raymond stood as still as a statue. Being ordered about by his underlings sent a bad message to the others. He almost looked over his shoulder to where Matthias forked his saddle, but refrained. Such a show of uncertainty filtered down through the ranks, and he always felt uneasy at the way Matthias constantly studied him.

One slip and Matthias would move up to lead the army that the Colonel had forged over the past year.

"I want to talk to Hutchins," he said. "Get him out here."

"Hutchins ain't here. He . . . I don't know where he got off to."

"But he was here?" Raymond pressed.

"He's gone." McCall's nervous answer bespoke of a lie.

"Show us the merchandise. Mr. Matthias needs to prepare it for transport."

"You haven't paid me for the last stack of crates I stored for you. I'm gettin' pissed off that you're holdin' us and the rest of the town in such little regard."

"Us?"

"Me and the marshal. And all his deputies, too. We're riskin' our necks hidin' what you stole. I've heard tell that Chief Marshal Bledsoe over in Denver's been complainin' about your ways."

Raymond snorted. "Bledsoe is no more than a distraction. After Paradise we encountered a posse of federal deputies that I assume were beholden to him." Raymond chuckled. "They are no longer even a minor annoyance." He sobered. "Our goods. Now, McCall, show us now."

"Well, I wish you'd let me know ahead of time. This ain't the best time to go pokin' around in the warehouse."

Raymond lifted his hand and gestured. Matthias trotted to the warehouse and dismounted.

"I don't need your permission, but your assistance would be welcome."

"It can be dangerous in there. My boys don't always stack those boxes right, and they can tip over and crush you."

"Colonel," Matthias called. "The door has been forced open."

"I can explain that," McCall said. He rested his rifle in the crook of his left arm. "Let's go on over and I'll show your man around. Your quartermaster, is he? I wish Hutchins was here to do a proper introduction."

The Colonel tugged on his horse's reins and turned to the warehouse. Matthias vanished into the dark building. He heard his quartermaster bumping into crates and cursing softly. McCall had been truthful about that. Raymond hoped the man hadn't set traps inside to fall over on an unsuspecting thief.

"There's a lantern," McCall said. "I'll fetch it and—"

"Don't bother," the Colonel said. He drew his Peacemaker, but didn't have to point it in McCall's direction. The man grumbled, but didn't openly protest. He still wasn't inclined to believe Raymond was going to shoot him for any of the lies he'd told or the obstacles he had so pitifully constructed to get back the stolen goods.

He went down the steps and preceded Raymond to the jimmied door.

"It wasn't anything, really. Some kids tried to get in. They damaged the latch, but nothing inside was taken."

"Did they open any of the crates?" Matthias asked, emerging from the warehouse.

"What'd they get if they did? Nothin' that'd do them a whit of good. Naw, I ran 'em off before they poked around too much. Marshal Welles knows about them. They . . . They're, uh, Lenny Larkin's kids. He's a second cousin, but knows which side his bread's buttered on. The whole danged town knows. We haven't been so prosperous since the Silver Emperor Mine closed down last year. Yes, sir, we appreciate the trade you brung us, Colonel. We certainly do."

"Much of the furniture I remember as taken from Paradise is missing," Matthias said. "I need to check, but at least two of the boxes of ammunition for the Gatlings are not in there, either."

"Ammo? I don't know anything about that, unless . . ."

"Unless what, Mr. McCall?" Raymond turned toward the man.

"Don't get your hackles raised, Colonel," McCall said. "Those must be the crates them old geezers hauled in."

"*Hauled in?* The crates were delivered and stored in your warehouse?" Matthias shrugged his shoulders and moved his coattail away from the iron dangling at his right hip.

"Yeah, yeah, they brung 'em, but they wanted too much money for the haulage, so I ran 'em off."

"Without paying?" Raymond asked. He closed his eyes and opened them slowly. "The door has been broken open, by children you say. But tracks in the dirt show a heavy wagon left here. A heavily loaded wagon, possibly owned by the men you cheated. You decided you weren't being paid enough, so you refused to pay simple freighters for their labor?"

"There's wagons comin' 'nd goin' all the time," McCall protested. "Ask Hutchins. He's the one what hired those thieves."

"*Thieves,*" Raymond said, rolling it over his tone like some bitter wine.

Colonel Raymond lifted his Peacemaker and fired once. He was a dead shot. And McCall was a dead man with an ounce of lead lodged in his heart as he crashed to the ground.

Chapter 12

"We ought to wait till morning," Slash said. "We've been on the trail too long."

"You sound like an old man. Next thing you'll be complainin' about is your achin' back and how your bones creak."

"Old pard, it ain't me I'm thinkin' of, because I'm such a fine, upstandin' fellow. It's you I worry about. You're the one who's showin' his age. Every time you move, the way your joints pop is enough to wake the dead."

"How'd you know?" Pecos shot back. "You're nigh-on deaf."

Slash drew rein and held up his hand to stop his partner.

"Ain't my ears that are fadin' with old age. I hear fine." He canted his head to one side. "You hear that?"

"Horses alongside the road, but where are they?"

"Their riders hid them," Slash said. "That's not the kind of thing neighborly folks do. But road agents? That's exactly what they'd do."

"Back in the day when we was robbin' banks and stickin' up trains, that's what we'd do. Can it be that Bleed-'Em-So knew what he was doin' by recruitin' us? We know all the tricks. Ain't that so, Slash?"

His partner pointed to a ravine cutting across the road. Together they urged their horses to the side. The ravine flowed down into a larger one. Fifty yards ahead, three horses nervously pawed at the ground and tugged hard, trying to free their reins. The bushes they were tethered to resisted with the tenacity of a plant surviving long, hard winters and occasionally fierce summers.

"Where're the riders?" Slash whispered, but he still made too much noise.

Rising from the darkness, what they'd thought were large rocks turned toward them. Starlight flashed off one of the ambushers' six-shooters.

Pecos swung his sawed-off shotgun around and fired before Slash unlimbered his two Colts. The blinding flash from the shotgun worked more against them than the storm of lead pellets ripping into the night. One man on the receiving end of that blast swore a blue streak. He'd been nicked, but not put out of action. His two partners fanned off six rounds each. In the dark the only way to find them was to wait for a muzzle flash.

The same shrouding velvet night saved Slash and Pecos. Bullets whined past their heads. The worst damage came when their horses began crow-hopping from all the noise. That made aiming from horseback impossible.

Both men kicked free of their stirrups and dropped to the ravine bottom. They had worked together for so many years, they instinctively knew where the other was. It didn't take them any long discussion to retaliate. They moved instinctively. After a couple more blasts, Pecos's shotgun fell silent, but his Russian .44 blasted back at the trio trying to reload.

All three had run dry at the same time. That wasn't a problem Slash and Pecos had. If one fired, the other hung back. When a pistol came up empty, the other fired away, giving cover to reload. This time both of them had their six-shooters loaded, cocked, and ready for action.

Slash used the lull in lead coming his way to rush forward, a six-gun in each hand. He alternated between the left smoke wagon and the right, until he came up empty. His frontal assault had ended the life of one owlhoot. The other two turned on him, weapons reloaded. With a smooth motion he tucked away both his Colts and drew the thick-bladed bowie knife sheathed at the small of his back.

He leveled the point and drove straight ahead. The tip pinked the nearest gunman's arm. The would-be ambusher yelped and dropped his popgun. Slash twisted viciously and ran the razor-sharp edge along the man's ribs. Warm blood spurted over his hand. Then Slash collided hard, and the two of them went down in a kicking, clawing tangle. With a quick yank he pulled the knife back and opened up an even deeper cut on the man's side.

Blood drenching him, Slash rolled over and tried to get a better grip on his knife. The blood turned the handle too slippery. He dropped the weapon as his attacker reared up. Slash saw the gun in the man's shaking hand.

"You gonna die," the man grated out.

Slash dived in a vain attempt to pick up his knife, although he was too far away to stab with it. The gore-slick handle made it impossible for him to throw it with any hope of accuracy.

A foot-long orange lance leaped into the night. A pistol fired a second time. This time Slash realized the gunshot came from behind him. His finger closed around the handle of his bowie knife, but there wasn't any call to use it now. The gunman who had thought to cut him down swayed, dropped to his knees, and then keeled over.

"The last one hauled ass like he knowed who we was," Pecos said, holding up his six-gun and blowing the smoke away. "Unless you want to take the time to scalp this one, we got to catch us one running-scared back shooter."

Slash rubbed his knife handle in the dirt, then sheathed it. He kicked the body Pecos had finished off. Not a twitch. Twin furrows in the man's side had turned black in the starlight—the color of blood in the night. The cuts no longer bled. The heart in that body had stopped pumping.

Taking the time to reload, Slash lost track of his partner. Pecos plunged into the darkness, hot in pursuit of the final ambusher. Turning slowly, Slash homed in on the sound of men blundering through the thorny vegetation.

Slash hadn't gone a dozen paces when a flurry of gunfire sounded. The hefty *boom-boom* of the Russian .44 sounded only twice. The sharper crack of a .45 kept coming for a full six times. He sucked in his breath and hurried toward the fight. The lack of reply from Pecos's gun worried him. The full cylinder of another pistol emptying worried him more.

A huge dark heap on the ground caused him to skid to a halt. He dropped to one knee and swung his six-shooters around. A formless ghost rose up and drifted toward him.

"Don't you dare shoot me, Slash Braddock. You'd never be able to explain it to your blushing bride how you gunned down your partner."

"I knew it was you," Slash said. "Nobody else smells as bad as you. Those buckskins need to be burned, not washed."

"You never noticed such things before Miss Jay started makin' you take a bath every Saturday night. You're gonna wear out your hide from all the soap and hot water." Pecos came over and lifted the corpse up to get a better look. "Lookee there. Why ain't I surprised?"

He reached down and ripped off a patch of cloth. He tossed it to his partner. Slash caught it and held it up so starlight reflected off two campaign ribbons. In the dim light the colors were muted and indistinct, but the ribbon design was all too familiar.

"Just like the ones Hutchins wore."

"Only thing was, he had more. We cut him down and

took out a senior killer. This one now, well, he's only got two, so he was a novice among them town rapers."

"We stomped on him and his friends in time to keep them from addin' ribbons to their chests. No tellin' how many folks died for him to earn these." With a savage backhand motion, Slash hurled the ribbons into the gloom.

"These three weren't road agents lookin' to waylay an unsuspecting pilgrim," Pecos said.

"Why were they here? Lookouts?"

"That's what I think they were. Guards to protect someone in Potero. Maybe they were supposed to warn whoever's there."

"I wonder if it might be somethin' more 'n that," Slash said.

"We're cogitatin' on the same idea. You reckon them town wreckers are on the way to Potero?"

They looked at each other. Even in the dark their smiles were obvious.

"If we hurry, we can catch ourselves a cutthroat responsible for razin' an entire town." Slash checked his six-guns to be sure they were fully loaded.

"Bleed-'Em-So Bledsoe'll be real proud of us for solvin' his problem so quick." Pecos started back to the ravine where they'd left their horses.

"All we have to do is find whatever cayuse is at the head of the owlhoots and take him out. One shot, maybe two. That'll dispirit the rest."

"I can hear 'em runnin' for the tall and uncut now," Pecos said. "We can't get too cocky, though. We got to take the boss out quick and dirty."

"Luckily, the dirty part's easy enough for you," Slash said.

They rode slowly into Potero. The town still slept, though the mouthwatering aroma of baking bread caused them both to slow down, then come to a halt in front of a dimly lit bakery. A woman with her hair caught up in a bandanna and wearing a long white apron stood in the window, kneading more bread for the town's daily fare. The heat from the oven made her sweat. She swiped away at her forehead and left streaks of white flour.

"It's been a spell since we ate," Pecos pointed out.

"The bread smells mighty good. My belly's grumblin' at the prospect of a few bites."

They shifted about in the saddle and Slash said, "If the locust plague's comin' to dine on the entire town, we can't waste time. Gettin' caught with a mouthful of fresh-baked bread ain't no way to go to the grave."

"I can think of worse," Pecos said. He heaved a big sigh and pointed. "McCall's place ain't that far off. Any self-respectin' town robber'd go there straightaway."

"We were intent on rummagin' around that warehouse anyway. It's a good way to spend a few minutes 'fore the horde sweeps down."

"Assumin' that's what'll happen. You might be wrong, Pecos. Them gents along the road might have been nothin' more 'n road agents."

"Don't you go gettin' into any game where you have to figger the odds. You're a natural sucker. You'd lose—" Slash cut off his appraisal of his partner's gambling ability when a gunshot rang out. It echoed down the street and disturbed the stillness.

They both galloped directly to McCall's in time to see a trio of riders leaving.

"What's that all about?" Slash asked.

Pecos knew the best way to find out. He rode to the open door into the warehouse, dismounted, and slid his Russian .44 from the holster.

"Hold your horses!" Slash called. "Don't go and get yourself all shot up without me."

Slash hit the ground. Both his six-guns popped free and

fit snugly into his fists. The former train robbers slipped into the warehouse. It was pitch black inside.

"Here's a lamp," Pecos said. "Close your eyes while I light it. No reason for us both to be blinded." He flicked a match along his thumbnail. A brilliant flare dazzled him as he held the flame directly over the lamp wick. A new light assault caused his vision to dance with spots of yellow and blue.

"Nobody's here," Slash reported. "You got your peepers workin'?"

"I do, old pard, I do." Pecos walked deeper into the warehouse to the spot where they had taken back the crates filled with the Gatling gun ammunition. He grunted as he pried off the lid of another case with similar markings.

"We took the wrong boxes," Slash said, peering over his partner's buckskin-clad shoulder. "There must be fifty Smith and Wesson pistols in this box."

"You fixin' on givin' up your Colts?"

"This many six-guns'd fetch a pretty penny."

"Sellin' 'em is easier than unloadin' all that Gatling gun ammunition we got back in Camp Collins. You have to have a Gatling for those magazines to be worth anything."

"They weren't stolen from the army. Where'd they come from?"

"I got a better question. Those men we saw ridin' off when we came up. Were they responsible for the gunshot?"

"I plumb forgot about them, Slash." Before he said another word, Slash put a finger to his lips and cautioned silence.

"I hear somebody sneakin' around outside," Pecos said, ignoring his partner's signal to stay quiet. "They musta come back." Pecos swung his sawed-off shotgun around and held it firmly at his hip.

"Let's give 'em a wee bit of a surprise." Slash cocked both his Colts.

The two made their way back through the cluttered warehouse. Slash set the lamp on a high crate so the light cascaded down. Both of them cast long shadows. Instinctively, they moved apart so they wouldn't betray themselves when they reached the door. They exchanged a quick look, both nodded and spun around, ready to get the drop on whoever prowled about.

They froze. Pecos uncocked his shotgun and raised his hands high. Slash wasn't far behind dropping his six-shooters.

A ring of a half-dozen leveled rifles threatened to add a couple pounds of lead to their guts if they put up any fight.

Chapter 13

"It's not right," complained Slash. "You can't toss us in the jug because it suits your fancy." He slipped his arms through the bars and leaned forward to watch the marshal's reaction.

Nothing. The lawdog sat at his desk, back to the four cells in the rear of the jailhouse, as he leafed through a tall stack of WANTED posters.

"He's right, Marshal Welles," Pecos said, hanging on the bars beside his partner. "The letter of the law's gotta be observed. Otherwise, why bother with laws at all? Just make 'em up as you go."

Pecos elbowed Slash to keep him quiet. His partner came close to blurting out that was exactly what the Potero marshal had done—making up his own laws. If they wanted to talk their way out of the jail cell, they couldn't annoy the marshal.

The marshal swiveled around in his chair. Welles held up a handful of arrest warrants and waved them around. They snapped like a blacksnake whip the way he thrust them toward his prisoners.

"I've been through these a half-dozen times. I swear I remember seeing that you owlhoots are wanted men. I just can't find the paper. But it doesn't matter, because I got you dead to rights. You don't need rewards on your head to commit new crimes."

"What are you talkin' about, Marshal? We're simple old galoots tryin' to make a livin' with our freight business. We were huntin' for more work from McCall."

"You were trespassing, that's what you were doing. My nephew's gone missing, but when I track him down, he'll prefer charges. You busted into the warehouse with the intent of stealing what doesn't belong to you."

"Hard for a body to steal somethin' from himself if he already owns it," muttered Pecos.

"I swear, I saw your ugly puss on a poster." The marshal glared at Pecos, then went back to hunting for their likenesses. He peered at every smeary photo and badly drawn picture, shaking his head as he worked. When he had exhausted the thick pile of warrants, he put on eyeglasses and started over again.

"Don't think any of 'em carryin' our likenesses are still makin' the rounds," Slash said softly to his partner.

"Been a while since we stuck up a train," Pecos said. "And Bleed-'Em-So set us up on that one. The other robberies don't really count no more. It's been too long, and they never had a poster out on us for any murders."

"We were honest thieves, I reckon. Peaceable enough, too, not mowin' down anyone who wasn't puttin' up a fuss."

Both men unconsciously ran their fingers around their necks where the hangman's nooses had been tightened before Bledsoe had saved them from death dangles.

"We kept a low profile back in the Snake River Marauder days, too." Slash sounded a little wistful about that.

"Not seekin' fame has its benefit," Pecos agreed.

"Fortune," Slash said. "Give me money over fame every time. You can't buy a drink with fame."

"I don't know 'bout that," Pecos said. "If you was a beautiful, famous actress and a bunch of cowboys wanted to rub up against your flank, you'd never have a call to buy a drink."

"You don't have to worry about turnin' down drinks, then," Slash said. "Not only aren't you no famous actress, you're so ugly that a mud fence looks downright pretty in comparison. And—"

A deputy kicked in the outer door and stood, out of breath, in front of the marshal.

"Don't you have any manners, boy?" the marshal snapped. He took out his frustration at not finding WANTED posters on his two prisoners. "You open a door. Maybe you knock. You certainly lift the latch and push open the door. You don't kick it down. Look at that. I gotta repair the busted upper hinge now. And—"

"Marshal, it's your nephew. We found him. We found him!"

"So tell him to get his worthless ass in here to file charges against them two varmints." The lawman glanced over his shoulder in the old, former train robbers' direction.

"He's dead, Marshal. He's been shot dead!"

Silence descended on the jailhouse. The only sound came from the regulator wall clock slowly ticking away the seconds.

In a voice so choked and low it was almost a whisper, Marshal Welles asked, "What are you saying?"

"We found him in his warehouse, stuffed into a crate filled with sawdust. He'd been cut down. He was all stiff, and getting him out of that danged box was hard and—"

The marshal shot out of his chair. He stormed back to the cells and, wild-eyed and flushed, bellowed, "You killed my nephew! You killed Earl! He was my favorite among all of Sweet Susan's urchins!"

Slash and Pecos exchanged a quick look. Both shook their heads in silent agreement about what they ought to do in the face of such accusations. Doing anything more to deny the murder would only set off the lawman. Not only was he sure they were outlaws, he was armed and they were penned up in a steel cage. Their odds of survival were lower than a snake's belly if he drew his six-gun.

Shooting white-bellied fish in a barrel became all too obvious a comparison.

"Get the circuit judge in town right now," the marshal said in a voice quavering with rage.

"But Judge Overstreet's somewhere up in South Park. He ain't supposed to come this way for another month," the deputy said. The man backed away a pace when the marshal spun on him and whipped out his six-gun.

"I will shoot you where you stand if you aren't outta here and on the way to find that law-spewing, drunken son of a buck in one second. One second! No more!"

The deputy let out a yelp and disappeared into the night. Marshal Welles swung back, his six-shooter aimed at his two prisoners.

"I don't need for you to stand trial to know you're guilty as sin. I ought to execute you right now. That'd save the tax-payers the cost of your trial and make me feel a hell of a lot better." He pointed the pistol at Pecos. His hand shook as his trigger finger drew back.

"Wait, Marshal, give us a chance," Slash called out, wanting to distract the lawman from his contemplated murderous ways. "Check our guns. They ain't been fired. How'd . . ." His words faded and ran away like a rabbit hunting its burrow.

He had forgotten he and his partner had shot it out with the men along the road leading into Potero. Their irons hardly had time to cool off since that gunfight. It was obvious they'd been fired. He hadn't reloaded, and neither had Pecos.

The outer door creaked back and another deputy poked his head inside.

"Hey, Marshal, I got another one for the back cell."

"Get outta here," the lawman grated.

"Better see what's eatin' at your deputy," Pecos said. "He looks mighty upset."

Welles whirled around. His six-shooter lowered when the deputy came in, dragging a woman behind him.

"She got into a fight over at the saloon. Smashed up the place and was goin' after one of the customers with a broken bottle. Ned claims she ain't one of his and that she just came into town all by herself."

Pecos poked Slash hard in the ribs to keep him from blurting something out that'd get them all in even hotter water.

"Lemme go. I was jist startin' to drink," the woman slurred. As she was escorted into the office, she faced the two startled men already locked up. "Don'tcha make me mad. I got a temper. So you two jailbirds bite down real hard on your tongues."

"Put her in that back cell, Marshal, and let her sleep it off?"

"Do it."

The deputy half dragged Jaycee Breckenridge to the far cell and shoved her inside.

"I'll get you a blanket to hang up for some privacy. We don't lock up many women in Potero. Mostly, the whores are bailed out right away by Madame Jane. Or Ned Fisk."

"Him the one what insulted me? The barkeep fella?" Jay hung on the bars of the locked cell.

"The two people in Potero most likely to bail out a woman ain't gonna be interested in springing you," the deputy said.

"Get out. Get back on patrol." The marshal was continuing to grumble under his breath. His fingers tapped out a nervous tattoo on the butt of his now-holstered six-shooter.

"Boss, I heard about your nephew Earl. Danged shame

him gettin' hisself kilt and stuffed into a box like that. Those the two what done the dirty deed?"

"Out!"

The marshal's sharp command sent the deputy scurrying for the door.

"Make yerself useful and fetch me a bottle, lawman!" Jay bellowed. "I came here to tie one on and ever'body's standin' in my way. What's with you people in this town? You never have any fun?"

The marshal stopped grumbling and started growling deep in his throat, like a dog fixing to attack. He spun and stalked from the jailhouse.

Jay sagged a little and shook her head. The mounds of gorgeous auburn hair fluttered about in wild disarray. She took a deep breath and looked over at the other two prisoners.

"You stepped in a fresh cow patty this time," she accused. "The whole town's buzzing how you gunned down the marshal's nephew."

"We didn't do it, Jay. Honest," Pecos said.

"It's a good thing I decided you weren't likely to come back in one piece without me looking in on you."

"Seems like your plan, whatever it is," Slash said, "don't work no better than ours. Only, we're bein' framed."

"We can talk this over after we get out of here," Jay said.

Slash rattled the bars. "As glad as I am to see you, Mrs. Braddock, you're not only in the same pickle as we are, we're not even in the same cell."

"Well, sir, Mr. Braddock," she shot back, "I put on an act to get in here. I haven't had a snort since I left the Thousand Delights."

"That was a real convincin' performance, Miss Jay," Pecos said. "Just listenin' to you carryin' on the way you did made me want to have a drink so we could set a spell and—"

"She's not drunk, and she's my wife," Slash said sharply.

"That don't mean I can't appreciate her," Pecos replied.

He craned around to look at Jay. "You must have a plan to get us outta here. What might it be?"

"I'm glad one of you appreciates me," the woman said. She snorted. "Too bad it's not my loving husband."

"I do more than appreciate you, darlin'," Slash said. "So, how're you fixin' to spring us?"

"How many different keys are there to jail locks?" she asked.

The two former bank robbers looked at each other and shrugged.

"You don't know," she accused. "The answer is not very many. That's why one of these is likely to open the cell door." Jay fished around in the folds of her skirts and pulled out a ring of keys.

Slash and Pecos watched silently as she worked through the keys, one by one. They held their breaths when she got down to the last couple keys and the lock hadn't clicked open.

And then it did.

"Hurry up. Get us out before the marshal comes stormin' back in." Slash sounded a trifle anxious. He explained in a low voice to his partner, "I gotta get her away from here, or the marshal'll take it out on all of us for escapin'."

"For two cents I should leave you locked up," she said. "That'd teach you a lesson."

"Bleed-'Em-So wouldn't like it," Pecos pointed out.

"I got him wrapped around my little finger. You can see it by the way he ogles me."

"He's an old lecher and looks that way at every woman," Slash said.

"Oh? So he'll come on to any old hag? Meaning *me*?"

"Please," Pecos begged. "Conduct your marital spat *after* we get out of town."

"If I could let him out and not you, too, I would," Jay said. She turned the key and the cell door swung open. "Get your shooting irons and let's go."

Armed and ready to fight it out with a pack of wildcats, they stepped out into the cool night. Fingers of pink lit the eastern sky as dawn clawed away at the night.

"I hear Buck protestin' out back. And that's your Appy answerin'," Pecos said. "Where's your horse, Miss Jay?"

"Dorothy's out back, too. Time to saddle up and ride, you two old reprobates."

"We wasn't the ones pretendin' to be drunk," Slash said. His arm circled her trim waist. He pulled her in for a quick kiss. "And I'm glad I married such a fine actress. But make this the last time you take your act on the road. I want you at home, where I can keep an eye on you."

They hurried around the jailhouse, and in jig time were leaving Potero. Slash and Jay rode knee to knee. Pecos hung back. He had an uneasy feeling and wasn't able to put it into words. Something went on in Potero that was more than one family running everything. Whatever it was centered in McCall's warehouse with all the furniture and household goods—and ammunition for Gatling guns.

Chapter 14

Colonel Raymond paced around the map pinned to the ground with jagged rocks. After the third circuit, he stopped and bent over, peering at the smudged ink in the faint light of dawn. He fished around in a vest pocket and drew out a lucifer. A quick flick of his thumb filled the air with a brilliant flame and nose-wrinkling sulfur. He knelt and held the flaring match inches above the paper, then tossed the match away when it burned down to his fingers.

He looked up. A dozen men stood nearby, nervously staring at him.

"Where's Matthias?" He stood. "I need his final report on the condition of the road in this stretch." He pointed out the area with his boot toe.

"I dunno, sir. He oughta be back anytime now. We ain't heard from Hutchins, neither."

"No sign of Hutchins, you say?" This made him stand ramrod straight. His most trusted scouts were absent without official leave. This wasn't like them. He almost asked after Harl Benson. Having a competent deputy beside him began to matter more. "So? Does anyone have an idea where he is?"

Deathly silence fell at this question. Raymond alternated between cold fury at the man's absence and the growing realization he had somehow, somewhere, lost his most capable field lieutenant. "Never mind. He can take care of himself." Raymond felt as if he lied to himself more than to his men.

He spun at the sound of a galloping horse. The rider made no effort to approach silently. It had to be Matthias. Finally.

"Report," he snapped when his second most trusted field officer drew rein a few yards away.

"You got the map all spread out, I see, Colonel," Matthias said. He dropped to the ground and came over. He oriented himself and then pointed. "There's the trouble." He traced his finger over a rocky stretch where Raymond had considered launching his attack on the cavalry column.

"Is it a bad road?"

"For our purpose, even worse. The soldiers can pull off the road and take cover in the boulders on either side of the road. If they're half as good as I've heard, they can swing their guns around in either direction and blow us to Kingdom Come."

"So," the Colonel mused, rubbing his clean-shaven chin, "we need a different location? What about here? Their wagons would be climbing a steep hill. They'd either roll back to the bottom or power on through to the summit if they tried to stop and fight."

"That's gonna be hard for them to do, Colonel," Matthias agreed. "The hill's too steep to see over. We take out their scouts—they only field two in advance of the column. They either lose half their men attacking uphill or they retreat. That'd be a disaster with the heavily loaded wagons, since they'd have to roll backward. There's no spot to turn around on that hill."

"Are there any level areas where they might place their guns along the road back to the bottom?"

"One. Here." Matthias pointed it out.

"Take ten men and command that spot, but don't engage."

"They'll set their howitzers if we don't stop them straightaway," Matthias protested. Then his face brightened. "I understand, Colonel. Ten men'll be more than I need."

"Ten," Raymond insisted. "This is the decisive skirmish. Take control and the battle is ours."

Matthias grunted something and vaulted into the saddle. He yelled orders. A half-dozen men who had been watching the Colonel pore over the map ran for their horses. By the time Matthias galloped away, his entire detachment of ten men trailed behind.

Raymond took one last look at the map to fix the terrain in his mind. Then he bellowed orders and assembled his main force. The fight was at hand, just as the sun peeked above the horizon.

"We ought to take the top of the hill," the man said timorously. "That's the way to keep them from attacking."

"You'll hold your fire until they are at the tip of the rise," the Colonel insisted. "Let them silhouette themselves against the sky. You'll have better targets."

"I reckon we'll know we done pushed 'em back, too, when no more poke their heads up."

"Exactly," Raymond said. He checked his six-shooters, one by one. He carried half a dozen today—a lighter load than usual. If thirty-six rounds weren't sufficient, his entire plan was in jeopardy. But he had no hesitation positioning his men. The plan was going to succeed. No fog of war. No confusion. It was simple enough, and felt like a chess match endgame, where every move was forced.

He moved, the cavalry had only one choice in response. Then he called checkmate and the skirmish was over.

The sun had risen far enough above the horizon to fully

illuminate the crest in the road. The soldiers would have the sun to their backs and think that gave them an advantage. Instead, using the hill to block the bright glare for his marksmen gave Raymond the true advantage.

He cocked his head to the side. A slow smile came to his lips.

"I hear them coming," he called to his men. "Rifles on full cock! Prepare to fire."

The Colonel never gave the order to fire. He expected some hothead to fire too early or maybe one of the greenhorns to get nervous and trigger a round unintentionally. His senior leaders always took note of who fired early. Having a sincere talk with them made them into better soldiers next time.

A volley sounded. Even though he steeled himself for the premature barrage, he still winced. At the top of the hill two cavalry scouts inadvertently revealed themselves. Both died with a half-dozen rounds pumped into their blue-uniformed torsos.

The firing died down; then the Colonel bellowed out the order to renew targeting the soldiers. Now a half dozen popped into view. Half died as their scouts had. The other three vanished back down the road. From the rumble and clank of caissons, the snapping of chains, and the loud displeasure of horses forced to turn sharply with stiff harnesses, Raymond knew the ambush had been a success.

Thus far.

"Hold, men. Don't go rushing up. Not yet. Not yet. Give them a chance to position their cannon."

He heard muffled cries of outrage and even fear. There wasn't any reason to give the cavalry column time to set up deadly mountain howitzers that would sweep the battlefield clean after only a few shots.

Raymond slowly counted under his breath. When he was sure a full minute had passed, he gave the signal to advance.

Just short of the summit, he halted his men. He rode on alone to survey the other side of the hill.

As Matthias had reported, there was a perfect flat area beside the road to set up the cannon. Raymond laughed aloud now. Matthias and his ten men had lain in wait until the soldiers prepared the cannon to fire.

The five-man cannon crew stretched out dead. Matthias was now gun captain and swung the muzzle around, toward the bottom of the hill.

"Fire!" Raymond cried. "Give them what for!"

The mountain howitzer belched white smoke, fire, and chain shot. The cavalry company farther down the hill was mowed down by the slashing, tumbling lengths of chain. The first blast brought down a half-dozen soldiers. By the time the lieutenant in charge of the squad regained control, Matthias reloaded and sent a second length of chain whirring through the disheartened command.

"Retreat!" The lieutenant might have been young, but he had no pretensions of facing his own artillery and surviving to win a medal.

Colonel Raymond gave the signal. The troopers behind him poured over the hill and rushed down, firing as they went. Together with the cannonade they laid down devastating fire. The rest of Raymond's men lay in wait at the bottom of the hill. When they cut loose, they caught the federal soldiers in a vicious cross fire. It took only seconds for the lieutenant to surrender.

"Cease fire!" the Colonel ordered. He rode slowly down to the bottom of the hill. His sharp eyes took in the half-dozen wagons laden with ammunition, Spencers, and two long, large boxes.

He trotted over and got the sunlight just right to read the stenciling.

"How many Gatling guns are there?" he asked the lieutenant. "From the size of the crates, you're transporting two."

"Sir, you have ambushed a U.S. Army detachment. I order you to surrender immediately."

Raymond glanced over his shoulder. "Was there only one howitzer? A pity you failed to deploy it properly. You might have held us off for a few more minutes."

"How did you know where the howitzer would be unlimbered along the roadside? I didn't know until you attacked."

Raymond ignored the question. Matthias had done well scouting the terrain and detailing possible defensive positions. The real question, unasked, was how he had learned the arms shipment was being made at all. The quartermaster had been paid a trivial amount for that information considering the firepower now lost to the army.

"There should have been another cannon. Will it be brought along in a separate convoy?"

"I will never divulge such intelligence to you!" The lieutenant turned red in the face. "You are the devil incarnate! You massacred most of my men."

"How many are left?" Raymond signaled for Matthias to round up the soldiers milling about on foot. Of the entire company, only eight remained. Three were wagon drivers entrusted with the heavily laden freighters.

Raymond kept his high-spirited horse from crow-hopping about. He stopped so he could look down on the three men.

"I need drivers. If you join up, you'll be paid top dollar."

The three men exchanged glances. A corporal spoke for them. "That'd be desertin', and we got no call to do that for a dollar or two. We're soldiers. They'd line us up in front of a brick wall and let the firin' squad have its way."

The corporal looked past Raymond to where the lieutenant stood stiffly at attention. The officer's hand rested on the hilt of his saber, gripping it so hard his knuckles turned white.

"I applaud your loyalty to the oath you've taken. However, it is foolish, given the circumstances."

Raymond inclined his head in the direction of the trio. Matthias drew his six-gun and dispatched the soldiers, each with a bullet to the head. Raymond trotted back to the outraged lieutenant.

"I commend you for the loyalty shown by your men, foolish as it was. I see by your insignia you are an artillery officer. An officer with your skills is very useful to me."

"Never!" The lieutenant whipped out his heavy cavalry saber and brandished it above his head.

Raymond drew and fired in a smooth motion. The first bullet knocked the sword from the officer's hand. The second ended the man's life.

Without another thought the Colonel signaled three of his men to climb into the driver's boxes. He had just liberated enough firepower to lay waste to a half-dozen towns.

"Matthias, see to the caisson and the howitzer. Excellent work. Yes, excellent. I commend you."

Colonel Belvedere Raymond rode at the head of the newly captured caravan, already planning on how best to use the additional firepower.

Chapter 15

"How long do you suppose?" Slash Braddock asked.

Pecos and Jay looked at each other; then Pecos asked, "What're you talkin' about?"

"The marshal's not gonna let us waltz out of town. He was fumin' mad," Slash said.

"Frothing at the mouth like a mad dog," Jay agreed. "You expect him to come after us?"

"How mad can an uncle get when his nephew's been killed? If it was my kin, I'd follow the miscreants to the ends of the earth. Or at least as far as Laramie. That's about what I'd call the ends of the earth, what with the way the local folks there treat strangers." Slash cleared his throat and spat. The gobbet arched in the air, caught the morning sun, and turned into a fiery meteorite as it arced out and spattered onto a rock.

"If he's as mad as all that, you're leavin' a trail any green-horn could follow," Pecos said glumly. "We need to hide our tracks. Trottin' along, as pretty as you please, pretendin' not to have a care in the world, will get us killed." He ran his fingers around his neck where a noose would fit just about right.

"It'd behoove us to figger out who done in Earl McCall. We didn't do it. He musta been killed before we swapped lead with those ambushers along the road, so they didn't do it."

"That doesn't mean others riding with those owlhoots weren't responsible," Jaycee pointed out.

"My lovely wife's got that right," Slash said. "Remember what Bleed-'Em-So said about them town killers. There was a huge army of them. If we've tangled with 'em and didn't know it, we might be up against an entire army."

"That's too big a bite to chew on right now," Pecos said.

"The way to eat an elephant," Jay said, "is to take tiny bites. There's no need to stuff it all into your mouth with the first bite."

"It never occurred to me that we had to eat a danged ellyphant. Where do we start? Tail or trunk? Maybe an ear?" Slash scowled as he thought on the matter.

"Well, Slash, my man, the way to clear our somewhat-tarnished monikers is to find who shot McCall and deliver him all wrapped up in a bow to Marshal Welles."

"We'll have to poke around Potero with the danged lawman howlin' for our necks. You have to admit, from that man's distorted point of view, we're the ones what done it."

"Aw, Slash, they ought to know it wasn't us," Pecos said glumly. "We're not that tidy. We'd never stash the body out of sight, when we could leave it for the buzzards out in the noonday sun."

"They don't know we wouldn't take the time to tuck him away in a box all dead and proper," Slash agreed. "I always let the undertaker do the plantin'. Why take away a man's livelihood, 'cept if the body's out on the prairie and coyotes are sniffin' around? That's something different. Ain't many varmints I'd leave to the buzzards."

" 'Cept maybe McCall. He deserved what he got." Pecos

sounded as if this was the final declaration to be made before they settled matters once and for all.

"You two can't be fixing to do what I think you're planning," Jay said. "You've done some scatterbrained things in your day, but this takes the cake."

"I wouldn't say that, darlin' wife. There was the time we got so soused we hardly found the floor."

"You talkin' about a couple years back? That firewater was the most potent brave-maker I ever did swill. After a couple shots we lit out and held up a stage," Pecos went on. "When we sobered up, neither of us remembered where all that money came from."

"Musta been close to two hundred dollars." Slash sighed in memory.

"And bundles of letters. Mail," Pecos went on. "That's the only way we knew we'd held up a stagecoach and didn't remember a second of it."

"There wasn't no way to ever forget those hangovers, though. The barkeep musta put knockout drops in our whiskey. It wasn't even good rye."

"A touch of chloral hydrate woulda improved the taste. It was something else. We ought to go back and find out," Pecos said.

"The only trouble with that, old pard, is that I don't recollect where we were. Do you remember?"

Slash shook his head.

"What a pair of cutthroats you were," laughed Jay. "You were so bad, you held up stages and didn't remember it. I wonder why Bleed-'Em-So recruited you."

"He wanted us because we're so talented," Slash insisted.

"It sure ain't because you're purty. Not only are you not purty, you're bowlegged," Jay said.

"That may be, but I'm not bowlegged and pigeon toed like you. When you walk, it looks like—" Pecos began.

"All I care about is how're you gonna look dangling from

the end of a rope. We got a special hanging tree just waiting for you." The angry voice carried in the still air.

Both Slash and Pecos went for their guns. They froze when they saw the marshal had the drop on them. And worse, two deputies had leveled rifles. Pecos considered the odds of sliding his scattergun around and taking out the marshal. That might create enough chaos for them to spook the deputies and get away.

"Boys, you got my permission to shoot them out of the saddle, if they so much as twitch." Marshal Welles drew back the hammer on his pistol, ready to join in the shooting gallery if his prisoners tried anything funny.

"The lady too?" asked a deputy. "She's mighty purty."

"Her too. She's the one that was creating the ruckus in the saloon. It looks like she's in cahoots with them."

"That's a damn shame," the deputy said to himself. "She's *real* purty."

"How'd you come to get in front of us to lay a trap?" Jay asked.

"You followed the road. We cut 'cross country. It didn't take much to find which direction you rode. And you've been real slow to high-tail it." Welles gestured for them to grab some sky. His deputies removed their pistols from the holsters.

"I sent a telegram," Jay said. "Before I went to the saloon and raised such a fuss."

"So?" The marshal sounded skeptical that this meant anything.

"I sent it to Chief Marshal Luther Bledsoe up in Denver. He'll vouch for us."

"What's she sayin', Marshal?" A deputy rode closer.

"Her hair may smell like sweet stinkum, but her stench is rotten. Don't you go believing a word she says."

"Satan's disciple," murmured the second deputy. "A honey-tongued viper come to tempt us."

"She's in cahoots with them two, the ones what killed my nephew," the marshal said. "You can count on that. Look at how cozy they all are. They didn't just meet for the first time back in the cells." He began looking around, studying every tree they passed, as if judging which was strong enough to support the weight of two hanged killers.

Luckily, all the nearby trees were spindly and flagged by the strong winds that whistled down relentlessly from the upper mountain slopes. The ones with limbs thick enough to take a hanging rope bent too close to the ground for a decent neck-breaking drop.

"I asked the chief marshal to send a federal deputy," Jay said. "Marshal Bledsoe won't take kindly to another lawman hanging his undercover agents."

"Now I've heard it all!" the marshal cried. "You expect me to believe these two owlhoots are deputies working undercover, like some Pinkerton agent? Next thing you tell me, they're not only Pinks, but are in disguise, like Mr. Allan J. Pinkerton himself is known to do."

"I've heard *stories* about the chief marshal," said the deputy, now into thinking Jay was the serpent from the Garden of Eden. "He's one mean cuss. You might think twice about doing anything to them, Marshal, at least till you find out if what the lady's sayin' is true."

"You don't wanna cross him if he thinks you've prevented one of his undercover deputies from performin' his bounden duty." Pecos looked at Jay, who shook her head to let him know he was laying it on too thick.

"My nephew's dead. Somebody's got to pay for that. You two are my best—my only—suspects."

"You got the wrong men, Marshal. We haul freight," Slash said. "We didn't have any reason to kill your nephew, since we wanted to collect our pay from him—"

"What he's trying to say," Jay cut in, since her husband was giving the lawdog a new motive to lay on his prisoners, "is that Mr. McCall was thinking on throwing in with them on their investigation."

The instant she spoke, she knew she had made a mistake worse than Slash's.

"He'd never cross the Colonel," the marshal said.

"Who's that?" Slash asked. He perked up and looked at his captors.

He got no answer. The marshal sank into a dark despair, mumbling to himself. The only words any of them heard were "hang" and "shoot the sons of bitches."

"How do you know we don't work for the Colonel?" Jay asked.

"You don't. We'd know if you did," the marshal said.

"How?"

"One more word out of any of you, and we'll roll your dead bodies into the ditch alongside the road."

They returned to Potero in silence. Slash and Pecos soon occupied the front cell again, but Jay kept up a constant verbal barrage that the marshal listened to.

"What's she sayin'?" Pecos wondered.

"She can talk a squirrel into givin' up its nuts," Slash said. "But she won't have to do more 'n get the lawdog to leave." He held up the key Jay had used to unlock the cell door.

"Good thing he's worryin' more on how to string us up than how we got away before."

"What's goin' on outside?" Slash asked. "Sounds like a parade."

"No window and I can't see out the door."

The two old cutthroats shook their head when a familiar figure pushed into the marshal's office. Luther Bledsoe's right-hand man, Deputy Marshal Curtis Donahue, stood like a Front Range peak, stolid and immobile, hand on his six-shooter and casting a stony stare on Potero's lawman.

"You're wearing a badge," the marshal said. "That don't cut it in this town."

"I want them released. Chief Marshal Bledsoe has a yen to keep them locked up himself."

"Nope, not happening." The marshal stood and squared off with Donahue.

"This ain't gonna end well," Pecos said. "Donahue's not my favorite mother's son, but I have to admit, I've never seen a man quicker on the draw."

His words reached the marshal, who reconsidered.

"Her. You can have her. Not them," Welles said.

"I'm not chattel! You can't barter away my freedom!" Jay protested.

"Her. Them too," Donahue insisted.

"I'm not arguing the point on an empty stomach. They made me miss breakfast."

"What a splendid idea!" Jay cried. "Let's get some steak and eggs." She looked past the marshal. Slash held up the key. "We can all sit down and discuss this misunderstanding. That's what it is. Don't you agree, Deputy Donahue?"

"The chief marshal sent me to fetch them. I do as I'm ordered."

"Breakfast first," the marshal said. "I think better on a full belly." He pointed. Jay smiled winningly, curtsied, and led the way from the jailhouse. Donahue trailed her. The marshal grumbled, but never so much as glanced back at the cell with his prisoners.

He had barely left the calaboose, when Slash had the cell door swinging wide. They wasted no time in once more retrieving their weapons.

"McCall's warehouse?" Pecos said.

"You called it, pard."

They took alleys and side streets to the edge of town. Pecos drew rein and stared at the warehouse and McCall's office.

"Something's wrong," he said. "It ain't the way it was earlier."

"Yeah, McCall's body's been taken to the undertaker's," Slash said. He paused, then rubbed his chin. "I see what you mean, though. I can't put a name to it, but things have changed."

They trotted to the warehouse door. Pecos stared down at the ground.

"Tracks. Deep ruts. Fresh," he said. With a hop he jumped to the ground. He slipped the Russian .44 from its holster and nudged open the door with his foot.

Slash took a position on the other side of the door. They exchanged a quick look; then Pecos spun around and entered. Slash followed, ready to shoot it out.

"I'll be damned," Pecos said.

"What's got your neck in a hump? My eyes are dancin' with yellow and blue dots from the sun."

Pecos walked into the warehouse. By the time Slash's eyes had adjusted to the dim interior, he let out a low whistle.

"This wasn't what I expected to find," he said.

His words echoed. The warehouse was empty.

Chapter 16

"Now if that don't take all," Slash Braddock said, shaking his head.

"You got that right. They took it all," Pecos said. "Who's *they*, do you think?"

"Whoever killed Earl McCall, they came back with wagons and loaded up, while the marshal had us locked up in a cell."

"Three wagons, I'd say, maybe four. The tracks are all mixed up when they ran back and forth, but all the crates stored here weren't loaded into one or even two wagons."

"Ammunition," Slash said. "That tells us plenty. McCall worked with the Colonel, whoever that is. He crossed him and got killed."

Slash didn't have any answer for that.

"And all the other rummage, too," Pecos said, prowling about. He kicked at a few nails and loose boards scattered around the warehouse floor. "It must have been loot from that town Bledsoe got so worked up over."

"Paradise," he said. "Where does the marshal come into

this? His nephew got gunned down, and he knows something about the Colonel. What's it all mean to us?"

"Standin' around, Slash, ain't gettin' us any closer to satisfyin' Bleed-'Em-So. It looks like we blundered onto the trail of the very man Bleed-'Em-So wants us to stop. Only thing is, this here Colonel has himself an army, and if he finds out we done killed his henchmen, he ain't gonna like it one little bit."

"I've got no idea what to do." Slash frowned, deep thought lines crossing his forehead. "You think we should poke Donahue about this or handle it ourselves?"

"Jay's safe enough from the marshal, as long as she's with Donahue. I don't like it one tiny bit havin' my lovin' spouse under Donahue's evil gaze, but he won't dare lay a finger on her. He knows Bleed-'Em-So would skin him alive . . . and that's bein' merciful, if I caught up with him first."

"He'll spirit her away from Potero so's she's all safe and sound. There's nothin' more we can do here," Pecos said.

"Unless I miss my guess, she'll coax Donahue into escortin' her back to Camp Collins. She's got a silver tongue when it comes to convincin' a man to do what she wants."

"That gives us time to follow those wagons. This is about the only lead we've got."

"There's one more. Remember how Bleed-'Em-So said somethin' about High Mountain? You ever heard about anyplace called that, Pecos?"

"Wherever that is, you two brand blotters aren't going anywhere again. You escaped twice. There won't be a third time."

"Aw, Marshal, we told you," Slash said. "We're innocent."

"Whatever you are, 'innocent' is not a word I'd ever use. If ever I saw a pair of cutthroats responsible for evil deeds, it's you."

"What was your nephew doin', storin' stolen goods for

the Colonel?" Slash took a wild shot at what was going on in Potero. The way Welles jerked, as if somebody had poked him with a needle, betrayed the extent of the thievery. McCall was involved, Marshal Welles provided protection and looked the other way, and probably their entire family was getting rich off the Colonel laying waste to other towns.

"This here town was drying up and fixing to blow away before the Colonel came by. All we had to do was store his boxes." The marshal panted as if he had run a mile uphill.

"You ever ask where it all came from?" Slash took a quick look around. The marshal had come alone this time.

"You never twigged to how all this was dinero from a robbery?" Pecos distracted the lawman by taking a step away from his partner.

"Did Deputy Donahue take Miss Jay into custody?"

"The two of them rode out and—" The lawman saw how his two captives worked him, badgering him with questions and forcing him to turn from one to the other. Whenever he did face one of them, the other scooted a few more inches away in the opposite direction.

Neither Slash nor Pecos knew who shot first. One of them might have. Or the marshal saw them slipping out of custody again. Whoever was responsible, all three ducked and dived for cover.

Slash filled his fists with both of his .44s and flung lead in the marshal's direction. Pecos began firing steadily, using his Russian .44 until he ducked back into the warehouse. The marshal targeted him, ignoring Slash entirely.

Hitting the dirt and rolling, Slash reached the corner of the warehouse. By the time the marshal turned his gun back on him, Slash was crouched out of the line of fire. He reloaded first one pistol, and then the other. A quick look showed that the marshal had taken refuge behind an overturned wagon across the yard.

Judging where the lawman hid, Slash filled that section

of wood with holes. He was rewarded with a loud yelp. But the string of curses that followed turned the air blue. He had winged the marshal, but hadn't taken him out.

"What're we gonna do, Slash?"

"Don't try rushin' him, Pecos," warned his partner. "I didn't wound him too bad. I just made him mad."

"How bad are you hurt, Marshal?" Pecos bellowed. "We'll let you go find a sawbones. It'd be a shame if you upped and bled to death."

"I'll see both of you with nooses around your filthy necks!" The marshal followed his intentions with six fast shots in Pecos's direction.

Slash took the chance to pop a few more splinters from the overturned wagon. The sudden thunderous reply drove him back around the corner.

"He's got a real barn-blaster, Pecos. Might be ten-gauge from the roar when it fires. Did you see him with it?"

"Nope, didn't," his partner called back. "He's a mite sneakier than I gave him credit for."

"Go on and get up into the loft so you can shoot down on him!" Slash called. "I'll pin him down!"

They had worked together for so many years, they knew what ran through the other's head. Pecos stayed where he was, keeping an eye out for a decent shot. Slash retreated, heading around the back of the warehouse to where their horses were tethered. Time ran out for them. So much gun-fire disturbed the sleepy town. Sooner or later, the two deputies would come running. It was too much to hope that Deputy Donahue and Jay Breckenridge would come, too.

Slash hoped they were far from town by now. His wife handled herself well in any fight, after being hitched to Peter "Pistol Pete" Johnson for so many years. He and his outlaw band guaranteed her an education in shooting ... and killing.

That had been years ago, he knew, but none of her skills

had turned rusty. Long hours running the Palace of a Thousand Delights exposed her to all manner of violence, but that didn't keep him from worrying.

Then he had something closer to home to worry over. The way the marshal used that scattergun threatened even the most cautious—and right now, that was one Slash Braddock.

A quick look at the warehouse's back wall showed a couple loose planks. The old bank robber put his foot against the wall, slipped his fingers under one board, and then wrenched. He tumbled back and sat hard when the wood broke. Slash recovered and aimed a six-gun at the hole when an eye peered out.

"Don't go shootin' me, you fool. You're not that blind yet." Pecos turned and drove his shoulder against the plank next to the one Slash had pulled free.

Pecos came stumbling out and caught himself before he fell alongside his partner.

"Let's ride," he growled. "I'm purty near fed up with this town."

"We've squeezed this lemon dry," Slash said. "All we got to go on are the wagons. If we ride hard, we can catch up with them."

"They can't be more 'n a few miles ahead of us, if that was them rumblin' out of town whilst we were locked up in jail."

Before the marshal twigged to what they were up to, they mounted and wended their way between buildings until they reached the outskirts of Potero. Open country ahead, they rode at a dead gallop for several minutes, to put as much distance between them and the furious Marshal Welles, then slowed to give their mounts a chance to regain their wind.

"You remember what Bleed-'Em-So said? About High Mountain? If we can't overtake the wagons, that's all we got left to think on, Slash."

"That's not a place I ever heard of. I don't cotton much to such a flimsy clue. I need somethin' more to chew on."

"It'd better not be too tough. Those old yeller teeth of yours'd fall right outta your head."

"Better my teeth than my eyes." Pecos lifted his chin to point ahead along the road. "You're goin' blind if you missed that. That there's dust risin' from a dozen wagon wheels."

"If we cut across country, we can catch them 'fore noon," Slash said.

"Besides catchin' up with the wagons, we gotta avoid the law on our trail, like before."

"Two things we need to do, then," Slash said. "You're still able to ride and think without hurtin' yourself too bad, aren't you?"

Silently they left the road and began using every trick they ever learned to hide their trail. If there had been a stream running nearby, they'd have splashed around awhile in it to hide their hoofprints, but they had to rely on dragging an uprooted bush and crossing rocky patches. By the time they'd hidden their trail the best they could, they came out in a low depression near the road.

"We got ahead of the wagons," Pecos said, looking up a steep hill. "What do we do? Stop them or follow along behind to see where they're going?"

"As much as I'd like to lay claim to everything they're carrying, we need to find where they think's a safe hiding place."

"It might be High Mountain," Pecos said.

"If that's their destination, we'll be done with what Bleed-'Em-So told us to do. He wanted us to find the varmints responsible, not kill every last one of them."

"That'd take more bullets than we've got. There's a young army followin' this here Colonel."

"Get off the road. There's the lead wagon toppin' the rise

already." Slash wheeled his Appy to get where he could hide, and let the caravan pass by.

"That's not as easy as it sounds, pard." Pecos swung his scattergun around and pushed the lanyard out of the way. His finger curled back and discharged one tube.

The sudden explosion of the twelve-gauge sent his buckskin dancing away, ruining a second shot. It also saved his life. Lead sang through the air where his head had been an instant before.

"It's that consarned marshal again!" Slash blurted. "There's no way we can lose him."

"Or his posse. There must be a half-dozen deputies with him." Pecos bent low and started to high-tail it away from the lawman.

He found his way cut off by another six men. This time the marshal had brought a posse large enough to capture his slippery prisoners. Slash and Pecos were caught between the halves of the posse.

Chapter 17

"They got us boxed in!" Slash wheeled about to face the marshal, then turned back to find the other half of the posse was just as determined to bring him and Pecos down.

"Uphill!" Pecos fired wildly in both directions, then got his buckskin turned uphill toward the wagons now cresting the hill. He tugged on the lanyard and brought his scattergun around. Both rabbit ears came back in full cock. He yanked hard on the triggers. The shotgun blared and sent buckshot ripping through the driver in the lead wagon.

The man screamed as he died. He half stood and flopped over the side of the driver's box. When he dropped the reins, his team bolted straight for the two former train robbers.

The out-of-control wagon rattled past, going between Slash and Pecos. Having been in so many tight spots over the years, without thinking, without the need to discuss what was best, they raced uphill toward the second wagon. Its driver tried to figure out what was happening. His head swiveled from side to side. Eyes wide and mouth open, he was at a loss over what to do. Then his expression changed. He must have recognized the marshal and tried to flag him down.

Seeking help from the lawdog didn't work out well for the driver.

Someone in the posse put a slug into the man's shoulder. He grunted with the impact and slid along the hardwood bench seat. His wagon's team bolted, too, creating even more furor.

"The third wagon," gasped out Pecos. "Head for it!"

Slash obeyed his partner. With the posse nipping at their heels, anywhere else was better. He lifted one of his pistols and discharged it as he rushed past the third wagon. Riding hell-bent the way he was, he missed, but came close enough to the driver, and a second man next to him, to sow more confusion. Both men tried to get their smoke wagons out and into action.

Controlling the team and shooting proved impossible to do together. They collided with each other, and the driver let go of the reins in his futile attempt to yank out his shooting iron.

This was all it took so that the third wagon veered off the road. Its bulk protected Slash from the hail of bullets coming his way from the posse.

"There's a fourth wagon. What do we do?" Slash's question was drowned out in the roar of guns. None of the bullets came his way. A quick look over his shoulder showed how the wagoners opened up on the lawmen. Confusion turned both sides into bloodied victims.

Whether Pecos had intended this hardly mattered. They dodged a leaden rain. For the moment.

"The Colonel!" Slash called to the fourth wagon's driver. "He sent us. They're tryin' to steal everything you're carryin'."

"That's the Potero marshal. He's paid off. Hutchins took care of it."

"Hutchins got himself ventilated. That other fella also."

"Matthias? Not both of them! What's going on?"

"They're all turned against us," Slash called. "They want your load. What you got? The ammo for the Gatlings?"

The driver's head bobbed up and down. Slash had given him enough information to seal the lie that the Colonel had sent him. The outlaw came to a wrong decision, with lead flying all around his head. Slash and Pecos looked to be his only saviors.

"Don't sit there with your mouth gapin' like that. You'll catch flies—and a few ounces of lead." Slash fired steadily over his shoulder at two deputies on foot struggling up the hill. He wondered if Pecos had shot their horses out from under them.

"What're we gonna do?"

Slash liked the way he had duped the driver. He emptied his right revolver and turned to the left, taking out a deputy intent on sneaking up on them.

"Thanks, mister," the driver said.

"You got a Gatling gun back there? Set it up and use it."

"Good idea," the driver said.

"Where were you takin' all this? All four wagons goin' to the same place?"

"High Mountain," the driver said, scrambling into the rear of the freight wagon. He tore through the tarp-covered boxes. He looked up at Slash. The forlorn look would have been pure delight for Slash to see, except he had recruited the enemy to his side—at least for a few minutes.

"What's wrong?"

"I need a couple others to help set up the gun."

"Rifles. Grab a rifle. There's some in there somewhere." Slash emptied his left pistol and jockeyed around to keep his horse from running away. The Appaloosa was accustomed to gunshots, but the Potero marshal and his posse made life especially terrible. Bullets tore into the wagon. It wouldn't be long before the team bolted.

The driver yanked a Spencer from a crate and began feeding cartridges into it. Just as he raised his weapon, he gasped, looked down, and saw the red splotch on his chest.

Slash fired both six-guns at the deputy who had shot the

driver. He missed, but drove the lawman back to take cover a couple yards away behind a tumble of rocks.

"Got me. They got me!" the driver cried. He dropped the rifle, fell to his knees, and crumpled over a crate.

Slash kicked free of the stirrups and got into the wagon bed. He pulled the driver upright. The man's face had turned pasty white with shock.

"You got anybody I should tell?" Slash asked. "Where are they?"

"High Mountain. One of the doxies. She took a shine to me. I liked her."

"How do I get to High Mountain to tell her?" Slash fired a couple times when a lawman poked his head around the wagon's tailgate. This time his aim was better. The deputy's hat went flying. Along with it went a chunk of hair and scalp.

"Her name's . . ." The driver shuddered.

"How do I get to High Mountain? Tell me!" Slash grabbed the man by the shoulders and shook him. Eyes flickered open and a smile came to the man's lips. He patted his chest, just above the bullet wound that robbed him of life.

"Dyin's not as bad as I thought. Tell her . . ."

Slash cradled a dead man in his arms. Snarling, he let the man fall to the top of the crate where he had taken out the rifle. He had come close to finding where the wagons were headed. The marshal and his posse had robbed him of finding what must be the Colonel's headquarters.

It had seemed that Potero was the storage depot and was now abandoned. Whether Slash and Pecos had caused the evacuation of Potero, or the Colonel had other plans, the only clue they had left was High Mountain.

"Damn you, Bledsoe." Slash got to his feet and worked to the front of the wagon.

The gunfight continued, heavier and more deadly than before. A quick count showed half the posse was stretched out dead, just like the wagon driver. How the others put up such a stout defense gave Slash pause. The Colonel recruited men willing to take a life and never think twice about doing it. The marshal's deputies weren't up to such death-dealing standards.

"There you are. I wondered if I'd have to dicker with the town undertaker for a grave site," Pecos said, riding up. He gave Slash a quick once-over and assured himself the blood on his partner's coat belonged to someone else. His pistol smoked from heavy use. "Even in Potero there's not likely to be a church willing to plant you in their graveyard."

"I'm not ready for the potter's field," Slash said. "Not yet." He looked over his shoulder at the dead wagon driver.

"The wagons are rolling on. The marshal's done quit."

The two old cutthroats exchanged a knowing look. They could high-tail it now and get away from the Potero marshal, once and for all.

But that wasn't the way former members of the Snake River Marauders worked. Slash dropped onto the bench seat and grabbed the team's reins.

"See to my Appy. We're joinin' a caravan that'll take us straight to where we want to go."

"Where's that?" Pecos asked.

"High Mountain. Wherever that is." Slash snapped the reins.

Pecos rode alongside, taking an occasional shot at a lawman, but not hitting any of them.

The other three wagons set a brisk pace. Slash was up to the challenge, having driven his own freight wagon for close to a year since they'd gone to work for Chief Marshal Bledsoe. But as expert as he was, his team was all tuckered out and his wagon fell farther behind.

"Go tell them owlhoots to slow down," Slash yelled at Pecos. "These horses ain't keepin' up."

"I did take note that you was fallin' farther behind. If you can't keep up, I'm gonna ride ahead as scout, and you just do your best."

Slash turned that over in his think box, then nodded. If he was being left behind, one of them had to learn how to find High Mountain. Chances were good, the other drivers were heading straight for what must be the Colonel's hideout.

"Get ole Buck gallopin'. I'll find you when I can." Slash reluctantly slowed as the team weakened even more. Having one of the horses keel over dead while in harness was worse than splitting up from his partner and the rest of the wagon train.

Pecos pinched the brim of his Stetson in acknowledgment and turned to overtake the others.

Before Pecos got fifty yards away, the wagon lurched and almost threw Slash from the driver's box. The loud screeching warned of damage that threatened to strand him if repairs weren't made.

Pecos galloped back, circled the wagon, and came up beside his partner.

"The back wheel's all cattywampus. It's fixin' to come off, 'less we do somethin' about it right now."

"With the heavy load, gettin' a wayward wheel attached properlike ain't likely." Slash looked around for a sign that the marshal had returned.

"He won't take kindly to havin' so many of his posse shot up."

"There's no way to get the others to help out, is there?" If they tried to convince the others in the wagon train to help, they'd draw attention to themselves. Chances were good, they all knew each other and had ridden together as they massacred entire towns. Seeing strange faces driving a wagon loaded with ammunition produced only one response. And Slash and Pecos didn't have a ghost of a chance to fight off men who'd just cut a wide, deadly swath through a determined posse.

"It ain't unfixable, not yet. We kin do some makeshift repairs and limp on. Or we can abandon it and try to overtake the other wagons. What do you want to do?" Pecos scratched his chin as he thought on it.

"Get the wheel hammered back into place before it falls off. There's enough booty in the wagon to make it worth our while. This is likely all the reward we'll see if we tell Bleed-'Em-So we can't finish his mission. If he decides to hang us because of that, at least we'll die with a considerable fortune."

"I was afeared you'd say that." Pecos dismounted and began fetching rocks to block the wheels.

"We're out of luck all around, otherwise. There ain't no way of trackin' the others to High Mountain, not on this road. It's too rocky for them to leave tracks." Slash worked his way over the cargo, grabbed the dead driver by the collar, and dragged him out.

"A friend of yours?" Pecos looked skeptically at the body.

"I'm gonna plant him. He seemed a good fellow."

"Other than bein' a bloody-handed butcher who slaughtered women and kids," Pecos said.

"Other 'n that," Slash agreed. He found a shallow depression to keep from digging in the hard, rocky ground. Piling small rocks on the body wouldn't keep a determined carrion eater away, but it was better than the man deserved. Everything Pecos said about him was the gospel truth.

Slash rolled the body into the shallow grave, then stopped and stared.

"Not every good deed goes unnoticed," he said.

"What's that? He had a spare wagon wheel in his pocket?"

"I'd settle for a sledgehammer. But unless I miss my guess, this is a map." Slash plucked a blood-soaked scrap of paper from the dead man's vest pocket.

He carefully unfolded it, then smiled even more broadly.

"He bequeathed us a map on how to get to High Mountain."

Chapter 18

"Should I let Del know what you got here?" Myra Thompson frowned as she peered into the rear of the captured wagon. "That's all stolen property, isn't it?"

"Now, little darlin', we don't know that," Pecos said. "Not exactly—"

"She's right about one thing," Slash cut in. "It was stolen from a bunch of murderin' thieves. How is it wrong to steal from thieves?"

"You ought to know," Myra said. "That's what you spent most of your lives doing."

"We're reformed. Why, you might say we're on the side of the angels now," Slash said.

"Some angels got bent halos," Myra retorted. "How can you ever mention the word 'angels' and Chief Marshal Bledsoe in the same breath? He's Satan incarnate, I'd say."

"We're doin' his work," Pecos said. "And if I remember my Scriptures, Satan is a fallen angel. So in that regard we *are* on the side of the angels. Or at least one of 'em."

"Maybe not a good one," Slash mused. "But what matters

is, we're still alive and kickin' and got a chance to complete Bleed-'Em-So's assignment."

Myra finished poking around in the crates and came out to sit on the dropped tailgate, her short legs swinging as she thought. She worked over the moral issues.

"There's no way to ever give any of the stolen goods back. Miss Jay would break my fingers if I tried taking back all that fancy furniture you gave her. And how can you ever find the folks who owned all this?"

"They're all likely dead," Slash said. "Besides, there's more than a few pots and pans in there. And that's just the stuff that ain't dangerous. I'd need to do some fancy countin', but there must be a thousand rounds of ammunition for those Spencers. And I can't count high enough to decide how many rounds of ammo are crammed into the Gatlings' column magazines, all ready to fire."

"You can't count higher 'n ten without takin' off your boots," Pecos said. "And nobody wants you doin' that. With smelly feet like yours, you'd choke half the town."

"The rifles and Gatling guns were stolen from the army," Myra said. "You should return them. But the rest?" She shook her head. "It's more trouble than it's worth, hunting down the owners."

"They're dead," Slash said firmly. "All those fancy silver knives and forks would look funny gettin' laid out on graves."

"If there are even graves to be found. From what Bleed-'Em-So said, the towns were looted after everyone in 'em got burned up." Pecos helped Myra hop to the ground.

"It might be all right you keeping everything if you use it to find this Colonel and stop him." Myra sounded as if she worked hard to convince herself that keeping stolen property was right and proper. Then, with more assurance, "Yup, that's what you need to do. I can see to selling the load, if you promise to go after those sidewinders."

"That's our mission," Pecos declared.

"Let me see what Del has to say about returning those rifles to the army," Myra said. "I won't say a word about the rest. Remember, you promised."

"Cross my heart," Slash said.

They watched their company manager hurry off to find her beau.

"She won't remember a thing about what's in that wagon ten seconds after her and Deputy Thayer get together. I never saw a pair so caught up in each other," Pecos said.

"You sound a tad pitiful," Slash said. "You need to find yourself a good woman, like I have." He cast a final look at Myra and said, "And like Del Thayer has. She's one fine filly."

"You're turnin' all maudlin on me," Pecos said. "We got ourselves quite a chore starin' us in the face. That map you took off the dead man don't give us anywhere near the information we need."

"Well, now, it might appear that way to the uninformed." Slash held up the map, now brittle from the dried blood. "They got maps because the regular road to their town's too steep for wagons. This here shows a back route into High Mountain."

"It does that," Pecos said, "but it don't put us any closer to figurin' out where it is. Nothing's marked. I've asked everybody I know if they've heard of a town with that moniker, and nobody spoke up."

"This here Colonel's got a mean streak. The way he destroys whole towns shows that. It must mean he thinks highly of himself. Takin' over a mountain town and renamin' it is exactly what a man like him would do."

"You've got a good idea there, sweetheart," came a dulcet voice. Jay Breckenridge came up and planted a wet kiss on her husband's cheek. "I've asked anybody coming into the Thousand Delights if they recognized the name. When nobody did, I asked if they had ever seen mountain peaks arranged like that." She traced over the lines on the map showing a cluster of five mountain peaks.

"That's right clever," Slash said.

"I have lots of good ideas, more 'n just marrying you," she said. "It turns out a mountain man who'd been hunting high up in the Rockies, south of Colorado Springs, claimed to know the place."

"Are you sure he wasn't cadgin' you for a drink?" Pecos asked. "Them grizzly hunters pine away for human contact, especially when it's a lovely lady like you, Miss Jay, and then turn downright surly if they put away a few shots of whiskey."

"It's a town not far south of Pikes Peak by the name of Altitude." Jay took the crumpled sheet of paper and turned it around. Her finger traced along the road, now at the bottom of the map, all the way up to the town marked with a small star.

"I've heard of that," Pecos said. "Never had occasion to go there, but I've heard of it."

"The Colonel might have renamed it, to keep it a secret," Slash said.

"That's what I'm thinking. The town's high up, situated in a mountain meadow high enough to make most folks gasp for air. If you take the road straight from Colorado Springs, it's steep. Too steep for a heavily loaded wagon."

"But this here trail's a gradual climb," Slash said, pointing to a second dotted line on the map. "So, what do we do? Straight up the steep hill or meander around and sneak in like the Colonel's plunder?"

"The old-timer who told me said there's something else to consider. Those are two ways to reach Altitude—High Mountain—from this side of the Front Range. And there's another road going west that crosses a Denver and Rio Grande spur line."

Slash smiled broadly. "The Colonel takes all this loot to High Mountain, then takes his sweet time to move it down to the railroad. Once it's loaded aboard a freight train, he can ship it danged-near anywhere."

"Why'd he take over that town, assumin' he did?" asked Pecos. "There must be other towns near railroad tracks that ain't so difficult to reach."

"It's an old mining town," Jay said. "I can't find anybody who's heard of an ounce of silver coming out of there in a year."

"The marshal said Potero was beholden to the money brought in. High Mountain must be, too. The place'd be a ghost town, without a steady flow of stolen goods." Slash endlessly traced out the roads with his finger, as if doing so would get him there without riding up a tall mountain.

"How can the people live with themselves?" Jay wondered. "They have to know everything pouring into town's stolen. They must have heard about how towns were completely destroyed."

"Maybe not. We hadn't heard anything about the Colonel and his army until Bleed-'Em-So told us," Pecos said.

"How do we beard the lion in his den?" Jay asked.

"Me and Pecos will get in there. You stay here in Camp Collins. You've got a saloon and whorehouse to run."

"You don't want me getting shot at."

"Or worse," Slash said. "You're my wife. It's my bounden duty to protect you."

"I can take care of myself," the fiery redhead said. She stamped a foot.

"It'd look mighty funny, you bein' along with a pair of . . . a pair of ironmongers," Pecos said.

"You reckon that'd be a good enough fib? I can tell you're makin' it all up as you go," Slash said.

"It explains why we'd be travelin' to a place like Altitude. That was a mining town. Miners need all kinds of iron for drill bits and ore-cart wheels. We take a load of metal scrap, actin' like we ain't heard the town's mines are all petered out."

"That's good, Pecos. Even the Colonel must need metal to work. For horseshoes or to repair his war wagons. Bleed-'Em-So said those wagons had iron plates on the sides to deflect bullets. They must get all banged up and need repairin'."

"It'll take us close to a week to get to this back road, if your wagon's loaded with scrap," Jay said.

"We don't have to carry all that much. Enough to make our story sound like we're for real, but not so much it gives our poor mules backaches."

"And, Pecos," Slash said, "*we* means you and me. Not the three of us."

"Do I have to leave you here in town?" Jay asked her husband. "I'm in this, up to my ears."

"As purty as those shell-like ears of yours are, you were lucky that Deputy Donahue got you away from Potero when he did. The gunfight where we found this map was bloody." Slash outlined the dried stain on the paper.

"It happens once a century," Pecos said.

Both Jay and Slash stared at him.

"My partner being right—that hardly ever happens, but he's right this time. You've got no cause to come along, Miss Jay. We'd both feel better if we knew you stayed here in town and looked after the Thousand Delights and our business."

"Myra does a fine job of that."

"She does," Pecos said, "but she's still a youngster. For all that she's been through, she needs a guidin' hand."

"Mine," Jay said. She pursed her lips. "She's capable, but I can see that this little adventure ought to be left to you two."

"Adventure?" muttered Slash. "Or *mis*adventure."

They started planning what types of scrap to freight up to High Mountain.

Chapter 19

"You did the right thing," Pecos said. "I don't know how you done it, but convincin' your wife to stay in Camp Collins keeps her out of danger."

"She wanted to stay there," Slash said. "Otherwise, it'd be like bangin' my head against Pikes Peak. I'd get a headache and not budge the mountain one little inch."

"The trail's been a sight harder than I expected." Pecos looked up at the towering, snowcapped Pikes Peak. "Comin' at High Mountain from Manitou Springs shouldn't have been so hard. I've got a real sense about such things, and I almost missed it."

"That means nobody takes the steep road up. This one's the way."

"You're right about that, pard. Deep ruts in the dirt, where there's any dirt at all. Even this trail's incline is almost more 'n the mules can handle."

The steel-rimmed freight wagon wheels slid and lost traction as they crossed a rocky patch in the road. The mules kept pulling, though they protested more, now that they were urged to pull ever higher into the mountains. The air was thin and cold, gusty winds whistled down from higher on the slopes. Even the marmots and other small critters had taken to their burrows to avoid the cutting breeze. Pecos took a deep breath and then let it out in a sudden rush.

"This is my land," he said. Then he sank down and stared straight ahead.

"Not yours," Slash said softly. "Not unless the lookouts all along the road are beholden to you."

"I only counted three."

"More," Slash insisted. "Twice that, and I think I missed a couple. You saw the flock of birds takin' wing? Something spooked 'em."

"A wolf," Pecos said.

"Two-legged wolves. We're drivin' straight into a wolf's den."

"You think this here Colonel's gonna be there?" Pecos tugged on the lanyard holding his sawed-off shotgun around his shoulder. "We don't even know his name."

"That hasn't stopped us from gettin' on the road to his stronghold," Slash pointed out.

"But them fellas might." Pecos shrugged and pulled the shotgun around to snug up against his hip. Two men with rifles resting in the crooks of their arms blocked the road.

"Don't go mentionin' the Colonel to them," Slash warned. "They're decorated with chest ribbons. That's got to mean they're old-timers in his service."

"It's a good thing we threw away all the ribbons from the men we killed. Answerin' questions about them wouldn't be something we could lie about."

"Lyin' is one of your better skills," Slash said. He fell silent when the guards blocking the road held up a hand to stop them.

"Where are you gents traveling?" The taller of the men swung his rifle around, but never—quite—pointed it at the freighters.

"Who wants to know?"

"You might say we're the gatekeepers for the city on the hill." The guard jerked his thumb over his shoulder in the direction of High Mountain.

"We ain't payin' no toll," Pecos said. "This is a free road. Nobody posted it back down in Manitou."

"No toll," the guard said. "Just a mite curious what brings you to this backwater. We don't see many idle pilgrims out for a stroll, so to speak. What's your cargo?"

"Scrap iron," Slash answered. "We heard tell there was a decent market in Altitude. You're right about this bein' outta the way for most folks. Gettin' supplies of any kind's hard this far up a mountain. I've lived in places like this and know a pretty penny's to be had sellin' hard-to-find things."

"This road's not one used too often," the guard said.

"The main road's too steep for this team," Slash said. He tugged on the reins to keep the mules from letting the wagon backslide. "This one's not much better when you're haulin' a load of iron. You folks need horseshoes and wagon wheels?"

"Good for kettles, too," Pecos spoke up. "The lady folks might appreciate new cookin' utensils."

"No need to sell us on that." The guard motioned. His partner went to the rear of the wagon and poked around.

Pecos watched him closely. For a moment their eyes locked. A shiver went up and down Pecos's spine. He had seen his share of cold-blooded killers in his day. This was one of the worst; he could tell from the utter contempt the man radiated like heat from the noonday sun.

Pecos didn't miss the four brightly colored ribbons pinned to the man's coat.

"They're telling the truth, Max. All that's back here are baskets of scrap iron."

The guard still blocking their way—Max—spat. He hitched up his blue jeans and swung his rifle back into the crook of his left arm.

"You gents appear to be on the up-and-up."

"If you're not here to collect a toll, that must mean you're the law. Who're you on the lookout for? If they're dangerous enough to take two of you, we should keep an eye out, too."

"Yeah, we're just a pair of old-timers tryin' to make a dime," Pecos said.

"Yeah, *old-timers,*" Max said sarcastically. To his partner he asked, "Any reason not to let them go on up to High Mountain?"

"Let 'em go."

Slash snorted. "That's mighty kind of you two. Can you pass that along to any other defenders of your town's honor?"

Max and his partner exchanged a glance. Then Max asked, "Why do you think there's anybody else out here?"

Pecos elbowed Slash to silence. He said, "No reason. We just thought it was peculiar bein' stopped by someone who wasn't either the law or a road agent."

"If you worry on things like that, pretend that we're the law in these parts," Max's partner said. He instinctively touched the ribbons on his chest.

"We'll consider that." Pecos touched the brim of his Stetson, then whispered to Slash, "Get us outta here. There's three more of them varmints in the rocks, to the left of the road."

"Three there and another on your side," Slash said. He snapped the reins. The mules brayed, then began pulling hard to defeat the incline. It was hard to think this wasn't the steeper road to reach the summit.

An hour later, the wagon rattled along the main street of Altitude—or High Mountain. They usually had a few gawkers whenever they rolled into a town. No one going about their business was the least bit interested in strangers. That told them more than the sign where ALTITUDE had been painted over and HIGH MOUNTAIN added in drippy white letters.

"This'd be a good place to peddle anything we hauled," Slash said. "If the place wasn't overrun by the Colonel's men." He stared at a trio of gunslicks swaggering along the boardwalk. All three of them wore one or two ribbons.

"Not veterans of very many campaigns," Pecos said. "But that don't stop them from lording it over the townsfolk who don't show off ribbons."

"Don't get betwixt them," Slash warned when he saw Pecos begin to jump down. One of the Colonel's men had shoved an old woman out of his way and then sneered when she complained about it. "We're outnumbered, and besides that, we want to finish Bleed-'Em-So's job."

"The Colonel must be in town. His men wouldn't act up like that, otherwise."

"I don't know about that, pard. They own High Mountain. The citizens look inclined to go along."

"Yep, that's true," Pecos agreed. "They're feedin' off the plunder brought here by the Colonel."

"Carrion beetles," Slash said. "We need to cut the head off the snake makin' it possible."

"Makes me a little sad thinkin' we'll be responsible for destroyin' this town. It looks like a good place to live. Other 'n they expect the Colonel to loot and pillage other towns to keep 'em from becomin' another ghost town nobody remembers or much regrets in passin'.'"

Slash craned his neck around and said, "Our good friends from the road trailed us into town. That's Max and his right-hand man watchin' every single, solitary move we make."

Pecos took a deep whiff and pointed.

"The smithy's in that direction. I can sniff out burnin' metal every day of the week."

"You saw the black smoke curlin' up. There's no way even that big honker of yours can take in the smell over the dead horses litterin' the street."

"Dead animals everywhere," Pecos said, nodding. "That means the marshal's not doin' his job, removin' carcasses."

"It might just mean that there isn't any law in High Mountain other than the Colonel."

"Campaign ribbons, not badges," Pecos said.

"That must mean the blacksmith's not hammerin' out lawman's badges. So what is he makin'?" Slash turned the corner and drove straight for the forge at the end of a short street.

A burly man stripped to the waist swung a ball-peen hammer to shape a strip of metal on an anvil. Beside him a forge blazed. A few feet behind him another glowed with intense coals. He looked up as Slash brought the wagon to a halt. With a quick move he quenched the metal, held it up with a pair of tongs, then tossed it into a box filled with sand.

"Howdy!" Pecos called. "You look to have a fair amount of work ahead of you." He pointed to unshaped pieces of iron.

"Unless you got something to say, mister, I'd rather hammer metal than make chin music with you." He used the tongs to pick up a new piece of iron. He thrust it into the forge amid the leaping flames. Green sparks wiggled around the metal and then became airborne.

"We got better than something to say. We've got something to sell you," Slash said.

This amused the blacksmith.

"That's about the worst sales pitch I ever heard, 'cept maybe for one potions peddler. He tried to sell me his bottled witch's brew, guaranteed to stop my muscles from wasting away." The smith flexed his massive biceps.

"It might be that he drank his own poison," Slash said, "and it turned him blind. Now, contrary to that, the scrap iron loaded into the rear of that there wagon's just what you need."

Pecos stepped away and let his partner make the pitch. Slash was a silver-tongued fox when he set his mind to it.

Pecos knew his limitations and was willing to let someone else do the talking. He stepped into the street and looked around, getting the lay of the land.

The town bustled with commerce. The accumulation of dead animals made his nose wrinkle, but it wasn't anything he hadn't smelled before. Pecos looked around for any sign that a marshal or sheriff only fell down on the job. Nowhere did he see a badge pinned on a vest, but quite a few men strutted around with their chests puffed out so everyone saw the ribbons fastened there.

"When do you get yours?" a voice, lilting and playful and very feminine, asked.

Startled, Pecos swung around to face a woman well into middle age. Time had been good to her. Only a few wrinkles danced across her forehead. As she smiled, her dimples looked positively angelic to him. Her auburn hair carried more than a few gray strands, but Pecos thought of them more as high-grade silver than proof she was within a few years of his own advanced age. At least that was his guess. The more he studied her, the less sure he was about her age. She moved with liquid grace, and a plain beige gingham dress fit her trim form nicely.

Pecos took it all in with a lingering look, but when he again studied her face, her gray eyes held him captive. They danced with merriment and something more. There was nothing shallow about her, and those penetrating eyes proved it.

"What's that, ma'am? When do I get what?"

"The Colonel's battle ribbons, of course. He's quite an Indian fighter. He and his men are making the entire territory safe for us."

Pecos had nothing to say to that.

"Colonel Raymond? You're not one of his army?"

"Reckon not. Me and my partner came to sell scrap iron. Are you sayin' all them dandies are soldiers?"

"It's a great honor that the Colonel chose High Mountain for his headquarters. Without him and his men spending so freely, we'd have vanished from the face of the earth a year back."

"The mines all petered out," Pecos said, pleased that he had hit the nail on the head.

"That's right. The marshal and his deputies left. The doctor left. The mayor and town council were fixing to go, too, when Colonel Raymond came. We were a bit frightened at first. So many armed men—*well*-armed men, I might say—and no law. But there hasn't been a single crime committed since he arrived. He and his troopers provide the best security possible."

Pecos soaked up every word.

She started to rattle on, then stopped suddenly. She reached out and laid a hand on his arm. "I'm so sorry. I shouldn't babble on like that."

"Ma'am, I could listen to that creek babble on for a long time."

She started to speak, closed her mouth, and smiled almost shyly. She touched his arm again and pulled it back as if it had burned her.

"You're not here to join the Colonel's company, are you?"

"I'd never heard his name until you mentioned it," Pecos said honestly. He blinked. Why he should confess such a thing was odd. The woman's openness and friendly smile lulled him into saying things best kept to himself.

"So, of course, you haven't ridden out on a campaign and earned a ribbon. Many of his senior officers have been with him for years. Why, Mr. Matthias has five ribbons. *Five!* And Mr. Hutchins has even more, being with the Colonel the longest of anyone."

Her bosoms rose and fell as she took a deep breath. Pecos found every movement enchanting.

"There I am, going on again. I'm Marianne Mertz." She held out her hand.

Pecos was slow to take it. He wasn't sure whether to shake it or kiss it.

"Melvin Baker," he said, giving the hand a squeeze as he gave her his real name.

"You don't look like a Melvin, if I may be so bold."

"Well, Miss Mertz, I go by the moniker of Pecos."

"Do tell. That suits you better. Yes, definitely. It's a sturdy name, a solid one." She reached out again and stroked over his biceps. Again she blushed and looked away. "I am so sorry. For some reason I can't keep my hands off you."

"Been a long time since a woman as pretty as you told me that."

"Go on. You have the ladies sniffing after you like a hound dog on a scent."

"If they all smelled as good as you, I wouldn't mind a whit. That's mighty heady perfume you're wearin'."

"Oh, you are such a flirt! I'm not wearing any perfume." She looked around, then sighed. "I must get back to work."

"Can I walk you there? My partner's still sellin' our scrap iron to the blacksmith."

"To Jacob? Jacob Nighbert? It might be a spell. Jacob takes forever to come to a decision. I needed a pot patched. Almost an hour passed before he got around to giving me a price."

"He's not slow. He just wanted to spend time with you," Pecos said.

Again she touched him. This time she playfully punched his arm.

"There you go again, teasing me." The way she beamed showed the compliment was well received. Marianne Mertz held out her arm. Pecos linked his through hers and let her lead the way.

The Galloping Garter Saloon seemed to be their destination, but Marianne kept up a steady pressure on his arm when he started toward it.

"I am sure you are thirsty, but I must get to my chores."

For once, Pecos did the right thing by not asking if the

lovely auburn-haired woman worked in the gin mill. He let her guide him past. They walked slowly to the edge of town.

"That's your place?" Pecos wondered. He had seen his share of cathouses. Something about this one didn't seem right.

"Mine free and clear. I've run the boardinghouse for nigh-on two years now, through boom and bust. When the mines were spitting out silver nuggets the size of your fist, I never had an empty room. Then, almost overnight, nobody was here."

"How'd you keep going?" Pecos asked. His heart about exploded from his chest at the answer.

"It's always full now. The Colonel and all his men stay here now."

Chapter 20

"What's wrong, Pecos? You jumped like I stuck you with a pin." Marianne Mertz smiled winningly. "That's not anything you like, is it? Being overstrung?"

"I've stepped on too many cactus spines in my day," he said. He hunted for any sign that the Colonel and all his men were in the two-story whitewashed boardinghouse. The upstairs windows were pushed open and a stiff breeze blew the curtains out and caused them to flap like someone inside was surrendering. The front door was pulled ajar, but he wasn't able to see inside the house. Located around back, a shed intended for stabling horses was obscured by trees growing in the side yards.

"Are you worried someone will see us?" She disengaged her arm. "There's no one in the house right now. The Colonel and his top aides are all out scouting."

"Do they use your house as a headquarters when they're in town?"

"I suppose you could call it that. They've built several warehouses around town and sometimes spend a great deal of time in them rather than here. That's where they keep their rifles and things. They use an awful lot of weapons to put down those Indian rebellions."

"Which tribes?"

Marianne Mertz frowned.

"I don't rightly know. We don't talk about it much. Let the Colonel and his men keep us all safe." She sounded hesitant when she asked, "Would you like to come in and sit a spell? I've got some lemonade. The last supply wagon they brought in had plenty of fresh fruit. Because the Colonel stays here, I got most of the lemons. And sugar. Sometimes that's hard to get, but I have plenty."

"Because of the Colonel," Pecos finished.

"Why, yes, of course. He is quite fond of lemonade and I try to oblige." Marianne took a step toward the house and paused, waiting.

"I'm new to High Mountain," Pecos said. "And I've bounced around on a hard wagon seat all day." He rubbed his hindquarters. "Sitting and talking with you—and drinkin' lemonade—is something to do. Later."

"Oh," she said, crestfallen. "I understand. When—"

"I meant, let's walk around. You show me the town. That way I don't have to set anymore." He rubbed his haunches again to give her the idea. She brightened. For Pecos it was as if the sun had risen in the morning to chase away the dark.

"I can't be too long. I'll need to fix supper soon, but right now, well, there's nothing I'd rather do than show Mr. Melvin Baker around town. You might come to like it more than driving all around delivering scrap iron."

"There's always a chance," Pecos said. Again he held out his arm and Marianne Mertz linked hers.

They started off down a side street. Pecos wanted to scout for where Colonel Raymond stored his armaments, but Marianne kept distracting him. Talking of nothing in particular proved strangely appealing to him. He wasn't much when it came to small talk. His conversations with the ladies usually had more to do with buying them another drink and dickering over their price. Plenty of the painted ladies flocked to him, but engaging in more than a little chin music was unusual.

"Those look new," he said. Located ahead, four medium-sized warehouses marched like soldiers on parade. Wagon tracks in the dirt betrayed the number of wagons coming and going.

"Brand-new, at least new since the Colonel arrived. Those are his armories I mentioned."

"That's a powerful lot of firepower to store, if he uses all four buildings," Pecos said.

"I suppose you're right. He must keep trail supplies in them, too. I don't really know. He's so very thoughtful."

"Come again?" Pecos looked at her. Her guileless face was about the prettiest thing he'd ever seen.

"He only moves his equipment after dark, when everyone's asleep, so's not to disturb us."

"So it's all secret?"

"Oh, I suppose you could call it that. Thoughtful is the way I'd call it."

Several men moved around the farther warehouse. Pecos recognized Max and his partner from out on the road. He steered Marianne down another street toward open spaces. Being seen poking around the place where Colonel Raymond assembled his arms only caused more suspicion. He wondered what Max had thought, though he and the other guards had let the old freight wagon, with its even older drivers, come into town.

"I so love walking through this meadow," Marianne said. "Here. This is my favorite flower of all." She bent and plucked an orange blossom and took a delicate sniff at it. "It's called a Cowboy's Delight. My favorite color and my favorite flower." She took another whiff and then reached up, standing on tiptoe, and tucked the stem behind Pecos's right ear.

He started to discard it, but her hand curled around his thick wrist.

"Leave it. My gift to you." Their eyes locked. "You are ever so tall, aren't you, Pecos?"

"Six foot six."

"I'm a full foot shorter than you. And so tiny in comparison." She stepped close, her firm, curvy body pressing into his.

Somehow his long arms circled her and held her close. The woman's warmth and gently yielding body made his heart race. She looked up and half closed her eyes. He bent down and his lips brushed lightly across hers. Marianne caught her breath and pressed closer.

"It's been so long, Pecos, so long since I found a man who makes me feel the way you do. I . . . I don't know you, but it feels like I've known you forever."

"I gotta get back. By now, my partner's wonderin' if I got myself into trouble."

"Yes, of course. And I have chores to do."

They returned to the boardinghouse. Marianne Mertz started to say something, then lowered her gaze and rushed to the house. Pecos watched her, feeling he should speak up, but not knowing what words to use. He caught his breath when she stopped at the door, turned, and looked back. She waved hesitantly, then disappeared into the house.

"Good to do business with you," Jacob Nighbert said. He thrust out his grimy hand. Slash took it, expecting the blacksmith to try to crush him. The smith's grip was curiously gentle. "Anytime you got more scrap, bring it my way. These days I'm making all the horseshoes I can. And rims for wagon wheels. Them boys surely do break a lot of wheels."

"Heavy wagons?" Slash asked, trying not to sound too inquisitive.

"Rough country where they go is my guess. They're all the time out there chasing down Injuns."

"This seems like an out-of-the-way place for that," Slash said.

"Altitude—I mean High Mountain—is handy to both sides of the Rockies. And the Colonel's about taken over all the supply business for the town. You're the only one not flyin' his colors that I've seen in more 'n a month. Or two."

"Can I buy you a drink to celebrate our business deal?" Slash wanted to find out more from the blacksmith. He was a man who was slow to start talking, but once he got rolling, stopping the flood was nigh-on impossible. That was exactly what Slash needed, to find out everything about the Colonel and the town he had commandeered.

"Thank you kindly, but I'm a teetotaler."

"Do tell?"

"Well, I wasn't always. Back in the day I'd drink anything that was poured over at the Galloping Garter. I tried working like that once, all soused." Jacob Nighbert held up his left hand and wiggled his fingers . . . or three of them. Two were as stiff as boards. "I mashed 'em up good and proper. Ever since then, I have taken the pledge. If there was a temperance movement here in town, I'd be a member." He stared at his hand and wiggled all but the damaged fingers. Then he turned back to hammering out the metal strips he had worked on when Slash and Pecos had approached him.

Slash patted the coat pocket bulging with greenbacks from the sale of every ounce of scrap metal. He felt pleased about the transaction, since they hadn't intended actually peddling it anywhere. It had been an excuse to get into High Mountain and nothing more.

He looked around for his partner, but Pecos had lit a shuck. Slash parked the wagon in an empty lot down the street from the Galloping Garter Saloon. He settled his six-shooters and stepped up to the double swinging doors.

It was getting close to twilight and customers trickled in. Slash went to the bar. The lady barkeep gave him a once-over and said, "You a new recruit?"

"Do you think that the Colonel might like to have a man such as me in his company?" he said to test the waters. The woman smiled broadly and rolled her bony shoulders.

"Welcome, then. You got the look of a scout. You fixing to track them redskins down? We'll all sleep safer in our beds if you help the Colonel run the lot of them off."

"Indians, yeah," Slash said. He had no idea what the woman was saying. The Utes had signed a treaty and the Arapaho were being quiet. Whatever tribe threatened the woman in her dreams, they were far off from High Mountain. "Give me a beer."

"Coming up." She drew the beer and slid it along the bar to him. "It's on the house, since you're joining up."

"Much obliged. I'd've signed on earlier if I'd knowed free beer was part of the enlistment."

He turned and leaned both elbows on the bar. He studied the men scattered around the room. None of them wore the flashy ribbons he now knew were the mark of the Colonel's army. Slash sipped slowly, wondering what more he could learn from the town's citizens. The buzz in the room was pleasant and encouraged him to get himself into a conversation with the men.

The saloon fell silent when a man entered. Slash looked at him, wondering if he had ever seen him before. While familiar, the impeccably dressed man was a stranger.

As he moved, he turned toward the barkeep and signaled silently. The woman hurriedly rounded the bar with a shot glass and a half bottle of whiskey. If Slash was any judge, this was bourbon worth drinking, and not some rotgut brewed up in the back room with rusty nails and nitric acid to give it a mule's kick.

The new customer sat down with his back to a wall.

"Here you are, sir. Can I get you anything else?"

Benson motioned her away. Then she scuttled off like a mouse hoping to reach its hole before the cat pounced. The man poured himself a shot of bourbon, delicately sniffed at it, then knocked the shot back and belched. A quick, sure move refilled the glass. He fished around in his coat pocket and took out a bound lambskin volume. He opened the notebook, with fussy precision, wet the tip of a pencil on the tip of his tongue, and began writing.

Slash looked around the room. The others pointedly ignored the man. If he had been a ghost, they couldn't have pretended to see through him any more. The ribbons proclaimed a man who had ridden with the Colonel for quite a spell.

Before he realized he was doing it, Slash went to the chair opposite the diligently writing man and pulled it out.

"Mind if I join you? You look like a gent in need of a friend."

The man never looked up from his careful annotation. The page was filled with precise handwriting, but all the additions were in the margins, as if expanding on the main text with details only now remembered.

"Go away."

"I'll buy you a drink. That'll set well with a man who's been on the trail for so long."

The man looked up sharply. He carefully laid the pencil beside his notebook and downed another drink. He repeated the mechanical process of pouring himself another shot before speaking. Slash had the feeling that every drink the man poured himself was precisely the same, down to the final drop.

"Why do you say that?"

Slash noticed how the man took a quick glance at his chest, hunting for ribbons, before he spoke. His cold eyes locked with Slash's.

"You wear fine clothes, but they're all covered in dust. You're not likely to be in a dust storm around here, not this high in the mountains." Slash chuckled. "High Mountain. That's a pretty tame handle for a town."

"I named it. You have a quarrel with that?"

Slash blinked. He might have been wrong thinking this was one of the Colonel's old-timers. This might be the Colonel himself.

"No complaint. It's certainly high up on the mountain. That must be how it got the name Altitude—before you renamed it, that is. Well located, even if the mines are all shuttered now."

"Who are you?"

"You're not a talkative cuss, are you?" Slash put the beer down on the table. "An unfeelin' gent might say you're downright rude." A thousand things flashed through his mind as the words slipped from his mouth. A quick draw and a few rounds fired across the table ended the death and destruction. Bleed-'Em-So hired him and Pecos to solve problems the entire legion of federal deputies couldn't. Sometimes that included being judge, jury, and executioner.

If anyone needed executing, it was the Colonel.

"Max!" The man called out as he closed his notebook and covered it with his almost-effeminate hand. "Get over here."

Slash felt cold wind against his back. The clicking of boot heels crossing the saloon floor warned him against starting anything.

"What can I do for you, Mr. Benson?"

Slash took a quick look over his shoulder. The sentry from the road and two others stood behind him. Worse than being unable to do anything about the chance of getting shot in the back by all three, the man across the table wasn't the Colonel. Nobody insisted on being called by an officer's rank and then allowed an underling to address him as Mr. Benson.

This was a high-ranking aide, but not the Colonel.

"He wants to leave. Right now."

Slash kicked the chair back into Max, causing the man to grab it or be bowled over. With a roundhouse that started halfway in the next county, Slash spun around and landed a hard fist on the side of a second man's head. The outthrust jaw went slack and bloodshot eyes rolled up in his head. By now, the other man with Max was going for his six-gun.

"Don't," Slash said. He was faster than the lot of them. He drew and leveled his Colts at both the man reaching for his piece and the man still seated at the table.

"You're mighty quick on the draw," Benson said, as if commenting on the weather. Staring down the muzzle of a .44 didn't cause him to blink.

"Quick to get my dander up, too. I was only tryin' to be friendly."

"I don't need new friends," Benson said. "Now leave me be." He opened his notebook again, read a line or two, and then looked up at Slash.

Slash slid his two six-shooters back into their leather dens and backed away. Max stepped over the man who'd been laid out cold, but it wasn't to protect his partner. He just as easily could have stepped on the man's belly. He wanted to get between Slash and Benson.

"Adios, amigos," Slash said. He pushed through the double swinging doors and stepped into the twilight. The cold wind turned the sweat on his forehead to ice. He had come close to weighing more by a few ounces of lead, and he knew it.

It was time to find Pecos and get the hell out of High Mountain.

Chapter 21

Slash Braddock felt eyes watching him as he returned to his wagon. He tried not to rush. That'd make it seem as if he was running away—or had something to hide. He hopped into the wagon bed and stretched out flat on his back, his heart pounding. Letting down his guard now wasn't in the cards. He and Pecos had to clear out of High Mountain fast.

He sat up, hands going for both of his six-guns. He took in the threat, then closed his eyes and shuddered.

"What's eatin' you, pard? Every time you move like that for your irons makes me think something's wrong." Pecos sounded downright cheerful. He stood at the rear of the wagon, leaning on the lowered tailgate.

"I stepped into a den of rattlers," Slash said. "I got out without exchangin' warm regards in the form of .44 slugs, but they're onto me. I know it."

"I found out a bunch about what's goin' on here," Pecos said. "All we need to do is wait around for the Colonel to show his face. He'll show up sooner or later. Then it'll be easy as pie. We kidnap him and drag him back to Bleed-'Em-So's tender mercies."

"I thought I saw him," Slash said.

"Colonel Raymond? What's he look like?" Slash remembered Marianne Mertz's worshipful description. If the Colonel had been a divine being, she wouldn't have idolized him any differently.

"I figgered it wasn't him when our ole buddy Max from back along the road called him Benson. You sure the Colonel's name is Raymond? That a first or last name?"

"From the way it was said, I'd reckon it's his surname."

"So Raymond Benson's not him?"

"Who's this Benson fellow you tangled with?" Pecos listened to his partner's tale. After a long pause he said, "This must be someone high up in his command, scribblin' notes and all. And he said 'jump' and our new friend Max was already five feet in the air obeyin'."

"I caught a glimpse of what he was writin'. It looked like an inventory. You know, them lists Myra's always insistin' we keep and never do. Only, it wasn't for any single business. More like what he'd find worth stealin' in an entire town."

"And I'd wager he had a chestful of ribbons. That makes sense. A man scoutin' a town for the Colonel would be there for every bit of the burnin' and lootin' and rapin'."

"He's important, but he's not their leader."

"I shoulda got a better description of Raymond," Pecos said. "I had my mind on other things." He blinked and remembered Marianne Mertz, being near her, feeling her body pressed into his, the fleeting kiss that should have been more . . . if he hadn't chickened out.

"We need to make tracks," Slash said. "Stayin' in town is too dangerous. Now that we know that Colonel Raymond is usin' High Mountain as a headquarters, we—"

A cold voice cut him off.

"Mr. Benson wants a word with you," Max said. He leveled his pistol at Slash. A slow smile crossed his lips. "If he knew there was the two of you, he'd want to talk with you both. I'll make him happy taking the pair of you to him. He don't like surprises, usually, but this one'll suit him just fine." Emphasizing his point, he cocked his six-gun.

"We're on our way out of town. If you need supplies, tell us now and we'll fetch 'em back," Slash said. "We can even negotiate a contract for a steady ration of whatever you need."

"Both of you. Out of the wagon. Now."

Pecos looked for a way out. If he scrambled forward the length of the wagon, the bench seat shielded him. He got his feet under him and froze. He stared down the double Damascus-wound tubes of a Greener held in the hands of another of Raymond's men already occupying the driver's box. The light from a fresh-lit gas lamp hanging outside the Galloping Garter reflected off the man's ribbons. Like Max, he was a veteran of slaughtering an entire town.

"Good decision," Max said as Slash lifted his hands. "Keep makin' good decisions and you'll live a bit longer."

Both Pecos and Slash moved away from the wagon and stood under the watchful eyes of Max and three others, all with drawn guns. The guard toting the shotgun tromped through the wagon to drop down beside Max. The double barrels never wavered from Slash's midriff.

"You fixin' to rob us?" Pecos prodded Max, wanting a response.

"Well, now, I hadn't thought on the matter. You have enough money to make it worth my while? Me and the boys don't come cheap."

"I asked the smithy. He forked over two hundred dollars for some scrap iron," the man with the shotgun said. "There's five of us. That's a pair of double eagles each."

"I've killed men for less," Max said thoughtfully. "But

such a piddly amount, now, well, I say pass that along to the undertaker. It don't hardly cover the cost of my bullets, much less my valuable time."

Pecos settled himself and widened his stance just a few inches. Every passing second came closer to lead flying. He and Slash weren't going to walk away, but he intended to take at least two of the Colonel's men with him. Pecos shrugged and loosened the lanyard around his shoulder so he could swing his scattergun around. One shot was all he was likely to get off, and to do that, he'd have to move fast.

From the corner of his eye, Pecos saw his partner squaring off. Three of the outlaws trained their guns on him, including the one with the shotgun. Slash was quick, but not fast enough to take out many—any—of his adversaries. Pecos vowed to do the best he could to avenge his partner's imminent death.

"There you are. I've been looking for you." The woman's voice caused Max to twist around. His finger tightened on the trigger, but he didn't fire.

"Good evening, Mrs. Mertz," Pecos called. "What brings you this way?"

The auburn-haired beauty pushed aside the shotgun and stepped up, boldly inserting herself between Pecos and Max.

"Your presence is requested at my boardinghouse." She glared at Max. "Right away. Mr. Benson wants to talk to you."

"You sayin' Harl sent you to fetch these two old reprobates? That wasn't what—" Max shifted and tried to shove Marianne Mertz out of the way. The woman stood her ground.

"I spoke with him about how the Colonel has lost several important men recently. Mr. Benson also mentioned not hearing from Mr. Hutchins in some time."

"You butt out," Max ordered. He lifted his cocked Colt and aimed over Marianne's shoulder. She reached up and pushed it off target.

Pecos felt sweat pop up on his forehead. She either had

no idea what a cold-blooded killer Max was, or she had courage enough for the lot of them. He had plotted out in his head how to kill most of the men around him, but with the woman standing so close, she'd be gunned down before he had a chance to do real damage.

And Marianne would die before he did. Where she stood shielded him from three of the men's trained guns.

"He's agreed to hire Mr. Braddock and his partner. Your fighting force seems to require a steady supply of trained wagoners."

"Benson hired them?" Max sounded confused. "We're talking about Harl Benson, right?"

"Who else?" Marianne's words carried just the right tone, mixing impatience with incredulity that Max went against Benson's wishes.

"Looks like we're ridin' the same trail," Pecos said. He thrust out his hand. "Let's shake on it, partner." He kept a keen eye fixed on Max. A word from him and the others opened fire.

"Mr. Benson actually hired them on? After what he said in the saloon?" He poked his six-shooter in Slash's direction. Max sounded perplexed. Then he growled deep in his throat like a dog preparing to attack. "Let's march on over there so I can ask him myself."

"You'll have to wait until after dinner. You know how he dislikes being disturbed while he's eating."

"Max, he cut the ears off that Granger kid for talking to him 'fore dessert was served. You remember that?" The man holding the shotgun lowered it.

"He done more 'n that when—" began another.

"Shut up," Max snapped. "There's a civilian here." He fixed Marianne with a hard stare. She turned away and didn't see it. "Maybe three civilians. The Colonel don't like anybody shooting off their mouth about things best kept to ourselves."

"Come along now," Marianne said to Slash and Pecos.

"Mr. Benson isn't a man who likes to waste time. Everything he does is on a strict timetable."

"I saw him writin' in his notebook," Slash said. "He does like punctuality."

Pecos shouldered past Max, putting himself between the man's six-shooter and Marianne. Things seemed right and proper now. If gunplay started, she wasn't going to be the first one to catch a slug.

Pecos mopped sweat from his forehead when they got far enough away that Max and the others would have to be better shots than he gave them credit for to do any damage.

"Thanks for pullin' our fat from the fire, ma'am," Slash said. "I take it you and Pecos here are acquainted?"

"You might say that," Pecos said hastily, not wanting to pursue the matter in any more detail.

"He's always keepin' secrets. Gettin' him to talk's always a chore."

"I hadn't noticed that," Marianne said, chuckling. "Though he never once mentioned you all afternoon."

"Fancy that," Slash said, getting a glare from his partner. They introduced themselves, much to Pecos's chagrin.

"Did you mean it about Benson wantin' to hire us on?" Pecos asked. "How'd that happen to come up?"

"Oh, I mentioned meeting you and how you were such a stout, strong man. You carry yourself like you know how to use that sidearm." Marianne sniffed just a little in disdain. "And that awful blunderbuss you have slung around your neck. For some reason, that interested Mr. Benson the most. Is such a weapon beneficial for hunting Indians?"

"It is," Slash answered. "They're terrified when they catch wind of it." Pecos's dark look didn't stop Slash. "Is Mr. Benson waitin' for the Colonel?"

"Their comings and goings are a mystery to me," the red-haired beauty said. "The Colonel pays me for the entire seven rooms I let, whether anyone sleeps here or not. Right now, only Mr. Benson is bedded down, and he just returned a few minutes ago."

"What about the . . . others?" Slash looked over his shoulder, back toward town, Max, and the cutthroats with him.

"No, no, my rooms are not for just any of his men. They're all reserved for the Colonel's 'senior staff.' I suppose that's the term, isn't it?"

"If you mean his 'senior Injun-fightin' officers,'" Slash said.

"Would he hire you as one of them? His 'senior officers'?" She looked at Pecos. "I could fix up a room all special for you."

"That's real thoughty of you, Mrs. Mertz," Slash said. "I doubt the Colonel needs our Injun-fightin' expertise so bad that he'd make us captains or majors. What rank's Benson?"

"No one's ever said. When the Colonel addresses him, it's always by his Christian name . . . Harl. Everyone else is respectful and calls him Mr. Benson."

She paused at the end of the walk leading to the front porch. Marianne laid her hand on Pecos's arm. He felt uncomfortable at the touch, but didn't draw back. That'd insult the woman, even if it meant his partner'd josh him about it for a long time.

"I . . . I didn't actually ask Mr. Benson about hiring you. The notion just came to me, but he's a difficult man to speak to. And he started supper. No one interrupts his meal. No one."

"Very prickly, that Mr. Benson," Slash said.

"That's one way of putting it," she agreed. "But I do think you riding with the Colonel would be so much better than hauling freight. I've heard gossip about what his men are paid. Three times what a cowboy gets. More even than a marshal. The work must be terribly dangerous to earn such a princely sum of money, but you have the look of a man able to take care of himself." She lowered her gaze and blushed. "And others."

"He can do that very thing," Slash said, grinning at Pecos's discomfort. "But we can talk to Benson. That's one thing we do real good. Talk."

"Him," Pecos said. "He's the one who talks better ever since he got married. Before then, he never uttered a word."

"You're married, Mr. Braddock? Would your wife like a town like High Mountain? We're very sociable here, and everyone's prospering because of the Colonel. He and his men spend freely."

Slash hemmed and hawed and was saved from answering when Pecos poked him in the ribs.

"Slash. Over there." Pecos pointed. A shadow moved across the front window. Someone stirred in the boarding-house.

"That's Mr. Benson," Marianne said, turning to see what caught Pecos's eye. "I recognize his silhouette. Let's hurry before he goes to bed. Once he retires for the night, no one disturbs him. He can be a very volatile man when it comes to disturbing his routine." She lifted her skirts, climbed the three steps to the porch, and hurried inside.

Slash and Pecos followed slowly. They slipped into the foyer as she reached the first landing on the stairs leading to the second floor. She heaved a sigh and shook her head.

"Too late. He's closed his door. You'll have to talk with him in the morning about employment."

"Is the Colonel likely to show up anytime soon?" Pecos asked.

"Only Mr. Benson is staying here tonight. Since he returned after a few weeks' absence, it wouldn't surprise me if the Colonel arrived soon, too. They do enjoy comparing notes and planning their next campaign against the renegade Indians."

"He assembles his staff for the, uh, powwow?" Slash asked, sucking on his teeth as he thought.

"Why, yes, of course. All the rooms would be occupied then, but—"

"But?" Pecos looked up the stairs at her. She stood on the landing in front of a stained-glass window that made it seem as if she were Madonna ascending to heaven.

"But since I have six free rooms at the moment, you can stay and wait to speak to Mr. Benson. He takes coffee at dawn. No matter when, always as the sun peeks over the horizon."

"That's not a good idea, us beddin' down in a place reserved for the Colonel and his staff," Slash said. "But you've got a stable out back. That'd be better 'n we've had for a month."

"Why, yes, that's fine," Marianne said. She descended slowly and stopped two steps up so she looked Pecos squarely in the eye.

Slash cleared his throat. Neither the boardinghouse proprietor nor his partner twitched a muscle. "I'll go see about catchin' some shut-eye. In the stable."

Marianne reached out. Her fingertips lightly brushed Pecos's cheek.

"And you can find a place to bed down on your own," Slash finished, speaking a little too loudly. He wasn't surprised when he awoke in the middle of the night and didn't hear his partner's snoring.

Chapter 22

"Who're you?" The cold voice froze Pecos. His bacon, securely impaled by his fork, halted halfway to his mouth.

"Good morning, Colonel," said Marianne Mertz, coming from the kitchen. She wiped flour on her hands off on a checkered apron secured around her trim waist. "It's good to see you're back all safe and sound from fighting those rampaging savages. Are you staying around for a while? The townsfolk would love to throw a social in your honor."

"I'm glad the church got a new room added," the man said. Then, ignoring the woman, he fixed cold gray eyes on Pecos and repeated, "Who're you?"

Pecos finished stuffing the meat into his mouth and used the fork to cut and corral a pile of the scrambled eggs.

"I'm a gent appreciatin' this lady's fine cookin'. I don't know how you make simple things like bacon and eggs taste so fine, Miss Mertz."

Colonel Raymond pushed his coat away from the Smith & Wesson slung at his right hip, butt forward for easy draw when mounted.

"Nice sidearm," Pecos observed, glancing at the Colonel. He turned his full attention to the boardinghouse owner. "Miz Mertz, are there any of your fine, fluffy biscuits left? I've got some bacon grease left that needs moppin' up."

"Don't bother," Raymond said. "You won't be staying."

Pecos carefully laid down his fork and stood. His six-foot-six frame intimidated most men. Colonel Raymond stood his ground.

Although six inches shorter than Pecos, the Colonel didn't quake. He took off his flat-brimmed black hat, complete with bright-gold braid, and laid it on the table. His long brown hair hung in sweat-soaked strings, giving him a wet-dog look. But his cold eyes showed no hint of fear. Pecos Baker didn't intimidate him.

"I've been on the trail a long time. I need a bath. I need to catch up on my sleep. And I certainly can use some of this woman's good cooking. What I don't need is arrogant back-talk."

"And all I need is for folks to be polite. I'm not huntin' for a fight."

"But you won't avoid it if one comes your way?"

Pecos nodded. He locked eyes with Raymond. He waited for the slightest hint that the self-styled military man reached for his S&W. Going for his own Russian .44 would only result in getting an ounce of lead in the gut. Pecos gauged distance and figured a punch to the face was his most effective response. Swapping lead in Marianne's house would be downright impolite.

"Please, Colonel Raymond, don't poke him. He's a good man." Marianne laid a hand on the Colonel's arm. He shrugged it off.

"What's he good for?"

"Well, now, Colonel, my partner's right good at puttin' away food enough for two men. You ain't et all my share of breakfast, have you?" Slash stepped into the kitchen behind

Raymond. If any trouble started, the Colonel was caught between two opponents.

He still didn't budge.

"This is Melvin Baker," Marianne said. "And that's his partner, James Braddock."

"And standing behind Mr. Braddock is Harl Benson. Mr. Benson has a six-gun trained on an exposed spine."

"Now, how'd we get around to pullin' iron on each other?" Pecos asked. "We're freighters, passin' through this fine town. The blacksmith bought a ton of our scrap, and we're willin' to sell Mr. Nighbert more, as he hinted."

"Gentlemen, please. Come on in, everyone, and sit down. I'll fix more breakfast for all of you."

"Count me in, Miz Mertz, if the offer includes seconds of everything. I worked up a real appetite last night," Pecos said.

The woman blushed and turned away, going to the stove to drop more strips of bacon into a skillet. The sizzle almost drowned out Harl Benson's question.

"What do you want me to do, sir?" he asked in a voice hardly above a whisper.

Colonel Raymond heard. The entire time he had fixed Pecos with his hard stare. Trying to look innocent wore on Pecos, but he succeeded.

"Join me for breakfast," Raymond said. "In the dining room. We have matters to discuss."

"Yes, sir."

Pecos heard the hammer on Benson's six-shooter uncock. An instant later, the sound of metal sliding across leather told him the Colonel's flunky ran his six-shooter back into its hideout under his coattails.

Benson pushed past Slash and trailed the Colonel into the adjoining dining room. Pecos settled down at the kitchen table and continued scooping food into his mouth. He looked up, loaded fork halfway to his mouth.

"Get yourself some food, pard. It's gonna be a long day." He glanced over his shoulder in the direction of the dining room. Muffled voices made his prediction seem all the more accurate.

Slash dropped into a chair. Marianne slid a filled plate in front of him.

"Did you sleep well out in the barn?" she asked.

Slash grinned crookedly and chuckled. "Not as well as Pecos, I'd wager."

"You'd win that bet." Both Pecos and Marianne spoke at the same instant. They fell silent, stared at each other, then laughed. The woman returned to the stove.

Pecos pushed back from the table to get closer to the doorway into the dining room. Slash slid his chair over, too.

". . . completed my reconnaissance," Harl Benson said in a low voice that still carried.

"Let me see your notes." Colonel Raymond leafed through the fancy lambskin notebook, muttering to himself. "Good work, as usual, Harl. I need to know about the disposition of the army units. Two of the targets are near posts."

"I can find out about patrols. The Cheyenne are causing a ruckus up north. That might draw the majority of the cavalry's firepower away."

"Two towns, yes. Would both send patrols?" Raymond asked.

Slash and Pecos exchanged looks. The Colonel was becoming bolder, planning a pair of attacks on towns and doing it under the nose of the U.S. Army.

"We'll have to be more selective," Benson said. "Moving so much loot is never easy. Two towns means twice as many wagons will be required, unless you intend to stash everything from the first town before hitting the second."

"We need to talk this over. I have an idea what we might do. I'd heard that . . ."

"What are you two doing?" Marianne asked. "It's too early in the day for a siesta. Get over here and help with the dishes. It's the least you can do, since I'm not charging you rent."

"On our way, Miz Mertz," Slash said. He heaved himself to his feet and stretched. "I do think you've got a decent idea, though. So much food's weighin' me down. I can use some shut-eye, in spite of just gettin' my eyes open from a good night's sleep."

"You wash. Pecos can dry," she said. "I need to clean up the counter and put away what food you didn't wolf down."

"It's not Pecos's fault there's anything left," Slash said. "The way he was shovelin' the chow down, you're lucky he didn't take off a hand, all the way up to your elbow, as you served him."

As the two former cutthroats worked on the fine china dishes, they kept a keen eye trained on the door leading into the dining room. Both Raymond and Benson had disappeared deeper into the boardinghouse. Benson's notebook lay on the dining-room table.

" 'Scuse me," Slash said. "I won't be a minute."

"My pleasure keepin' Marianne company." Pecos began stacking the dishes.

"Put them in the cabinet, will you, Pecos?" Marianne came over. "Here. I'll show you where." She reached around him and opened the cabinet door.

Slash kept from chuckling at how his partner blushed. If Jay Breckenridge had moved like that on him, he'd be turning beet red, too. Women did that to men like him and Pecos, men used to spending all their time alone in the mountains or out on the prairie. Slash wasn't even sure how long his only companion had been the old galoot now being fawned over by Marianne Mertz, but it was a long time.

A quick look assured him that Raymond and his scout were gone. He stepped over to the table and opened the notebook. A quick move let him run his calloused fingers over the soft lambskin cover. Harl Benson was something of a dandy. If he hadn't obviously dressed like a fashion plate, just looking at his choice in writing papers said that. Slash remembered the cold look in the man's eyes. The cold, *dead* look. Benson was not a man to cross, no matter how much the clotheshorse he looked.

He flipped open the book and slowly scanned the pages. Benson's handwriting was almost as perfect as newspaper print. Every word was perfectly written and distinct. Slash shook off the admiration when he got to the bottom of the first page. Then he leafed through faster.

"Sweet Jesus, no," he gasped out when he came to the second section detailing how best to loot another town.

The sound of the two men returning sent him running for the kitchen. He barely slid around the corner when Raymond and Benson entered the dining room. They argued, and the topic was suddenly of vital importance.

"The second town is a quick raid," Benson said.

"It's farther to go and we'd have to come south to continue," Raymond said.

"The fort is farther away and might as well be abandoned. That makes it an easy target, one ripe for the plucking."

The two bickered over details of shipping their booty and how many wagons were needed.

"What's wrong, Slash?" Marianne turned from fussing over Pecos. "You look like someone's walking on your grave."

"Got a bit lightheaded from standin' too quick," he said, sinking into the chair he had pulled close to the dining room. Try as he might, he wasn't able to overhear Raymond's objections. The thunderous pulse in his temples drowned out ordinary conversation.

He jerked around when Raymond and Benson came into the kitchen. Slash reached for his two six-shooters, but checked the move. There wasn't any way to take out Raymond before Benson filled him with lead.

"Are you going out, Colonel?" Marianne asked. "Should I expect you for lunch? Or supper?"

"Supper," Raymond decided. "I need to do some recruiting."

"How's that, Colonel?" she asked. She pulled Pecos back a half step and moved in front of him, squarely facing Raymond.

"The Indians have put up spirited defenses, ma'am. My forces have been depleted. And we need support."

"Support?" Marianne grinned. "Do you mean wagon drivers?"

"We are in need of those, yes," Harl Benson said suspiciously. "Why do you ask?"

"My two friends are freighters. They have a strong team of mules and their own wagon."

"These two?" Benson looked from Pecos to Slash.

Slash didn't quail under the man's gimlet stare. He tried to fathom what went on in the depths of the man's think box and failed. Playing poker with Benson would be a one-way trip to the poorhouse.

Or the graveyard.

"They hauled a load up for the blacksmith. You know Mister Nighbert."

"You vouching for them?" Raymond asked. "And would the smithy? I've been well pleased with the ironwork from Nighbert and consider him trustworthy."

"I haven't known these two scallywags long," Marianne said, "but they have shown themselves to be hardworking and honest."

"And you have your own wagon?" Raymond pressed.

"They do," Marianne cut in before Pecos could answer.

Slash shook his head to silence her, but she ignored him. She thought she did them a boon.

"Very well, Mrs. Mertz, I'll hire them both. And their wagon and team. At competitive rates."

"If you have anything more to offer, I'm sure they'd be willing to listen," she went on.

"Indeed," Colonel Raymond said, eyeing first Pecos and then Slash. "They have the look. If my recruitment doesn't provide me a full regiment, perhaps the two of them would be interested in fighting."

"Indians," Benson said hastily.

"We've done our share of Injun fightin'," Pecos said.

"Excellent. Come along, Mr. Benson." Colonel Raymond seemed to turn invisible. One instant he stood in the kitchen, the next he was gone like a puff of smoke. Benson was hardly less elusive as he left.

"There. You two old reprobates have fine-paying jobs now. Jobs that'll keep you in High Mountain for a while longer." Marianne gave Pecos a quick peck on the cheek and hurried off into the dining room before disappearing into the boardinghouse.

"I ain't sure this was what I expected, but it works out for us," Pecos said. "If we hang around Raymond long enough, and do it without all his men thinkin' we're outsiders, finishin' Bleed-'Em-So's little chore is easy as pie."

Slash swung around and looked into the dining room. Benson's notebook was gone.

"I saw it. I saw what that sidewinder had all writ down. They're fixin' to massacre two more towns. Two!"

"That's nothin' Bledsoe didn't expect."

"You don't understand, Pecos." Slash's mouth felt as if he had stuffed in a bale of cotton.

"What don't I get?"

"The towns." Slash swallowed hard, then blurted, "Jay! One of the town's they're fixin' to burn to the ground is Camp Collins!"

Chapter 23

"If you get us killed, we won't be worth spit to anybody," Slash said peevishly.

"Complaints, that's all you're givin' me. Do you have a better idea?" Pecos stepped back into the shade and looked across the street at the saloon. When they had come to town, there'd been few customers in the Galloping Garter. Now the gin mill was half filled with more men on the way inside. From the horses tethered in front and around the back, at least ten riders had come into High Mountain.

They had to be the Colonel's men returning from whatever looting and plundering they'd been engaged in. Within a week, at this pace, a hundred men or more would cause the small town to burst at the seams. Whatever Slash and Pecos decided to do, it had to be done before then—sooner.

"It's broad daylight. We should wait till sundown. Later. Midnight," Slash ruminated.

"Slash, old pard, you're losin' your nerve in your old age. And you're forgettin' somethin' I never believed you would."

"Jay," Slash said in a low voice. "These prairie pirates are gonna destroy Camp Collins. We don't have any way to get a warning to her."

"Or to Bledsoe. We spent the last hour huntin' for some way to let them know. The telegrapher's been told not to send out any wires. He's like some kind of religious crazy when he talks about the Colonel. If he'd been paid not to send a telegram, we'd have a chance to outbid Raymond."

"You got that right, Pecos, dammit. I saw the look on his face. It's like he is on a holy mission because the Colonel told him."

"Stealin' a horse ain't somethin' I've done in a while, but it'd be noticed quick as a jackrabbit. There ain't much of a chance to escapin'." Pecos stood a little straighter. "If Marianne didn't come with us, and stayed behind, the Colonel would think she was in cahoots. There's no tellin' what vengeance he would deliver on her head."

"It's not the Colonel you should worry about," Slash said. "Benson is worse. It's not hardly possible, but he is. Raymond might feel a twinge as he killed you, but Benson? He'd worry more about the cost of replacin' the ammo he used."

"He'd consider it a waste," Pecos agreed. "So we got ourselves bottled up in this here town. It's swarmin' with owlhoots all willin' to kill us, just for practice."

"All right. You got me. We have to do somethin' fast. What's rattlin' around in that pea brain of yours?"

"There are three buildings just past the blacksmith's. Who needs them?"

"And for what?" Slash continued, playing along with his partner's thinking out loud.

"Armory," they both said.

In silence they made their way past the smithy's forge. It had died down. The blacksmith was nowhere to be seen or they'd have asked him what he saw being stored in the buildings.

"It's better to find out for ourselves," Slash said. "We don't want to cause trouble for any of the townsfolk if we get caught."

"You make it sound like, just because we're decrepit old has-beens, that we can't sneak around and scout on our own."

"One of us has knees that pop so loud when he walks that a bystander might think it's Gabriel fixin' to sound the Second Coming."

"Glad," said Pecos, "that it ain't me." He motioned his partner back. They stepped into shadow at the side of the first warehouse as two riders passed within ten feet. Neither of the gunmen saw them.

"Big-time killers," Slash said. "They got ribbons galore on their coats."

"Four each. You think that means they've helped wipe out four towns?"

"Like Quantrill, 'cept that crazy Ohioan only murdered the citizens. I never heard of him strippin' houses and businesses and cartin' it all off as spoils of war."

"Once you're dead, what you owned don't worry you none," Pecos observed.

Slash peered out and signaled that the riders had turned the corner, heading for the Galloping Garter Saloon.

They circled the building and found a locked door at the rear. Pecos rattled the shiny, new padlock. "What do we do if we bust the door open?"

"That depends on what's inside. If it's all the ammunition for the next attack, we blow the place to Kingdom Come."

"The town would burn to the ground. We wouldn't be any better than them."

"Think of us like a sawbones. If a leg's all black and rotten with gangrene, sawin' it off saves a life. Otherwise, leave the leg attached and the patient dies," said Slash. "What are you willin' to risk?"

"We have to get Marianne out of the way 'fore we light the place up," Pecos said.

"You're always crossin' the river 'fore you get to it. There might be nothin' inside but furniture and the plunder, like McCall stored."

Pecos swung his shotgun around and hammered away at the lock with the short stock. The third whack broke the hasp. The lock fell to the ground. He kicked it out of the way and slowly opened the door.

"Sure is dark in there," he said. With a quick step, he entered. He swung the sawed-off shotgun around, in case guards prowled.

"There," Slash said. Both his six-shooters slid out of their holsters. He went into a crouch, the pistols pointed to the left.

Pecos laughed. "It took me a second for these tired old peepers to see after all that sunlight. Put your guns down. It's a mangy tomcat chasin' down a meal."

A furious hiss punctuated Pecos's description of the life-and-death pursuit.

"Sounds like we gave his food a chance to get away."

They advanced and wound around the stacked crates. Pecos came to a box and pried off the lid.

"Lookee there. Just as I thought." He reached down and filled his fist with loose cartridges. He tossed them into the air so they cascaded back into the box. "There're enough Spencer rounds to fight off every Indian this side of the Canadian River."

"There's another pile of crates. All marked dynamite. If we blow this entire place, it'd cut a hole a mile deep."

"Not that much," Pecos said. "We're on top of a solid mountain. This much explosive'd only blow a hole a half mile deep."

Slash chuckled, then sobered.

"Should we see what's in the other two warehouses?"

"No reason," Pecos said. "We blow up this one and the Colonel's sorely in need of more ammo. And dynamite. And from the look of the cases piled along the wall, fifty or more rifles."

"This all looks to have been stolen from the army," Slash said. "What reward would they give us to get it all back?"

"How long have you been settin' beside me in that driver's box haulin' freight?" Pecos sounded disgusted.

"Close to a year now, more or less. Why?"

"Eyeball the contents of this here building. There're ten wagonloads. More. The Colonel's not about to let us load up, much less drive off with even one shipment."

"You just want to see how big a bang it makes when it blows up," Slash said.

"Think of it as the Fourth of July. Or maybe the final shot in a war most folks in Colorado don't even know's bein' fought."

"Jay," Slash said to himself. Louder, "You see any fuse? I've got a match."

"Nary an inch of miner's fuse anywhere," Pecos said. "We'll have to start a fire. Do you think you can run fast enough so you don't get swallered up in the blast?"

"You'll be lost in my dust cloud." Slash rummaged about and found a crate filled with excelsior. He pulled a double handful out and dropped it on top of a box of dynamite. "That oughta get things rollin'," he said.

Both men froze when they heard loud voices outside.

"Light it. Get that danged match into the box." Slash grabbed Pecos's arm and shook. The taller cutthroat yanked free.

"Hide. They're comin' in!"

Both of them crouched behind a wall of boxes. Whatever was in these crates had been disguised by someone using a knife to scratch out the lettering.

"We got enough, Matthias. The Colonel said so."

"I need to load wagon number three with the ammunition for the second wave. We lost five hundred rounds when that fool Jessup dropped a cigarette into the stockpile I'd put out near the target."

"That much? He was damned lucky he didn't blow himself all up."

"I wanted to use up one more round, but Benson said no. I think him and Jessup have some kind of deal going on," Matthias said.

"Are you accusing them of hiding all the inventory that's gone missing?"

Slash chanced a quick look around the crate where he hid. Matthias and three others moved through the warehouse, using knives to mark the crates they wanted with deep-cut X's. He fumbled to find a match. With luck he'd rob the Colonel of an entire warehouse of arms and ammo and four men who'd ride at the head of his deadly column.

Before he had a chance to strike the match, a powerful hand clamped on his wrist. Slash tried to pull free, but Pecos held on too tightly.

"Don't be a danged fool. We'll go up with 'em."

"If we don't destroy their stockpile, Camp Collins will be leveled." Slash swallowed. His mouth had filled with cotton wool. "And Jay. If we can't warn her or Bledsoe these killers are on the way, the whole town's in danger."

"Gettin' ourselves kilt dead won't help your missus," Pecos pointed out. "We need to find another way to stop them."

Slash grumbled, chanced another look where Matthias and his henchmen continued to mark crates for removal, then slipped back. He reluctantly stuffed the lucifer back into his pocket. His shoulders sagged; then he perked up.

"We can shoot 'em. They got their backs turned. We cut 'em down and then set off the dynamite. The blast will hide what we done to 'em."

"Too late," Pecos said. "Two more are comin' in."

"Your scattergun. You can take out the lot of 'em if they get all bunched up. I can decoy them."

"We're clearin' out. There's got to be another chance that won't land us both in shallow graves." Pecos shook his head ruefully. "With this bunch they'd only dig one grave for the pair of us. I don't want to spend eternity sharin' a grave with you."

"I'm the one who'd suffer. Your snorin' is loud enough to wake the dead," Slash said. But in spite of his arguing, he pressed back and followed Pecos to the back door, where they'd entered.

"Ready?" Pecos asked. "We got one shot at leavin' without them spottin' us."

With a surge both men rushed for the door.

Both froze when Matthias called out, "You two. Stop!"

They turned around slowly to meet their fate.

Chapter 24

"Where are you two going?" Matthias's cold voice demanded an answer.

Slash and Pecos turned. They worked well in tandem, stepping away from each other. They had been in dangerous situations before, and when lead began flying, they wanted to be far enough apart so a shot missing one of them wouldn't wing the other. Make the enemy work for his kill. That was as close to advice as either ever gave.

Pecos blinked. Matthias hadn't thrown down on them. A hundred ideas flashed through his head. The Colonel's gunman wouldn't have hesitated to shoot them in the back. There wasn't any reason to call them out, so he had something else in mind.

"What do you want?" Pecos said, his voice gravelly with stress. He cleared his throat, but there wasn't any call to ask again. Matthias waved his arms around like a windmill.

"You're the new freight haulers Colonel Raymond hired, aren't you? This is the freight we need loaded right away." He peered past them out the door they had broken through to get inside. "Are you two the village idiots? What do you think we want you to do? Where's your wagon?"

"Got it parked down the street," Slash said. "We weren't sure where you wanted us to load the cargo."

"What the hell do I care if you load it out back or in front? If the crate's got an X carved on it, get it onto your wagon. Now!" Matthias glared at them. Three of his partners moved to flank him.

"On it, boss," Slash said. When Pecos tried to complain, he elbowed his partner.

Outside, Pecos flared, "He ain't our boss. Nobody is!"

"We got people tellin' us what to do from all sides. Bleed-'Em-So says 'frog' and we jump. While we're bidin' our time in High Mountain, the Colonel's got the last word."

"Until we clamp the shackles on him," Pecos said.

"That's hard to do with an army all around him. Let's get our wagon and start doin' what we're told. We might get the chance to arrest Raymond if we play along."

Pecos grumbled the entire way, but quieted when they pulled up in front of the warehouse.

"Bigger doors," Slash explained.

"Ain't as likely to notice how we busted in, either," Pecos added. He jumped down and peered into the warehouse. "Are any of them weasels gonna help us?"

"Can't say, don't care," Slash said. "We need a plan to stop them from burnin' Camp Collins to the ground."

"And murderin' every last mother's son," Pecos said. He spat. "And Miss Jay. And Myra and Del and—"

"Hush up. Stop your thinkin' out loud. We got plenty of work to do."

Three hours later their freight wagon creaked under the load of ammunition and dynamite. None of the crates they'd identified as having rifles carried Matthias's mark.

Slash stepped away when the last crate was stashed securely.

"If our wagon goes up, they don't want to lose any of the rifles."

"Or Gatling guns," Pecos said. "We don't have shells for the howitzers, either." He stepped away and looked down the street at the other two warehouses. "You reckon those are stored there?"

"If they are, we just lost our chance to find out," Pecos said. He squinted into the sun at the five riders trotting up.

"It took you long enough," Matthias said. He spat. "Get those mangy mules pulling. We've got a lot of ground to cover 'fore sundown."

"Where are we headed?" Slash wanted to throw a little sand in the air and make it sound as if they hadn't been spying.

"You'll go where I say, that's where," Matthias said. "Me and the boys will be your escorts."

"Escorts?" Pecos said, as if the idea was something unusual. Under his breath he added a few choice curses and pungent descriptions of the men and their ancestors.

"Yes, sir, that suits us just fine. With this freight we wouldn't want road agents tryin' to steal it. Why, a determined band of outlaws would have enough ammo to hold up a hundred banks."

All Slash got in reply was a cold stare. He smiled insincerely and shrugged. "Just makin' conversation."

Matthias snarled something crude, wheeled his horse around, and trotted off with the rest of the "guards" trailing him.

Pecos and Slash had delayed as long as they could. Anything more would draw unwanted attention. They climbed into the driver's box. Pecos settled the reins in his hands and convinced the mules to start the trip out of town. All the way down the steep hill, he stomped hard on the brake to keep the heavy wagon from rolling over the team. When they reached the bottom of the hill, he moaned.

"My leg's about ready to fall off, and them mules don't have a kind word for me."

"While you've been pretendin' to drive this wagon, I've come up with an idea," Slash said.

"If it's half as good as my expert handlin' of the wagon, it's bound to be a big joke."

"Matthias and his cronies are ridin' way ahead, scoutin' for us."

"This is the road to Camp Collins," Pecos said. "As if we needed guides to get there."

"They don't know that, and the whole town's survival depends on us not givin' a hint where we hail from." Slash got a far-off look in his eyes. Pecos knew his partner was thinking about Jay.

"Every second takes us closer to town," Pecos said. "If you ain't got an idea about how to stop them, I do. Look ahead."

Slash stood in the box and shielded his eyes. He sank back.

"Three war wagons. They've got Gatling guns mounted on all three. The armor's good enough to keep anything smaller 'n a Sharps .50-caliber slug from getting through the walls. And they're all turning down the road, so they'll be at Camp Collins before us."

"They need the ammunition we got. Those are just the wagons. The Colonel sends through an army all firin' six-shooters. We've got their ammo. That means we'll rendezvous somewhere outside town for all of 'em to load up before the attack."

"Is there fuse in the back, Pecos? We didn't find none in the warehouse."

"Don't much matter. We pull into the middle of them war wagons and I let loose with a few rounds." He patted his shotgun slung over his shoulder. "The dynamite's old. I saw a couple of the sticks drippin' nitro. Some of them sticks are so bad, they look like they're spinster ladies at a wedding,

all weepy. I'm surprised we're still of this earth and not ar-
guin' with St. Peter about gettin' through them Pearly Gates.
The bouncin' around's been fierce."

"The road's a mite rougher than I remember," Slash said.
"But then, we don't come this way often. The main road's
on the other side of town, toward Denver."

"There're the raiders," Pecos said. "The Colonel's ral-
lyin' them for the fight. You want to jump out and find a spot
to ambush any of them cowardly jackals when they try to
high-tail it?"

"What are you talkin' about?"

"I knew it'd happen. All the bouncin' 'n bangin' along
this poor road's addled your brains. You get off and find a
spot to snipe them. I'll blow up the wagon when I'm smack
in the center of the war wagons. When the men line up to
collect their ammo, *boom!*"

For a moment Slash sat speechless. His mouth opened
and closed like a fish trying to swallow a hook. Then he
shook his head.

"I'm not lettin' you kill yourself."

"You got a wife to think about," Pecos said. "I can stop
the attack and satisfy Bleed-'Em-So if I blow up Colonel
Raymond, too. You're entitled to my share of the reward.
You and Miss Jay."

"Whatever happened to us bein' partners? We've rode
along together for . . . well, forever. You're not gonna do
anything as stupid as . . ." Slash's words trailed off.

Matthias and a dozen men galloped up in a cloud of dust.
They surrounded the wagon.

"Head on down that side road," Matthias said. "We got
problems with the attack."

Both Pecos and Slash sucked in their breaths.

"What kinda problem's that?"

"Ordnance problems," Matthias snapped. "That's all you
need to know. Kirk, Manny, you two climb on in the back
and ride along."

"Wait, there's no call for you to do that," Slash started.

"Why not?" Matthias's hand drifted toward the pistol holstered at his side.

"It's . . . Well, it's downright dangerous, what with all that loose ammo and the dynamite. Them sticks are leakin'. Jostle 'em wrong and . . . *blooie!*"

"That's real kind of you to take the risk," Matthias said in a nasty tone. He motioned. Two men hitched their horses to the rear of the wagon and climbed in.

Pecos cast a look over his shoulder. Both men sat staring straight ahead. If either he or Slash tried to set off the explosives they carried, the guards would ventilate them before they had a chance to maneuver around to take out the Colonel and his senior officers.

"Watch 'em real close," Matthias said. There wasn't any question who the order was for—or who was to be the object of that scrutiny. "Follow us."

He wheeled his horse about and trotted off. Slash squinted to see where the raider went. He pointed.

"I see it," Pecos said. He turned the mules down a steep trail that lead off in a peculiar direction. The road twisted and turned. It wasn't long before he lost track of the direction. The sun sank and the cold shroud of night pulled itself around wagon and driver.

"I can't get my bearings," Slash said. "The clouds buildin' up block out the Big Dipper and danged-near everything else."

"I'm all turned around, too, but we must be gettin' close to town. We've been rollin' along for hours."

Slash fumbled about in his vest and pulled out his pocket watch. Holding it up within an inch of his face let him read the time.

"It's past midnight. We coulda been in Denver by now."

"I don't recognize anything out there, pard," Pecos said.

"You two, keep your yaps shut. The Colonel says no talking." One of the men riding behind them added a curse to his orders.

"You're the one makin' all the noise," Slash said loudly.

"You hush up." The sound of metal slipping across leather warned that either Kirk or Manny had pulled iron.

Pecos started to warn him about firing while sitting in the back of a wagon creaking under the weight of so much ammunition and dynamite, but Slash elbowed him to silence.

"There. Up ahead," Slash said.

Their escort split into two columns, letting them roll ahead with only Matthias leading the way.

"There must be fifty men camped here," Pecos said in a choked voice.

"And we're bringin' 'em all the ammo they can carry when they hit the town."

Colonel Raymond rode to Matthias and spoke rapidly, then galloped away. In the flare of a half-dozen campfires, Pecos and Slash watched him go from one war wagon to the next.

Matthias came back and said, "We attack at dawn. Help Kirk and Manny unload your cargo. The boys have a few hours to be sure all their guns are ready for some hot action."

Kirk and Manny hooted with glee.

Pecos and Slash stared at each other. They had to do something to stop the attack on Camp Collins, but there wasn't anything that would be effective. Jay and Myra and the rest of the town would be gunned down—and there wasn't a damned thing they could do to stop the slaughter.

Chapter 25

Thirty men, all armed to the teeth, lined up behind their freight wagon. Manny sat on the dropped tailgate, while Kirk pried open boxes inside the wagon bed. Hundreds of shells were pushed out to the eagerly awaiting army.

Slash and Pecos stood by helplessly, watching as the men took enough ammunition to load a half-dozen six-shooters, then stuff handfuls more into canvas bags slung over their shoulders. Every last killer had the cartridges to reload ten times over. The firepower in front of them made even Chief Marshal Bledsoe's legion of federal deputies look puny . . . and Bleed-'Em-So fielded armed-to-the-teeth men when he went after outlaws.

"What chance is there against all them killers?" Pecos whispered.

"We got to think like them." Slash shifted nervously from one foot to the other. "How can we kill the most of 'em as quick as we can? If we leave their partners' bodies strewn all over the place, the ones left might scatter."

"Do you think any of them wolves will get scared by the

sight of a dead body? Even if it was the weasel ridin' beside 'em?"

"I reckon not," Slash said.

He looked around the shallow bowl holding the bivouac.
Campfires caused shadows to dance along the sides of the
war wagons. He tugged at his friend's sleeve.

Pecos quietly stepped back. The Colonel's men were too
busy loading their six-guns and stashing extra ammo to notice. Even Matthias had ridden away, probably to palaver with
his leader. That meant the attack was due to launch soon.

The two reformed train robbers edged closer to the nearest war wagon. The armored sides showed deep pockmarks.
The wagon had survived at least one assault. Slash gave up
counting when he got to twenty dents in the thick steel.

"The back door's open." Pecos shrugged his shoulder
and worked the lanyard around to bring his shotgun up to
bear. A brush on one of the triggers would blast apart anyone
inside the war wagon. Once it had been cleaned out of the
Colonel's crew, they had a chance to wreak all kinds of
havoc on the entire camp. All they needed was for the
Gatling gun to be prepared for the attack, the magazine column snapped down into the breach.

His hand itched for the feel of the wood crank handle. A
few spins would unleash a torrent of lead among the raiders.

Slash gripped the edge of the door, then yanked it wide.
Pecos whirled around. Both of the rabbit-ear hammers were
pulled all the way back, cocked and ready to drop on the
shells waiting in the twin barrels.

"Nobody's in there," Pecos said in a hoarse voice.

"That ain't a bad thing, even if we don't get to kill any
of 'em. We can do more damage using the Gatling gun."

They climbed in and lowered a steel panel from inside
the wagon. A narrow window opened wide enough to get a
good shot at a quarter of the camp when they primed the
Gatling gun and aimed its rotating barrels outward.

"There's something missin'," Slash said.

"The magazines." Pecos snorted in disgust. "I don't see them anywhere." He gripped the handle and gave it a crank. The octagonal barrels began rotating, but firing pins dropped on . . . nothing.

"They must be hid somewhere." Slash began rummaging through the blankets piled inside. When he reached the wood planking that made up the floor, he shoved the last blanket aside and sat heavily. "No ammo columns."

"They must use the blankets to cover themselves when they get to firin'. There's got to be a powerful lot of sparks and gunpowder fillin' the wagon when they get down to the attack."

"Pecos, we gotta get outta here. They can't catch us here. If we don't have any bullets for the gun, we are trapped prey inside this cage."

In frustration Pecos cranked a couple more times on the handle and turned away in defeat. He jumped from the wagon, sure someone must have noticed them.

"We still got a chance, Slash," he said after a quick look around. "They're all too busy loadin' their guns to notice us."

"We didn't bring the Gatling gun rounds. They've got to be in another supply wagon."

"Where?" Pecos looked around. "I don't see any other supply wagon. Ours is the only one in camp." He shuddered and stood stock-still.

"What's wrong, pard?"

"That way's east. The sun'll be up in a few minutes."

The need to do something to stop the attack on Camp Collins sent them both away from the war wagon and looking around like prairie dogs popping up out of their burrows. A final reconnaissance caused them both to despair after they found what they sought.

"The other war wagons got too many men around them for us to take over," Slash said.

"It don't look like they've got rounds for the Gatlings, either. What do you think the reason is? The Colonel's not the kind to go into a fight without all his ducks in a row."

"That, Pecos, was my thought, too. He's waitin' for more supplies to arrive. We didn't see other wagons leavin' High Mountain, but those other two warehouses musta been crammed chock-full of what he needs for the attack."

"If we sneak away, we can warn everyone in town," Slash said. "We shoulda done that instead of workin' ourselves up into a lather over blastin' away the entire army."

"Good," came the cheerful voice. "I like to see my men all eager to get into the fray. There comes another freight wagon. It should have everything we need to proceed." Colonel dropped down heavily onto his saddle. He had been standing in his stirrups to survey the entire camp. When he sank down and looked forward, he spotted the two old cutthroats.

Pecos reached for his scattergun. Slash put a hand on his forearm to stop him.

"Look around," Slash said softly. "Matthias and his henchmen are all behind us."

"I can take Raymond out before Matthias or any of the owlhoots with him can draw," Pecos said. Slash had to crush down hard on his partner's wrist to prevent him from lifting the shotgun.

"They've got their guns out," Slash warned. "And the way Matthias is eyein' us, we don't stand a snowball's chance in hell of pluggin' the Colonel."

Pecos craned his neck around and saw a dozen weapons pointed in his direction.

"It's like they don't trust us."

"We ain't the only ones. The four crowded together just beyond the wagon are under the guns, too."

"Freighters, Pecos. All of 'em are like us . . . civilians. Not a single one of them's sportin' a ribbon on his chest."

"The ammo for the Gatlings must be in their wagon."

"No way can we fetch it without causin' a ruckus," Pecos said.

"Men!" Raymond bellowed. "We are on the brink of making history. We prepare to sweep through our ninth town. Many of you have been with me the entire long road. Some of you fight with me for the first time. Each of you is a valuable part of the invasion."

"How much we gonna get, Colonel?" The voice came from the back of the crowd, behind Matthias. The Colonel's henchman nudged two men with him. They slipped away, hunting for the rabble-rouser.

"You'll be amply rewarded," the Colonel said. "More than this, you are part of history. You are a key element of this army. Look around. Those are your friends, comrades, your blood brothers in arms. We will enter this town and we will prevail. We ride to glory!"

A cheer went up that caused Pecos to cringe. He saw the stricken look on his partner's face. This was the horde ready to murder every last living soul in Camp Collins.

"I can decoy them," Pecos said. "Get away. Go to town and get Miss Jay and Myra, and anyone else you can, to safety."

"Jay won't desert the town like that. She'll want to fight it out."

"There's no way to fight off an army like this, not when the Colonel has rapid firers and riders each wieldin' ten six-shooters."

Pecos growled deep in his throat when he saw a dozen men lugging ammo boxes from somewhere on the far side of the camp. The cartridges for the Gatling guns were being loaded into the war wagons. He saw the one that he and Slash had tried to commandeer filled with men. A crew broke open the crates. Three others prepared the revolving-barreled guns. Once, there hadn't been anything loaded into the deadly weapons.

Now columns of bullets were being seated into the receivers. Two of the crew wrestled the weapons to the gun ports on the sides. When the war wagons rolled and those deadly repeaters started spewing their leaden death, an entire population would die.

Raymond called out to Matthias. "How long to the town?"

"A half hour, sir."

"Let's roll! We'll be there just at dawn. We attack from the east so the sun's behind us."

Slash hardly spoke. When he did, his voice was hoarse with emotion.

"Anybody spottin' 'em will be blinded. He's a clever son of a bitch."

Pecos jumped when Matthias shoved a six-shooter into his back.

"You and your partner, get on back to your wagon. Bring up the rear of the column."

Pecos exchanged a quick glance with Slash. They were the cleanup crew. Their empty wagon would be loaded to the top of the canvas canopy with the spoils ripped away from town.

"Where do we take the loot?" Pecos wanted to stall. Most of the Colonel's army rushed to mount. Many of them checked the pistols slung around their torsos, but the real threats rattled from the camp. All three of the armored, armed wagons headed west cloaked in clouds of swirling dust.

"Don't fret none about that," Matthias said. "Get it loaded. You'll be told where to take it."

"Back to High Mountain?" Slash asked. "We got all turned around. I don't know how to backtrack."

"The Colonel hasn't decided yet. We got one more town to take down before moving on."

"Leaving Colorado?" Pecos started to grab for Matthias,

but the gunman was too quick. He stepped away and pointed his iron at the former bank robber.

"Don't go asking questions. You just do as you're told. You'll be a lot happier not knowing until you have to."

Five of Matthias's bullies fanned out around them. Pecos took a quick look at the other freighters. They were all treated as virtual prisoners. Matthias—or more likely, Colonel Raymond—didn't trust any of them.

"Looks like we're the backbone of this here operation," Pecos said.

He and Slash silently returned to their wagon. The guards surrounding them pointed where they were to go.

"We've got to do something," Slash said, sounding more desperate than ever.

"Ever try to race a man on horseback while you was drivin' a mule team? Ain't possible," Pecos said. "We don't even have the dynamite in the back of the wagon anymore. They unloaded everything."

"Something will happen," Slash said. "Lady Luck has to smile on us after bein' so mean up till now."

They drove for a half hour. As the Colonel had predicted, the sun was just peeking over the horizon at their backs. This made for a perfect attack on a helpless, unsuspecting town.

Pecos started to pull back on the reins. He wasn't going to be part of such slaughter.

Slash grabbed his arm and yanked him around.

"Pecos, look! Look! *Look!*"

A cry of disbelief escaped Pecos's lips.

Chapter 26

"This is Whiskey Creek!" Slash exclaimed. "It ain't Camp Collins!"

Pecos peered at the sign alongside the road. The rising sun caught the white-painted letters and turned them into blazing beacons.

"We're miles from Camp Collins," Pecos said, "but that don't help the folks in Whiskey Creek one little bit."

Sporadic gunshots from ahead reached them. They sat a mite straighter. The assault began and they were powerless to stop it. After the first hesitant volley came a thunderstorm of discharges. Battles had been fought where fewer rounds were fired.

"What do we do?" Slash stirred uneasily on the bench seat. One of the Colonel's men rode directly in front. He craned around and saw others on either side of their wagon. "We can't do anything to stop them."

"It's too late to warn the townsfolk, too," Pecos said. He almost shouted to be heard over the thunderous roar of guns now coming from the town. They were barely a quarter mile off.

Pecos caught his breath. So many rounds were being fired, a huge white cloud of gunsmoke rose in the dawn, as if the entire town had been set ablaze.

"You two, drive the wagon right down the first street you come to." The rider held up a sheet of paper and carefully read it in the increasingly blinding dawn sunlight. "Stop when you get to a general store."

"What do we do then?" Slash ran his fingers over the butts of his twin six-guns.

"Somebody there'll tell you what to load. It's likely to be food and all the usual stuff you find in a mercantile."

Slash frowned and whispered, "That means we're gonna be sent back to High Mountain."

"And it means something else, too." Pecos smiled crookedly. "They won't be descendin' on Camp Collins like a plague of locusts for a spell."

"It might be they have to sort through the plunder. We might have to take something to Potero. McCall's warehouse is standin' well nigh empty."

The two argued over where the Colonel would send them after they'd stripped the general store of everything of value. They fell silent for a moment; then a disturbing thought crossed Pecos's mind.

"If they have us load food for an army, they might intend to finish off Whiskey Creek and go direct to Camp Collins. From what we overheard, they're movin' on real soon."

"It must be gettin' too hot for 'em in Colorado," Slash said. "They want what they can grab and take on the trail to somewhere else."

"Utah, maybe, or Montana. It don't matter. I can't believe Bleed-'Em-So or the army's anywhere close to runnin' them to ground."

"The Colonel's a cautious one. He knows better than to go to the well too many times. His welcome in Colorado is past bein' worn out." Slash rubbed his chin as he thought. "We got to stop him before he clears outta Colorado or he'll keep up his murderous ways, only doin' it somewhere else that don't expect it."

"'Cautious' ain't hardly the word for it. Him and Harl Benson are like peas in a pod. They figger out every little detail before striking. They might know somethin' we don't. I hope it has to do with Bleed-'Em-So and his deputies."

"I can't believe you'd ever say you was hankerin' to see that murderin' old badge-wearin' derelict." Slash sucked in a deep breath. "I can't believe I'm agreein' with the sentiment."

Pecos tugged on the reins and urged the team down the first street.

Around them the buildings had been turned into heaps. Hundreds of rounds had ripped through wood plank walls and blown out glass windows. The front of a bakery had been ravaged by a Gatling gun so badly, they saw all the way through the shop and realized the slugs had created an equal amount of destruction on the back wall. The wood creaked and protested and slowly snapped apart under its own weight.

Both men had seen their share of killing and death. In some cases they had been responsible, but never had they intentionally cut down a woman or unarmed man. An early bakery customer sprawled on the boardwalk, filled with so many bullets he had been cut in half. Just inside the front door sprawled a woman. Her blood mingled with an ample dusting of flour. Cases of bread inside were smashed.

Pecos drove faster to avoid thinking too hard about the two dead citizens of Whiskey Creek. He drove past even worse scenes of carnage. The proprietors of a half-dozen stores had been preparing to open for a day of peaceful commerce. There'd never be another chance for any of them.

"Up there," called their guide. He pointed. A general store had escaped the violent onslaught dealt out to the other stores. That only meant the walls were untouched by the prodigious outpouring from a Gatling gun. Three bodies, two men and a woman, were flopped over a hitch rail and spread out like Saturday washing.

The proprietor and his clerical help had been individually murdered rather than perishing in a leaden storm from the rapid-firing Gatlings.

"Get to it. Load what's needed to keep us on the move."

Slash started to ask what supplies were needed, but he was cut off. The raider made a cutting motion with his left hand. He rode closer and bent over to give them a sheet of paper.

"You can read, can't you?" Before he got an answer, the man yelled to his partners, "Get on over to the bank! We're on a timetable, and thanks to these two dawdling, we're gonna be late. The Colonel won't like that."

Matthias never looked back as he and his companions galloped off down the street, leaving Slash and Pecos alone amid the destruction.

"This is Benson's doing," Slash said, holding up the list. "I recognize his handwriting. It's all cramped up and every letter looks like it was cut out from some damn newspaper."

"Them two don't leave anything to chance. Imagine givin' us a shopping list."

"What are we gonna do?" Slash started to crumple up the sheet and throw it away. He stopped before he destroyed the list.

"We've robbed banks and trains. This is the first time we've ever held up a general store." Pecos snorted in contempt. "Feels like we're backslidin'. Us, the two best damn train robbers in the West, reduced to stealin' penny candy from a jar."

Gunfire in other parts of town slowly faded away. The two looked at each other.

"We save whatever folks we can," Pecos said.

"If anyone's still alive. How're we gonna do that? The raiders are everywhere I look."

To prove Slash's point, a half-dozen men rode past, flash-

ing their guns and laughing as they fired at shadows. Three
rode close to Pecos and one peered down at him. He cocked
his six-gun and pointed it.

"You'd best think twice on where you point that hogleg,"
Pecos said, standing his ground.

"Old man, you ain't tellin' me what to do. You might—"
That was as far as he got before Pecos swung his shotgun
around. The short barrel collided with the front leg of the
man's horse. The animal let out a wail of pain, sounding almost human. Then it collapsed forward, the injured leg
buckling under it.

Pecos whirled in a circle, letting his shotgun swing out
full length on the lanyard. The metal barrel crashed into the
side of the man's head as he fell from horseback.

"Now, boys, you don't look stupid. So don't make a stupid mistake," Slash said, resting his hands on the butts of his
twin Colts as he addressed the man's partners.

"We're not lettin' a pair of freight haulers push us around."

Both of them trained their guns on Slash. They were too
late pulling their triggers by a scant second. Slash never hesitated. He cleared leather and started firing. If his first bullets didn't hit the pair, his second or third did the trick. They
flew off their horses and lay kicking in the dust. One showed
a spark of fight and tried to raise his iron. Slash shot him
through the head.

"That settles their hash," Pecos said. "Now, how do we
explain away three dead bodies?"

"Get 'em out of sight. Stuff 'em in the rain barrels alongside the store," Slash said. "Who knows what kind of trouble these three found as they rode around, prob'ly intent on
killin' anyone not already dead!"

"You shot the pair of them. You have to lug them outta
sight," Pecos said. He wrestled the one he had hit so hard
that it crushed his skull.

By the time he loaded the barrel, Slash had added one beside his. Pecos grumbled and helped his partner get the third

man into another barrel out of sight if any of the Colonel's men came by. It'd take a dedicated search to find them.

"Let's get the shoppin' done, then see if those murderous back shooters left anybody alive and kickin'." Slash didn't wait to see if Pecos trailed him inside. He grabbed a couple boxes and carried them to the wagon.

His partner was nowhere to be seen. After a few seconds spent thinking on the matter, he returned to the store and kept loading boxes. He carefully arranged them in the wagon to provide hidey-holes. By the time he had completed the list of goods to steal, he saw that his foresight paid off.

Pecos herded four children ahead of him. The youngest was four or five, and the oldest not over ten. The two tow-headed boys were clad in rags. The two girls wore matching brown muslin dresses. They all tried to hang on to one another in spite of Pecos hurrying them along.

"Into the wagon," Slash said. "Hide behind the crates. I'll throw a tarp over you so you won't be seen if anybody looks in."

"Where's Mama?" the smallest girl said, tearing up.

Pecos took the oldest boy aside and gave whispered instructions to him. He slapped the boy on the shoulder when he finished and said, "They're yours to protect now. We'll get you outta town."

"What do we do, mister?"

Pecos picked the boy up as if he were feather light and put him into the wagon.

"I don't know," he said softly. "Grow up, I reckon, the best you can. Let me and my pard there even the score with the men who killed your ma and pa."

"And Ginnie," sobbed the smallest girl. "She was shot."

"She was our big sister. She was fifteen," the next-to-oldest boy said.

Slash wanted to tell the little boy that death was preferable to what Matthias and Colonel Raymond and the rest of those cutthroats would have done if she had lived. He held his tongue and pointed silently into the wagon. However, the four children worked out the disaster that happened to them this day, their futures were dim unless they got out of Whiskey Creek right now.

"You stay quiet, all of you," Pecos cautioned. "No matter what you hear, don't make a peep." He stared straight at the oldest boy, who fearfully nodded.

Pecos and Slash hurried around to the driver's box and climbed up.

"You didn't find any other survivors?" Slash asked.

"Nary a one. They were hidin' under straw in a stable. It was a lousy place to hide. Lousy." Pecos gripped the reins and snapped them. The mules began pulling slowly. He didn't rush them.

"Where do we go?" Slash asked.

"It's all writ across the bottom of that list. We head back the way we came."

"What about them?" Slash tilted his head toward the rear of the wagon. "We can't haul them back to High Mountain."

"We play it by ear. It's all we can do." Pecos lifted his chin to point out a dozen raiders moving restlessly ahead of them. Matthias led them.

The wagon rolled along. Pecos made no effort to slow it when he came to the knot of riders.

"Get on back to High Mountain!" Matthias called.

"We don't rightly know how," Pecos answered before he realized what he said.

"I'm heading back. Me and the boys'll escort you." Matthias bellowed for others to join him.

"That was downright dumb," Slash said. "We coulda let the kids out somewhere along the road. Or we coulda hunted around and found the way to Camp Collins. It's not more 'n fifteen miles off. We don't have a tinker's damn chance of gettin' away from all of them now."

"Especially Matthias," Pecos said. "Sorry. I never thought—"

"That's right. You never thought. This is a worse pickle than the time you insisted we hold up that bank, and a sheriff and ten deputies was inside, all countin' money they were escortin' to Laramie."

"How was I to know Wells Fargo hired 'em rather than lettin' the shipment go out unguarded?"

"That drunk what told you about the shipment was . . . was . . . a drunk. What'd he know?"

All the way back to High Mountain, they argued. Not once did the opportunity to let the children escape present itself.

Chapter 27

"Get that wagon unloaded," Matthias ordered. "Me and the boys are gonna wet our whistles. It's been a long ride."

"What about us?" Slash asked. "We got a real thirst, too."

"Do as you're told." Matthias moved his hand to his Colt. Then he laughed. "It's been a good raid. Don't you go expecting to see a ribbon, though. The Colonel only gives those to the troops who actually participate."

"We've done more 'n just shoot up a town," Slash protested. He grunted when Pecos elbowed him. "All right, all right. We'll fill that ole warehouse till its wall bust out."

Matthias and his henchmen galloped off to the Galloping Garter.

"Why'd you want me to hush up?" Slash asked.

"We got some cargo in the back that needs to be unloaded—without any of them buzzards seein' it," Pecos said. He inclined his head in the direction of the children. The oldest boy poked his head from his hiding place and looked around fearfully.

"If I hadn't kicked just a little, Matthias would think it was strange. As it is, him and his partners are all boastin' on how they burned down a town *and* got us to do what they want."

"None of them'll come watch us," Pecos said. "You're not as dumb as you look, pard."

"We can't hide 'em in the warehouse. What're we gonna do with them?"

Pecos and Slash looked at each other. Both smiled as the answer came to them. They drove past the road leading to the warehouses and drove to Marianne Mertz's boarding-house. They jumped down. As Pecos kept watch, Slash hustled the four children from the wagon and herded them to the front door.

Marianne opened it as he started to knock.

"Slash! Is Pecos with you?" The woman blushed just a tad when she mentioned Pecos. Her cheeks grew roses and she averted her gaze. It was only then that she saw the four urchins.

"You got visitors," Slash said. "Just for a while."

"Where'd they come from?" She blinked, then looked past Slash as Pecos rushed up.

"Get 'em inside. There's a patrol comin' this way." Pecos grinned at the woman and pinched the brim of his hat. "Good to see you again, Marianne . . . Miz Mertz."

"Who are they? These children aren't yours, are they, Melvin Baker?"

"Not perzactly," Pecos said.

She turned her hot gaze on Slash.

"Not mine, either, Miz Mertz. Not by blood, but we're kinda responsible for them."

"Inside," she said, hearing the thunder of hoofbeats approaching. As the children hurried in fearfully, she reached out and grabbed a handful of Pecos's buckskins. She pulled him toward her. "Why do I have to hide them from the Colonel's men?"

"It's a long story, darlin'," Pecos said. "I'll tell you the best I can."

"While you're pourin' oil on troubled waters, I'll take the wagon to the warehouse. We don't want Matthias wonderin' what's become of all his plunder."

"*Plunder?* Whatever are you going on about? This is going to be a long story, I fear." Marianne tugged on Pecos and pulled him inside.

The four children cowered under the kitchen table, peering out like rabbits being hunted by a wolf. Getting them to safety was going to be a big chore, and not one Pecos looked forward to doing. But he'd had no choice but to save them from the Colonel's destruction of Whiskey Creek.

Slash closed the door and heaved a sigh. The kids were as safe as they could be for the moment. He made his way back to the wagon. His knees creaked as he pulled himself up into the driver's box, and his hands barely closed on the reins. Getting old was a chore. He usually let Pecos drive, not only because he was a better muleskinner, but because the arthritis didn't vex him near as much. Keeping his fingers flexible and free of aches and pains was doubly important now—if he had to use his six-shooters.

Caught up in the middle of High Mountain, surrounded by stone-cold killers, he knew the chance of having to use those matched Colts was nigh-on a certainty. As he drove, he swapped the reins from one hand to the other, flexing the fingers of the one not gripping the leather straps. It helped keep the hands moving and ready for action. A little.

The team pulled at his command. He turned the wagon around and rode past the dozen riders who'd been galloping toward the boardinghouse. Some he recognized as having taken part in the Whiskey Creek massacre. One or two of the newcomers reached up way too often and ran their fingers over a colorful decoration pinned on their coats.

The Colonel had already passed out new battle ribbons and inducted the greenhorns into his merciless army. The way they all had stupid grins on their faces told how much they valued this bloody distinction. Crossing any one of them would be a mistake, Slash saw. Even after the heat of battle and slaughter faded, they'd be dangerous—and completely under the Colonel's spell.

Slash found the side street and pulled the wagon up near the main door. He sat for a moment, wondering what to do. The crates of food and other stuff stolen from the store were too heavy for him to unload alone. At least many of the crates were. He heaved a sigh and jumped down. Unloading what he could showed Matthias he was obeying orders. That kept the henchman from getting too suspicious.

Playing for time was Slash's only goal for the moment, since no *scheme* blew up full-blown in his think box. If he put off dealing with any of the predatory wolves until he had a chance to talk things over with his partner, he'd count that as a win.

He dropped the tailgate and pulled out a twenty-five-pound sack of flour. Before he turned and hoisted it to his shoulder, his bane trotted up.

"Don't bother none with that." Matthias kept his horse from dancing about—it was as if the animal had other places to go and cared nothing about its rider agreeing.

"Leave it in the wagon?"

"Them's orders from the Colonel. Get on over to the boardinghouse. You know the one. He wants to talk to you."

Slash caught his breath.

"He's there already?"

"On his way. Now git!" Matthias let the horse have its head and galloped back the way he had come.

Slash pushed the flour back onto the tailgate and brushed off white dust from his hands and shoulder. Groaning with the effort, he lit a shuck, slid between buildings, and ran as hard as he could for the boardinghouse. With any luck he'd arrive before the Colonel and warn Pecos and Marianne Mertz to hide the children.

His luck wore mighty thin. The Colonel's horse was tethered to the side of the house, alongside three others.

Matthias had told him to hie on over here, but Slash scouted the house before going to the kitchen door. He knew the Colonel and at least one other, probably Harl Benson, were in the dining room. With a quick movement he made sure both his pistols slipped easy and free in his holsters. If his luck changed, taking out the Colonel and his top aide was in the cards.

Slash stepped in and knew his luck had not changed. Two more of the Colonel's men lounged in the doorway. And the way they slouched wasn't too encouraging for him to take the Colonel prisoner or even start a shoot-out. Their bodies were loose. Their eyes darted about, taking in everything—and him.

"Come on in," the Colonel greeted. "Have yourself a seat."

Slash walked slowly. Pecos sat in a chair in the corner of the room. At the dining-room table Harl Benson and another of the raiders attentively listened to their leader's every word. Slash saw that the man beside Benson wore four ribbons. He wasn't a newcomer to the slaughter.

Slash sat on the edge of a chair, alert for any movement of the gunmen behind him. In a quick exchange of lead, he was destined to lose. But if his bullet-riddled body was going to leak blood all over Marianne Mertz's fine rug, he'd take at least one of the jackals with him.

If his luck changed for the good, it'd be the Colonel preceding him to the burning-hot nether regions.

"I got reports of how you and your partner did such fine work back at . . ." He turned to Benson.

"Whiskey Creek," the man supplied. His eyes fixed cold

and dark on Slash. Slash didn't flinch. He had faced worse men and come out on top.

"Yes, there," Raymond went on. He reached into his coat pocket and pulled out a battle ribbon. He slid it across the table in Slash's direction. Then he tossed the second one to Pecos, who caught it. Both of them stared at the colored ribbon.

"Go on. Wear it proudly. You're blooded veterans now. I want you to come with me when I move on in a few days."

Slash held the ribbon. He felt like puking at the notion of pinning it onto his coat.

"That's mighty decent of you, Colonel."

"Wagon drivers are always needed, but after . . ."

"Whiskey Creek," Benson said again.

"After Whiskey Creek, we lost a couple war wagon drivers. You and your partner will be in line for a bigger cut of the spoils."

Slash only nodded. He didn't trust himself to say a word.

"You want us to join up?" Pecos spoke softly, but his words shook with emotion. Only Slash recognized that it was anger, not eagerness.

"You're the type of men I need. Stalwart, dependable. You finish what you start." The Colonel looked smug with his praise. He had given this speech many times before to get what he wanted.

"We're all that," Slash said. "We get a job, we never quit till it's done, no matter who's givin' us the orders." The veiled reference to Chief Marshal Bledsoe wasn't lost on Pecos.

He started to add a soothing word or two so they could high-tail it. A distant crash and the sound of glass breaking stopped him.

"What's that?" Harl Benson was out of his chair, hand on his six-gun. "There's somebody else in the back."

"Go find out," the Colonel said. "Take care of it, as you always do, Harl."

Slash had heard the children moving around, too.

"I'll go with him." He was halfway out of his chair when the Colonel froze him with a single word.

"No."

"But if there's trouble . . ."

"Mr. Benson is capable of handling it. I want you and your partner to completely load your wagon with food and supplies. We have one more objective before leaving the territory."

"Where're you—I mean, we—goin' then?" Pecos asked.

"First things first," Colonel Raymond said, obviously annoyed at being questioned. "We pacify the next town, pack our equipment, and divvy the dividends from the work, then I tell everyone."

"What's the next town?" Slash blurted the question.

"Mr. Benson will brief us after his reconnaissance. Now you have your orders. Don't disappoint my trust in you." The Colonel pushed away from the table and left the room before Slash got his wits about him.

He started after Raymond, but the sound of horses galloping away warned him he was too late. The Colonel and his tight knot of bodyguards were on the trail again.

"Benson's still here," Pecos said. "Marianne's with them children in the bedroom." He drew his Russian .44 and plunged into the corridor leading to the far end of the house.

Slash was a step behind, both his six-guns drawn and ready.

His vision collapsed until he saw nothing but his partner's broad back. Pecos was like a cyclone blasting across the prairie. Nothing was going to stop him, not even Harl Benson. Slash had to do whatever he could to back him up in what would be an all-fired deadly gunfight.

He swung around into a bedroom just behind Pecos.

"Are you all right?" Pecos demanded.

Marianne sat on a bed, pasty-white and clutching her hand to her throat. She tried to speak, but only a croak came out. Pecos swung around and sat beside her, causing the bed to sag under his bulk. She naturally slid toward him. He circled her quaking body with his long, muscular arm and held her close.

"I heard Mr. Benson coming. He had his pistol drawn and looked like he was snorting fire. I . . . I hurried the children out. The older boy had knocked a vase off my bedside table. That made Mr. Benson come rushing in, fire in his eye."

"The kids?" Slash prompted.

She pointed out the open window. "I don't know where they'd go, but I didn't warn them about the rest of the Colonel's men." She looked stricken. "He'll hurt them, won't he?"

"Benson?" Pecos asked. He nodded.

"I meant Colonel Raymond. And his men. They'd always been so nice and polite, but . . . but they're different. Changed. I see it in the way they look and walk. They strut around like *killers*."

"Did Benson take out after the kids?" Slash asked.

Marianne nodded mutely.

"Two birds with one stone." Pecos jumped to his feet, leaving the woman still shaking with fear on the bed.

"What do you mean?" she asked. She turned her pale, drawn face up to Pecos.

"Keepin' them chillun safe's one thing," Slash said. "We need to catch Benson 'fore he forks that horse of his and goes on his scoutin' mission." Slash peered out the open window, then worked his creaky legs over the sill and landed outside.

"Where's he going?"

"If the kids come back, you take good care of them," Pecos said. "Promise me that. Keep safe."

He left Marianne begging to know more. It took long strides to catch up with his partner. He caught up at the corner of the house.

"What do you think, Slash?"

"Benson might be goin' to a different town than Camp

Collins, but it don't matter, does it? We stop him, and the Colonel won't raid whatever town's next."

"They fooled us with Whiskey Creek. The Colonel might have his eye on some other town than home." Slash worried about his wife as much as the rest of Camp Collins. The town was filled with friends, and if he stopped the attack, none of them need ever know of the brutality visited on the other Colorado towns.

"We should get the kids to a safe hidey-hole," Slash said, looking around. "What do you think? Did they run for the woods?" He pointed to a stand of lodgepole pines just beyond the boardinghouse.

"They hid in the stable before, back in Whiskey Creek. Everyone does what's natural, again and again." Pecos kicked open the stable door and looked around the dimly lit interior. All the horses were gone. The Colonel mustered his troops.

"Come on out. It's just us. Slash and his decrepit ole partner. We won't hurt you." Slash wandered back and forth, trying not to look too intimidating as he hunted for the four children.

"I'm not as creaky and flea-bitten as you," Pecos snapped. "We might have seen better days, but there's still a finger or two of whiskey left in *this* bottle."

"They're not here, Pecos. I don't even see any trace that they have been."

"If they took to the hills, that's about as safe a place for 'em as I can think of," Pecos said. "But you know where that leaves us?"

"On foot while Harl Benson's on the trail, headin' for . . . the next target." Slash's throat tightened as he spoke.

"Spit it out, pard. We both know where he's goin'. Camp Collins."

Chapter 28

"Are you sure, Jay?" Myra Thompson leaned against the bar. She had to stand on the brass rail to rest her elbows there, since she was such a short drink of water. "I've bothered Del so much about it, he's taken to avoiding me. I don't like that." The young woman scowled and drummed her fingers on the mahogany bar.

Her words were muffled by the roar of customers in the Palace of a Thousand Delights. It was still early on Saturday night, but cowhands from a half-dozen nearby ranches had already come to town. The usual townsfolk who frequented the bar moved around with an electric intensity that reminded Jay Breckenridge of how animals milled about anxiously just before a big thunderstorm. They were nervous and uneasy, and had no idea why.

"You want a drink, Myra? I know you're not one to imbibe, but it might calm your nerves."

"It's not my nerves that need calming, Jay. It's my downright worry about those two. I wouldn't expect much from Pecos. He never says much anyway. But Slash is a horse of a different color." The young woman balanced precariously on the rail and stared straight at Jay. "I can't believe Slash hasn't gotten in touch with you."

"All I know is that they were hauling freight high up in the hills," Jay said, as worried as her friend, but not willing to show it. Spilling all she knew of the chores Bledsoe had set for her husband and his partner would only upset Myra. She was edgy enough. "There's not many telegraph lines heading up above ten thousand feet."

"They always send messages, somehow," Myra said. She chewed at a fingernail, then realized she was doing it and jerked her hand away. She smiled wanly. "Del doesn't like it when I do that. He says it tears the sheets."

"The *sheets*?" Jay had to laugh. "That explains the scratches on his face. I thought he got them rescuing a kitten from a tree."

"The only kitty he needs is me," Myra said, smiling lopsidedly. Then the smile melted away. "You wouldn't keep back bad news, would you?"

"Myra, girl, I have *not* heard from Slash. Or Pecos, for that matter."

"They're out working for that old devil Chief Marshal Bledsoe, aren't they? They try to keep it secret, like it's something disreputable, but considering what all they've done robbing banks and trains and riding with the Snake River Marauders, this is, well, it's almost honorable. It's certainly legal if the chief marshal tells them to do something, right?"

Jay danced around telling Myra the truth. The only times Bleed-'Em-So sent Pecos and her precious Slash out was when it required illegal tactics. He wanted the law upheld, but sometimes the very law got in the way of justice. If the two old former cutthroats wanted to keep their freedom—and their necks free of a knotted hemp rope—they had to do as they were ordered. Jay hated Bledsoe for such blackmail, but, like Slash and Pecos, couldn't think of any way to escape his bony grip.

"It wouldn't do much good asking around about them,

would it?" Myra sagged, stepped down from the brass rail, and looked up at the much taller woman. "Tell me if you hear, will you? I've got a business to run and need to talk to the bosses now and again."

"I will, Myra. I promise. Are you sure you don't want a drink?"

"I'll be getting on home to Del, if he's not out on patrol, this being Saturday night and all. I think the marshal takes advantage of him."

"Go," Jay said gently. "I've got people asking around about them."

Myra nodded solemnly, turned, and left the saloon. The slouch made her look smaller than she was. Jay started to have the bartender set her up with a shot of whiskey, then changed her mind. Myra hadn't outright said it, but keeping a clear head right now was a better choice than knocking back a shot or two of whiskey.

The night was young, and from the size of the crowd, it was going to be rowdy. Keeping her wits about her made more sense than drowning her sorrows.

Right now, at least.

She moved lightly around the floor, steering some men to the cribs upstairs and coaxing others into drinking more heavily. She led these men astray. The preacher delivering tomorrow's sermon would call her a harlot, a demon, an agent of Satan. At the moment all she wanted was to find a way to stop worrying about her husband and his partner.

Around midnight she sank into a chair at a vacant table, the first to appear in close to two hours. The others were crowded with men drinking up their wages or busily losing their money to keen-eyed gamblers with nimble fingers and skill beyond any cowboy's. Before the night was out, she'd collect a fee from each of those men so busily scooping up money and pocketing it.

As long as they weren't cheating, she wanted them in the Palace. They provided excitement, entertainment, and were certainly one of the "Thousand Delights" advertised in the saloon's name.

"Mind if I sit here?"

She looked up at the man and frowned. Strangers coming into her drinking emporium weren't an uncommon sight, but ones dressed as well as this one was. Some trail dust made the fancy green coat a little duller, but he wore a flashy black vest chased with silver threads. A long gold watch chain dangled from the pocket where the watch resided in a loop to a buttonhole, and then through to fasten on the other side of the expensive waistcoat.

For a man just off the trail, his trousers were mighty clean. And the tooled leather holster at his hip held a well-maintained gun. She smelled the oil, betraying that it had been cleaned and oiled within a day or two.

His flat face carried a few small scars, but the eyes made her shiver. A rattler wouldn't have stared at her with colder, flatter eyes. He tried to hide his inner soul. Jay had worked in a saloon long enough to size up a man with a single glance. And if that wasn't experience enough, she had been the woman of Pistol Pete Johnson, one of the most notorious outlaws in Colorado for years and years. Riding with his gang had exposed her to some of the worst scum ever to sit astride a horse.

This one would fit in well with the most vicious of those cutthroats.

"This is about the only free chair in the place," the man went on. To his credit, he didn't immediately sit. He waited for her approval, showing some manners were hidden away inside.

Or was it all camouflage? A man adapted to his surroundings like a chameleon, being as nice or as nasty as the company required.

This one had the potential to be very, very nasty.

"All yours. What's your poison, sir?" Jay started to stand and leave.

"I'll buy you a drink. It's the least I can do, intruding on your thoughts."

The way he said that carried more than a hint of contempt. This gave her a clue how to deal with him.

"Why, li'l ole me's not likely to have much of a thought. I'm just a dance hall girl waiting for you."

This caused him to take a half step back; then he checked himself and smiled. Jay wished he wouldn't. The smile was one-hundred-proof evil.

"False modesty," he said. "What may I call you?"

"Anything but late for dinner," she said lightly. The small joke irritated him. "Jay. You can call me Jay. Everyone does."

"I'm Harl." He reached into his coat pocket and pulled out a bound leather notebook. A short pencil used as a bookmark allowed him to open to a page in the middle. He began writing. She wasn't able to read what he wrote, but saw his handwriting was precise and letter-perfect.

"Can't remember my name?" Jay asked.

"What?" He looked up, eyes flashing anger. "What do you mean?"

"I told you my name and you're writing it down."

Something shifted in the way he studied her. Before, contempt had been hidden away, but it boiled out now. A new appraisal lit his face. With painstakingly slow, precise penmanship, he completed one page and began writing on another.

"This is a prosperous establishment," he said. He went to the margin of his page and entered a few numbers. "On a night like this, more than a thousand dollars passes through your till."

Jay almost choked. He guessed the revenue with astounding accuracy.

"I wouldn't know about such things. I just entice men to have another drink."

"Men like me?" He chuckled and wrote several more lines before looking up. "Your inventory must consist of at least fifty cases of whiskey. How much beer is on hand? Does a local townsman brew it for you?"

"Are you a whiskey peddler, Harl? Most men who sit across a table from me aren't interested in talking about what's in the storeroom." Jay flashed an insincere smile. "They aren't interested, that is, unless they're in the back room with me."

"You may be a whore, but you're not a common one," he said. He closed the notebook and tucked it into his coat pocket.

"Aren't you the charmer?" she said.

"I don't appreciate your tone," he snapped.

"And I'm not fond of your crude language. That's no way to talk to a lady."

He stood and glared at her.

"I know how to talk to a lady—if I ever find one." He spun on his heel and stalked out.

Jay felt as if she had been drenched in slime. Shaking hands with a shepherd dipping his sheep wouldn't have been as unpleasant as her brief encounter with this stranger.

"Mr. Benson. Mr. Benson! Let me buy you a drink!" Gustav Reinking waved at the departing man to get his attention. He failed.

Curious, Jay went to the bar and pressed in close to Reinking.

"Enjoying yourself after a long week of foreclosing on widows' mortgages?" she asked.

"Now, Miss Breckenridge, is that any way to talk to your banker?"

"I don't need a loan. I'm doing just fine, Gustav," she said. "Let me buy you a drink." She signaled the barkeep to draw another beer for the banker.

"You won't make a profit giving away your merchandise," Reinking said.

"I don't see you turning it down," she said, laughing. "And the real merchandise is upstairs. My girls *never* give it away."

"Don't I know it?" he muttered. Louder, "Thanks for the beer. What's the occasion?"

"The man who just left. The one you called out to. Harl. Has he been in town long? I haven't seen him in the Palace before."

"Already on first-name terms with him?" The banker sipped his suds and licked his lips in appreciation. "Harl Benson opened an account yesterday afternoon, just before I closed for the weekend. I wish there were more customers like him."

"Why's that?" Jay studied the pudgy banker's face for any hint he was lying. The man meant what he said about Harl Benson. He positively beamed with joy.

"Such trust! Most strangers won't trust a banker straightaway. Not Mr. Benson. He opened an account with five hundred dollars. In gold!"

"That is a princely sum," she agreed. "That must mean he's fixing to do some business in town."

"I asked about that. Always a chance to make a loan, you know. But no. He wanted a secure vault to stash his gold."

"And you showed him your safe?"

"Of course! He was hesitant about making the deposit until I assured him we have the finest safe in Colorado, other than ones in Denver, naturally. It's a Marvin Safe Company Chrome Iron Spherical Mini-Cannonball. A real beauty."

"Heavy too," Jay prodded.

"Weighs more than six hundred fifty pounds," Reinking boasted. "Nobody's going to waltz in and drag it out, not unless they get a team of mules into the bank."

"It'd take a howitzer to blow it open," Jay said. A cold knot grew in her stomach. "And you showed him every little detail."

"He was knowledgeable. Quite so, actually. It's surprising to find a gentleman so well informed about safes," Reinking said. He took another sip of the beer. "He knew a great deal about the banking business. While he didn't say, I have the impression he spends a great deal of time in banks."

"Unless he's in the business."

"Why, yes, that's possible. He might be a banker like me. I never inquired. He might be willing to make a deal for a newer model. This one is an 1865. If he works at a Denver bank, many of them have newer models they might sell to buy larger ones. Business is good, Miss Breckenridge, very good these days."

"You misunderstand me. I meant he might be in the business of blowing open a safe."

"A bank robber?" Reinking's eyes went wide, he choked on his beer, then regained his composure. "No, that's not possible. He was too much a gentleman. A businessman. What robber deposits such a large sum of gold?"

"One who intends to get it all back, plus anything else stored in the safe."

The banker sputtered a bit more. Jay made him even more flustered by giving him a quick peck on the cheek. "You're such a trusting man, Gustav."

She went to the double swinging doors and looked out into the night. Jay hardly expected to spot Benson, but she was wrong. He walked slowly to the far side of the street, half hidden in shadows cast by the gas lamps. Across the street he made an entry in his notebook. He began walking—pacing—deliberately down the street.

At the intersection of the two largest streets, he entered more in his notebook. Jay stepped out and watched curiously. Benson paced off the width of each street, then cut catty-corner and measured that distance. More entries followed.

If a man wanted to be certain a large wagon had the proper turning radius, this is what he'd measure.

Finished with pacing off distances, Benson disappeared

down the cross street. Jay walked quickly to the corner and peered after him. Benson continued to measure halfway down the street and stopped in front of the bank. He recorded the width of the bank, then the distance across the street to a haberdashery shop. He paid no attention to the merchandise in the window. Only distances mattered. Satisfied at last, he disappeared around the side of the sturdy brick building.

As Harl Benson trotted off into the night, Jay ducked back and pressed herself into a recessed door leading into a feed and grain store. She stepped out of her hiding place and stared at his well-clad back until he vanished past the last gas lamp at the edge of town.

Whatever he was up to gave her the willies. She wished Slash was here to tell her it was nothing, that her imagination ran wild for no good reason. But Jay knew it was something. What, she didn't know, but it was an important something. She pushed back into the Palace of a Thousand Delights, hoping to change her mood. The gaiety and drinking did nothing to change her dark premonition.

Chapter 29

"This ain't for me," Pecos said. "I got to do something." He flashed his bowie knife around to catch the light from a coal oil lamp on Marianne Mertz's dining-room table. He made a few stabs with it. He wanted Colonel Raymond to be out there as his target instead of thin air. Or Harl Benson. Or even Matthias. Pecos wasn't feeling too fussy about which scoundrel he wanted to stop.

"We can go hunt for the kids," Slash said. "When they lit a shuck, they just vanished."

"They're prob'ly in the mountains somewhere near. How far can they get on foot, without supplies? For all we know, they done froze to death already."

"They escaped the raid on their hometown. Gettin' by is what they do. Still, I wish we could help them." Slash chewed on his lower lip as he thought on the matter.

"Might be enough to put out blankets and food and let them sneak it away from town."

Slash nodded in agreement. This was about what he considered doing to help the four frightened children.

"They'll be a whole lot safer if we find a way to do Bleed-

'Em-So's biddin' and stop the Colonel dead in his tracks."
Pecos grinned wolfishly. He made a couple more quick
moves with the knife. "And I mean *dead.*"

"We couldn't even catch Benson, and he rode out all by
his lonesome," Slash said.

"He's the linchpin holdin' the Colonel's schemes together. Without his scoutin' reports, they'd sweep on into a
town and find every man pointin' a rifle or shotgun at 'em."

"You're right about that. *Surprise.* Knowin' where the resistance is, that's what keeps the Colonel's army together.
One big defeat, and not a man would follow him again."

"Sorta like what we was up against in the Snake River
Marauders, if you consider it real close, Slash. All the new
recruits thought we was too old—"

"And too tame," Slash cut in. "They knew we was old-
timers and thought that meant we'd lost our nerve."

"That," said Pecos, "was what broke up the gang."

"*We* broke 'em up because Bleed-'Em-So ordered us to."
Slash stood and began pacing. He and his old partner were
alike. Neither of them had much in the way of patience
when action was called for.

"It didn't take any convincin' after what the gang did to
us," Pecos said.

Slash spun and looked hard at his partner.

"Reminiscin' about the past don't do a danged thing to
stop Raymond. What're we gonna *do*?"

Both turned at the sound of hooves pounding like thunder
outside. Slash went to the window and peered out. His hands
dropped to the butts of his Colts.

"We're at the point of fishin' or cuttin' bait. That's
Raymond. He's got a few guards with him. What do we do?"

"I'm for cuttin'," Pecos said. He flipped the thick-bladed
knife around and caught it by the blade. Whoever walked
into the dining room would be on the receiving end of a
powerfully thrown razor-edged knife.

Pecos froze as he drew back to make the toss. Marianne

Mertz came into the dining room, looking flustered. Right behind, Colonel Raymond pushed her forward. By the time Pecos recovered, and had his knife back in its sheath as if nothing had happened, Raymond and four of his bullies were stationed around the dining-room table.

"Good that you're here," Raymond said. "We've got plans to discuss."

Slash considered his chances of throwing down on the men. He could take out Raymond—he hoped. Marianne remained in front of him as a shield. The others would slap leather and drop him before he had a chance at a second shot.

"Whoa there, Slash," Pecos said. He shook his shaggy head and looked past Slash.

The reflection from a glass cabinet door showed Slash how close he had come to pushing up daisies. Harl Benson stood behind them in the doorway leading toward the main section of the boardinghouse. He rested his hand on his pistol. Even if Slash was the fastest gunman in the West, he'd never have gotten off a first shot at Raymond before taking Benson's slug to the back of his head.

"Fetch us some coffee, Mrs. Mertz." Colonel Raymond swung her around by her shoulders and pushed her toward the kitchen. He pulled up a chair at the head of the table and motioned for Harl Benson to stand beside him.

"This one's going to be a cakewalk," Benson said. He spread out a hand-drawn map on the table. His finger stabbed down. "We go in at dawn, as usual, and this piece of ripe fruit falls right into our hands."

Both Slash and Pecos held their breath. They knew the town's layout all too well. Benson had drawn the map with his usual precision, detailing distances and locations of the bank, mercantile—and the Palace of a Thousand Delights.

"The marshal's office won't be open. The law will be home in bed. Go straight for the bank. They have one of those cannonball safes. A howitzer round will blow down the wall behind it. A few sticks of dynamite will open it like a can of sardines." Benson pointed out other locations, including Pecos and Slash's business, and concluded with, "The saloon's got plenty of booze. Be careful shooting up the downstairs. The two upper stories?" He shrugged. "Whores. No loss if they catch a few rounds."

Slash almost blurted that the top floor was where he and Jay lived. Pecos elbowed him in time to turn the protest into a grunt.

"You have something to say?" Raymond glanced toward him.

"Will we be drivin' in with the freight wagon? To take the inventory in the saloon?"

"No," the Colonel said slowly, as if considering a weighty matter. "I told you to expect more. You'll be in the middle war wagon. Two experienced men will use the Gatling gun. You only need to drive according to plans." He reached out. As if by magic, Harl Benson leafed through several sheets and handed him one from the middle of the stack.

"Here're your orders. Follow the route exactly. One of you has a watch? Good. You'll be timing the route. You must be at every spot marked on the map at precisely the right time."

"That makes us into nothin' more 'n train conductors," Pecos said.

"Oh, yes, you're responsible for keeping everything on the tracks and on schedule. And you'll punch a lot of tickets!" Raymond laughed uproariously at his own joke.

Benson smiled and the rest of the Colonel's cortege hesitated long enough to understand he wasn't ridiculing them, then laughed with him.

Colonel Raymond stood, whispered something to Benson, then blew out of the room like a fierce mountain wind. His men trailed along behind, ducklings trying to keep up with their mama.

Harl Benson grabbed the map and rolled it into a cylinder. His expression put both Pecos and Slash on guard. The Colonel trusted them to drive one of the war wagons, but Benson had no faith whatsoever in them.

"Don't make a single mistake," he said. "I'll be watching your every move." With that, he left.

"It won't do any good puttin' a slug through that rattler's head," Slash said. "He's already passed along what he knows and Raymond's made a battle plan."

"Looked like a good one, too," Pecos said. "What are we gonna do?"

"What we can, pard, what we can."

Slash ducked into the kitchen, where Marianne boiled a pot of coffee.

"Have they all gone? I hate to waste so much coffee," she said.

"Miz Mertz," Slash said, "there's something you've got to do."

"You're leaving, aren't you? You and Pecos?" Her stricken look told Slash he was the wrong one to talk to her.

"Not right away," he said. "We need you to get blankets and food to the four kids we brung in."

"But they ran away. And I don't blame them. That awful Mr. Benson yelled and went around with his six-gun drawn, like he was hunting them. Like wild animals! He seemed so polite when he first came to town, but now?" She shook her head. "He's changed."

"Marianne, he ain't changed one tiny bit," said Pecos. He stepped in front of his partner. Slash got the idea and backed into the dining room to let them talk.

"I don't understand, then. What are you telling me, Pecos?"

"What Slash said. Can you do it? Trackin' them kids down takes more time than we got. The Colonel is launchin' an attack on our home."

"Camp Collins?" She stared wide-eyed at him. "An *attack*?"

"You think him and the rest with him are fine folks keeping Colorado safe from renegade Indians. I can't say it any clearer. There aren't any Injuns on the warpath."

"But . . ."

"The Colonel and his men? They're jackals. They're killers."

"But they've brought new life to High Mountain. They've kept businesses going that'd have gone bankrupt after the mines petered out, and me? This boardinghouse is all I've got. Without the Colonel renting it all out, I'd have gone under months ago. If Altitude—excuse me, High Mountain—becomes a ghost town, who'd ever buy the place? What will I do?"

"The food for the kids," Pecos insisted. He tried to keep her focused on things she could do now, and not to worry so about the future when Colonel Raymond was gone. "You'd know where to leave it better 'n I would." Pecos held her by the upper arms and looked into her eyes. "You don't have to believe what me and Slash say about the Colonel. But don't let them kids starve."

"You're going to stop him, aren't you? Or try. Are you a lawman?" She almost laughed at the notion. Then the smile melted away.

"You might call me a lawman. It ain't exactly what I am, but me and Slash work for the federal chief marshal over in Denver."

She shook her head in disbelief.

"This is all too crazy. I—"

He kissed her. For a moment she resisted, then returned as good as she got.

"You're the best thing that's come my way," Pecos said. "I can be content with that, whether or not you believe me."

"It's far-fetched," she said in a low voice.

"Put out the blankets and anything else you can for the children. If one of 'em will talk to you, ask about their ma and pa and Whiskey Creek." Pecos stepped away.

Marianne touched her lips where he'd kissed her. She started to speak, but Pecos left to join Slash in the front hallway.

"We can steal a couple horses and ride to Camp Collins," Slash said.

"That's the best you can come up with for a plan?"

"Yup."

"That's good enough for me," Pecos said. They slipped out the front door. He cast a last look back. Marianne stood in the kitchen window, her fingers still touching her lips.

Chapter 30

"What do you mean the marshal's out of town?" Jaycee Breckenridge clenched her fists and wanted to hit the deputy for being so smug. Being left in charge fed his sense of importance. Del Thayer was a decent fellow and, in ordinary times, made a competent deputy, but she had misgivings about how effective he'd be listening to her premonition of doom.

"Just that, Miss Jay," the bucktoothed deputy said. He hiked his feet up on the marshal's desk. Del leaned back and laced his fingers behind his head. "He left me in charge. That's worked out real good for me and Myra, bein' able to get to spend more time together. We don't have to worry about, you know, being interrupted."

"I'm sure it works out for you, but this is serious."

"You still goin' on 'bout that gambler fellow that breezed into town yesterday?"

"His name's Harl Benson, and how'd you know?" Jay stared at Del. First impressions were sometimes accurate, but she wondered if hers were wrong about Del Thayer.

Him and Myra Thompson sparking had been a surprise.

Myra was cute and full of life. Del dragged around and looked . . . dull. Only, there might be more to him than she'd thought, even when she had given her unofficial blessing to Myra to pursue the deputy. Myra looked up to her more as a big sister than a mother. Jay was glad of that. She was middle-aged. The wrinkles and occasional gray hair that snuck into her auburn locks showed that. But she had miles left.

It would have made her mad if a young woman like Myra thought of her as her mother.

"I asked around about him. He was polite and spent money. The curious thing 'bout him was how he writ down every last thing people told him. I watched as he measured the width of the street in front of this here jailhouse, too."

"He did more than that. He surveyed the width of the streets and made a map showing the location of the bank and other places where a lot of cash money passed through the till."

"Well, now, that sounds like a businessman wantin' to set up shop here. Might be he just wants to be sure there's enough money in Camp Collins to support a new business. That's nothin' to get worked up over, unless you think he's plannin' on openin' another saloon and bein' your competition."

"I've got plenty, already," Jay said, her anxiety turning to anger. Del missed the point entirely.

"Oh, them other cathouses," Del said. He waved his hand as if shooing them away. "They don't hold a candle to your place. Everyone knows you have the best liquor and the purtiest girls."

"Benson noted all that and was especially interested in my inventory in the back room."

"Did you consider he might be a whiskey peddler lookin' for a new market?"

"He was up to more 'n that. He wasn't any kind of businessman I've ever met. And he was . . . slimy." She shivered remembering how he looked. And those cold, flat snake eyes that never missed a detail before he wrote it all down in his damnable notebook.

"What do you want me to do? I owe Slash a favor, and helpin' you goes a ways toward repayin' him. Him and Pecos, but mostly Slash. Slash—"

"I think Harl Benson is a bank robber. He measured everything about the approach to the bank. He pumped Gustav Reinking for details about his safe."

"And he made a note about your liquor inventory?" Del shook his head, as though all of this was beyond him. "I reckon I can let the marshal know when he gets back from wherever he went. He's been talkin' about that little Gunnison girl. I think he's taken a shine to her. He must have rode out to the farm to see her, although I hear tell that Mr. Gunnison's got plans for marryin' his daughter off to—"

"Del!" Jay spoke more sharply than she intended. The deputy's face went pale. "We've got to tell everyone in town that trouble's stampeding our way. If everyone doesn't prepare for it, we'll end up like . . . like other towns," she finished lamely.

"What do you mean? What other towns?"

"Paradise," she said in a small voice. Slash had told her what Chief Marshal Bledsoe wanted them to investigate. It was unimaginable that such a plague would ever descend on Camp Collins, but Harl Benson fit into the picture too well to ignore.

"What about Paradise?"

"It was destroyed. Everyone in it was murdered and the town was burned to the ground."

"Are you feeling all right, Miss Jay? I haven't heard a peep about any such thing happening. You know Dirty Tom? The telegraph operator? He'd've heard for certain sure if anything like that happened. You know how he is with gossip. He—"

"If everyone's dead, who would be left to spread the word of the massacre?"

Del pursed his lips and nodded slowly. He dropped his feet off the marshal's desk and leaned forward, more attentive now.

"That's a good point, Miss Jay. Myra always says you're always thinkin', always tryin' to stay a lap ahead of everyone else."

"You don't want anything to happen to her, do you, Del? If we get folks to barricade their places and make sure their guns are close at hand, we might save a lot of woe."

"If nothin' happens, I'd look like a complete fool. The marshal'd fire me so quick, my head'd spin like a top."

"That's better than letting everyone in town die. I promise, if the attack doesn't come and the marshal fires you, I'll see you get a better job."

"A lot better?" Del got a dreamy look. "Me and Myra are talkin' about more 'n courting. I can see myself hitched to her. I don't know what's in her purty little head, though. She likes me, but—"

"Several places around town can be fortified and hold off a small army," she said. "The Grand Hotel is one. Men on the second-story balcony with rifles can command most of Main Street."

"The top floor of your saloon is a good place for that, too. If this Benson fellow is comin' for your booze, you'll want to keep any robbers out. Only, gettin' armed men to post themselves in both places is gonna be hard."

"My girls are capable of firing rifles and six-shooters, if the need arises."

"Soiled doves with guns," Del said thoughtfully. "The marshal won't cotton to that idea, me seein' them all armed. He always says—"

"The road into town crosses the bridge over the Cache la Poudre River. It's been threatening to give way for a year or more. If it happened to collapse, the town council'd have to repair it." Jay silently changed that to "replace it."

"That's goin' a bit far, considering it as a casualty 'fore

any shootin' starts, but you're right about its condition. Pecos complains about it every time he drives that old Pittsburgh wagon of his over it. I tell him not to load so much into the wagon, but he never listens."

"You go up and down Main Street and let the merchants know that trouble is brewing. Some will listen, others won't. Don't argue. Move on to the next store."

"You'll talk to Mr. Wilks at the hotel? He doesn't much like me, not after I arrested his son for beatin' up on one of the girls up on the third floor. A soiled dove. He claimed it was all right because she bad-mouthed him, but I disagreed. She left town right after, and I had to let Mr. Wilks's son go scot-free."

"I'll talk to him. And I'll see that the Palace of a Thousand Delights is turned into the Palace of a Thousand Guns." She swallowed. "The worst one to convince will be Gustav Reinking. He's about the most hardheaded man I ever did see, and I married one who can give him a run for his money."

"I'll do some talkin', Miss Jay. But when should I say to expect this horde to come swoopin' down on all of us? They'll want to know." He cleared his throat. "Truth to tell, I want to know, too."

She thought hard. Harl Benson had left town the day before. It'd be two or three days before any attack formed. Or so she hoped.

If only Slash would get in touch with her!

"Soon," was all she said.

"You never steered me wrong," Del said with some reluctance. "You wouldn't say these things if you didn't believe 'em."

"Get Myra to help you. She can coax folks into about anything," Jay said.

"That's the gospel truth. Why, just last week she—"

"Time's a'wasting, Del."

"You're right, Miss Jay. Time has feet, as they say. Or

maybe that's time has fleas? I don't think I heard it right when—"

"Get moving, Del. *Now.*"

The deputy heaved himself to his feet and escorted her out. He looked around, then headed for the stores lining Main Street.

Jay wasn't happy to deal with the hotel owner. She and Wilks had locked horns often enough for the man to bristle whenever he saw her. The last time, a few days earlier, he had crossed the street rather than pass her on the boardwalk outside the general store. Such disdain was understandable. More than once, she had ragged on him about the way he treated his doxies. The matter had come close to a fistfight when she had hired one of his battered soiled doves.

Wilks reared back to hit her, then saw the fire in her eyes. Hitting a woman was wrong. Wilks would never have lived down hitting a woman and then being decked when she struck back. Jay had been in more than one bout of fisticuffs in her day. She hadn't always come out on top, but she had won enough to put fear into the hotel owner.

"Mr. Reinking. Gustav!" She waved at the banker as he shook hands with a departing customer.

"Miss Jay," he greeted. "What can I do for you? A loan? Looking to sell that fine property?" He looked past her down the street to her saloon and brothel.

"I've been through that recently, Gustav, and decided the matter with some finality."

"So I've heard," he said, chewing his lower lip. "Most unfortunate, kidnaping and nooses and all that."

She launched into her fears about Harl Benson without revealing what she knew of Paradise and the hints that other towns had been looted and razed totally.

"What you're asking for is nothing short of martial law," the banker exclaimed. "Unless you know for certain that my bank is to be robbed, I'm reluctant to hire additional guards. The expense. I have stockholders to think of and can't spend money on frivolous . . . suppositions."

"It won't be permanent. For a day or two. Or a week, to be on the safe side. If I'm wrong, I'll reimburse you."

"You feel that strongly?" The banker stroked his short, well-trimmed brown beard. A gleam came to his eye. "Are you willing to put up the deed to the Palace to defray my expenses?"

"The deed? Hardly, Mr. Reinking. But perhaps you'd be interested in a visit or two on the second floor?"

"Just one or two?"

"You have yet to be introduced to Cara and Tara. They're twins. Blond and shapely." She saw the blaze in his eyes spread throughout his body. "Did I mention they are identical twins? It's hard to tell them apart, except for . . . Well, they'd have to show you, Gustav."

"My entire expense hiring guards?" he pressed.

"For a week. I'd say a half-dozen guards will be adequate, if they are well-armed and have plenty of ammunition. Finding cowboys this time of year shouldn't be too hard, since most of the herds are taking to pasture and don't need constant tending."

"For a siege?" Gustav Reinking nodded and looked over his shoulder at the brick bank.

"Twins," Jay reminded him. "Like looking in a mirror."

"A mirror," he mused. He stood a tad straighter and smiled broadly. "I need to begin recruiting immediately," Reinking said. "Miss Jay." He pinched the brim of his bowler and went off, whistling a bawdy tune.

Jay sighed and shook her head. Some men were too easily manipulated. She'd have to pay the twins a bonus—if the raid she feared didn't happen. Any time with the banker meant they'd earn their fees.

And if the attack occurred, everyone would pay the price. She lifted her skirts to hurry along toward Slash and

Pecos's freight yard. Jay called out to Myra when she saw the young woman going into the warehouse.

"What brings you by? Any word from Slash?" Myra asked.

"Nothing, and it worries me." She looked into the dark interior. "Did they store any of Osborne's cargo here?"

"He was blasting stumps, wasn't he? There's a case of dynamite left because he refused to pay for it. They took out four cases and he only used three. We need to figure out a way to make cheapskates like him pay up. You have any suggestions?"

"Where's the dynamite?"

"Are you fixing to blow up something?" Myra laughed. Then the merriment died when she read the answer on Jay's face. "What are you going to do?"

"I don't think you should know. Del might ask. It's better if you have no idea what's going to happen."

"Don't worry about Del and me. What happens if I give you the dynamite?"

"You work for Pecos and Slash," Jay said carefully. "I'm married to Slash, so that makes you one of my employees, too. Show me the explosives and run along. You might ask your beau about what he's been doing all afternoon."

Myra stood, feet wide and fists on her flaring hips. She fixed Jay with a hard stare. When it didn't budge her and squeeze an explanation for her lips, Myra changed tactics. She looked a little pouty.

"I'm hurt, Jay. You don't have much faith in me. If I work for you, like you say, go on and fire me. I'm manager and ought to be trusted with about anything."

"Stop trying to wheedle it out of me. You're a greenhorn, girl, compared to some of them who work for me." Jay locked eyes with Myra, then said, "All right. Here's what I'm afraid will happen."

She laid out her suspicions and danced around revealing much about Pecos and her husband's mission for Luther

Bledsoe. In spite of the times she'd gone over the story, it still seemed incredible that anyone destroyed entire towns just to pillage them.

"That's mighty audacious," Myra said when the tale had run its course. "Are you thinking to throw dynamite at the raiders when they come into town?"

"Something more. A few sticks of dynamite against what might be a company-strong horde won't be too effective." She hesitated, then plunged on. She already had told Myra more than was safe. The rest of her crazy plan might as well be put on the table.

Myra shook her head and said, "You want to blow up the Poudre Bridge?"

"It's about ready to collapse," Jay said, as if trying to justify the demolition.

"If these invaders have such heavy armored wagons, the bridge would collapse under their weight," Myra said.

"Pecos has driven fully loaded wagons across. During the last few trips, the wagon was busting at the seams, it was so heavily loaded."

"The river's low this year. Can't they drive their wagons off the road, ford the river, and then get back on the road to reach town?"

"I know that river bottom," Jay said. "It's got silt a foot deep. If they tried to cross at the wrong spot, the muck might grab hold of their wheels. Anything that slows them works to our benefit."

"Are there lookouts posted to warn us?"

"I've left that up to Del," Jay said. "There's so much more that can be done."

"Over there," Myra said, pointing into the corner of the warehouse. "A case of dynamite sticks. And some of that black miner's fuse. You know about it?"

"It'll burn a foot a minute, so I'll have time to get away."

"So *we'll* have time," Myra said. She waved off Jay's protest. "If my bosses—and that's Slash and Pecos—want to fire me for not doing my duty, they can. With you, I'm just looking after property stored in the company warehouse."

"Are you sure you're not going to blow up?" Myra asked. "That dynamite looked . . . old."

Jay glanced back at her saddlebags, where she'd stuffed twelve sticks. None of the paper looked wet, as if the dynamite was sweating. She had seen sticks with yellowed tears dripping down the sides. That was the nitroglycerin oozing out. But these were free of that. Still, jostling around detonated dynamite—that's why a blasting cap was used.

"The bridge looks even older."

The rickety bridge over the Poudre River creaked and moaned in the twilight wind blowing down from the distant Front Range.

"I don't know anything about how to blow something up," Myra said.

"Watch and learn, girl. I've helped blow new stopes in mines and . . ." Jay hesitated to finish what she was saying. She and her first husband, Pete, had blasted open more than one bank vault. Bragging about her sordid past wasn't going to get her anywhere. The fewer people who knew, the better off she was.

It was bad enough that Bleed-'Em-So Bledsoe knew and used that knowledge against her, and to keep Slash and Pecos in line.

"The strongest supports will be where I set the dynamite," she said. "There's no point in knocking out the weaker ones. If the weight brings down the bridge, fine. And if it doesn't—"

"And a heavy wagon tries to cross, with the strongest struts out, the whole shebang comes crashing down!" Myra sounded downright enthusiastic about such destruction. "I want to light the fuse!"

"You're turning into a firebug," Jay said, laughing.

They dismounted. Jay gentled her horse, Dorothy, since it

tried to rear at the smell of the dynamite. Carrying the sticks to the bridge, she looked up into the shadows. Saying she intended to blow the strongest part of the structure was one thing; doing it was something else. She had no idea what was strong and what was weak.

"Those supports are about rotted through," Myra said, pointing to the ones in the center of the bridge. "Do you plant the explosive where the bridge fastens to the ground on this side?"

"I don't want to wade across the river." Jay watched the river churn and boil. It wasn't running as high as usual. The high-water marks left chalky white lines on the riverbank, but that didn't mean this was a gentle stream.

She wormed her way up under the bridge and began stuffing parcels of three sticks into crevices offering the most blast upward. She positioned rocks on the sides of the sticks and then she placed the blasting caps carefully.

"Those are dangerous, Jay. I've seen more 'n one miner who blew his hand off because he was careless."

"You don't see miners who're careless with the dynamite all that much," Jay said. "That's because only bloody bits of them are usually left to mark their graves." She finished crimping the blasting caps and miner's fuse.

Edging back, she carefully played out the waxy rope of black fuse. The main fuse led to four branches. Each of those branches was the same length, which meant all the explosive should detonate at the same instant. Jay ran out another three feet, then cut it off with a knife she carried in her skirts.

"That's about four feet," she said.

"Four minutes gives us plenty of time to high-tail it," Myra said. She blinked and asked, "Doesn't it? How big will the blast be?"

"Not that big," Jay told her, not having any idea about the size. She fumbled around in her skirts and then asked, "Do you have a match?"

Myra did a quick search and came up with a single lucifer. She held it out.

"Go on. You wanted to light the fuse," Jay said.

Myra let out a squeal of glee, dropped to her knees, and took the end of the fuse in her left hand. It took a few seconds to find a dry rock. She dragged the match tip across. It flared brightly. Within seconds the black fuse sputtered, hissed, and began its slow march toward the sticks hidden under the bridge.

They hurried back to their horses and mounted. They trotted a dozen yards away and turned to watch.

The explosion rocked the earth. A small tidal wave rolled down the river and then a shower of burning embers and splinters came raining down.

Myra's eyes were wide and bright in the blaze of the burning bridge.

"So much for having a heavy wagon bust the weak supports."

What the explosion didn't destroy, the fire did.

Chapter 31

"**D**o you think she'll do it?" Pecos tried to keep up with Slash. "Do you?"

"Even if she doesn't get the children food, they'll survive. They dodged a lot of death back in Whiskey Creek."

"But the town's swarmin' with the Colonel's men, and has been for a couple days. They know this is the last raid before clearin' out of the territory. They might take it into their heads to burn High Mountain to the ground . . . after shootin' every last livin' soul in town."

"I'm more worried about Camp Collins. You should be, too." Slash stopped suddenly. Pecos collided with him. "I got a wife there. You got all your friends in Camp Collins. How're we ever gonna stop the attack?"

"You're right," Pecos said grudgingly. "There's nothin' in High Mountain to take that'd be worth their time. Besides that, haulin' it down would fill up all their wagons."

"They'll keep 'em empty for plunder from . . . Camp Collins," Slash said. "If they wanted to move their loot from High Mountain, they'd get it over to the D and RGW spur line and ship it west. The Colonel might already have taken everything he wants from this town. Squeezed it like an orange till nothin' but pulp remains."

"I don't like the way that sounds," Pecos said. "We've got to do somethin' before Raymond high-tails it. There must be a way to tell Bleed-'Em-So how to nab him."

"It'd take an army—more!—to stop the slaughter. There's no way even a chief marshal can get that many men together in a posse, much less move 'em all to Camp Collins."

"The U.S. Army. They got robbed. They'll want their cannon back."

"They got the men, they can move fast when the mood strikes, but, Pecos, this is up to us. *Us,* and nobody else."

"We're just a pair of retired train robbers. All we can do is rescue Jay. Get her outta town before the fur starts to fly." Pecos stepped around his partner. "And even a meager thing like that's beyond us now."

Slash spun. He cursed when he saw Matthias and at least ten riders coming toward them. From the determination Matthias showed, he had found the victims he sought— them.

"Don't do anything dumb, though I admit I'm thinkin' on the same thing," Pecos said. "We might be makin' a mountain out of a molehill."

"You two. The Colonel wants you to get the war wagon moving now. *Now!* You deaf?"

"They will be, come morning, Matthias," a rider called. "The crews in them tin-plated wagons go deaf from the sound of so much shooting. The sound bounces around in the steel cage something fierce. I heard of one gunner whose ears started to bleed. Fancy that!"

"Better deaf than stupid," Pecos said. He stepped up and tugged at the lanyard on his shotgun. It was foolish on his part to challenge the man on horseback, but his temper reached a boiling point.

"What's that?" The man who had joked with Matthias reached for his hogleg. "You mouthing off to me?" The man thrust out his chest. He displayed five of the Colonel's combat ribbons. Such a history made him feel entitled.

"You'll get us both killed," Slash whispered. "Jay wouldn't like that any more than I would."

"Just feelin' my oats," Pecos said. He took a deep breath and tamped down his ire. "Rarin' to get to the fight. I didn't mean nothin' by it."

"We're all keyed up," Matthias said. "It's always this way before a campaign. You two save it for the fight."

"Ain't gonna be much of one, not if what Benson said's right. They're little birds just waiting to get plucked." The raider with the five ribbons laughed. The sentiment spread through Matthias's squad.

"Over yonder," Matthias said to Pecos and Slash. "Pretend somebody's lit a match on your boots and burned your soles. There's a lot to learn about the war wagons, and you don't have much time. You have to roll out right now to be in position by dawn."

Pecos saw a wagon pulled up beside the saloon. Men swarmed all over it. Two men lugged a Gatling gun from a case, while another gathered an armful of magazines. He hesitated, but Slash prodded him forward.

Matthias watched them as they greeted the supply crew. The two with the Gatling poked their heads out of a panel behind the driver's box.

"The gun's all bolted in place. We've loaded the ammunition. Let's get a move on!"

"You fellas all right back there in that sweatbox?" Slash asked as he settled on the bench seat. "Bein' locked up in the hot sun turns that into a cooker."

"We're used to it by now. Drop the side panels and keep this window open and we got all the air we need." The scrawny man slid the steel plate behind the drivers up and down. He left it where he and his partner peered out.

"I want to—" Pecos began.

"You want to drive. We got orders about you." The skinny raider touched the six-shooter hanging at his side. "Benson thinks you're slackers."

"Slackers?" piped up the other man. "That ain't what he said. He thinks you're lily-livered cowards, that's what. If you run or try to hang back, we're supposed to shoot you."

Pecos and Slash exchanged a glance.

"Thanks for lettin' us know where we stand. You boys ain't gonna have cause to pull those six-shooters on us." Pecos took the reins and snapped them. The wagon lurched. He kicked out with his foot and dislodged the brake. "Sorry 'bout that. It takes a spell for me to get the hang of a new rig."

Slash chuckled and looked straight ahead. Pecos drove the heavily armored wagon to the steep trail leading to the main road and considered driving off the brink. This would wreck the wagon before it plunged halfway down the slope.

"The other way. The road that's nowhere near as steep. We have to be there if we want to save anybody," Slash said.

Pecos grumbled, but guided the team around to the back side of town. Even taking the less steep road required him to ride the brake all the way down to keep the heavy wagon from overrunning the team. He took one last look uphill at High Mountain and then got the wagon rolling toward Camp Collins.

"You're goin' too slow. We won't make it to the assembly area before dawn if you don't whip the team." The scrawny raider pounded on the steel sheet between the compartment with the Gatling gun and the driver's box.

"Now?" Slash said softly.

"Not yet. Let him gripe some more. What's he gonna do? Shoot us? I don't think he's a teamster. He'd never get to the fight if he shot us."

"That, Pecos, would be interestin', watchin' an inexperienced village idiot fight a balky team. But pluggin' the pair of them now gives us some breathin' room."

"You come up with a clever plan to save the town yet?" Pecos asked. "I've had my think box workin' so hard, it's overheatin'. Sweat's pourin' down my forehead into my eyes, I've been cogitatin' so hard. I haven't come up with any good ideas."

"That's me, too. I have lots of ideas. They're all bad ones."

"What's with you two?!" the man screamed. His words echoed around inside the steel box. He began banging on the steel plate with the butt of his pistol.

"If the gun discharges, it'll save us a bullet or two," Pecos said. "But the way our luck's run lately, it'll bounce around inside and then go through the side panel."

Slash nudged Pecos and pointed into the darkness. Ahead, alongside the road, two dismounted men stood beside their mounts.

"What's that all about?" Slash wondered. He leaned back and shouted through the window, "There's a pair of men ahead. What do you want to do about it?"

"We'll take care of it," came the eager answer.

One of the men ahead stepped into the road and waved his hat to flag them down. Barely had he moved to block the road than the Gatling gun ripped out a line of deadly lead. The scrawny gunman cackled as he spun the crank. In seconds the magazine came up empty. His partner yanked out the empty and stuffed in a full magazine. The throaty roar sounded again and gunsmoke billowed from inside the compartment.

"What the hell are you doing?" The man in the road dived for the ditch running along the left side. His partner on the far side raised his rifle and got off a round. The slug tore past Pecos's head and disappeared into the compartment.

The crew there screamed in anger and surprise as the bullet ricocheted around.

"Gimme another magazine. We're being attacked!"

Both Pecos and Slash slid down into the foot well and peered out. Both men ahead were firing at them, while the Gatling gun continued to chatter its deadly message. Interrupting the fight, a grinding sound, followed by metal breaking, warned that the Gatling gun was out of commission.

The crew cursed each other as they worked to repair whatever had gone wrong.

"You danged fools. The Colonel posted us here to tell you the attack's postponed for a day. We don't hit the town until dawn tomorrow. Damn you!"

"Ain't us shootin' at you," Pecos called. "It's them two in the back of the wagon."

"Matthias gave the order," one of the men in the road shouted. "If you don't shut down that gun, I'll tell him. Hell, I'll tell the Colonel! You know what he does to traitors and idiots who foul up his plans."

The whispered argument going on behind Slash and Pecos ended abruptly.

"What's the secret password?" The skinny man pounded on the inside of the steel compartment. "You tell us and we'll believe you. Otherwise, we open up with the Gatling gun again."

"They can't," Slash called to the men in the road. "They busted it. We believe Matthias."

"It's good somebody in the wagon's got the sense God gave a goose. There ain't a password. There never has been!"

"Don't shoot. We're coming out." The two in the back unlocked the rear door and jumped down. They rounded the wagon, hands in the air. "That you, Eddie? Eddie McMillan?"

"I shoulda knowed you'd be in there, Goodman. Nobody else is stupid enough to buck Matthias's orders." The man who had dived into the ditch came over, brushing dirt from his clothing.

"I didn't go against anything he said. I never would."

Goodman and McMillan faced off in the middle of the road, shouting at each other. The second man sauntered back and looked up at Slash and Pecos.

"Come on out. The worst of it's done."

"Why'd you stop us?" Slash angled around in the driver's box so he could draw either of his six-shooters, should the need arise. He eyed the two guards' horses. Kill the Colonel's four men, steal the horses, and they'd be in Camp Collins long before noon.

"There's a problem getting into town. Looks like a crate of dynamite blowed up and took a bridge out. The Colonel and Mr. Benson are plotting out a new way around it. They don't reckon it'll be more than a day's delay."

"Are we supposed to go back to High Mountain?" Pecos asked hopefully.

"Naw, there's a lake not a mile off. Camp there, water the horses, and maybe hit the road again, around four in the morning."

"We'll get mighty hungry waitin' that long," Slash said. He rubbed his belly to emphasize the problem.

"You won't starve, not eating for a day. Hell, go hunting. Bring down a deer and feed a couple dozen of us. Just don't use that Gatling gun. It'd blow a deer into hash." He laughed at the idea, then settled down. "It jammed up, didn't it? Can you fix it before the attack?"

"Neither of us is a gunsmith. Those yahoos in the back are supposed to know about these things. If they can't repair the rapid firer, should we go on back to High Mountain?" Pecos kept pressing to return to the lofty town.

"Not my call, but Matthias would never order a retreat. He's like that. Always advance, never give up ground you've taken. Now, you got a line on the North Star? Over there? Head directly for it, maybe two miles across country.

You'll find the lake there, along with the Colonel and most all of us in a bivouac."

"It's dangerous crossing open prairie with a wagon that weighs this much," Pecos said.

"Ain't no hurry. Just get there. I'm told there are guides along the way. Hell, why not? We've got close to a hundred men with nothing else to do for another full day."

He saluted and turned away to where the two men in the road still argued.

"What do you think, Slash? Can we sneak away if we plug the four of them?"

"Nope," his partner said. "There's a platoon ridin' this way. The gunfire drew 'em."

Pecos spat.

"So it's play out the hand and see if the next one's any better? Our luck's gotta change eventually."

He took the reins and guided the team off the road in the direction of the approaching knot of riders. Goodman screeched at being left behind and ran to catch up. They heard him and his partner continue the argument from the rear of the wagon.

Pecos was getting to the point of shooting them both, just to get some peace and quiet.

Chapter 32

"If we shoot the crew on another wagon, we might take out the third one," Slash said. "The one we're drivin' ain't in commission. Goodman and his partner are still workin' to fix what they broke."

Pecos grunted. He sat on top of the war wagon, long legs dangling over the edge. The entire attacking force was spread out around the lake. Animals drank noisily and more than a few fires blazed. His belly growled from lack of food, but he wasn't inclined to hunt for dinner.

"Somebody's comin'," Slash said. He slid from the bench seat and dropped to the ground. High above him, Pecos got to his feet. "Who is it? They're makin' straight for us."

"Matthias," Pecos said. "Him and his usual flock of buzzards."

Slash worried that they had given themselves away somehow. A word was all it took to turn the Colonel's men against a traitor. Matthias watched them like a hawk, but Benson worried him more. The Colonel's tactician had given them a single glance and disliked them.

"You two!" Matthias called. "You left your wagon back in High Mountain, didn't you?"

"That's where it is, unless somebody stole it," Slash said.

"I wouldn't put it past half the town, either," Pecos said. He edged closer and peered down. From his vantage point he towered above the mounted raider.

"Go down to the lake and get a couple horses. We're going back to High Mountain."

"Why?" Slash moved to get a better look at the riders with Matthias. The smallest twitch from any of them and he was filling his fists with Colts and shooting his way out of camp. Slash was relieved to see that they all looked bored, rather than excited, at the idea of shooting up somebody on Matthias's orders.

"We got more problems to fix." Matthias rode to the side of the wagon and rapped on the steel plate until Goodman poked his head through the side loophole. "You having any luck fixing the gun?"

"It's too busted up," Goodman said. "There's no way either of us can fix it without a lot of tools."

Matthias put his palm on Goodman's face and shoved him back into the compartment. Goodman screeched angrily, but did nothing more.

"Horse. Go on, you two. We're heading back to High Mountain to fetch a replacement Gatling gun."

"Do you need it?" Pecos asked. "There's plenty of firepower without us causin' a ruckus."

"We need it. The second Gatling gun is jammed up and the lead war wagon's busted an axle. That's what caused us to put off the attack."

"Why not forget about it? The Colonel said we was movin' on," Slash said. "We don't need another notch on our gun butts . . . or a new ribbon to pin to our chests."

"You shut your mouth. You're not in command. We'll

load up a couple more guns, get a spare axle and some other equipment."

"You're hirin' us to move freight?" Pecos laughed at the irony. This was the job they'd started.

"You're moving supplies because that's what a loyal soldier does in this army."

"Army?" scoffed Pecos. "I never signed up for a hitch in any army."

"If Benson assembles all the materiel we need, and you're not in High Mountain to load it onto your wagon, there's gonna be hell to pay."

"Benson's goin' with us?" Slash asked.

"He's already on the trail. He forgot some of the maps he drew. Now, are you obeying my orders, or are you traitors?" Matthias rested his hand on his six-gun.

Slash saw the rest of the squad follow their leader's move. He motioned to Pecos to come down. This wasn't what they'd planned, but it might work out fine for them. Matthias and a handful of raiders, along with Harl Benson, reduced the number of men they had to shoot their way through.

Pecos landed with a thud. He stood painfully, rubbing his back.

"The knees are a bit achy, too," he said to Slash.

Matthias and his men trotted off toward the lake.

"This gives us a chance to catch Benson," Slash said. "If Raymond finds out the man who planned all his raids is under arrest, he might high-tail it."

"We'd have to chase him down," Pecos said. "Bleed-'Em-So ain't gonna let us off the hook by catchin' only one of them small fishes."

"It's a start. And we can ruin the plans for hittin' Camp Collins. I'll try anything to keep Jay safe and sound."

"No attack, no danger," Pecos agreed.

They hiked in silence to the lake. Matthias had cut out

two horses from the remuda. It took a few minutes to adjust the stirrups and find a comfortable spot in the saddles. By then, they were a mile behind Matthias.

"We can split up. You go on to Camp Collins and warn 'em all," Pecos said. "I'll go to High Mountain and—"

"And nothin'. There's no excuse you could make that'd convince Matthias you had no idea where I'd gotten off to. He'd shoot you out of habit."

"Your horse pulled up lame? How's that? And—"

"What's keepin' you owlhoots?" A trio of riders came up behind them. "Matthias told me you'd try to duck out. I don't like it that you got ribbons for the Whiskey Creek raid and I didn't. Just 'cuz I was guardin' the rear, I didn't get noticed."

"We're on our way," Slash said. He and Pecos turned their mounts' faces toward the road and set out at as fast a pace as possible in the dark, overly rugged prairie.

"Let's make it count," Pecos grumbled.

"You know what the Colonel needs," Matthias said. "Get to loading your wagon."

Pecos and Slash said nothing as Matthias and his henchmen trotted off in the direction of the saloon. It was close to dawn—the day they had been scheduled to attack Camp Collins. All the failures of the Gatling guns and other war wagon had given a reprieve.

"What about us?" Pecos called after Matthias. "We're thirsty, too."

Matthias made an obscene gesture and kept riding.

"Mighty early for the saloon to be open," Slash said.

"There won't be a problem. It'll be opened one way or the other." Pecos kept riding along the main street, then trotted down the road where the warehouses filled with all the war materiel stood dark and silent.

"That was good, calling out Matthias about giving us a drink or two," Slash said. "He'll have an extra one just to spite us."

"It's finally payin' off that none of them like us." Pecos spat. "And none of them ever consider us part of the gang."

"I never wanted to be part of the Snake River Marauders, leastways not after the new blood flowed in and they started callin' us old-timers," Slash said. "We showed them. All of them."

"Time for us to do the same for these cutthroats." Pecos circled the warehouse. Their wagon was parked out back. The mule team was in a stable, back down the street.

"We could steal the Gatling guns," Slash suggested. "Or just blow this whole danged place to hell and gone."

"They'd be on us like buzzards on a fresh carcass. Better to grab Benson. We can use him to flush out Raymond."

"You think the two of them are friends, Pecos? Like me and you?"

"Nothing like us. I had to get liquored up to stand as your best man. There's not enough whiskey west of the Big River for Benson and Raymond to go through with—"

The scream cut through the still predawn. Pecos raked his heels across the horse's flanks and shot like a rocket down the street and out toward Marianne Mertz's boardinghouse. It was everything Slash could do to keep up. By the time he reached the house, Pecos had already hit the ground running and had reached the front door.

"Marianne! What's wrong?" Pecos pushed into the house.

More screams came from the back of the house. Pecos drew his pistol and plunged ahead.

"You don't understand," Marianne cried. "Don't hit me again!"

The sound of a fist hitting flesh made Pecos even more frantic. Nothing in the first room. Or the second. He skipped the next two and went directly to Marianne's bedroom. As he whirled around the door, pistol leveled, he took in everything in a flash. Pecos dropped his Russian .44; firing endangered the woman.

Harl Benson was choking her neck. As Pecos came into the room, he swung her around like a rag doll, using her body as a shield.

Marianne's face turned purple from the arm strangling her. Benson put his other hand flat on the back of her head, ready to break her neck.

Pecos yelled, "Let her go!" He backed up the command with a fist the size of a canning jar. He punched Benson squarely in the face. The man's head snapped back and blood spurted. Pecos had broken his nose with the first punch. The second knocked out a tooth.

Benson stumbled away and sat heavily on the bed. Pecos caught Marianne as she sank to the floor.

"Are you all right? Did he hurt you?"

Her eyes focused on him. She tried to speak, but only a frog's croak came from her damaged throat. Pecos read her lips. He lowered her more gently to the floor.

"I'll do that for you, love," he told her. She had mouthed that he was to kill Benson.

Pecos saw red as his fury mounted. He kicked out and knocked Benson's foot from under him as he tried to stand. The raider bounced on the bed, still trying to stanch the blood spurting from his nose. If Pecos had put an ounce of lead through the man's head, there wouldn't have been a bloodier scene.

He dived onto Benson, trying to give the would-be killer the same medicine he had delivered to Marianne. His massive hands sought Benson's neck. Pecos had driven mule teams constantly over the past eighteen months. He could crush rocks with those powerful hands. Soft flesh closed under his punishing fingers.

Benson gagged. Pecos forced him back onto the bed. The feather mattress let the writhing Benson slip to one side. He drove his hand against Pecos's elbow, forcing him to release his grip. Gasping, Benson flopped onto the floor. On hands and knees he presented a vulnerable target. Pecos kicked him as hard as he could. He felt flesh and bone yield as his foot lifted the man off the floor.

Benson gasped in pain and landed on his belly. Pecos heard Marianne moaning. This gave him new strength, added fury. He drove his hard fist down into the middle of the prone man's back. Benson was smashed flat onto the bedroom floor.

"No, stop, I give up," Benson grated out. "You can't beat me to death."

"Like hell I can't," Pecos said between clenched teeth. He towered above the fallen man. Then he regretted putting aside his six-shooter.

Benson rolled onto his side. He clutched a double-barreled derringer in a surprisingly steady hand. Death flashed before him. Pecos never slowed as he plunged downward. Marianne screamed as the derringer fired once, twice.

Twin arrows of pain drove into Pecos's chest. He made no effort to break his fall on top of Benson. For a moment they wrestled. Blood flew everywhere, from Benson's broken nose and from the two gunshot wounds in Pecos. Pecos turned into a mindless fighting machine. His fists pummeled the man under him.

Then he realized Benson had slipped away and he only pounded on the floor. His fists began to ache from hitting solid wood.

"Come back. I ain't finished with you," Pecos snarled.

No answer. He scooted across the bedroom floor and grabbed his six-gun. Pecos rolled onto his back and clutched the weapon in both hands to steady his aim.

Benson had crawled through the window and stood outside. He held his own six-shooter now. For a mere second both men stared at each other. Then one of them fired. Pecos wasn't sure who shot first. He tried. He tried and missed.

His slug broke glass. Benson returned fire. His bullets hit the mattress and sent up a flurry of white feathers.

Pecos kept firing until his gun came up empty. The hammer fell on one empty chamber after another. He switched position and got his barn-blaster pulled around. Hardly realizing what he did, he cocked the shotgun and yanked on both triggers. The roar deafened him. A two-foot section of the bedroom wall vanished in a fog of plaster and wood.

Then a curious calm descended. He had done all he could. Pain crept into his chest, and his hands shook too hard to hang on to his shotgun. It fell, dangling from the lanyard slung over his shoulder.

"Pecos, Pecos!" Hands shook him. "Don't you dare die on me. I will never forgive you if you do!"

"Aw, Marianne, I won't leave you." He struggled to get to his feet. All he managed was to prop himself against the bed.

"Let me stop the bleeding. He shot you. He shot you twice!"

Pecos felt frantic hands working to pull back his buckskin jacket so fingers could probe his wounds.

"It ain't as bad as it looks," he said. He moaned. "Or as bad as it feels. It takes more 'n a couple shots to stop me."

"I don't believe it, but you're right. You're right. One bullet destroyed your watch. It went clean through and cut your belly. It's hardly a scratch. But the other bullet went into your shoulder and came out the back. I won't have to dig around to get it out."

"Just patch me up, little darlin'. I got work to do. Me and Slash."

"You stay still. I declare, I've never seen so much blood before."

"Most of it was his. Did I plug him? I know I whumped up on him good and proper, but I wanted to put a bullet through his rotten heart."

"There's blood outside on the windowsill. You must have hit him at least once."

"Too bad I didn't kill him." Pecos pulled himself up onto the bed. "Are you all right? I saw how he choked you. What happened?"

"He surprised me. I was giving one of the children a gunnysack with clothing and food. He recognized them as being the ones you saved from Whiskey Creek. Benson went crazy. Henry got away, but Benson caught me."

"Henry?"

"The oldest boy. They're hiding . . . somewhere. I never asked, and Henry never told me."

"The Colonel and his killers will be gone real soon. Him and his brother and sisters can stop hidin' then." Pecos winced as Marianne poured whiskey onto his shoulder wound. It burned like hellfire.

"Your left arm's going to be numb for a while. I need to put it into a sling. Where, where—"

He caught her arm and spun her around. Pecos pulled her down and planted a kiss on her lips. Her eyes widened in surprise.

"Aren't you full of unbridled energy? If I didn't know better, I'd think there was a teenage boy hiding in an old man's body!"

"*Old man?* I'll show you what an old man can do." He kissed her again.

She pushed away from him.

"I've about got you patched up, but all the gunfire will bring the rest of Colonel Raymond's men running."

Pecos was ready to tell her it didn't matter. For her, he could whip his weight in wildcats. Then another voice echoed in the room.

"We've got to clear out, pard. Matthias and every last black-hearted demon trailing around with him's on the way."

"Slash!"

His partner leaned through the destroyed window. He touched the brim of his hat in Marianne's direction.

"Much obliged for patchin' him up, but we've got to go. It might be best if you came with us. We can get you out of town and—"

"No, no," she said, shaking her head. "I'm not letting them run me off my home." She took a deep breath and rubbed her bruised throat. "Besides, I need to stay to be sure nothing happens to those children you brought here."

"They've done a good job lookin' after themselves," Slash said. "But you need to think of more 'n them—and yourself."

Pecos started to object, then saw what his partner was getting at.

Pecos held her close and said softly, "We need you to find an army patrol. Or get yourself to a cavalry post. Tell them the Colonel's fixin' to attack Camp Collins."

"But, Pecos . . ."

"You can save a whole passel of lives, Marianne. Do it. Warn people that what happened in Paradise and Whiskey Creek's gonna happen in Camp Collins, unless they stop the Colonel." Pecos held her at arm's length and looked at her. She started to answer, but was interrupted.

Slash drew back from the window, then leaned through, reaching for Pecos. "We've got to go. Now, before Matthias sees us."

Pecos dallied long enough to kiss Marianne once more, then lumbered to the window and tumbled through it. With Slash helping him, they disappeared into the early dawn before Matthias spotted them. They still had a town to save.

Chapter 33

"I can walk. You're slowin' me down," Pecos said. He took a few steps on his own and found his balance. "The way my left arm sorta dangles is worse."

"You shoulda let Miz Mertz fix you a sling."

"That makes me look like a cripple."

Slash shook his head and said, "You *are* a cripple, old-timer. With a busted wing you're floppin' around, no matter how good you think you look."

"Do you think she'll go fetch help?" Pecos looked over his shoulder, but kept walking back to the warehouse where they'd left their wagon.

"That's the smart thing to do, but she talked about them kids like they were hers. She might want to stay in town to help them."

"We should go find Benson. I swear I put a round or two into him." Pecos tried to lift his left arm. He only got halfway up before he winced in pain. He quickly lowered it and cast a sidelong glance to see if Slash noticed.

"As much as I want to catch that skunk, we've got an entire town to save," Slash said. "The Colonel's wolves are fixin' to leave High Mountain and move on—after they take down Camp Collins."

"Benson's a big part of Raymond's attack," Pecos insisted.

"He's done all the damage he can. That notebook of his has all the details about Camp Collins in it. The Colonel's made his plans and by now has told his men what they need to do."

Pecos held out his good arm and halted his partner. He waited until Slash saw the danger ahead of them. Matthias supervised three of his men loading crates from the warehouse into Slash and Pecos's wagon. The mules had already been hitched and noisily protested a new muleskinner holding their reins.

They reloaded their six-shooters. Pecos worked open the shotgun and dropped in a pair of shells, pinning the barrel between his left arm and chest as he worked. Sweat beaded his forehead, betraying the pain he still felt. He dropped the shotgun and let it dangle on its lanyard. He nodded to Slash.

The pair of them walked forward, watching to see what their reception would be. Matthias spotted them first and waved them over.

"You two shirkers need to help out. There's trouble around town and we have to get out of here pronto."

"We heard gunfire. What was it all about?" Slash asked. He looked into the warehouse and saw most of the crates were gone. A quick look at Pecos got a nod.

"The Gatling gun's on its tripod in the back of the wagon," Pecos said.

"We might need to use it. There's no telling what trouble we'll run into. Nothing's gone right this time."

"Maybe Benson is fallin' down on the job." Slash stepped back to get the pair in the back of the wagon into sight.

"Or Colonel Raymond's lost his touch," Pecos said.

"You two have pushed me too far with talk like that," Matthias said. "Benson warned me that—"

Everyone grabbed for their guns at the same instant. The two old cutthroats had swapped lead more times than all of Matthias's men combined. Slash fired both his smoke wagons at the men in the wagon. Pecos unlimbered his Russian and hit Matthias, spinning him around. Before he was able to deliver a killing shot, the gunman inside the warehouse took a shot at him. Pecos flinched away.

That was all it took for Matthias to flop forward and roll away. By the time Pecos regained his balance, Matthias had joined his henchman inside the warehouse. Pecos tried to make them out in the dark. Unless they took a shot at him, nothing betrayed their location.

He heard both of Slash's guns come up empty.

"I'll cover you. Did you get the two in the wagon?"

"Both of them," Slash said. "I hit what I aimed at, you blind old bat. Are both of yours hidin' from us?"

"I'm not blind. I'm injured. That slowed me down, but not so much that I didn't wing Matthias."

"That's a start," Slash said, snapping shut the loading gates on his pistols. "I'm ready to go huntin' for bear."

Pecos said, "Hold on. Let's think this out."

"Don't hurt yourself."

"As much as I'd like to plug Matthias, what happens if we let 'em get away? We take the wagon and drive out. That steals one of their rapid firers," Pecos suggested.

"They'll come after us. We can't let him get his men together. I don't know how many are around High Mountain, but it's more 'n I want to shoot it out with along the trail."

"Slash, old pard, you've got a point, but what if we get ourselves killed right here? What happens to Camp Collins then?"

Slash took a couple shots into the warehouse. Matthias

cursed him, but didn't return fire to betray his location with a muzzle flash.

"You gettin' an idea?" Slash asked.

"I can turn a crank," Pecos assured him. He slid under the wagon and pushed up the canvas canopy. Wincing as pain shot into his left arm, he came to his knees. Working his fingers through a tear in the canvas, he ripped open a foot-long rent.

He swung the Gatling gun around so it pointed into the warehouse, and peeked through the loophole. Pecos grabbed a magazine and jammed it down into the receiver. Hand on the crank, he shouted at Slash, "Now!"

Slash opened up. Matthias and his henchman returned fire this time. Pecos squinted, saw the foot-long yellow-orange muzzle flashes, and swept the crank in a full circle. The Gatling spat out a dozen bullets.

"You got 'em!" Slash shouted.

"I hit one of the varmints," Pecos said. "The other one dodged the bullets."

Slash slipped through the door and went to the body on the warehouse floor. He prodded with his toe. It was definitely a corpse. Lifting the head up, he took a quick look at the man's slack face.

"It ain't Matthias."

"The slippery worm wiggled away," Pecos said. "But I'm sure I hit him. Or you did. He was slinkin' around like he took a bullet."

Slash made a quick dash behind a stack of crates. Pressing his ear to the floor, he heard a distant *thud-thud.* The footsteps were going away. He backed off, then ran to the wagon. With a big jump, he vaulted into the driver's box.

"He's goin' out the back door. Get ready." Slash snapped the reins. The nervous mules lurched forward.

The wagon rounded the warehouse.

"Get him. There he is. Runnin' for the next warehouse."

Slash ducked as Pecos began spinning the barrels of the Gatling gun. The bullets ripped past his head and danced all around Matthias. The raider went to one knee, turned, and fired wildly. Slash kept whipping the mules to race forward; Pecos cursed when the Gatling came up dry. The metallic clicking warned that he had discarded the empty magazine and loaded a full one. Slash leaned far out to the side so Pecos could fire past him at Matthias.

"Got him again," Slash cried. "I saw him jump when the slug tore through his leg."

"He won't be runnin' then. Good. I'm not sure I've got it in me to run him to ground." Pecos cranked off a few more rounds. The hammering bullets tore a large hole in the side of the warehouse.

Slash drove away from the hole and then cut back, giving Pecos a better angle to shoot into the warehouse. Pulling up parallel allowed the Gatling gun to fire through the tear in the canvas side and rake the door and all the wood around it. Splinters flew everywhere under the leaden onslaught.

"I see him movin'," Slash said. "He's . . . he's pointin' a cannon at us!"

Matthias finished ramming a three-pound cannonball down the throat of the mountain howitzer. He stepped back and fumbled with a match to light the fuse.

Slash tried to get the mules pulling to get out of the line of sight of the cannon. They decided they wanted to stand and bray, rather than work to save the wagon, the men in it . . . and themselves.

Slash began firing with both his pistols until he came up empty.

"Jump," he cried to his partner. "This here wagon's gonna be blown to splinters!" He stood, but didn't jump. Pecos wasn't budging in the rear of the wagon.

Pecos rammed in another magazine, bent low, and aimed along the rotating barrels. Then he gave a powerful turn to the crank. All thirty of the rounds in the column seemed to fire at the same instant. The deafening roar drove into his skull like a railroad spike and gave him a powerful headache. If his skull didn't split open, he was sure his eyeballs would bulge out from the pain.

Then came an explosion that rocked the wagon and blew Slash out of the driver's box.

He picked himself up and ducked under the wagon. The warehouse was in flames. From its depths came gunshots. A few stray bullets sang overhead. Slash pulled himself up and used his knife to cut away a section of the canvas that had been set ablaze.

"I nailed him before he could light the fuse," Pecos said. He let out a loud yell. "He dropped it into the keg of powder beside the cannon."

"The whole place is explodin'," Slash warned. "We gotta move or we're gonna be fried." He ducked back under the wagon and clawed his way up the far side to get to the driver's box. With a sweep of his hands, he caught up the reins.

The mules shied away from the heat and errant bullets set off by the fire. Slash got them pulling hard. Rather than turn the team, he drove straight ahead toward the third warehouse. Firing behind Slash, Pecos cried out in glee as he spewed more slugs from the Gatling. Either a spark from the burning warehouse or one of Pecos's rounds set off a case of dynamite.

The explosion rocked the wagon on its wheels. The mules staggered, but kept running at full speed until they were well past the last warehouse.

"We showed them," Pecos said. He clumsily crawled from the rear and plopped down on the bench seat beside his partner. "Never seen a Fourth of July fireworks display to match that."

Underscoring his words, a new explosion erupted. Flaming splinters rained down around them. Slash wanted to turn the team, but in their fright the mules weren't obeying any of his commands, no matter how he yanked on the reins. He let them have their head.

For once, providence was with them. The mules found the back road from High Mountain and started down it.

Slash fought the mules, while Pecos braced himself and used both feet on the brake to slow their descent. The heavy cargo normally would have required them to drive poles between the spokes, keeping the wheels from turning at all. Skidding down the hill was preferable to a runaway wagon.

But together the two teamsters reached the bottom of the hill. When they looked back, towering flames licked at the sky.

"We certainly done in that town," Slash said.

"Let's do it to the Colonel and his men," Pecos said. "I've still got a half-dozen cases of ammo for the Gatling gun."

Slash drove into the dawn, since Pecos's arm wasn't up to handling the team. Every mile they left behind took them closer to the final showdown with Colonel Raymond and his army. They both knew the penalty for failing to stop the crazed raider and his legion of murderers.

Chapter 34

"Town," Slash said, slamming his hand down on the bench seat between them.

"The rendezvous," Pecos said, equally as adamant.

"If we hurry, we can be at the town 'fore the Colonel attacks. We'll be able to warn everyone and take out the raiders 'fore they know what hit 'em."

"You want to be sure Miss Jay's safe. Your way'll get lots of our friends killed. Maybe even Jay," Pecos stated.

"So, why ain't your way worse? Let the raiders attack?"

"Nope," Pecos said. "Like always, you're not payin' a whole lot of attention to anything but that little voice inside your head. It must be screamin' like a banshee—for you not to see the brilliance of my plan."

"Lettin' the lot of them form their battle formation ain't much in the way of genius. And I can hear just fine, voice or not."

"We can sneak on into their camp. We got a Gatling gun in the back. Remember what we done to Matthias and his boys. We drive on into the middle of the camp and open up with that rapid firer. Take them by surprise. They won't be ready for us, and most of 'em won't be festooned with all those six-shooters, like they are when they attack a town. If we kill enough, they'll scatter."

"This is a wild bunch used to bein' shot at," Slash said. "There are a few mossyhorns in camp, but not too many. The Colonel's been tryin' to recruit and ended up askin' *us*. Most of his men have ridden—and killed—with him three, four, even more, times. I've seen a couple with nine ribbons. They aren't inclined to turn tail if we shoot up the camp. They'll be the first ones to come for us." Slash grumbled some more and stared straight ahead.

Although Pecos had a bad arm, he'd insisted on taking over the driving. Now, to Slash, it was obvious why. He wanted to sell out Camp Collins and everyone in it.

"If we plug Colonel Raymond, it's like loppin' off the head of a rattler," Pecos explained. "The rest of the body just thrashes around, but it's harmless."

"Snakes don't die till sundown," Slash said. "Everyone knows that, you consarned fool."

"I don't know that," Pecos said. "And neither do you. That's an old wives' tale. We kill Raymond, and who's to tell the rest of them where to ride, who to shoot, when to cut and run after lootin' the town?"

"We can't be sure he's even in camp. What if he's out there scoutin'?" Slash gestured in the general direction of Camp Collins.

"He's all wound up, wantin' what we got bouncin' around behind us. The broke axle, the busted guns, he won't budge from his tent until those are squared away."

"Maybe," Slash said reluctantly. "That don't mean we can kill him. Or even arrest him. He's settin' smack-dab in the middle of an army of cutthroats. They don't get paid unless they plunder Camp Collins . . . and then have their way with whoever's not been killed."

Pecos drew back on the reins and brought the team to a halt. The lead mule snorted and stamped its foot. If the wagon kept rolling, it didn't have to put out much effort. It knew how hard it was to get the heavily laden freight wagon moving again after it had stopped dead.

"This is where we decide," Pecos said. "If we keep goin' along the road, we'll be in Camp Collins before we know it. Or we cut across the prairie and hunt down Raymond. What'll it be, old son?"

"I hate it when you argue so good," Slash said. He drummed his fingers on the bench seat and muttered to himself. Finally he said, "I wish there was a voice in my head dispensin' nothin' but good advice."

"That's why you got me as a partner," Pecos said.

"A really good voice in my head wouldn't sound anything like you."

"If we break the back of the attack out here, nobody in Camp Collins need ever know how close they came to disaster. They won't be riled, and they won't be upset. They just won't know what a narrow scrape they'd had."

"Whiskey Creek showed how downright evil they are, the Colonel bein' the worst of the bunch."

"From what Bledsoe said about Paradise, it suffered even worse. The smell of cookin' flesh made him gag from twenty miles off."

"Anything that makes Bleed-'Em-So puke has got to be bad," Slash said. "You believe we can do this so nobody in Camp Collins ever knows how close they came to endin' up like Paradise and Whiskey Creek?"

"Well, Slash, old buddy, I think we can. But we might not come out of it alive. The odds against us are worse than in that gamblin' house in Denver."

"The one just off Larimer Square?" Slash snorted. "I don't think there's a game in that house that ain't crooked. The cards are marked, the roulette wheel's wobbly, the dice don't have all the right spots on 'em." He half stood, then sat again. "Well, what're you waitin' for? We can get to the lake in less than an hour. I want to get this over with."

Pecos snapped the reins and leaned to his left, to get extra power pulling in the direction of the outlaw camp. Their wagon bounced and rolled as they crossed the rugged prairie. Neither said a word. They were all talked out and knew what they faced.

"Drive right smack-dab through the middle of camp. I'll swing that Gatling around and we can mow down most of 'em," Slash said.

"They'll never knowed what hit 'em," Pecos agreed. He steered the wagon past a deep gully and found an easier route into camp.

By now, the sentries had spotted them. Word spread like spilled whiskey. In less than a minute, most of the camp was standing around, staring at the wagon as it made its way into the bivouac.

"I don't see Raymond anywhere. If he'd come out to greet us, this'd be right near perfect," Pecos said. He glanced over his shoulder. Slash worked furiously to seat the Gatling gun's magazine. He took a deep breath. If they came out of this alive, it'd be due to divine intervention.

Slash knelt on a crate of dynamite as he swung the rapid firer about and positioned it to shoot through the hole in the canvas. Other boxes rattled about. Pecos wasn't sure what they were, but knew they all contained explosives of some kind. Shells, cartridges, maybe rockets. He'd never seen such a weapon, but the Colonel had wanted it or Matthias wouldn't have loaded it.

"Ready to give 'em what for?" Pecos called back to him. "Just like we did Matthias and his cronies?"

"I—" Slash lurched to one side and pushed the crank down, firing a single round.

The men in camp would have reacted. Every last one of them carried a rifle and had several six-shooters slung around his shoulders and waist.

They would have fired back—if they had noticed. The thunderous boom that sounded did more than rock the wagon, it caused it to slew to the side. Pecos fought to keep it upright, to no avail. The left side dragged along a few feet, pulled by the diligent mules. Then a second explosion sounded and the wagon keeled over entirely, throwing Pecos free.

He hit the ground hard and lay stunned. His left arm was pinned under him. If it had been in bad shape before, it wasn't able to move at all now.

He winced in pain and sat up, staring at the wagon lying on its side. Slash fought his way out through the back and staggered as if drunk.

"What happened?" Slash croaked out. He swung around. The Colonel's men rushed over.

"I seen it," one cried. "The back axle broke clean through. It sounded like cannonade when the other axle busted, too, a second or two later."

"What's in there?" another asked cautiously.

Others crowded close and poked about in the wagon.

"Enough dynamite to blow us to hell and gone!" came the answer.

This caused most of the men to edge away. They were stopped in their tracks by Colonel Raymond's sharp command.

"Halt! Stand your ground, you sniveling cowards."

"But, Colonel, they got a wagon filled with dynamite and—"

"Retrieve it. Go drag it out. Those are the supplies we need for the assault. What's with you men? Have you turned cowards because we postponed the attack for a single day? Unload the wagon! Unload it, or I swear I'll see you flogged!"

Pecos tried to draw his pistol. Shooting Raymond was pure suicide, what with the entire army around him, but Pecos felt too much pain for anything else. His shoulder hurt and the spill caused double vision. If he took a shot at the Colonel, he'd have to decide which image to hit.

"Don't," a distant voice said. He tried to ignore it. A hand clamped around his wrist and kept him from throwing down on the Colonel. Pecos jerked free and turned on . . . Slash.

"Why're you stoppin' me? This is our only chance to—"

"Shut your trap," Slash said. "He's got fifty men all around him. You don't have a good shot. Not only would you miss, you'd end up dead. Me too."

"That's fine with me. About now, not havin' your whiney voice tellin' me what to do, and not do, seems like heaven on earth."

Slash released his friend's wrist and shoved him back so hard, he lost his balance and sat. The impact of hitting the ground caused his double vision to go away. Pecos saw that his partner was right. The Colonel directed unloading the wagon, but never presented even a sliver of a target. Shooting through a couple dozen men in hopes of hitting their leader was a fool's errand.

"We want to do what Bleed-'Em-So told us to," Slash said. "And, unlike you, I want to be alive to brag on it."

"Miss Jay'd find it real entertainin' late-night conversating," Pecos said.

"You have no idea." Slash grabbed him by the shoulders and heaved him to his feet.

Pecos wobbled a little, then carefully pulled his left arm around so he could tuck it into his jacket, where it wouldn't flop around and give him distracting jolts of pain.

He was so engrossed in securing his injured arm, he didn't hear the first words.

"I said, good work!" Colonel Raymond shouted at him. "Are you all right?"

"Buzzin' in my head," Pecos lied. "Hard to hear."

"We don't know what happened, Colonel," Slash said. "We was headin' into camp and it sounded like lightning. Or maybe a cannon."

"One of the boys said the axle rear snapped. That caused the wagon to tilt. The front axle wasn't up to the strain and it broke, too. You are lucky to be alive." He slapped Slash on the back. He started to duplicate the move with Pecos, but a quick move on the injured man's part positioned the raider's leader to only shake Pecos's hand.

"I reckon we'll have to call off the attack now," Slash said.

"What's that? Why? You delivered the goods. Nothing in the wagon was damaged."

"But, Colonel, the wagon's ruined. We can't drive it no more." Slash sounded a tad desperate. Pecos considered going for his pistol again. At this range it'd be impossible to miss putting a bullet into Raymond's rotten heart.

"The ammunition and explosives were what mattered, not the wagon. And, of course, the Gatling gun. It's already moved to the war wagon that needed it."

"But the attack . . ." Slash wasn't giving up on trying to convince the man of the futility of continuing.

"It will begin in three hours. At dawn."

"Did Benson say it was all right?" Pecos shot his partner a quick look.

"Mr. Benson has not returned yet," Raymond said testily. "That's not unusual. He'll put in an appearance before we attack, I am sure. He enjoys seeing how well his planning works during the actual combat. What about Mr. Matthias? He was supposed to escort you."

"Matthias tied one on and passed out back in High Mountain," Slash said quickly. "He'll have to sleep it off. Even then, he won't be much good. I've never seen a fellow that soused."

Colonel Raymond's face turned into an expressionless mask.

"He got drunk?"

"One thing's for sure," said Pecos, "he won't be in any condition to join in."

"It looks as if I'll need more reliable lieutenants." Raymond stepped into the center of a cadre. "You two fit the bill nicely. You delivered supplies we needed at great risk to your lives and you never wavered. You've proven that I can depend on you when I need it most."

"We can ride with you, Colonel?" Pecos worked through all the ways they could capture Raymond if they acted as his personal guards. Not only could they arrest him and satisfy Bledsoe, removing him broke the back of the attack.

"Better than that, my loyal men. You can command the war wagon. After all, it wouldn't have been usable if you hadn't brought the replacement Gatling gun."

"Wait, Colonel, we—" Slash never got any further with his protest.

Colonel Raymond bellowed, "Form attack columns! Get on the road immediately. We strike at dawn! To victory!"

Slash and Pecos did not join in the earsplitting shout that went up from the small army. The Colonel was carried off in a welter of men congratulating one another and cheering, as if they had already wiped out another town.

Chapter 35

"Del convinced a couple wastrels to stand lookout along the road," Myra Thompson said, "but he's worried they took a bottle with them." The young woman shook her head sadly. "By now, they might be passed out." She fixed a hard stare on Jay Breckenridge, daring her to object to such a conclusion.

"Worse," Jay said, "they might see things that aren't there. All we need is a false alarm." She looked around Camp Collins. Not many citizens had heeded her warning.

Deep down, she wondered if she wasn't the little shepherd boy shouting "wolf" when the flock was safe.

"Hallucinations might liven things up," Myra said, "but nobody'd ever listen to you again."

Jay worried that her thoughts had become so transparent. She lacked the confidence to go out and present her case without solid evidence. But how did she show the skeptics a burned building, or a looted business with bodies scattered all around, when she hadn't seen them herself? The horrendous descriptions had come from Slash, and he had gotten them from Bledsoe, a known prevaricator. The skeletal marshal ruled from his push chair through fear, intimidation, and outright lies.

The notion of a horde sweeping through and wreaking such destruction was the stuff of campfire tales meant to scare and entertain.

"The bridge being blown up will slow any army marching on us if they come," Myra said.

"If," Jay cried in frustration. She threw up her hands. It was all "if" and not "when." Even Myra carried a seed of doubt that she was doing the right thing for Camp Collins.

"I'll see what Del's rounded up, in the way of a greeting party," Myra said. "He won't be able to keep them long, even with your promise of free drinks."

"I might sweeten the pot a mite," Jay said. She had already offered the services of some of her soiled doves as incentives to some key defenders. The bank was as secure as it could get. Gustav Reinking had hired five marksmen and stationed them around his establishment.

"The Grand Hotel's going to be a hard nut to crack, too," Myra said, giggling. "The girls look like porcupines, all spiny with rifles and pistols."

"How many can use them?"

"From the way a couple of them waved their guns around, well, I'm glad Del doesn't have to face them down. Enough of them have run with outlaw gangs before ending up on the third floor." Myra hugged Jay and said, "Look at the bright side. If nothing happens, the town's still standing." She turned and hurried off to talk to her beau.

Jay heard grumbling from the men in the Palace of a Thousand Delights as they worked to board up the windows and move tables forward to serve as barricades. Anyone trying to burst through the front doors would catch a bellyful of lead from a dozen different directions.

She stepped off the boardwalk and into the street. Looking up and down turned her apprehensive. Most of the businesses were open for customers as usual. They'd be easy pickings for the vultures Slash warned about.

She skirted the bank. Reinking had posted three of his riflemen on roofs across the street. Anyone trying to break in faced not only a barrage from the guards in the bank, but from others behind them. Such a cross fire worked well if the attackers were mounted. Jay wondered how effective it would be against an armored war wagon.

How effective would any resistance be?

She lifted her skirts and hurried down the street, taking a couple shortcuts to reach the church. It had been quite a spell since she'd been here, and then it had been to attend a funeral. Jay hesitated going to the open front doors. She felt like a bug squashed by a swatter when a soft voice called out to her.

"Miss Breckenridge," the pastor said, stepping from shadows. "I wondered when you'd come by."

"Reverend Smith." She took a deep breath. She saw this man of the cloth wasn't one of those who claimed celibacy from the way he watched the rise and fall of her bosoms. "You've heard what I have to say."

"I've heard the rumors how a huge army will smash through town, destroying buildings, raping women, and stealing what's not broken." The reverend came from the church and stood in the wan morning light. He was taller than Jay by half a head. His brown hair was greased into place and showed more than a few strands of gray, belying his youthful looks. He reached out to her with a hand calloused from work and showing a pattern that surprised her.

The calluses hinted at a man who wasn't any stranger to using a six-shooter—often.

"You've only been in town a few months," she started.

"A year," he corrected somewhat sharply. He withdrew his hand as if he realized what impressions ran through her mind.

"About the time the Clarkson Gang left the territory."

"An odd statement. I suppose you're right," he said cautiously. "I prefer to use an ecumenical calendar rather than such a secular one."

"A leopard can't change its spots," Jay said, "but can a man change his occupation?" She saw how close this jab came to hitting a target. The reverend carried a pile of guilt about something. Naming the Clarkson Gang illuminated what that might be. They had been as bad a bunch of desperadoes as any robbing throughout Colorado since . . .

. . . since the Snake River Marauders.

"Are you asking if a man can stop stealing and begin giving? The answer is simple, if not easy. If it is the Lord's will, anything is possible." His voice hardened. "I had a calling that brought me here to this congregation rather than to the end of a hemp rope."

Jay rushed on. A man's background made no difference to her, especially considering her own running with a pack of cutthroats that made the Clarkson Gang look like choirboys. Many in town would argue that she hadn't progressed much, going from robbery to running a saloon and whorehouse, but she wasn't using a six-gun to get money anymore.

"Can you fortify the church? Get some of your parishioners to defend it like a fort?"

"Such a sturdy place slows an advancing tide of destruction. Is that it?"

"Making them commit as many men as possible lets others in town see the danger and organize enough to fight back."

Reverend Smith nodded. He glanced over his shoulder into the church, then said, "I haven't considered turning my church into an Alamo or recruiting as Colonel Travis did. Such a defense of this building would likely end the same way as the Alamo did."

"The Texicans held off a huge army long enough for others to prepare. That's my goal here." Jay held her breath. The reverend's face had become a mask. She had no idea what he was thinking.

After what seemed an impossible length of time, he said, "I can do that. It will take some time, though. My flock is scattered all over town."

"I'll warn everyone I see to take sanctuary here. If you are prepared for that, it'll save lives. I think I can depend on your experience to post fighters in the best places to defend the church."

"If this attack happens." Reverend Smith smiled, just a little. "Or has it begun already? I heard gossip that the bridge leading into town out west was, shall we say, prematurely brought down."

Jay said carefully, "I heard the same thing. It must be someone caring very much for Camp Collins and willing to protect it, however he can."

"However *she* can," he corrected gently. "I should see to—"

They both whirled around and faced west. The thunder of cannon fire rolled through the town.

"Ring the bells!" Jay cried. "That's got to be enough to warn everyone what's on the way!"

She pointed to the carillon in the church steeple. Without waiting to see if the reverend sounded the tocsin, she lit out at a dead run. She wanted to get back to the Thousand Delights and defend her own property.

Before she had reached the bank, the three-bell assembly carillon began chiming. Once melodious, it now sounded like the peal of doom.

Gustav Reinking stepped from the bank and looked around wildly.

"Get your men in position. They're coming!" Jay shouted. "They're coming!"

She ran until she gasped for breath, rounding the corner

onto Main Street and almost ran smack into the attacking vanguard. A war wagon rumbled along, its team of draft horses snorting and straining against the heavy load. Jay stared in mute horror as the armored sides dropped on the wagon and a Gatling gun began chattering out its deadly load. She watched all the carefully nailed-up boards over the windows in the Palace turn to splinters. Anyone banking on the wood to protect them was likely dead.

Then the real assault began.

Chapter 36

"The bridge is out!"

Slash and Pecos grinned. This would prevent Colonel Raymond from advancing on a helpless Camp Collins.

"I always knew that bridge'd collapse one day," Pecos said. "It picked about the perfect time to fall down."

Slash shook his head.

"You're smokin' locoweed again if you think this just happened all by its lonesome. Now? This very day? Something happened to reduce it to this sorry state." He jumped from the driver's box and cautiously went to better see the burned wood remains.

Pecos joined him. They hadn't gone more than a few yards when both of them turned their noses up and took a deep whiff of the predawn air.

"Dynamite," Slash said. "It warn't no accident. It was blowed."

"Miss Jay?" Pecos asked in a low voice. He stepped aside as the Colonel galloped past, shouting orders as he went.

They trailed his mad dash to the place where he urged his horse down the steep embankment to the river. Slash pointed to evidence that the explosive had been planted to do the most damage. The creaking old wood, long dried out, had turned to flinders from the blast. Repairing it would take a week, if there had been the timbers required for replacement. Most of the trees within twenty miles had been chopped down for use in building Camp Collins or carted off to use as supports in mines along the Front Range.

"You want us to turn around, Colonel?" Pecos bellowed enough for not only Raymond, but all the men crowded in a knot at the edge of the destroyed bridge, to hear.

"Of course not. Mr. Benson is not so careless. He always plans for such setbacks."

"We can't ford the river here. It's too deep," Slash argued. "Our wagons'd be up to the roof in water 'fore we got halfway across. We might try floatin' 'em across, only they're steel armored. No float will support weight like they carry."

Slash judged the impact of his words not on the Colonel, but on the men around him. Any discontent among them reduced the chance for a successful attack. Who in their right mind wanted to drive a war wagon across what looked to be a raging river?

He and Pecos knew better. And they knew a half-dozen places to ford the river this time of year. Keeping that from Colonel Raymond and his men delayed the assault enough for the town to be up and moving about. Somebody had to see the danger building up on the horizon like a nasty thunderstorm ready to sweep through.

"North," Raymond ordered. He urged his horse up the steep embankment and glared down at Slash and Pecos. "A quarter mile to the north is a rocky patch where you can cross with little more effort than driving across this bridge." He wrinkled his nose in disgust. "Considering the condition of this bridge, it'll be safer crossing there."

"If somebody blew up the bridge, that means . . ." Slash let his words trail off. The Colonel hadn't heard him. Luckily.

"Don't give him the idea the whole danged town's wait-in' for us," Pecos whispered.

"I figgered that all by myself. We have to slow him down." He stared east toward the town. Sunrise would put the new day's light squarely in their eyes if they delayed another couple hours. It wasn't much of an advantage for everyone in the town, but it was something.

"To your wagons. Earn your pay," Raymond ordered.

They expected him to gallop off to give more orders. Instead, he rode alongside them, back to the armored wagon. Both men inside tending the Gatling gun complained loudly. They hushed their grievances against their drivers when they spotted their leader.

"I'll show you the way," Colonel Raymond said. He pulled one of Benson's notebooks from his coat and held it up to get a better look at the map.

Pecos caught sight of it and elbowed Slash.

"I swear, that Harl Benson is Satan incarnate. That's the exact spot where they forded the river when Camp Collins was built back in '62. Ain't nowhere else less than two feet deep for ten miles in either direction."

Slash reached for one of his pistols. His intent was clear. A single shot now ended the Colonel's life, and the leader of the attack.

Pecos stopped him. Both the men in the rear of the wagon leaned out the front window with six-shooters in their hands. The hesitation was all it took for Raymond to ride away into the dark, out of sight, out of range.

"Get this here wagon rolling, you two." The older of the two in the rear motioned with his gun. Slash and Pecos had no choice but to climb up and get the team pulling.

The wagon rattled and almost turned over. Pecos steered toward the worst path off the road in hopes of doing that very thing. Luck ran against him again. The wagon reached a flat stretch along the river. Far ahead the Colonel waved them forward. All around rode the attackers, once more chattering about how many people they intended to kill and how rich they'd get after pillaging the town.

Slash tried not to hear the owlhoots bragging on the women they'd rape and kill.

"Across! This is the spot," Raymond shouted. He led the way.

The water rushing over the rocks here wasn't even two feet deep. The current caused the wagon to shift, but not enough for Pecos to steer it into deeper water where it'd sink. All too soon the wagon lurched as its wheels bit into drier ground. The entire column crossed and returned to the main road in less than an hour, the destroyed bridge behind them now.

"What's that?" Slash looked around at the sound of gunfire.

"Must be shooting travelers along the road," the man behind him said. "That happens from time to time."

"Or lookouts," Pecos said sourly.

He was greeted with a cruel laugh. "They won't be seeing nothing ever again. Our scouts hardly ever let a sentry pass along a warning. We're on the road to getting filthy rich!"

"Filthy, yeah," Slash said.

They hadn't driven another fifteen minutes when the rising sun made them squint. And another five minutes passed when a cannon sounded.

"They done opened fire on the town."

"What?" Slash spun on the man in the compartment.

"The Colonel don't do it often, but this time he sent in a mountain howitzer at the head of the column to soften up resistance. He must worry about that blown-up bridge and men watching along the road."

"He's not one to take chances," said the other man. "Time to get the gun ready to fire. We got us some serious killing to do!"

Slash turned as both men went to prepare the Gatling gun. Their backs were exposed. With a single swift draw, he leveled his weapons on them and said, "Get those hands up."

"What—" The older man wheeled around, saw his problem, and grabbed for the six-shooter thrust into his belt.

Slash fired four times. Each bullet ripped through the man's chest. He danced around and managed to pull his six-shooter—only to have it slip from lifeless fingers. He was dead before he hit the wagon bed. The other gunner stared at his partner and made an equally bad decision. Slapping leather to get his iron out, when Slash already had the drop on him, proved equally as fatal. Two slugs ended his life.

"Keep on drivin'," Slash said. He holstered his six-shooters and crawled through the window into the rear of the wagon. He braced his back against one wall and shoved the bodies to the rear of the wagon.

"Don't leave 'em in there," Pecos said. "Them bodies'll bounce all around and distract you."

"I hate it when you're right," Slash said. He flung open the rear doors and shoved the two corpses out. Another war wagon rolled immediately behind them. The driver half stood and gaped at the bodies as he ran over them.

Slash drew his six-guns again and fired at the driver. He should have reloaded. Each shot missed, but the reports spooked the other team and caused the driver to fight to keep from racing off in a direction away from Camp Collins. Seeing he had done as much damage as he could, Slash slammed and barred the back door.

He dropped the side shields and poked the gun out.

"Turn, Pecos, turn! Get us turned sideways. I ain't got a good target otherwise!"

Pecos steered at an angle so Slash caught a quick glimpse of the wagon trailing them. A quick spin of the firing crank sent a stream of lead hammering into the steel plates. White lightning jumped from every spot where a bullet hit. Slash kept working the crank until the smoking Gatling gun came up empty. He had worked with the rapid firer enough to have the movement down pat: old, empty magazine tossed aside. A fully loaded one slammed into the breach. A single turn dropped a new cartridge into the firing chamber.

Slash was thrown off balance as Pecos veered in the opposite direction.

"Watch what you're doin'! I almost wasted a round or two." Slash cringed when heavy fire slammed into the rear of the wagon. Then bullets sang through the open ports on either side.

The Colonel's men twigged to the danger in their midst. Mounted riders raced past, firing as they went. The war wagon behind them managed to send another stream of bullets against the rear door. This time one slug penetrated. It whined through the ruptured steel and bounced around inside the steel-walled compartment.

"Dang, get us out of here!" Slash shouted.

"We got big troubles, pard. Jump. Do it now!" Pecos turned and pointed for Slash to get out. Then he vanished from sight.

Slash didn't have to be warned twice. He kicked open the back door and dived headfirst. He landed on his belly and slid a few feet. The rocks on the road tore at his clothes and flesh. He covered his head when he saw how close the following team was. The horses reared. He was going to get stomped into the ground.

Then the world erupted all around him. Overhead he saw the wagon he'd just abandoned sail through the air. Parts of it tore at the team trying to trample him. And then a second explosion covered him with dust and bloody hunks. He hoped they were from the horses that had been pulling his and Pecos's war wagon. He was afraid some of them were human.

Strong hands lifted him from the ground. His legs kicked feebly, then got traction.

"We gotta run. We're exposed out here." Pecos shoved him toward the boardwalk near the Palace of a Thousand Delights. He stumbled and fell flat on his face.

That saved him from being stitched with a long volley of bullets from a Gatling gun.

"Where'd that come from?" He shook himself to clear his head.

"The first wagon into town's coming back. Drop flat!"

Pecos shoved him to the ground. The edge of the board-walk hid them from sight. The war wagon raced past. The Gatling fired so fast, the rotating barrels smoked. The com-partment filled with choking white fog and had to be hotter than Hades, but the crew kept firing. Stores all around slumped in on themselves, wooden walls blown into splinters. Faint cries of men and women inside being struck made its way through the cacophony of fighting.

"Look. Look!" Slash shook Pecos and forced him to peer around the edge of the boardwalk. "The Palace is all forti-fied. They're shootin' at anything in the street. Jay's got 'em fightin' back."

Another boom sounded as a howitzer discharged. A col-umn of smoke rose from the direction of the bank.

"Let's help 'em out," Pecos said. He got his feet under him, then launched himself into the air. He collided with a raider galloping past. The two of them crashed to the ground.

Slash kicked as hard as he could. The toe of his boot con-nected with an exposed chin. The raider's head snapped back, and he flopped about on the ground. The crazy angle where his head met his shoulders told that he had murdered his last town. Slash helped his partner up.

"You do that purty good for an old feller," Pecos said. He plucked a couple pistols from the dead man's holsters and tossed them to Slash, then added a couple more to his own arsenal.

They set out at a run, occasionally shooting at a rider try-ing to murder some of their neighbors. When they reached the bank, they stopped and stared.

A mountain howitzer had been positioned across the street from the bank. But the area was strangely quiet in the middle of a roar of gunfire from everywhere else.

The cannon crew sprawled over the caisson. One man, tasked with lighting the fuse, sprawled on his back. Sightless eyes stared into the clear blue morning sky. A sliver of sunrise crept between buildings and softly touched the cannon itself. Silver streaks on its barrel showed how many slugs had hit it and bounced off.

"On the roof," Slash said, pointing. "A couple riflemen."

"In the bank, too. They kept the crew from firing the cannon and blowing a hole in the sidewall."

"Pecos! Slash! Hallo!" Gustav Reinking hesitantly poked his head out from inside the bank. Two gunmen flanked him.

They hurried to the bank president. He hugged them, much to their discomfort. Slash finally pushed the man away.

"How'd you come to have such protection?" He pointed to the men backing up the president and then the others on the roof across the street.

"Jay convinced me. I didn't believe her, but . . . she can be very persuasive."

"That she can," Slash said.

"Uh, Slash, is the Palace still standing? I mean, what are the casualties?"

"Among the girls?" Slash shook his head. "We didn't check."

"I can send some men to help defend the, uh, saloon. And all the building's occupants on, uh, the upper floors."

"Go on. And on the way over, shoot anybody on horseback luggin' around a half-dozen pistols. They're all the Colonel's men."

"Colonel?"

"He calls himself that. None of the raiders are in uniform." Slash involuntarily ducked as new cannon fire sounded.

"That came from the direction of the church," Pecos said.

"The church? That don't make any sense. Why'd Raymond want to attack the church?"

"Unless, Slash, Jay convinced the reverend to turn it into a fort. Raymond can't let a place stand that holds men capable of rushing out and attackin' his rear."

"Yeah, he'd lose his rear end for certain." Slash avoided Reinking hugging him again.

He and Pecos cut through buildings, some on fire now, others shot up, and burst out into the clearing in front of the church.

"That puts a whole new meanin' on 'church social.'" Pecos stared at the Colonel's men scattered around the field. More than a dozen lay unmoving. They had been mowed down by defenders hiding inside. He grabbed Slash by the arm and pulled him around to see the danger threatening the church.

A gun crew had set up a howitzer not twenty yards distant. They worked with smooth efficiency. Swabbing down the hot barrel, dropping in powder and three-pound cannonball and wadding, took only seconds. The loaders turned away and clapped their hands to their ears as the man behind the cannon applied a match to a fuse.

The cannon bucked. The deep-throated roar rolled across the cleared space. Then the church spire blew into a thousand pieces. For a frightening instant the carillon rang as if summoning the faithful to services. Then those three bronze bells exploded as the shell crashed through them.

The shrapnel from the bells and cannonball rained down on Slash and Pecos. They beat out tiny fires nibbling at their clothing. Safe again from turning into human torches, they turned back to see the efficient crew ready to fire again.

Both men began firing, a six-gun in each hand. The front crew sagged as the old-timers' bullets found vital organs. But the man with the fuse lowered the lucifer just as Slash's two captured pistols came up empty. He watched in horror as the fuse again simmered.

A new shell exploded from the cannon. This one was aimed lower. It crashed through the church wall. The impact caused the roof to sag and then collapse. It all looked as if it happened in slow motion.

Slash ran hell-bent for the surviving crewman.

"Get 'em from the church!" he bellowed at Pecos. Then he was occupied with staying alive. He crashed into the gun crewman trying to pull a Colt from his waistband. The two of them tumbled over the cannon's hot barrel. Slash hardly noticed the added pain as his flesh singed. The gunner yelped and reached to touch his burned legs.

Slash reared back and punched down hard. In an awkward position his blow didn't carry its usual power. It still caused the man's head to snap to one side. But rather than knocking him out, it infuriated him. With a powerful kick he lifted both of them off the ground. A savage twist sent Slash rolling away.

Slash came to his feet. The Colonel's man again went for his pistol thrust in his belt. Slash dipped, then picked up a cannonball stacked beside the howitzer. The muscles in his arm screamed in protest. The powerful toss sent the three-pound iron ball smack into the man's gut. He doubled over and grabbed for his belly.

Slash kept driving forward. His arms circled the man's and pinned them to his sides. He caught the raider up in a powerful bear hug, then lifted. Twisting in midair, he slammed the man down, full-force, across the barrel. A new thunder filled the air. This time it was the gunner's spine snapping. He let out a strangled sound. His arms flailed about, but they were no longer connected to his body.

The light of life drained from his eyes. He lay draped backward over the cannon he had used to blow up the church.

"You got what was comin' to you," Slash grated out. "Another man might call it divine retribution." He straightened and tried to stretch his cramped limbs. Every muscle in his body ached or hurt or burned. It'd take a good long soak in a hot bath to work out the knots.

That and a loving massage from Jay.

"You. I should have known it was you. Benson warned me, but I didn't listen."

Slash turned. Standing not ten feet away, Colonel Raymond faced him. The man sported a half-dozen six-shooters dangling around him. He, like his men, came to kill dozens of innocents. Now he faced off with an old cutthroat who had been ordered to arrest him.

Or stop him.

Fair play meant nothing when facing a monster like this. Slash whipped out both his six-shooters and fired. And fired. And fired. Every time the hammers fell on empty chambers.

He went cold inside. He had used up all his rounds ridding the war wagon of the Gatling gun crew. And he had never reloaded. The pistols he'd used were ones taken off a fallen raider.

A wicked smile crossed Colonel Raymond's lips.

"You don't deserve any quarter." Raymond's hand flashed for a six-shooter thrust into a cross-draw holster.

Slash moved with liquid grace. His hand reached behind, to the small of his back. Fingers closed on the hilt of his bowie knife. He half spun and sent the wicked blade spinning through the morning sun. It flashed three times, like a Catherine wheel, and then found a sheath in the Colonel's gut.

Raymond triggered a round, but it went harmlessly into the dirt at his feet. He looked at Slash, surprise blossoming on his face. His lips moved, but no words came out. Then he died.

For a dozen heartbeats Slash was unable to do anything but stare. Only when he calmed his pounding heart, the energy of the fight draining from him, did he walk over on achy, shaking legs. He rolled the town killer onto his back and plucked out his deadly knife from its bloody sheath. Two quick swipes on the Colonel's chest cleaned it of blood.

"I don't reckon I earned one of your campaign ribbons." Slash spat, turned, and went to see how Pecos fared.

Then he had a wife to find.

Chapter 37

Sporadic gunfire sounded throughout Camp Collins. Slash reloaded his six-shooters as he walked. Pecos caught up with him.

"That was about the finest knife toss I ever did see," Pecos said. "But you had to use the bowie knife 'cuz you forgot to reload. Ain't that the truth of the matter?"

"I wanted it over. Raymond wasn't gonna give himself up. This saves Bleed-'Em-So the need to pay for a judge and jury and hangman."

"You make it sound like you planned it out," Pecos said, joshing his partner. "Next thing you know, you'll tell me all the stores burned to the ground are your idea, too."

"Why'd I do that?"

"To get better-lookin' stores put up in their place. Some of them firetraps what burned down needed repair. This does away with the need."

"I only wanted to stop the Colonel because of Jay. You seen her?"

Pecos shook his shaggy head.

"She wasn't in the church. If she'd been in the bank,

Reinking would have said something. She must be in the saloon."

"Good. I need a drink."

"I need to wet my whistle, too, but them gunshots tell me the Colonel's cutthroats are puttin' up a fuss. We should help out."

"Yeah, Pecos, that's a good idea. After all, we led 'em here."

"Don't you go sayin' damn-fool things like that. Someone might take it to heart. We snuck in, workin' undercover like some damn Pinkerton agent, so we could stop them. Think what Camp Collins would look like if we hadn't. Because of us, two of the war wagons got taken out of action early."

"Until the cannon was turned on us and blew the doors off our wagon," Slash said.

"You might say we forced them to shoot at us instead of usin' the howitzer against targets in town. We saved Camp Collins businesses that little bit of cannonade." Pecos sounded pleased with himself and puffed out his chest. His smile faded as he ran his hand over the spot where the Colonel's ribbon rode. He yanked it off, tearing away some of the buckskin. With a savage toss he cast it away, as if ridding himself of a fanged snake chomping at his flesh.

Slash grabbed his partner's arm. For a second he thought Slash wanted him to leave the despised ribbon in place. He calmed down when Slash cocked his head to one side, turned slowly, and pointed toward the road they'd taken into town.

"We got more to do," Slash said.

"I hear the Gatling gun firing. We destroyed two of the war wagons. The third musta lit out when it met some fire."

"Thanks to my lovely wife. I know Jay's responsible for this. Who else in this jerkwater town could whip up such a defense?" Slash grinned proudly. Then he drew his six-shooters. "The shooting's not gonna stop, is it?"

"Not till we make it stop." Pecos reloaded his Russian .44 and set out with his partner.

They ducked between buildings, avoided some on fire, then took a shortcut to the road into town. The remaining war wagon had lost a wheel and canted onto its side, but that didn't stop the crew from firing through both the front window and out the back doors.

"They don't want to get taken alive," Pecos said. "I don't blame 'em. They got a lot to answer for, especially if they're wearing more 'n a couple of the Colonel's ribbons."

"We could toss a stick of dynamite into the compartment," Slash said. "Or just wait 'em out. They can't have much ammo left, and when the sun gets high enough, they'll cook their fool brains out in that steel kettle."

"Or—" Pecos broke off his thought and listened hard. "Do you hear that?"

"It sounds like a bugle," Slash said. "The cavalry's on the way. I can see a dust cloud bein' kicked up along the road."

They took a few potshots at the Gatling gun crew to keep them in the wagon until the U.S. Army column arrived.

"Now look at that," Pecos said. "The lieutenant's gold braid about glows in the sun."

"He ain't been in command long. And not in the field. That braid's not been bleached by sun and wind, not one teeny bit."

The two old reprobates sat in the shade and watched the lieutenant order his men around. Most of his orders were ignored. The sergeant deployed the men and pretended to do as his commanding officer said. Then the two raiders in the war wagon finally surrendered.

"That's smart of 'em," Slash said. "Give up and let the army take them into custody. They'll be stood in front of a firing squad, but considerin' how the army operates, there's a chance they might escape."

"Ain't a ghost of a chance of gettin' away from me. Or Chief Marshal Luther 'Bleed-'Em-So' Bledsoe," added Pecos.

"Are you two Baker and Braddock?" The lieutenant trotted over and squinted as he studied them.

"See, Slash, we're famous again. This shavetail recognized us right away."

"I had detailed descriptions from the lady. You two closely match her account." The lieutenant barked a few more orders that went unheeded. His sergeant made sure the two from the war wagon were properly shackled. Then a corporal and two privates climbed into the rear of the wagon and wrestled out the Gatling gun.

"You reclaimin' your property? There's a few mountain howitzers scattered around town, too," said Slash. "All belongin' to the U.S. Army."

This time the lieutenant's orders were obeyed without being modified. He dispatched half his column to find the cannons and other Gatlings. He turned his horse back to where Slash and Pecos lounged on the boardwalk.

"Don't expect a reward," the lieutenant said sternly. "You had nothing to do with recovering the stolen weapons."

"Yup, the army's takin' full credit for savin' us. That all right with you, Slash?"

"I'm happy to be rid of Raymond and his pack of wolves."

Pecos sat a little straighter in the chair, then came to his feet and stopped just in front of the officer.

"You said you had descriptions of us? How's that?"

"A lady alerted my scout about all this and said you were likely to be in the middle of it. A Mrs. Mertz, she called herself."

"Marianne!" Pecos blurted. "Is she with you?"

"She gave us detailed instructions on reaching Camp Collins, as if we needed them, the deserted fort being close by and all, and then she told me she was going home. Something about orphans, which I didn't understand."

"She went back to High Mountain?" Pecos reached up and grabbed the lieutenant's wrist in a vise grip. The officer tried to pull free, but a hand tempered by driving a team of mules proved too strong.

"If that's where the orphans are. Does she run an orphanage? I never heard of one in High Mountain. Truth to tell, I've never heard of any town by that name."

Pecos was halfway down the street by now. Slash called after him, "You want me to come along?"

"You find Miss Jay and get settled. There's plenty to do in this town."

Pecos disappeared, on his way to their freight yard and the livery where they stabled their horses.

"I'll do that, old partner, I'll do that. You can be sure I'll see that Jay's in tip-top shape." Slash grinned ear to ear and said softly, "And you do the same for Miz Mertz."

Chapter 38

Pecos's Appaloosa strained as he trotted up the steep road to High Mountain. It was quicker than taking the less steep back road, and the sound of gunfire turned him anxious to see what was going on. Colonel Raymond's small army of raiders had been crushed and dispersed by the cavalry back at Camp Collins. With any luck the shavetail lieutenant in charge of the army detachment ordered his men to run down the town killers, who had run away like scalded dogs and scattered like cockroaches after their failed attack.

There was no way Raymond's men would shoot up High Mountain. This was their refuge. They came here to plot and plan and hide out, and not have to worry about the law catching up with them.

The Appy let out a loud, wet whinny as it topped the incline. High Mountain stretched out before Pecos, a jewel set in a green mountain meadow. He heaved a sigh of relief when he saw only the thin white curl of cooking fires around town. Nothing burned that wasn't supposed to. But the sporadic gunfire continued to worry him.

He drew rein in front of the Galloping Garter Saloon. A

fistfight raged inside. From what Pecos saw, at least four men exchanged wild punches. This wasn't unusual in any saloon. Then came a single gunshot. Silence fell inside.

Pecos swung down, secured his horse, and cautiously peered inside. The barkeep held a rifle with a sawed-off barrel. Gunsmoke drifted from the muzzle branding him as the shooter.

"Enough. You buzzards, take your fight outside!"

"We own this place," snarled a man with two of the Colonel's campaign ribbons on his chest. "We brought you money and kept the town from drying up and blowing away."

"Have the Colonel come discuss how you're bustin' up my place."

Pecos swung his shotgun around and fired from the hip. The barn-blaster ripped apart two men, sporting the campaign ribbons, as they went for their six-shooters. The man confronting the barkeep also slapped leather. The barkeep ended his life with another shot.

"What's goin' on?" Pecos called. "They turnin' on you?"

"Ain't many of them in town, but they're stealin' with both hands," the bartender said. He leaned over the bar and looked at a customer knocked down by a punch. "You got your senses back, Hank?"

"Did I win?"

The barkeep looked over at Pecos, shrugged, and said, "They whaled away on Hank here for no reason other than he refused to buy them a drink."

"Is that what happened?" Hank rubbed his jaw and took a step that betrayed how wobbly he was in leg and brain. The bartender grabbed him by the collar and pulled him around to lean on the bar.

"How many are still in town?" Pecos asked.

"Whenever the Colonel goes Injun hunting, he leaves a handful behind to watch over things here. We don't need a marshal. Not till now," the barkeep said, staring at the bodies on his sawdust-covered floor.

Pecos snorted. In spite of everything the barkeep still believed Raymond ranged across Colorado putting down Indian revolts. But there wasn't any cause for him to think otherwise. News of Paradise and Whiskey Creek never made it into a town run by the very men responsible for those atrocities. After getting whupped good at Camp Collins, the Colonel's legend would take a nosedive. Folks would have to ask his followers what they had been doing attacking a town that didn't have more than a dozen Indians, and not a one of them on the warpath.

"There's more gunfire," Pecos said. "What's that about?"

The barkeep answered with a vague gesture before he grabbed the nearest body under the shoulders and started dragging it toward the back door. Pecos looked around. Other than him, Hank, and the barkeep, the saloon was empty of anyone still drawing a breath.

Pecos swung around, reloaded, and considered the small pockets of gunfire. The Colonel's men were trying to pick clean the skeleton of High Mountain. That meant they'd been given orders. This was the Colonel's nest, and messing with it without his authorization was unthinkable.

Unless they'd been told they were moving out—and to hell with High Mountain and its duped citizens.

He took the reins in hand and vaulted into the saddle. He grunted at the impact. Getting old turned his joints rusty. Pecos looked around to see if anyone noticed. Everyone in High Mountain was occupied elsewhere. Did the Colonel's men now view the town residents as potential foes? And how did the Colonel's army see him? Still a member or a traitor?

He touched the ripped spot on his chest where he'd torn off the single ribbon given him by Raymond. Cold anger flooded him.

"Giddyup."

* * *

Pecos put his heels to the Appy's flanks and rocketed through town to reach Marianne Mertz's boardinghouse in record time. He hit the ground running and went to the front door.

He hesitated. The door stood ajar.

"Marianne?" He stepped inside and listened. A scuffle from upstairs echoed throughout the deserted house. Then he heard Marianne scream.

Pecos had his Russian .44 out and took the steps three at a time to reach the second-story landing. A quick look right, and then he turned left in time to see Harl Benson vanish into a room at the end of the hallway.

Again a woman's scream filled the silent house. He recognized fear. Worse, he recognized Marianne's voice.

"Stay away!"

"You sold us out. You warned them!"

"You . . . You're a thief. A killer!" The sound of a fist hitting flesh gave wings to Pecos's feet.

He burst into the room to see Marianne sprawled flat on a bed. Benson towered over her, ready to punch her again. In a flash Pecos saw one of the woman's eyes swelling shut. An ugly green-and-purple bruise sprouted on her chin. Before Benson delivered another punishing blow, Pecos roared and launched himself.

His Russian .44 swung around in a long arc and slammed hard into Benson's forehead. The Colonel's scout reeled away and crashed into the wall so hard, it knocked a picture to the floor. Pecos glanced at Marianne, who moaned on the bed and held her injured face. Rage welled up inside him. He swung the pistol around, ready to empty it into Benson.

Benson was down, but not out. From his position on the floor, braced against the wall, he reared up and kicked hard. His fancy tooled boot caught Pecos's gun hand and sent the six-shooter flying. Pecos half turned, then loomed over Benson. He dropped onto the struggling raider. One hand closed around Benson's throat.

Then Pecos screamed when Benson punched him hard in the shoulder where he'd been injured. Dynamite exploded in his head and his grip loosened enough for his enemy to twist free. Pecos tried to recover, but the tide had turned. Benson drew his pistol and landed it squarely on the top of Pecos's head.

Between the pain from his still-healing shoulder and the crack on his head, he wasn't able to see straight. Benson danced around—two Bensons, as double vision blinded him.

"I always thought you were a traitor," Benson said, gasping out the insult. "You're a traitor and she betrayed us!"

Benson aimed the six-gun at Pecos. Pecos flinched when the gun fired. Only he felt nothing.

"Am I dead?" He patted his chest to see if a bullet had torn out his heart and instantly killed him. Nothing.

"Oh, Pecos, I've never shot anybody before." Marianne sobbed. She still lay on the bed, but she clutched Pecos's .44 in both hands. A curl of smoke rose from the barrel.

"What happened?"

"I shot him. He was going to kill you, and I shot him." She sobbed so hard now that her entire body shook like an aspen leaf.

He pushed the pistol away and held her in his arms. He felt her tears soak into his shirt.

"Why'd he come for you?"

"He caught me giving the children food. They're still hiding. I . . . I think they're fixing on leaving town, and I wanted to convince them to stay."

"Benson was a skunk, through and through," Pecos said.

"He also said I betrayed him." She looked up. Tears welled in her eyes and spilled down her cheeks. "I found the army patrol and told them what you'd said to me."

"You saved an entire town," Pecos said, though he knew he and Slash had done far more. The two of them, and Miss Jay, and the banker, and the reverend, and so many others. But it soothed her.

"I did? Maybe you can show me around Camp Collins sometime soon, Pecos."

"I'd like that. In fact, I was thinkin' that we—"

The gunshot tore between his left arm and his chest, leaving a bloody gully on both. Pecos fell forward to protect Marianne. He fumbled around, hunting for his iron. When he had pried it from Marianne's fingers, he had tossed it aside. Somewhere.

"You ruined everything. Everything!" Benson screeched like a hooty owl in fury as his face turned livid.

Pecos found his Russian, slid his trigger finger through the guard, and jerked around. On his side he pointed the gun at Benson, who fumbled with his own six-shooter. Both of them fired at the same instant. Benson's slug tore up a pillow on the bed. Pecos's bullet caught the man in the arm and spun him about.

For a moment Benson fought to keep his balance. Then he once more cut loose with his shrill, ear-piercing cry and tumbled through the window. Pecos heard a sick thud as the man hit the ground two stories below.

"That's gotta settle his hash," Pecos said. He sat up and almost blacked out. The pain in his shoulder and the new bloody scratch worked to drain him of both determination and vitality. Worse, where he'd been hit on the head still made him see double.

"Pecos," Marianne said, gently tugging on his sleeve. "It's so cold."

He rocked to his feet and yanked a blanket off a shelf by the bed. He had no idea whose room this was. Since it was upstairs, and Marianne's bedroom was downstairs—as he well knew!—this one was occupied by a raider whenever Raymond brought his men back to High Mountain. Carefully tucking her in, he bent over and gently kissed her.

"You're so good to me, Pecos. So good. Lie down beside me. For a while." Her eyes fixed on his. He kissed her again.

As he stood to move around the bed to the other side, he

lost his balance and stumbled backward. He grabbed the window frame to steady himself.

A bullet blew splinters into his face. If it had been an inch closer, it would have blown splinters of his skull throughout the room. Pecos sank and twisted around.

"I don't believe it," he snarled. Harl Benson held his six-shooter in both hands to steady it and fired again.

"H-he's not dead? How's that possible, Pecos?" Marianne tried to sit up, but wasn't strong enough.

"He won't be among the livin' much longer," Pecos said. "This time I'll take care of him."

"Don't leave, Pecos. Please."

He rushed from the room, looked around, and saw the back stairs. His stride strengthened as he reached the head of the stairs leading out back to the stables. Pecos chanced a quick look out. Getting his head blown off because he was too anxious wasn't how he wanted to end his days. Being with Marianne meant more than showing his raw courage now.

Pecos went down the steps, wary of any creaking that might give him away. He reached the ground. A quick peek around set the scene firmly in his head. Benson stretched out behind a large rock, his legs splayed at a curious angle. Pecos blinked hard to clear his vision.

His enemy came into clear focus.

He had done more damage to Benson than he thought. The man's legs were both broken, maybe from the spill he took falling out the window. His fancy green coat was a mess, blood and dirt mixing into a gory mud. With the scratches on his face, he could be used as a checkerboard. His hair was wild and one eye had swelled shut.

And he held his six-shooter with deadly steady hands.

From his angle Pecos had a slim chance of hitting the man. The rock shielding Benson was fortuitously positioned. Benson steadied his pistol butt against the rock and centered his aim on the second-story bedroom window.

Pecos never gave it a thought. He cocked his revolver and started walking steadily, not hurrying, not dallying. He covered more than half the distance between him and Benson before the man caught the movement from the corner of his eye.

"You're not upstairs!" Benson flopped about like a fish out of water. His pretzel legs twisted about as he tried to bring his gun to bear.

Pecos kept walking. He raised his Russian .44, aimed, and fired. He kept walking and fired again. A third bullet tore through Benson's chest before Pecos came to a stop.

He stared down at the still body. His last round had gone smack through the middle ribbon on Benson's chest. Pecos lifted his pistol and took aim, then lowered it. Dead was dead.

And Harl Benson was as dead as they came.

Pecos returned the six-gun to his holster and looked up at the window where Benson had been so focused. A smile crept to his lips.

"Comin' back, Marianne, on my way back."

Climbing the stairs proved harder than he expected. His legs felt like Benson's had looked. But his pace picked up when he reached the second floor. Pecos hurried toward the bedroom, where Marianne lay under the blanket.

"I'm back, my love. I'm back." He sat on the bed beside her. He reached out, but his hand stopped inches above her head.

Pecos turned on the bed and drew back the blanket. The bed was drenched in blood. Benson's bullet that had grazed his inner arm and side had found another target. The hunk of lead had drilled into the woman's chest. Pecos gently reached out to wipe away the pink froth on Marianne's lips and nose. The bullet had punctured a lung.

"Oh, Marianne," he said softly. He stretched out beside her and took her in his arms until long into the night.

Chapter 39

"I don't want to be here," Jay Breckenridge said peevishly. She paced back and forth in the deserted Saguache saloon. "It's too ghoulish for me to tolerate."

"You know how me and Pecos feel. Bleed-'Em-So doesn't ask, he demands." Slash turned toward the swinging double doors at the far end of the saloon and rested his hands on the horn handles of his Colt six-shooters.

A tall, lanky deputy marshal pushed through and looked around.

"Checking to see if the withered old weed's gonna get shot from ambush?"

"Something like that," the deputy said. His tone showed he was as bored as Jay was irked at being here. Beyond him, out in the hot sun, stood two more deputies, looking like weather-beaten statues.

"When I take him out, I won't shoot him from ambush. I want to see his face when I fill him with bullets," Slash said.

"Dear, be quiet. You know how he gets if he hears anything like that." Jay clung to his arm and squeezed in warning. If his wife was annoyed, he was straight out pissed.

"What do I care?" Slash fumed. He squared off when the deputy pushed the two swinging doors open and held them open.

Slash squinted at the blazing figure coming in. Abigail Langdon wore a dress of the purest white that clung to her trim figure as she moved. She might have been one of those fancy Italian marble statues, only no cold stone ever radiated such sexiness. Her jade-green eyes fixed on Slash, then darted to Jay. A tiny smile crept to the Nordic goddess's lips, and she nodded ever so slightly. Then she left, returning to wheel Chief Marshal Luther Bledsoe into the dim interior.

Utter silence descended until only the squeak of his push chair's wheels betrayed Bleed-'Em-So's presence.

Bledsoe slapped his hands on the arms of his push chair and grinned wolfishly.

"I see you got new china clippers," Slash said. "These teeth don't fit any better than the old ones."

"It's good to see you, too, Slash. You're lookin' fit as a fiddle." Bledsoe cackled. "As long as you dance to *my* tune, you'll keep that way." Bleed-'Em-So turned his lustful gaze in Jay's direction. "You're as beautiful as ever, Mrs. Braddock."

"Marshal Bledsoe," Jay said carefully. She looked from the chief marshal to Abigail and back. She got no hint as to the lawman's mood. Playing poker against Abigail would be quite a challenge. The blond beauty's lack of emotion betrayed no hint about what ran through her head.

Her scheming head, Jay amended. No one worked as closely as Abigail did with Bleed-'Em-So without playing politics like a maestro.

"I got that son of a bitch's body you sent me down in Denver," Bledsoe said. "Good riddance, I say."

"He decapitated Colonel Raymond and has his pickled head in a jar," Abigail said. A hint of disapproval showed on her finely boned face, but the emotion quickly vanished behind her neutral mask.

"You coulda had him stuffed and put on display like they did that Sauk Indian, Black Hawk," Slash said.

"Now, then, Slash, you jangling bag of old bones, don't get yerself fancy ideas like that. Besides, all that was put on display was his skeleton. I'm more inclined to send Raymond's head to the Army Medical Museum for them squinty-eyed doctors to examine the fee-no-ology of his head."

"Phrenology," Abigail corrected softly.

"Whatever that is. I want 'em to measure the bumps on his head and find why he done such horrible things. He killed hundreds of people." Bledsoe slumped in his wheeled chair. His bony fingers began weaving in and out, making intricate patterns in his lap. He looked up. "You and your partner done good stopping him. You took on a whole damned gang and beat 'em like redheaded stepchildren."

"That's hardly what the army claims," Jay said. "Slash and Pecos brought him down. Slash especially."

"And my wife stiffened the spines of everyone in Camp Collins. When Raymond rolled into town, it was like slammin' into a brick wall," Slash said.

Bledsoe leered at Jay.

"That's not all she stiffens in that miserable town," he said. Bledsoe perked up when he saw Slash's reaction. "No offense. I meant she pours stiff drinks in that saloon of hers. What's it called, again? Something about Delights?" Bledsoe cackled.

"You've got proof that Colonel Raymond's dead," Slash said. "Why're we here?"

"We? I only see you," Bledsoe said. "You and your lovely little wifey, but she don't count. Where's your cloud-scrapin', tall-hatted partner? The one who wears dirty buckskins and smells like he's just mucked the stables? Where is he?"

"Around," Slash said.

"Him and you's my property, old man. I want to know where's he got off to? I ordered you both to come to this here meeting." Bledsoe stabbed a bony finger in Slash's direction, demanding an answer.

"He's tidying up," Jay said when she saw the chief marshal was pushing Slash a bit too much. After all he had been through, taking on three deputy federal marshals to strangle Bleed-'Em-So must seem worthwhile odds to her husband. "Raymond's right-hand man tried to get away. Pecos lit out after him."

"I wanted both of them here so I could personally congratulate them on a job well done." He looked up over his shoulder at his secretary. Abigail stared straight ahead, unmoving, unmoved. "Unless I miss my guess, I'm not the only one wanting to thank him."

"I'll send him around your Denver office when he gets back. You want him to lop off Harl Benson's head for your collection?" Slash made no effort to hide his disgust.

"No need, unless he wants to visit . . . friends," Bledsoe said. He reached up. Abigail handed him an envelope she had carried in some hidden pocket in the snow-white dress.

"I got a thousand dollars each for you wastrels. This here's a bonus from a grateful population of the state of Colorado, in addition to the money I already gave you." Bleed-'Em-So held it out. When Slash stepped over to take it, the old marshal yanked it back. "It's money for each of you. How do I know you won't steal it? You and him were train robbers. You rode with the Snake River Marauders."

"We did. Me and Pecos killed all of 'em for you."

"That's right. You did. My old brain's failing on me. Why, I might accidentally tear up that pardon. You and Pecos would swing, if I did." He tilted his head to one side and stuck his tongue out, mimicking an executioner hoisting him on a hangman's rope.

"You owe us a couple teams of mules, too. Ours got run off."

"Take it out of your fee," Bleed-'Em-So said. He sent the

envelope spinning. Slash fielded it. "Be sure that your no-account partner sees his share."

Slash handed the envelope to his wife. Jay rapidly flipped through the greenbacks inside, then nodded.

"It's all there. Two thousand dollars."

"I may be many things, but I ain't a cheater," Bledsoe said.

"Yeah, you're right," Slash said. "You're many things."

Bledsoe's eyes flashed angrily; then he laughed.

"You and your truant partner will be hearing from me. I think I got another job coming up real soon I want you to handle." He snapped his bony fingers and laughed like a rusty hinge swinging in the wind.

Abigail's eyes went a little wider and her lips parted, but she said nothing to either Slash or Jaycee. She braced herself and pushed against the bar running across the back of the push chair. Without a backward glance she steered a snickering Chief Marshal Luther Bledsoe from the saloon. The deputies left, too.

An almost-painful silence crushed down on Slash. He spoke after Bledsoe's fancy wagon pulled out of town.

"One day he'll push me too far."

"Darling, don't say that. He's an evil man, but every time he sends you and Pecos out on one of his missions, you show how much better you are than him."

"I knew there was a reason I married you, Mrs. Slash Braddock. I just don't know why you married me."

Jay showed off her pearly-white teeth in an ear-to-ear grin.

"Why don't you let me find out? Again," she said, pressing warmly against him for a kiss.

Chapter 40

Pecos led his horse along the mountain trail, moving slowly to avoid disturbing the contents gently bouncing on the travois. Now and then, he glanced back and took a deep breath. He had wrapped Marianne's body in the blanket from the bed after dressing her in a bright orange dress he found in her wardrobe.

"You said orange was your favorite color," he whispered.

He had put the orange dress over the one that she had been killed in; disrobing her had seemed wrong. Besides, her blood had dried. Removing her bloodied dress would have meant he peeled it off, like skinning a deer. That didn't just seem wrong—that *was* wrong.

The path curled around and came out on a grassy knoll overlooking High Mountain in one direction, and one of the tallest peaks in the Front Range in the other. He stared off into the distance. The purpled peak brought a small smile to his lips.

"You'd have liked this place," he said. He wished they had come here on the walk they'd taken together. Seeing her reaction would have been special. Seeing her beauty against the splendor of the Rockies would have been even more special.

For him.

He untied the rawhide thongs holding a shovel to his saddle. The spot where he dug the grave dictated itself. It was the only place on the knoll where he didn't hit rock a few inches down. He dug and dug, taking his time. The grave wasn't as deep as it would have been, had he buried her in the town cemetery. That was a barren place, though, and not one Marianne would have appreciated for the rest of eternity.

Pecos led his horse up to the grave and then rolled the blanket-shrouded body over and into the grave. Lowering Marianne proved harder than he thought. She landed hard. He stared down into the grave and took a deep breath. Then he shoveled back the dirt, moving as quickly as he could now. In less than fifteen minutes, a mound of fresh dirt outlined where he had buried her.

He sat on a stump with a pine board brought from town and took out his Barlow knife. Painstakingly, he carved her name into the soft wood. This wasn't permanent. Wind and rain and fierce winter storms would quickly erase his work. That didn't matter to him. Marking her grave, even for a short while, was the right thing to do.

Whispers and quick footsteps caused him to look over his shoulder.

Four children, the ones he had rescued—and the very ones Harl Benson had killed Marianne over—crept forward. They all clutched freshly picked wildflowers.

Pecos didn't speak. They gave him a wide berth and hesitantly laid the flowers on the grave.

"You got blood all over you," the oldest boy said. Henry— that's what she had called him—stared hard at Pecos.

Pecos only nodded.

"That yours? Or hers?"

"Some of mine," Pecos allowed. "Too much of hers." He stood. The children backed away like frightened feral animals. He placed the carved plank at the head of the grave, then leaned heavily on it. The marker sank almost a foot into the soft dirt before he stopped pushing.

When Pecos looked up, the children had melted away, as if they had never been there. But the yellow flowers were scattered on the dirt mound as evidence that he had not been visited by ghosts. Marianne had tried to help them after their tragedy, and had brought tragedy on herself. The children would survive. Somehow.

Pecos looked around, then hiked to the edge of a small flower-festooned embankment. He used the shovel to dig out a plug of earth with a cluster of orange Cowboy's Delights.

He walked back to the grave and planted it about where her heart would be.

"Your favorite color. Orange," he said. "Your favorite flower." He hunted for other words to say over her, but none came. Nothing seemed enough. Or right.

Pecos unfastened the travois and left it. He mounted, turned his buckskin's face downhill, and rode off slowly. He left behind his new love and rode ahead to where his old-time partner waited.